Praise for the novels of Rick Mofina

"Rick Mofina's books are edge-of-your-seat,
thrilling page turners that don't let up."
—Louise Penny,
#1 *New York Times* bestselling author

"*Six Seconds* should be Rick Mofina's breakout
thriller. It moves like a tornado."
—James Patterson,
New York Times bestselling author

"*Six Seconds* is a great read. Echoing Ludlum and
Forsythe, author Mofina has penned a big, solid
international thriller that grabs your gut—and your
heart—in the opening scenes and never lets go."
—Jeffery Deaver,
New York Times bestselling author

"*The Panic Zone* is a headlong rush toward
Armageddon. Its brisk pace and tight focus remind
me of early Michael Crichton."
—Dean Koontz,
#1 *New York Times* bestselling author

"Rick Mofina's tense, taut writing makes every
thriller he writes an adrenaline-packed ride."
—Tess Gerritsen,
New York Times bestselling author

"Mofina's clipped prose reads like short bursts of
gunfire."
—*Publishers Weekly* on *No Way Back*

"Mofina is one of the best thriller writers in the
business."
—*Library Journal* (starred review) on
They Disappeared

"*Vengeance Road* is a thriller with no speed limit!
It's a great read!"
—Michael Connelly,
#1 *New York Times* bestselling author

RICK
MOFINA

MISSING
DAUGHTER

mira

ISBN-13: 978-0-7783-6919-6

Missing Daughter

Copyright © 2019 by Highway Nine, Inc.

Recycling programs for this product may not exist in your area.

For questions and comments about the quality of this book, please contact us at CustomerService@Harlequin.com.

www.Harlequin.com

Printed in U.S.A.

This book is for my brother, Stephen.

MISSING
DAUGHTER

Grief fills the room up of my absent child...
—King John, Act III, Scene iv,
William Shakespeare

BOOK ONE

1

It was almost midnight when Ryan and Karen Lane returned home after dinner and a movie, neither of them knowing that within a few hours their lives would be changed forever.

Ryan parked their Ford Escape in the driveway beside his pickup truck. Karen got out first, a little ticked because he'd been sullen much of the night. She shut her door with more force than was needed, leaving him to take a long breath. He looked at the lettering painted on the doors of his truck—Lane & Sons Drywall Contractors—and considered everything that those words signified, feeling the full weight of them before he followed his wife into their house on the west side of Syracuse.

Inside Ryan noticed the smell of pepperoni and onions mingled with what he thought was a hint of marijuana. Karen was in the kitchen talking with Crystal, their seventeen-year-old sitter.

"Oh yes, they were good, Mrs. Lane," Crystal said. "Tyler kept telling me that now that he's turned thirteen you won't need me to sit."

"No, not true. Not yet. I've been over that with him."

Ryan counted four empty soda cans on the table. He knew that the kids and Crystal never drank more than one soda each with pizza. Then he spotted a large empty Doritos bag on the counter and looked at Crystal, who'd caught his observation. She started running water to wash dishes, and collected the pizza box and soda cans quickly as if hiding evidence.

"Oh, don't worry about cleaning up," Karen said, "I'll do—"

"Did you have anyone over tonight, Crystal?" Ryan asked.

Crystal looked at him, blinking several times.

"No, I didn't, Mr. Lane."

"Did you invite your boyfriend over after the kids went to bed?"

"No, Mr. Lane."

"Because there are four soda cans and only three of you were home tonight."

"The delivery guy brought four. They came with the order. I drank two."

"You know our rules and what it means if you break them."

Crystal's gaze bounced from Ryan to Karen.

"Oh my God, are you firing me?"

"No," Karen said, glaring at Ryan. "What's this? Nobody's getting fired. Ryan, she said she didn't have anyone over. We're sorry, Crystal, we're just a little tired." Karen reached into her bag for her wallet and pulled out two twenties. To Ryan that was a lot of money, especially now. But Karen had continually assured him that Crystal's rates were low. Extending the cash to Crystal, Karen said: "I can drive you home, honey."

Crystal didn't move or speak, staring at both of them for an awkward moment that ended when headlights raked across the walls.

"Thank you, Mrs. Lane, but I texted Zach. That's him now."

"Boy, that was fast," Ryan said.

"I texted him as soon as I saw your lights. He doesn't live far. Thank you, Mrs. Lane." Crystal snatched the money, grabbed her jacket, shouldered her bag and started for the door.

"Crystal. Wait," Karen said.

Karen caught Crystal at the door. "Don't mind my husband. It's all right."

Fighting tears, Crystal said, "Mrs. Lane, I like Maddie and Tyler."

"And they like you. Listen, everything's fine. We're just going through some things right now that have nothing to do with you, okay, sweetie?"

Crystal absorbed her explanation, nodded, then reached for the door.

Karen left Ryan to brood in the kitchen while she went down the hall to check on the kids, starting with her daughter, Maddison.

Quietly opening the door, she found her asleep on her side. One leg had escaped from her blankets. Karen pulled the sheets over it then took in the room, fragrant with shampoo, the ceiling a galaxy of glow in the dark crescent moons and stars. In the dim light, Karen surveyed her posters of singing idols; shelves populated with her stuffed bunnies and bears, her phone in her hand. Taking care, Karen gently pried it from her daughter's fingers and set it on her night table.

Kids these days.

Karen's heart ached a little because like her brother, Maddison was growing up fast, and Karen was not ready to see her little girl become a full-fledged teen. Lately their arguments over Maddison wanting to date boys were becoming more pointed and echoed in her mind.

"The answer is no. No dating. You're only twelve, Maddie!"

"I'm mature for my age! You don't understand anything, Mom!"

Karen smiled a tired mother's smile as she gazed upon her.

Oh, I understand, sweetheart. There's so much in this life you've yet to learn, believe me.

Tenderly she stroked Maddie's hair.

Bottom line, kiddo: I love you more than you'll ever know.

Karen closed the door, stepped across the hall and opened the door to her son Tyler's room. It was all hard-core boy; his walls were papered with posters of the flag, Black Hawk choppers, Humvees and a Hercules warplane deploying flares.

His shelves held trophies, plaques, photos, comic books and his collection of hunting knives. On his desk was his gaming stuff, and his computer covered with stickers. Tyler kept nagging them for a new laptop, an expense they couldn't afford right now. Karen met the empty eyes of the skull on his bookshelf, a full-size plastic model he'd gotten from a friend.

That thing always creeps me out.

In one corner, Tyler's skateboard rose like a rocket from his clothes heap.

Karen touched one photo she'd taken the time they went camping near Lake Placid, Tyler and Maddie laughing their heads off. Tyler's arm was wrapped around Maddie. Now here he was, sleeping on his stomach, Maddie's big brother and protector.

Love you, sweetie.

Karen kissed his cheek and left, closing the door behind her and reflecting on her life. Maybe it wasn't perfect, like in movies and books.

And maybe I'm not perfect. Who is?

So her dream of being a nurse instead of a grocery store cashier didn't come true; so they were facing tough times with Ryan's business. Karen was still thankful, acknowledging that while she didn't get what she wanted, she had what she needed and considered herself a blessed woman.

* * *

Alone in the kitchen Ryan poured himself a glass of milk.

What the hell am I gonna do?

Drinking at the sink, he looked through the window and searched the night for answers while replaying the meeting he'd had earlier that day at the bank. He'd sat across the desk of Henry Driscoll, the manager who'd assessed his application for the loan he needed to save his drywall business.

As Driscoll clicked at his keyboard and calculator, Ryan's eyes went to the diplomas and awards on the wall, then the credenza with photos of Driscoll and a smiling attractive woman standing in front of the Colosseum in Rome and the Eiffel Tower in Paris.

Ryan took stock of his own life. He and Karen didn't have college degrees. She was a cashier. They'd never been to Europe. He twisted his wedding band and stared at his callused hands. The corners of his thumbs were dried and cracked. He hadn't cleaned off all of the tiny white flecks of compound on his scarred knuckles. These were his diplomas, earned from his work as drywall contractor, a job he loved; a job by which he defined himself.

My hands look like my old man's.

Ryan thought of his father, dead seven years now, and how he'd started the drywall business dreaming that his boys, Ryan and Cole, would take over. Cole wasn't interested but Ryan was, ever since he began learning the job working summers while in high school. He remembered hefting four-by-eight sheets of plywood, hoisting bags of plaster, mastering how to plumb a site, hang and align drywall, make the right mix, how to feather, how to make seams invisible. Ryan saw the art and honor in creating smooth new walls and ceilings, enclosing the spaces in which people work and live.

Driscoll's chair creaked and he sat back, shaking his head.

"I'm sorry, Mr. Lane. But we can't support your request for a working capital loan."

"I'm only asking for short-term."

"The interest rates are too high for your current financial situation."

Ryan stared at Driscoll, a new guy who'd been assigned to him after the bank's merger with a bigger one. Driscoll leaned forward.

"Mr. Lane, I'm not going to sugarcoat it. Surely you know the facts. The loan on your business has been extended a number of times. Your revenues have decreased for the last three quarters, your cash flow is weak and the recent cancellation of two major jobs has hurt you. Your debt load is straining you. You've got payroll for five employees, including yourself. You have rent and insurance payments on your shop and payments on your truck."

"But once the city approves the three new developments things will move fast. We'll get contracts. I just need capital to see us through this rough patch."

"The proposed developments are no guarantee of contracts. That's not collateral."

"What about our life insurance policies, on me, my wife, my son and daughter? Could I use those as collateral?"

"In some instances, some banks will accept them as collateral, but it won't work here. I'm sorry, but right now more debt is not sustainable given your weak income statements. It costs the bank as much to process a small loan as it does to process a big one. The truth is that since consolidation the bank has been extremely risk averse."

"This business has been in my family for thirty years, and we've always met our obligations. Always."

"I understand and respect that, but your numbers are diminishing." Driscoll read the figures he'd jotted on a yellow pad, worked on his calculator, then tapped out a verdict on Ryan's company. "Look, it's almost certain that Lane & Sons will only be viable for another eight months, nine at best. You risk foreclosure. You may have to consider selling or ending operations."

"Shut it down?"

Ryan's memory rushed back to winter mornings watching his dad at the kitchen table drinking coffee before heading to work in the dark. Coming home in the dark, carrying an empty lunch box, plaster dust in his clothes, the creases in his hands caked white.

On his hospital bed, tubes going into him as the cancer took him.

Ryan stared at Driscoll's crisp button-down shirt, his tie precisely knotted, and the bandage on his baby finger, likely from a paper cut. Driscoll, with a few clicks pronouncing a death sentence on all his old man had worked for, all he had entrusted to Ryan.

Driscoll cleared his throat. "I'm sorry, Ryan, but that's the reality."

"That's the reality, is it?"

Indignation burned in Ryan's face with such intensity Driscoll was taken aback, and his Adam's apple rose and fell as Ryan stood and glared at him.

Now, in his kitchen staring into the night, Ryan was still reeling, even after the movie Karen had suggested they go see, "to take your mind off things for a while," a thriller about spies and assassins that he'd barely paid attention to.

A hand touched his shoulder.

"Hey," Karen said. "You were a little hard on Crystal, don't you think?"

"She had Zach here."

"We were seventeen once. Besides, she's not the thing you're mad at."

Ryan turned to his wife, knowing she was right.

"I can't lose the business."

"I told you, ask Cole for help. There's not much else you can do."

"I would never go to him for this."

"But after what the bank said, don't you think maybe—"

"I will not go to him for this. Not for this."

"Okay." Karen surrendered for now.

She rubbed his shoulder, letting the moment pass.

Ryan downed his milk before they locked up and went to bed.

Sometime later that night, Tyler woke.

Thirsty from all the pizza he'd eaten, he dragged himself to the bathroom for a drink of water. Outside Maddie's bedroom door he froze.

He heard voices talking in softened tones.

What's she doing in the middle of the night? he wondered. Half asleep, he shrugged, got his water, then got back into his bed. *She must be playing a video or talking to someone on her phone. She's always on that thing.*

2

In the morning Ryan was at the kitchen table scrolling through his tablet, studying state and local financing programs for small businesses.

Karen glanced at his screen as she poured more coffee into his chipped mug, a Father's Day gift bearing the words *Awesome Dad*.

"How's it looking?" she asked, reaching for her cup on the counter.

"Not good."

"You should talk to Cole."

"Karen." His voice was cold.

"You don't have many options, Ryan."

"I will not go to him," he said, raising his cup to drink and looking at her, suddenly puzzled at why she was wearing her ShopToSave City cashier's smock. "You're going to work today? It's Saturday."

"I told you yesterday that I was taking an extra overtime shift."

"It got by me, sorry."

Karen released a borderline groan. She didn't

want to fight, but she was frustrated that he wouldn't ask his older brother for help. She closed her eyes for a moment then switched gears.

"So you're on chauffeur duty today," she said. "You've got to get Maddie to gymnastics this morning for nine and Tyler to the school for nine thirty. He's helping build sets for the play."

"All right."

"I need to get going," she said.

Tyler appeared, dressed in jeans and a blue hoodie, with his hair mussed, pulling his face from his phone.

"Mom, can you make me French toast?"

"You have to ask your dad, hon. I'm going to work."

"But it's Saturday."

"Does anyone hear a word I say?" Karen rolled her eyes, smiling and finishing her coffee.

"Dad," Tyler said, "can you make it?"

"Give me a sec, buddy." Ryan was back on his tablet checking on a contract bid. "Hey, go wake up your sister, please."

"Maddie!" Tyler called, then worked on his phone to text her.

"Go get her up, Ty," Ryan told him.

Tyler pivoted and returned down the hall. Karen was rinsing her coffee cup. "And tell her to put her leotard in the bag with her towel," she called after him. "If she forgets it again, Dad's not going to drive home to get it!"

Tyler returned in seconds.

"Maddie's gone."

Karen and Ryan ignored him because he was always joking.

"I'm serious, she's gone!"

The unease in his voice seized Ryan's and Karen's attention. Their heads snapped to him.

"Did you get her up already?" Ryan said.

"No, Dad—she's not there!"

Karen hurried down the hall to Maddie's room. Her bed was empty. Unmade. Karen checked the kids' bathroom. Nothing. Her stomach tightening, she called Maddie's name as she searched Tyler's room, then hers and Ryan's room, their bathroom and every closet before returning to Maddie's again, this time to check the closet and under the bed.

Nothing.

"Oh my God, Ryan!" Karen yelled for him.

Ryan rushed to Maddie's room with Tyler where they found Karen running her hands through her hair, worry creasing her face.

"Her phone's gone. So are her shoes and hoodie," Karen said.

"Did you have a fight with her yesterday?" Ryan asked.

"No, I mean, it was the usual. I told her she couldn't date boys, but we didn't *fight* and she was sleeping when I checked on her last night."

Ryan left to check the doors. They were still locked, bolted and chained from the inside.

What the hell?

The house was a ranch-style bungalow. Ryan hurried to the basement, quickly scouring every room, window and storage area in vain. He ran out to the garage and searched there, too. Then he searched their cars.

Nothing.

His pulse quickened as he returned to the house. In Maddie's room, Tyler was on his phone and shaking his head.

"I called and texted her. She's not answering—it goes to voice mail."

"Did you see or hear anything last night, Ty?" Ryan said.

Tyler blinked several times as if trying to contain a mistake squirming in his head.

"Tyler!" his father shouted. "What do you know?"

"I got up in the night to get some water, and I thought I heard voices in Maddie's room."

"Voices? What? Whose voices?" Ryan said.

"I don't know. They were quiet, like whispers."

"Why the hell didn't you tell us?"

"Dad." Tyler's chin was crumpling. "It was like she was talking to someone on her phone. She does that sometimes. I didn't think it was a big deal."

"Who was she talking to?"

"I don't know!"

"So she took off in the night, then, with a friend?" Karen said.

"I don't think that's what happened," Ryan said,

"because all the doors are still locked from the inside."

"Oh my God!" Karen slumped to the bed.

"Hold on, there's a way to find her." Ryan trotted to the kitchen and began working on his tablet. He went to a folder where he stored key information for the kids' phones, and applied it to a phone locator app for his daughter's phone.

As it worked, he rebuked himself for not monitoring the kids' phone use as carefully as he'd done when they first got them. He'd become lax.

An icon flashed, "Maddie's Phone," over a blurred map of the city, along with the message: No Location Available. Ryan's heart sank. He knew that meant her phone was off-line, or had no access to GPS, or Wi-Fi, or something else. But it might come back online, he thought. And it might not. He tried running a quick recovery system update, but it failed and he cursed. That was the extent of his skill with wireless technology.

Ryan grabbed his phone and hurried back to Maddie's bedroom, a sickening feeling rising in his stomach as he stood next to Karen.

"I tried tracking her phone but it didn't work," he said.

"This is bad," Karen said.

At a loss, Ryan scrutinized the room and the floor. His eyes narrowed when he detected a faint streak of mud on the carpet, and followed it to a tiny smudge on the wall under the sill. Then he noticed the sliding vinyl window was not fully closed.

Ryan ran outside to the backyard, his heart thudding in his chest as he wrestled with fear and anger. He'd wanted to install a home security system, a good one with cameras, but he kept putting it off because of the cost. And he was angry, because in a far corner of his mind he wanted to believe that Maddie had just run off in the night with a friend, pulled some sort of tweener stunt. Oh, he'd be pissed at her.

But I could live with that.

Now, however, as he felt the cool, dewy grass on his bare feet, icy, dark panic coiled around him, crushing his hope as he stopped in his tracks.

His six-foot stepladder, the one he'd kept behind the garage, was folded shut and flat on the ground under Maddie's window.

Someone used it to get to her bedroom.

He was stabbed with the image of the ladder from the Lindbergh baby kidnapping he recalled from seeing a documentary on the case.

"Ryan!"

He turned to see Karen and Tyler rushing to him.

"We need to call the police!" Karen said.

In that instant, he looked at Karen in her *cashier's* smock, her horror-stricken face. Tyler's eyes circles of alarm. His stomach lurched as he looked down at his phone. His fingers were numb, and he couldn't feel them press the three numbers that made it all too real, especially when the emergency dispatcher answered his call.

"We need police." Ryan dragged his hand over his face. "Our daughter's missing. She's twelve years old. We think she was abducted from her bedroom last night."

3

The first police car arrived within seven minutes of the call.

No sirens, no flashing lights. Two uniformed officers.

Ryan and Karen met them at the door.

A man in his thirties of defensive tackle proportions extended his hand. He was warm, confident and serious. He offered a hint of a smile and turned down the squawking portable radio clipped to his belt.

"Dalvin Greer and my partner, Eve Porter."

Porter appeared to be in her early twenties, fresh-faced with freckles, red hair pulled back in a tight, all-business ponytail.

"We understand your daughter's missing," Greer said.

Ryan and Karen quickly summarized Maddie's disappearance. "Somebody used my ladder to climb into her bedroom window and take her," he concluded. "We need to get everyone looking for her now. We're wasting time."

"Okay, hold on, we'll get to that," Greer said. "First we're going to take a quick look through the house and walk around the property, then we'll get all your statements separately."

"We've searched everywhere!" Karen said. "She's gone!"

"Ma'am, bear with us, please," Greer said.

The officers made a cursory check of the entire house, the property, garage and the family vehicles, using their force-issued camera to video record the rooms. Then they separated the family, quickly arranging for Tyler to wait with the Coopers, the retired couple who lived next door, while the officers talked with his parents.

In the Lanes' home, Porter took Ryan to the kitchen and Greer went to the living room with Karen, who clutched her cell phone in case some of the mothers of Maddie's friends she had called got back with any word.

"We're separating you because we don't want your individual statements tainted," Greer said, withdrawing his notebook, requesting Karen outline her family's last twenty-four hours, giving him a time line of events.

Interrupting to ask questions, Greer seemed to take inventory of her demeanor as she answered.

"Now," Greer said, "you say you saw your daughter holding her phone in her hand and that she often fell asleep while gripping it?"

"Yes, I took it from her and put it on her night table."

"And despite your husband's efforts, you can't locate her phone or determine the last person she communicated with?"

"That's correct."

"Okay, we'll have our people pursue tracking her phone. Do you think it's possible Maddison ran off with a friend and that she lost her phone or its battery died?"

"No, maybe, I don't know. Maddie's never run away," Karen said.

"If her phone's missing, it suggests she may have run away."

"She didn't jump out the window. You saw how high it is. You saw the mud stains, the ladder. The doors were locked from the inside. Someone took her."

"Or could she have left with someone, someone she knew?"

"No, she wouldn't do something like this. She just wouldn't."

"But wouldn't she have cried out if she saw a stranger climbing into her room?"

"We don't know what happened. Tyler heard voices. Maybe a stranger got in quietly while she was asleep then threatened her? Or gagged her, or stole her phone." Karen's voice was breaking. "Oh God, I don't know!"

"Okay, I understand," Greer said. "Have you had any arguments with your daughter recently?"

"We disagreed about her dating boys. Beyond that nothing serious."

"Did she date boys?"

"No, she wasn't allowed, not at her age."

"What about any recent instances of people following her, calling her, harassing her? Anything that sticks out in your mind?"

Karen shook her head. "No."

"What about people Maddison texts or talks to? Is it possible she's been communicating with strangers or older people online?"

"We set controls on the kids' phones and computers. They can only talk to people they know."

"Yes, but kids can usually figure ways around the rules. And they can be pretty good at keeping secrets."

Karen's knuckles whitened around the balled tissue she was gripping. As Greer continued his questions, she touched her fist to her mouth in anguish.

This isn't happening. I'm not really sitting on my sofa with armed police officers describing what Maddie was wearing the last time I saw her. The last time! Oh God, I'm having a nightmare and I'm going to wake up. I have to wake up—

"Mrs. Lane?"

"I'm sorry."

"I said we need the most recent picture you have of Maddison to go with her description so we can circulate it as soon as possible."

Karen began swiping through her phone as tears splashed on the screen, coming to a beautiful photo of Maddie with a mile-wide grin, her eyes bright, snuggling Ice Baby, her stuffed polar bear.

"I took this one of her yesterday."

Ryan's patience with Porter was slipping away. She looked to be straight out of the academy and couldn't be much older than a high school senior, he thought.

We're losing time here.

As Porter reviewed her notes, he leaned back against the kitchen counter, arms folded across his chest, his cell phone in one hand, their cordless landline in the other. He examined them constantly, praying that Maddie would respond to their calls and texts.

Now, standing there, barefoot, still in his sweatpants, a Buffalo Sabres T-shirt, unshaven, hair uncombed, watching Porter flip through pages, Ryan fought to keep calm as she went over her notes again.

"To be clear, Mr. Lane, you and your wife got home about midnight?"

"Yes."

"Then your sitter, Crystal Hedrick, left and you both went to bed at approximately twelve fifteen, after Mrs. Lane checked in on the children?"

"Yes."

"And you suspected that Crystal secretly had her boyfriend visit after the children went to bed, contravening your rules about visitors?"

"It was a feeling I'd had, yes. And I smelled a faint odor like marijuana in the house."

"But Crystal denied having a visitor, and you have nothing to support your suspicion?"

"Yes. It had been a long day. We were tired."

"And during the night you didn't hear Maddison cry out for help?"

"No."

"And you don't believe her bedroom window was locked?"

"No. Karen let Maddie keep it open a crack for fresh air. You saw there's a screen, but it slides open like the window."

"And you didn't hear or see anything to indicate a stranger was in Maddison's room?"

"That's not correct. I told you Tyler heard voices."

"I understand that, sir, and we'll interview Tyler. But with respect to you, you didn't hear or see anything to indicate a stranger was in the house, say, the floor creaking, a door or window opening or closing, voices, other sounds or smells?"

"No."

"And you suspect an intruder used your ladder to gain entry to Maddison's unlocked window?"

"Yes. I keep that ladder behind the garage, and I found it on the ground under Maddie's window. I didn't move it. Karen and Tyler didn't move it. We've been over this, dammit! Shouldn't you guys be looking for her, getting search parties together with helicopters and dogs, Amber Alerts, door knocking, calling the FBI—isn't that what you should be doing?"

"Yes, sir, we'll look into all that as soon as we talk to your son and take care of a few matters."

Ryan's and Porter's attention shot to the living room.

Karen's phone was ringing.

4

The call to Karen's phone was the first since Maddie's disappearance.

Ryan and Porter rushed to the living room, joining Karen and Greer, who'd held up his hand cautioning Karen to hold off answering as he pulled out his phone and set it to record.

"Would you agree to put yours on Speaker for us, Karen?"

"Yes, I will."

Her phone rang a second time and she checked the caller.

"It's my work," she said, pressing the answer key then placing her phone on the coffee table next to Greer's and leaning forward. "Hello?"

"Karen, Bill at the store. You're late."

At a loss for words, Karen started shaking her head. "I can't come in today, Bill, I—" Her voice trembled as if the magnitude of what she was dealing with crushed down on her.

"Is something wrong?"

"It's my daughter, Maddie."

"What is it?"

"She's gone, Bill. Someone took her from her bed in the night."

A long silence passed.

"Are you serious, Karen? I mean, jeez, really?"

"I've got police officers in my house right now! We need to search for her!"

A tense moment passed.

"Okay, okay, Karen, um, listen, listen." Bill was thinking fast. "I'm going to call Parcell at home. We'll alert all the staff on duty and off and get people over to your house ASAP to help you look for her, okay? Okay?"

"Yes, thank you, Bill. I have to go."

"Karen, you hang in there. We'll help you!"

"Thank you."

Karen covered her face with her hands and sobbed.

Ryan moved to comfort her. Greer and Porter watched them closely and updated their notes.

After the call, Porter brought Tyler back from the Coopers to the Lane house. Karen hugged him long and hard before the officers took him to his bedroom and shut the door.

Tyler sat on his bed. Porter joined him, pen poised over her pad. Greer perched on Tyler's desk chair, dwarfing it.

"Just tell us in your own words about last night, son," Greer said. "Start from when your parents left you and Maddison with the babysitter."

Tyler's eyes darted to their utility belts, their guns, handcuffs, radios, thinking how small his room had become, thinking that this was so freaking serious it scared him.

"It's all right son, we know you're nervous but we need you to help us."

For the next several minutes Tyler related the history of the last hours as best he could, detailing playing video games, getting the pizza, watching a *Jurassic Park* movie with Maddie and Crystal, going to bed, then coming to the most critical time.

"I was thirsty and got up in the night to get water from the bathroom, and when I was outside Maddie's door, I heard voices."

"Was one of the voices hers?" Greer asked.

"I'm pretty sure she was talking to somebody."

"Who?"

"I don't know."

"Was the voice that was not your sister's familiar to you?"

"I couldn't hear it that well."

"Was it a male or female voice?"

"I couldn't tell. They were talking low, like in whispers and I was still pretty sleepy."

"What were they saying?"

"I don't know. I thought maybe she was watching a video or something."

"Could you tell anything by the tone, like if someone was scared or threatening, that kind of thing?"

Tyler thought for a moment then shook his head. "Not really."

"Does your sister ever climb in and out of her window, even just kidding around?" Greer asked.

Tyler shook his head.

"Have you ever known anyone, any friends to come to your sister's window, maybe talk to her from there, or try to come in?"

"No."

"Do you know what time this was when you heard the voices?"

"I don't know. I was pretty sleepy, but I think it was late in the night."

"Could it have been your mom or dad talking to Maddie?"

"Maybe, but Maddie's door was closed, and I really couldn't tell about the voices because they were whispery. I also thought maybe she was talking to someone on her phone."

Greer nodded, thinking, his eyes going around Tyler's room and noticing the skull and other items.

"That's quite a collection of knives you have there."

"I like knives."

"Tell us, son, what do you think happened to your sister?"

Tears filled Tyler's eyes. "Someone came in our house and took her, and it's my fault."

"Your fault?" Porter looked to Greer then Tyler. "Why do you say that, Tyler?"

"I should've told Mom and Dad when I heard

voices. I'm her big brother. I should've got one of my knives to scare off whoever was in there. If I did that, maybe she wouldn't be gone."

Having secured initial statements, Greer and Porter requested Ryan, Karen and Tyler to wait in the driveway while the officers tugged on latex gloves and again examined every room of the house, this time with greater scrutiny.

Beginning with Maddie's room, they studied her bed, the sheets, night table, her closet and dresser. They video recorded it all, including the mud traces and noting that the window was ajar. Then they looked closely in every other room before moving to the basement.

They searched every corner of the rec room then the furnace room, moving to a storage room, looking through a closet filled with old clothes then a shelf unit jammed with boxes of board games, old lamps, radios, computer keyboards, extension cords, cables and spare bulbs for the Christmas tree. The unit was also crammed with rows of old books, stacks of ancient magazines and a row of photo albums.

In one corner they found a nook with a sewing machine on a table adjacent to a cutting table, fabric stored neatly on shelves, and an ironing board standing next to a dress form.

The heavy fragrance of powdered soap filled the damp air when they came to the laundry room. Sheets, towels and clothes were piled on a large folding table. Greer looked at the washer and dryer and stopped.

Three years ago he'd been part of an investigation where a missing boy had been murdered. The parents had lied to investigators from the get-go, claiming their son was kidnapped. Greer was the one who'd found the child's body stuffed in a dryer. The boy had been horribly abused.

Now, Greer braced himself before opening the doors to both machines and probing the insides with his flashlight.

Empty.

The officers moved outside, checked the garage and vehicles again before walking the perimeter of the house, looking for anything out of place, ending in the back at Maddie's bedroom window and the ladder.

After recording it they turned and walked along the Lanes' neatly trimmed lawn to the edge of the backyard. Their lot was large with aging, flimsy chain link fencing lining the property that backed onto dense woods.

"Lucifer's Green," Greer said, taking in the forest wall.

"What?" Porter asked.

"It's the nickname for the woods. The property used to belong to a farmer who grew food for the Union Army. Then bootleggers ran an operation in there during Prohibition. That's how it got its name, for people using it to do the devil's work for money. Now it's municipal property. It's not really a park. It's webbed with overgrown paths. Nature groups sometimes use it. So do young people who want to party, or whatever."

"Well, thank you for the history lesson, Professor." Porter turned back to the house. "So what do you think happened here?"

"I don't know. We've got to get the tape from our car, seal the place, protect this as a potential crime scene, get more help and turn this over to Criminal Investigations."

"Right."

"And I'll tell you what you never do at this stage in cases like this, Eve." Greer turned to look at the Lane house.

Porter followed his gaze to the driveway. They could see between the house and garage and glimpsed Ryan, Karen and Tyler Lane huddled in the driveway, talking and checking their phones.

"Never ever rule out anything or anybody."

5

Ryan stared at the yellow crime scene tape stretched around their house, watching it quiver in the morning breeze.

His phone was pressed to his ear. He was on hold with a tech supervisor with his service provider, attempting to locate Maddie's phone. The hold music was Glen Campbell's "Rhinestone Cowboy," and Ryan had heard most of it when the supervisor came back on the line.

"I'm sorry, sir, we're unable to locate the phone."

"I don't understand. I've got map locater and phone finder features for all of our phones—we're damn well paying for them!"

"Sir, I understand your situation, but for those features to work, a phone must be on a data network and right now your daughter's does not have a connection, and that could be for any number of reasons. We'll keep working on things here."

"What about giving us the numbers or names of the people she last communicated with?"

A long silence passed between them.

"Hello? Are you there?" Ryan said.

"Sir, we can't provide that information due to privacy restrictions."

"What? Our daughter is a minor—she's missing, and your priority is to protect the people who may know where she is?"

"I'm sorry, sir, my hands are tied."

"Un-freaking-believable!"

"Again, my apologies, perhaps you could work with police and—"

Ryan hung up and dragged his hand over his face, his heart sinking with every passing second.

A few hours ago they were living their lives, doing the best they could like any other family before their world was ripped apart.

This can't be happening! Maddie can't be gone!

But each moment that passed made it more real. Ryan's stomach tightened as if clamped in the jaws of a bench vise, and questions burned through his mind.

Who could've taken her? Why Maddie?

For an instant he considered Crystal and her boyfriend, Zach. Ryan didn't know Zach's last name but had seen him a few times, most recently when he and Karen had bumped into them at the mall. He recalled Zach had a lot of tattoos and piercings, earrings, eyebrow ring, lip loops and a nose stud, and that he had trouble making eye contact when you spoke to him. Ryan got a bad vibe from the guy.

And I can't shake the feeling Crystal snuck him

into the house last night against our rules. But the kids were in bed after Crystal left with him. Maybe Zach came back? Maybe he got the ladder and—

Ryan stopped himself.

I can't point fingers at people with no proof. Wait. Wrong. I sure as hell can! Our little girl's gone. They should question that tattooed little— Stop, think. We've gotta search for her. I know who I should call but—

More people had converged on their home.

Jeff and Jean Cooper, their neighbors who'd briefly watched over Tyler, were among the first.

"We're here to help," said Jeff, a retired firefighter.

Then a dog barked, and Ryan's thoughts shifted as he, Karen and Officer Porter were joined by Officer DeDe Cook and her partner, Hitch, a male Belgian shepherd dog.

"We'll need something your daughter wore or kept close to her," Cook said, stroking Hitch, who was panting as she fixed a tracking line to his collar.

Porter was still wearing latex gloves. She reentered the house and returned with Maddie's pillowcase. Cook ran it under Hitch's nose. He yipped, acknowledging he'd registered Maddie's scent, then led Cook to the back of the house.

Hitch kept his snout to the ground under Maddie's window. His tail wagging as he worked, the dog soon pulled his partner across the yard until they disappeared into the dense woods of Lucifer's Green.

As Karen watched the police dog pursue a trail into the woods, a measure of hope rippled in her heart.

Maybe Maddie called a friend and ran off because she's mad at me? Maybe it's a stunt and they're hiding in there?

Karen turned to Porter, standing beside her and Tyler on the street at a spot from where they saw the K-9 team disappear among the trees. Ryan had stepped away to talk to Greer and other arriving officers.

"The dog's picked up Maddie's scent, right?" Karen said. "We should run after them and help search."

"We'll let them work alone first. We're setting things up for a search here now, and we've put the advisory out."

"See, Mom?" Tyler showed her his phone. "It's posted everywhere online."

Maddie smiled back at Karen from the notice.

Missing Person—Possible Abduction

Maddison Lane. Age: 12 years old. Gender: Female. Height: 4' 11". Weight: 87 lbs. Hair: Brown. Eyes: Brown. Scars/Marks: Half-moon shaped birthmark above right ankle, Clothes/Wearing: Pajamas, two piece, black long-sleeved top w/ matching pants. Top has multicolored hearts spelling "Time To Chill." Pants have matching hearts pattern. Also wearing yellow hoodie and white sneakers with pink polka-dot laces. In possession of a pink cell phone with a glitter butterfly pattern case with name "Maddie." From: Syracuse, NY USA. Anyone with information please call your local police.

Karen stared hard at her daughter's face, at her pretty smile, at how her eyes sparkled as she crushed Ice Baby to her. Here she was just yesterday, your average twelve-year-old girl before she'd tried to convince Karen, yet again, that she was on the cusp of womanhood and should be able to bring boys home.

Not on your life, young lady. Not till you're older. That's what I told her.

Emotions surged in Karen, and she covered her mouth with her hand. Then her phone rang. It was Lauren Webb, the mother of Maddie's friend Nicole.

"Karen, I was in the shower when I got your message! Oh my God, is Maddie really missing?"

"Yes! Did she go to your house? Does Nicole know anything?"

"No, Maddie's not here. Hang on, I'll get Nicole."

"Mom." Tyler had been texting friends nonstop since Ryan had called police. "I asked Nicole already. I'm asking everybody, and so far nobody knows anything."

A few seconds passed and Lauren came back.

"No, Karen, we don't know anything. What happened?"

"We think someone took her from her bedroom last night."

"Oh my God!" Lauren shouted to someone in her house then came back to Karen. "Where are you? Are you home?"

"Yes, with the police. They've got a dog looking for her in the woods."

"Okay, we're coming over to help."

Karen ended the call and her phone rang again. This time it was Valerie Morber, the mother of Maddie's friend Amanda.

"Karen, I just heard from Amanda. She's been talking to friends asking around about Maddie. Are you home? We want to help."

As word spread, Karen received more calls, then suddenly she and Tyler were hugged by Mary Ling and Sarah Ramirez, her coworkers.

"We came as soon as we heard from Bill at the store," Sarah said.

"More people are coming," Mary said. "Sidra and Latonya are at the copy shop. They're downloading the missing notice to make posters. We'll put them up everywhere in the neighborhood. We'll do whatever it takes to find her."

Karen thanked them and through her tears she now counted six police cars parked on the street in front of their house. Ryan was nearby huddled with police officers, neighbors and people Karen didn't recognize.

I hope he called his brother. Maddie's life is at stake. We need help.

"You're not listening to me Officer Greer." Ryan struggled to keep himself together. "You have to work with our carrier to track Maddie's phone, find out who she talked to last. And you've got to talk to our babysitter, Crystal Hedrick. I'm certain she had her boyfriend over here last night, and I don't trust that guy. He may have come back. His name is Zach somebody. Why aren't you questioning him? We're losing time here!"

Police radios crackled.

The eyes of the officers who encircled Ryan went to him, then to Greer. Greer reached for the microphone clipped to his shoulder, confirmed a message to his dispatcher, then nodded to Ryan.

"Mr. Lane, we're bringing in more expertise and resources to help us on all fronts." Greer was calm, respectful. "And I can assure you, we've sent officers to Crystal Hedrick's residence to obtain a statement from her."

"What about Zach?"

"We'll confirm his whereabouts as part of the investigation."

"Okay, that's good." Ryan indicated the woods behind their house. "Did the dog pick up anything yet? Shouldn't you have more people in there?"

"We have to let the K-9 team do their work first. We're requesting the county's helicopter, and we'll get drones up."

Ryan was nodding as Greer continued.

"We've circulated our missing person alert online for Maddison, we're about to launch a canvass here and we're preparing to issue an Amber Alert." Greer raised his chin beyond the half-dozen officers. "Excuse me, and you are?"

"Chuck Field," the first man said. "This is Red Baldwin and Phil Demarco. We work with Ryan."

Ryan was happy to see them. Chuck was his right-hand man.

"We came as soon as we could. We're here to help," Chuck said. "And don't worry about the job we're on, or the business. We'll help you here and take care of work, so don't worry."

Ryan nodded his thanks, then Greer's attention shifted to the five other men from the neighborhood who'd joined the group. Two stepped forward to make introductions. The first was Ryan's neighbor Judd Salter, a retired armored car driver who headed the local neighborhood crime watch group. The other man, Angelo Darnado, who Ryan didn't know, was from the neighborhood association. Salter and Darnado identified the others as members of neighborhood groups.

"Ryan, we just heard and our prayers are with you and Karen." Salter gripped Ryan's shoulder then turned to Greer. "Sir, we've been alerted about

Maddison's disappearance and we're standing by to activate our call out and help."

"Thank you. Here's what's going to happen," Greer said. "Our people will knock on doors in a canvass and check for residential security cameras. Mr. Salter, can you get your people to get neighbors in the surrounding area to check their property for anything that might help. Do you have forms?"

"We do."

"All right, all of this must be logged and recorded with names, times, dates and turned over to us. Remember to show your crime watch identification."

"We'll get on it."

"And what about the other side of the Green?" one of the officers asked Greer.

Something in the officer's tone betrayed to Ryan that a secret exchange of information had passed between the officers, something important.

"Yeah," Greer said. "We'll get our people to start a canvass along DeBerry Street and the others that border the woods."

"Hold on. Isn't that where the new halfway house for paroled criminals is supposed to open next month? On DeBerry?"

"It's been operating for about six months now," Greer said.

"*Six months?* What the— Six months? Why didn't we know?"

"It opened quietly. They wanted it low profile. Mr. Lane, take it easy."

"Take it easy?"

"Those residences are monitored under tight restrictions. This will be a matter of routine that we'll check everyone, everywhere."

Ryan bit his bottom lip, angry at himself for not thinking, not remembering about the halfway house and not putting up a better fence and security. How could he let his guard down? His mind had been focused on his business.

More people had arrived from Karen's store and were gathered around her, comforting her and Tyler.

The nightmare's real, Ryan thought as he stood there, helpless amid the chaos of the growing search, stubbled face, hair messed, still wearing a T-shirt and sweatpants, although he'd managed to get sneakers on his feet.

Time is ticking down on Maddie, and we need more help.

Feeling his phone in his hand, he made the call he had to make and it was answered on the third ring.

"It's me," Ryan said.

"Hey bro, what's up?" Cole Lane said.

So positive. That can-do, climb-any-mountain drive of his just floods through—I don't know if I can say it. How do I say it?

The silence hissed until Cole broke it.

"What is it, Ry? Why're you calling?"

"Maddie's gone."

"What? What do you mean, Maddie's gone?"

Ryan took a breath and slowly relayed all he knew to his older brother.

"We've got police but we need your help, Cole."

"Okay. Who's there from the Syracuse police leading things at the moment?"

"Officers Dalvin Greer and Eve Porter."

"Don't know them. Did they protect the scene, seal the house?"

"Yes."

"All right, I'll call some of my guys. I'll get Jill and Dalton and we'll be right over. Hang in there. It's going to be fine, okay? You hang in there."

Hang in there.

Ending the call and taking stock of everything around him, Ryan thought it was ironic because "hang in there," were the words he and Karen had used all those years ago to help save Cole's life.

6

Miles across the city in Sparkling Brook Ridge, a relatively new upscale community of large homes—some would say mansions—Cole Lane looked out the glass doors of his kitchen breakfast room at his patio and his pool, and processed what his brother, Ryan, had just told him.

Maddie was missing, taken from her bedroom in the night. He read the police advisory on his phone to confirm it was true, and his breathing quickened.

This is a nightmare.

He sent prayers to Maddie, Karen, Tyler and Ryan, then thought of his own son, Dalton, thankful he was sleeping in his room.

At fourteen, Dalton was a handful. In full-blown adolescent rebellion. He'd given Cole and his wife, Jill, plenty of attitude these days, but at least he was home and he was safe. Cole couldn't imagine what his brother, sister-in-law and nephew were going through right now.

I've got to help them find Maddie.

He needed to alert Jill, but she was out for her morning run. He scanned their long driveway, which twisted through their treed lot to the street.

She'll be home soon. I'll tell her then.

Cole walked through their spacious house to Dalton's room. The door displayed the handmade sign reading Danger Zone and was shut, signaling that Dalton was sleeping, or wanted privacy. Cole and Jill couldn't enter without knocking in keeping with what Jill called the "period of respect and trust" they'd all agreed upon.

Cole banged his fist on the door.

"Dalton, get up! We've got bad news and I need you."

A groggy groan seeped from the room, then nothing.

"Dalton!"

"What!"

"Maddie's missing. I'm coming in."

Cole was hit with the smell of cologne and body spray, and he nearly tripped over a bowl of corn chips, buried in the pants, shirts, dirty socks and underwear strewn on the floor. The place looked like a disaster site. Dalton's computer games, paintball stuff, his charging stands and schoolwork were cluttered on his desk, dresser and night table.

Dalton was under the blankets, and Cole shook the bed.

"Maddie's missing, and we've got to get to Uncle Ryan's to help look for her. Let's go, son."

Dalton sat up. "Maddie's missing? Are you serious?"

"Dead serious."

Dalton reached for his phone and began tapping and swiping.

Cole said, "Police are with them now. Someone took her in the night."

Dalton rubbed his face, studying the police advisory he'd found online. His mouth opened slightly with disbelief. As Dalton read it, Cole took quick stock of his son's messed hair. He wore it long, parted in the center with the sides that nearly covered his face to his chin, some kind of rock-star style. Dalton had blotchy skin, his eyes bloodshot, and Cole's pulse kicked up a notch with suspicion.

Dalton broke his curfew and he wasn't tired—he looked hungover.

In working together during this "period of respect and trust" to allow Dalton to demonstrate his maturity and improve his behavior, Cole and Jill had set his Friday night curfew at midnight. Last night Dalton went to a friend's birthday party and was to be picked up and dropped off by a friend's older brother. Cole was disappointed with himself because after he and Jill came home from going out to dinner, he'd been exhausted, had gone to bed and never heard Dalton come in. Jill was up this morning before Cole, and he hadn't asked her if she'd heard Dalton.

"What time did you get home last night?"

"I don't know."

"Did you break your curfew? Hey, look at me when I'm talking to you."

"It was late, Dad. The Slades' car died, and it took a long time to get it going again, so I got home late. I'm sorry."

"Why didn't you call me? I would've come for you."

"I didn't want to wake you up."

"Were you drinking at the party?"

Dalton looked his father in the eye. "I had a couple beers."

"A couple beers." Cole shook his head. "How many?"

Dalton shrugged. "Two or three maybe?"

"Any drugs?"

"Just beer."

"Don't lie to me."

"Want me to pee in a bottle?"

Cole pursed his lips and inhaled to diffuse the situation and set the matter aside.

"We don't have time for this. Get up, get dressed." Cole tapped Dalton's phone. "Ask around about Maddie, see if anybody's heard anything."

"What do you think happened? Maybe she ran away or something?"

"Don't know, just get moving."

Cole walked to his den, sorting out what he needed to do to help find Maddie, still upset with Dalton for testing his patience. He'd come clean on the beer, but it troubled Cole that Dalton was running with the wrong crowd. Their agreement to give him the freedom to make the right choices was not working.

I should be harder on him, Cole thought before the truth pricked him with the memory of his own wild teen years, and he realized what goes around comes around. *But you got your shit together, and if you can do it, so can Dalton.*

Yeah, but it's not easy.

Cole was thinking who he had to call as he passed the wall in his home office with the gallery of cherished framed photos and awards marking the achievements and triumphs in his life.

There was Cole, the young Syracuse cop in uniform, Cole the US soldier in Afghanistan. There he was in hospital getting the Purple Heart after he was blown up when his unit was attacked. There he was learning to walk on his prosthetic legs at Walter Reed. There he was with the president. There was Cole and Jill on their wedding day, then the two of them with Dalton. Then the framed cover of Cole's bestselling memoir, *One Man's Victory Over Adversity*, and pictures of Cole interviewed by network news celebrities. There was Cole cutting the ribbon opening his first private security office in Syracuse, with pictures of the satellite offices in Chicago, Miami, Seattle, Los Angeles and Manhattan.

At his desk he made calls to the senior investigators in his Syracuse office, all of them ex-cops, detectives who worked twenty-four hours a day, seven days a week. Cole's first call went to Vince Grosso, who was conducting surveillance on an infidelity case.

"Grosso," he answered on the first ring.

"Vince, my niece is missing."

"What?"

"I need you to put your case aside and help me."

"Absolutely."

"I'll text you my brother's address. Meet me there as soon as you can."

"Sure thing, boss. I'll see you soon."

Cole scrolled through his phone, then called Sally Beck, who was wrapping up a child custody case.

"I just saw SPD's advisory," Beck said. "I'll be there."

Then Cole's phone rang. The caller was his investigator, Grant Leeder.

"Cole, Grant. I saw a post about Maddison Lane, a missing girl on the west side. Isn't that your brother's daughter?"

"Yeah, Grant, Maddie's my niece."

"What can I do to help?"

"I'm pulling the senior team together to help find her. We're meeting at my brother's home as soon as possible. I'll send you details now."

"I'm there, buddy."

Cole released a long, slow breath and looked at the framed photos next to his computer monitor. There was one of him with Jill and Dalton at

Niagara Falls, then another of Ryan, Karen, Tyler and Maddie.

Cole stared at his niece, at the light in her eyes, shining like stars.

I'll move heaven and earth to find you.

Then Cole looked at his brother.

It was no secret that Cole and Ryan had their differences. Ryan had never forgiven him for his falling out with their old man—*talk about a hard-ass*—in the last years of his life, and Cole's refusal to partner with Ryan to carry on their dad's dry-wall business.

Ryan never accepted that I couldn't do it because I didn't get along with dad the way he did. I needed to go my own way.

But the path Cole followed had nearly resulted in the end of his life.

Nearly—if it hadn't been for Ryan and Karen.

Cole was grateful for what they had done, but his attempts to reconcile with Ryan over the years were futile. Sure, their families got together on holidays, birthdays, barbecues, and everyone got along. Karen and Jill liked each other. Maddie and Tyler looked up to Dalton. But Ryan's resentment toward Cole simmered just beneath the surface.

He'll never let go of it.

Still, it would be forever fused in Cole's DNA that he owed Ryan and Karen for what they did for him during the darkest days of his life. That's why he was glad that, despite Ryan's bitterness toward him, that now, when it really mattered, his brother had reached out to him.

I swear I'll bring Maddie back to you.

Cole heard Jill in the house and hurried to catch her in their bedroom before she got in the shower.

"Jill," he said. "Ryan just called. Maddie's missing. They think someone took her from her bedroom last night."

"Oh, dear God!" Jill covered her face with her hands, worry filling her eyes. "We have to find her, Cole!"

"We will. I've called people in. I got Dalton up. We're going to meet at Ryan's house just as soon as we can."

Several minutes later, Cole, Jill and Dalton were in Cole's new Land Rover cutting across the city to the west side.

7

The sky above Ryan and Karen Lane's home thundered as Air-1, the helicopter for Onondaga County, approached Lucifer's Green.

The pilot, Deputy Ken Nulone, and flight observer, Deputy Gary Blay, calibrated the Bell 407's equipment as they made several radio dispatches with the county deputies on the ground assisting Syracuse PD in the search for Maddison Lane.

"We've got some pretty dense cover down there," Blay said, scanning the trees flowing under them as they made their first flyover. "We'll use the infrared on the next pass."

Nulone banked, they came around and Blay activated the aircraft's infrared camera, which sensed heat sources in low-light conditions and transformed them into light images on a video monitor.

They slowed over the woods, and soon the glowing ghostly image of a figure and a four-legged animal with its tail swinging appeared on the screen in Air-1's cockpit. The human figure waved at the chopper.

"That'll be SPD's K-9 team," Bray said.

Nothing else appeared on the monitor. SPD and deputies had set up a perimeter around the woods. Would they find the girl or would they find a body? In the past two weeks, the flight crew had helped locate an escaped convict; then a suicidal woman; and then a ninety-five-year-old man who wandered from a seniors' home.

Bray scoured the patchwork of rooftops, yards, alleys, parks and vacant lots as they turned above the west side and made more passes over the forest. Occasionally he would raise high-powered binoculars to his face to check an area. They'd nearly completed a pass over the east side of Lucifer's Green and were banking for another when something streaked on the infrared camera's monitor.

"Hold on there. We've got something. Roll back, Ken."

Nulone flew them over the northeast corner of the forest and brought the helicopter to a crawl until two glowing figures materialized on the center of the screen.

"Air-One to dispatch, we've spotted two subjects on the northeast corner about one hundred yards due southwest of DeBerry. Request units move directly under our position now."

Nulone moved the helicopter over the thick forest cover and hovered over the two figures concealed below, and stared at the screen that had captured them. One figure was clearly adult size. The other was much smaller.

Both were looking skyward.

"Fourteen-five, copy!"

Syracuse Officer Jimmy Holmes cranked up the volume and shouted over the chopper into his shoulder microphone while running through the thick woods toward the location.

"I'm coming from DeBerry from the north."

Every few seconds he glanced up to the canopy of maple, oak, spruce and pine trees, some reaching upward of ninety feet. Through patches of blue he glimpsed Air-1 hovering in a holding position as his radio spurted transmissions.

"Sixteen-twenty, we're closing in from the east, Jimmy."

Branches slapped and tugged at Holmes as he got closer, almost directly under the helicopter.

Splotches of color, yellow then light khaki, flashed through the trees and Holmes's pulse hummed. Maddison Lane was supposed to be wearing a yellow hoodie.

"Fourteen-five, I've got a visual on the subject." Holmes unholstered his gun.

"Sixteen-twenty, we see them too."

"Sixteen-twenty and fourteen-five, check for cross fire." A commander's voice came over the air as Holmes stepped into a clearing, arms extended, his gun pointed at the two people standing before him.

"Police!" Holmes shouted. "Hands up! Get on your knees now!"

A man who appeared to be in his seventies, with a white beard and wearing a safari hat and a khaki vest, slowly lowered himself to his knees. His palms shook, his face a mask of alarm.

At the same time, the person with him, wearing a yellow hoodie, jeans and straw hat, appeared to be the same age, but petite, no more than five feet tall. Her face flushed with fear as she got to her knees and looked at the officer behind them who was also pointing a gun at them.

Holmes held them at gunpoint while the second officer handcuffed them, patted them down for concealed weapons while Air-1 thumped overhead.

Each of them had binoculars strapped around their necks, and had small knapsacks. The officer found identification, field manuals, guidebooks and logs as they explained their presence in the woods.

The officer took notes then reached for his shoulder microphone.

"Sixteen-twenty to dispatch. Our subjects are bird-watchers," he said. "They say they haven't seen or heard anything related to our search. We'll run the names, get full statements from them."

"Copy, Sixteen-twenty," the dispatcher said.

Air-1 thundered away and resumed searching.

"Bird-watchers?"

Syracuse Officer DeDe Cook's radio gave a

static-filled squawk, and Hitch barked over the chopper's roar.

"You heard that, Hitch. It wasn't the girl, it was birders. We gotta keep going, buddy. You're doing great."

The dog was panting, enthused as he worked, making Cook confident they were tracking Maddison Lane. The conditions were good. The woods were dry, and the temperature was not too hot.

Tracking dogs like Hitch had phenomenal smell receptors at least twenty-five times more powerful than those of humans. He could smell one microscopic drop of blood in two gallons of water.

Hitch followed human smells, which could take form in skin rafts—near-invisible particles of skin that humans shed. Rafts could be determined by the soaps and perfumes used, the food eaten, all combining to form scents unique to individuals.

If Maddison was afraid, she'd likely put out more rafts, Cook thought, growing hopeful as Hitch led her deeper into the woods, almost bisecting Lucifer's Green, leading them toward DeBerry Street.

He halted, his tail wagging fast.

"What is it, pal?" Cook said.

Hitch's ears perked up as he circled an area, snorted then barked at his partner as if to say, "Here!"

Cook's brow furrowed. The area in question was a clouded puddle of dark water about five feet long and three feet wide.

Hitch barked again.

"Okay, okay. Give me a sec."

Cook tugged on latex gloves and reached around in the dark pooled water, which was nearly a foot deep. Feeling nothing, she noticed that it was next to a heap of branches and underbrush. There was nothing there, she thought.

Hitch punctuated his panting with another bark.

As Cook continued probing the puddle, she wondered if the mound of deadfall was natural or had been piled that way—*by an animal maybe, as if to bury something.*

That's when her fingers grazed something in the water.

8

Syracuse police detective Stan Zubik sat in the booth of Big Ivan's Diner looking at a picture on his phone, lost in a pair of beautiful eyes. Lucy had lived with him for fifteen years until she passed away last summer.

"You all right there, Stan?" Detective Fran Asher asked.

"I'm fine, why?"

"Why? Look at you. We've been partnered, what, more than two years now, pushing three, and I gotta say something."

Zubik put his phone down.

"It's been three years since Thelma left you to marry that car salesman from Ithaca and about a year since Lucy—" Asher indicated Zubik's phone "—your golden retriever died. My heart aches for you, but Stan, you've become a country song."

Zubik, the descendant of Polish professors, was a severe, intimidating cop, with icy, penetrating eyes that had stared down lying killers, rapists, drug dealers, pedophiles and psychopaths. Now they narrowed at Asher and he said, "Your point?"

"You need to get out there. You're five years from hanging up your shield. You need someone in your life. Did you try those online matchmaker sites I showed you? And that community center I told you about with the singles bowling league? Don't wince like that, Stan. I'm saying this because I care."

"I'm content, leave it at that." Zubik indicated Asher's laptop and reached for his coffee. "Did you finish reading the new information on the Mitchell case? If so, we should go."

"Give me a minute." Asher's attention shifted to her computer.

Zubik and Asher worked in the Criminal Investigations Division, assigned to cold cases. Zubik held one of the department's highest clearance rates, and Asher, who grew up on a farm before getting a degree at Syracuse University, had earned a near-record high on the detective's exam. The fact she was gay and lived with another woman was of no concern to Zubik. He always shut down anyone he caught making idiotic comments. Zubik respected Asher because she had one of the best analytical minds of any investigator he knew, and he liked her, cared about her, because she had a good heart.

In working their cases, the two detectives often met Saturday mornings at Big Ivan's, Zubik's preferred greasy spoon, to review notes before conducting interviews. Weekends worked well for them to locate witnesses.

The Mitchell case concerned the unsolved murder of Jeremy Mitchell, a clerk shot to death in a jewelry store robbery twenty years ago. Some of the unique rings stolen at the time had recently surfaced at a flea market, giving them a new lead.

"See," Zubik said, "photo five shows these markings and—"

His phone rang.

"Zubik."

"It's Tilden. We've got a missing twelve-year-old girl, possibly abducted from her bedroom by an intruder last night at her home on the west side."

"Who's the primary on it?"

"You are, with Asher. Could be a runaway, could be something bigger. We need this done right from the get-go, Stan. Responding officers, Greer and Porter, already got K-9 searching and sealed the house to preserve the scene."

"Good."

"I'll alert Missing Persons and Crime Scene. Onondaga's already supporting."

"Does the girl have a phone? Can we track anything?"

"No phone located yet, but we're getting the Computer Forensic Unit to get on the family's service carrier. As we get rolling, I'll call state police, FBI and pull in anyone else we need."

"Okay."

"Just sent you details. By the way, it looks like

the girl is Cole Lane's niece, so expect him to want to play a role."

"That so?" Zubik fished out a fresh notebook from his portfolio case and started a log with time and date.

"I know I don't have to tell you, Stan, but I'll say it anyway. Keep things tight. We don't know where this will go. Don't share key fact evidence, and protect the investigation at all times."

In that instant Zubik's mind raced back over his cases, heartbreaking, soul-destroying cases involving children, dead children, and how he had vowed on their graves that he would see that justice was done. They were his hardest cases, where parents, upstanding people, had reported children missing but were later proven to have lied to cover up abuse, an accidental death or a homicide. He had looked into the eyes of mothers, fathers, sisters, brothers, aunts, uncles and friends as they lied, watched their tears, even believed that they were convinced in the truth of their own lies until the facts, the evidence, emerged and the incontrovertible truth was revealed.

"I know the drill, Captain."

"You have the details so haul it over there now. Every minute counts."

Twenty minutes later, as Asher wheeled their unmarked sedan onto the Lane family's street, Zubik's phone rang and he answered.

"Detective, Officer Greer. The K-9 unit's found

something in the woods that you should see. Once you arrive, I'll meet you, let you evaluate things, debrief you, then guide you in."

9

The number of Syracuse police, Onondaga County cars and other vehicles lining the street outside the Lane home was growing.

Cole Lane and his family had to go three doors down, passing two TV news vans and a car from a radio station, before they could park. They hurried to the house and searched the groups clustered there.

Jill saw Karen, went to her and they hugged for a long moment.

"Oh Jill, I don't know where Maddie is," Karen said. "She was in her bed last night and now she's gone! This can't be real."

"We're here and we're going to help." Jill gave an encouraging smile.

Jill brushed back a strand of Karen's hair that had curtained over her face, an intimate, warm gesture that surprised Karen a little, for she had always thought that there was a thin, invisible wall between them. Jill was a physical therapist, so pretty, so shapely, confident and poised. At any other time, Karen would be self-conscious of Jill seeing her in her ShopToSave City smock, which she hadn't been able to change out of yet, but not today. Today, Karen's world was tumbling out of control, and she took comfort in having her sister-in-law near.

"Karen, listen to me. We're family, and we'll get through this together. We're here, and we're going to find Maddie, okay?"

Karen nodded and thanked Jill, secretly wishing she could be in control, like her.

Nearby, Dalton and Tyler exchanged a bro hug. They were cool with each other as they studied their phones, sharing what they were finding online, pausing to check messages.

"This is freaking us all out," Tyler said.

"It sucks," his cousin said.

Dalton was a bit taller, a year older and way more cool, like he knew more about life. Dalton was always giving him expensive gifts—like knives for his collection—at Christmas and birthdays because he could afford that sort of stuff.

"When we were driving here, my dad said somebody used a ladder and took Maddie from her bedroom," Dalton said. "Is that for sure?"

"Yeah, it's pretty scary," Tyler said. "Check this out. Some kids at school put up a Find Maddie page."

"On the drive over I heard my dad on the phone

trying to arrange with police and people for a reward to help find her."

"That's good," Tyler said. "We gotta do everything to find her."

"My dad's going to help," Dalton said.

"You know what some of the kids from school are saying?"

"What?"

"That guys that just got out of prison, including pervs, live in a place on the other side of the Green. That makes me nervous, you know."

"Yeah, what do the cops say?" Dalton asked.

"They asked me stuff."

"What kind of stuff?"

"Well, I heard Maddie talking to someone in her room last night."

"Seriously? Who?"

Tyler shook his head. "Don't know. They were whispering."

"So you didn't recognize them?"

"No."

Dalton looked at the woods, waiting as the helicopter passed overhead then said, "Do you think it could be one of the convict guys?"

"I don't know, but the police have got a dog sniffing around in the woods. They think Maddie went that way."

A few feet from the boys, Cole clasped his brother's shoulders, and Ryan, on the brink of tears, took a firm grasp of his brother's forearm.

In that moment, Ryan's anxiety over his business, along with any residual resentment he'd held for Cole, evaporated in the monstrous event that had befallen him.

"Thanks for coming."

"We'll find her and bring her home, Ryan. Whatever it takes, I promise."

"This is my fault. I should've put up a security system and a new fence with that forest and that new halfway house across the way on DeBerry. I got a bad feeling about that place."

"You can't blame yourself." Cole searched his eyes to ensure he had his attention. "Tell me what you know so far."

As Ryan recounted everything that had happened, the police helicopter thumped overhead and he nodded toward Lucifer's Green, then he indicated Chuck Field and his guys from his business, Karen's coworkers, friends, neighbors and people from the community groups. The private investigators who worked for Cole had arrived and were taking notes and talking with the community officials, getting up to speed.

After Cole took it all in, he took charge of the family and neighborhood-volunteer effort to find Maddie.

"Ryan, I'm arranging to put up a page with a reward that leads to her safe return. So far we can put up ten thousand dollars. We'll solicit donations and we'll get them, don't worry."

"Really?"

"Yes, we have to move fast and it might lead nutcases and fraudsters to us, but we can't hold back, okay?"

"Yes, okay."

"With the neighborhood association's help, we'll set up a search center immediately at the community hall, on Lime Tree Street. You can see it, three blocks that way." Cole pointed. "Direct everyone there. We'll coordinate everything at the hall."

As people moved toward the base of operations, the lights of TV news cameras fell on Ryan.

"Excuse us, Ryan. Harry Hanlon, Channel 52." A tall man with neatly combed hair and white teeth held a microphone near him. "Could you tell us what's happened and your thoughts concerning your daughter's disappearance?"

Ryan saw a second TV news camera; then a woman with an expensive-looking digital camera aimed at him. Three or four other people thrust their phones in his direction as they tightened around him.

"We're doing all we can to find our daughter, Maddison," Ryan said.

"We understand that someone took her from her bedroom, used a ladder to climb to the window, is that correct?" asked one serious-faced newswoman, her sunglasses perched on her head.

"It appears that's what happened."

"Any idea who could've done this, Mr. Lane?" someone else asked.

"No."

"Any ransom calls?"

"No."

"Any contact from anyone, a text, a call?"

"No."

"Has your daughter ever run away before?"

"No."

"Is it possible she met someone online and arranged to meet them?"

"We don't know." Ryan shook his head. "We've told police everything we know."

"Thanks, guys." Cole stepped in. "We may have more to say later."

"You're Cole Lane, the Purple Heart guy who wrote that book."

Hanlon and a few of the other reporters gave Cole a subtle, quick head-to-toe look as if they couldn't believe he was standing before them on prosthetic legs. Cole was used to that look.

"Yes, I'm Ryan's brother and that's all we can say for now."

"Wait," Ryan said. "I just want to say if anyone out there knows anything, anything at all, please call us or call police, please. And Maddie, if you see this, just call us and I'll come get you, please, honey!"

Knowing Ryan's last comment would play well, the news people moved on, seeking other people to interview while Cole took Ryan to join Karen and the rest of the family.

While the Lanes comforted each other, Grant Leeder, one of Cole's most experienced investigators, pulled Cole aside.

"We better look at the sex offender registry, cross-reference names and addresses and create a map listing offenders residing in the area."

Cole nodded. "Get on it. We'll subcontract for help. I'll cover the costs."

"Then there's that halfway house on DeBerry."

"Yeah, that's a concern," Cole said.

"I know some people in Corrections. We'll shoot for a list of names."

"Good. Have Vince help there. He's good on ex-cons," Cole said. "The key is her phone. You know anybody in the department who might help?"

"I do, but we shouldn't push SPD too hard on that aspect. It could be seen as interfering."

"I get that, but we can sure as hell nudge them," Cole said. "We need everyone to push their sources and contacts on the street and online with her picture. We need everybody working every angle."

"Got it," Leeder said.

"And," Cole added, "can you call that web team and tell them to get the site up with the contact info and reward offer as soon as possible?"

Cole's attention shifted to the Onondaga County helicopter. It had been hovering over one area of Lucifer's Green for a long time. The transmissions bouncing between the portable police radios had increased with an underlying tone of urgency.

"Are you guys seeing this?" Ryan asked Cole and Leeder.

"Yeah," Cole said. "Something's up."

Then a transmission came through on the radio

of an officer nearby, loud enough for them to hear clearly. *"What's the ETA on Crime Scene? We need them in here."*

A barking dog and the sounds of a commotion could be heard in the background of the radio call. The officer near Cole and Ryan moved quickly to silence his radio and insert his earpiece. Other cops nearby did the same, indicating the message should not have been heard beyond police at the scene.

"What is it? What did they find? Let me go in there." Ryan started to lift the tape to head toward the woods, but two officers blocked him.

"Sir, don't."

"Did they find my daughter?"

"Please wait here, sir."

Ryan, Cole and the others concentrated on the space between the garage and the house, which gave them a line of sight to the forest. After several long moments, they saw a man and a woman in plain clothes, and two detectives wearing latex gloves walking out of the woods toward the house.

As the two investigators neared, the man looked toward them. Ryan locked on to his eyes, and with each step the detective took, Ryan struggled to read if the answer to his worst fear was written in the investigator's movements.

10

Stan Zubik and Fran Asher walked out of the woods, ducked under the tape and went to the officers who were blocking Ryan.

After one of them introduced Ryan as Maddison Lane's father, Zubik pulled off his latex gloves and shook his hand firmly. Asher did the same.

"Mr. Lane, I'm Detective Stan Zubik. This is Detective Fran Asher, my partner. We're leading on your daughter's case, and we'd like to talk with you and your wife."

Ryan's breathing had quickened and his face was taut—he was pissed.

"What did you find out there?"

"Mr. Lane," Zubik said, "let's get your wife and go over by that patrol car where we can talk privately."

"Tell me now! Tell me what the dog found!" Ryan cast his hand in the direction of the groups of concerned friends and neighbors. "We've got fifty people ready to search the woods, but they won't let us in. Why?"

At that moment, Zubik and everyone else saw three members of the crime scene team emerge from a truck, suited head to toe in white coveralls and carrying equipment into the forest, following the path the detectives had used. Zubik then saw fear rising in Ryan.

"You tell me right now! Did you find her?" Ryan's voice got louder and Karen now stood next to him, alarmed. "We have a right to know if you found our daughter out there!" Ryan said. "Tell me now or I swear to God, I'll go out there to look for myself and you'll have to shoot me to stop me!"

The air tensed.

Zubik, the seasoned detective, knew it was critical to protect evidence, to be strategic when revealing and playing his cards, that knowledge of the facts was essential to controlling the case. And while he also knew the pain the victims' families suffered, he knew too that in most cases a family member was behind the crime.

"I understand you're upset, Mr. Lane. But we need to talk privately. There're matters we need to discuss. Please."

Zubik allowed a moment for Ryan's blood to cool and for him to yield to his request. Then, before he and Asher led Ryan and Karen away to talk, Cole Lane moved to join them. Zubik recognized him and said, "We've got this, Cole, just Ryan and Karen."

Cole knew Zubik from the old days and didn't push it. He resumed talking with his investigators.

* * *

Standing next to a patrol car at the edge of their driveway while other officers kept people away provided the detectives and the Lanes privacy.

"We did not locate Maddison in the forest," Zubik said.

"You didn't?" Ryan said.

"No."

"Oh thank God!" Karen said. "We thought she was—"

Zubik held up his palm. "I know. What we found could be part of the investigation, so we're treating it as potential evidence. You have to appreciate that I can't tell you what it is at this time, but what we found may or may not help us. Do you understand?"

Ryan and Karen nodded.

"Now, we've got a lot of people working flat-out to help us locate Maddison. We've got people here from our Missing Persons unit, who can coordinate search efforts with the community, but most important, Fran and I are going to need your full cooperation."

"Of course, whatever you need," Karen said.

"Thank you. We're going into your house. We'll evaluate things. It'll take a little time, but when we come out, we'll tell you what we need next."

Ryan stared hard at Zubik.

"Detective Zubik," he said. "Do you believe Maddie's okay? Tell us what your gut tells you. We need to know."

Zubik looked into Ryan's eyes, then Karen's.

"We've found no evidence that she's been harmed. At this stage, she's missing, and we'll continue investigating until we locate her and bring her home to her family."

"Thank you." Karen blinked back her tears. "Thank you."

Careful to follow the same paths taken earlier by the officers, Zubik and Asher carried out a preliminary investigation of the Lanes' vehicles, the garage and the yard surrounding the house, the ladder and the area under Maddison's bedroom window.

"Greer and Porter were smart to seal the place right away," Asher said as they pulled on shoe covers and fresh latex gloves.

They went inside and continued examining rooms in the house, concentrating on Maddie's bedroom. It smelled mildly of soap, Zubik thought, as he and Asher examined it. They first focused on the muddied carpet, the mud streak near the sill and the window, taking photos and notes.

"That's a strong indication someone from outside entered and exited through the window," Asher said. "Dad says all the doors were locked and chained from the inside."

"It's a possibility."

"What're you thinking?"

"She could've climbed out. Jumped."

"Jumped? Stan, that's a six- to eight-foot drop."

"She could've hung down from the window.

The grass is soft. Then she could've got the ladder, climbed back in and out, or she could've had someone's help."

"Boy, you won't rule anything out, will you?"

"It's early. We don't have all the facts. We'll have to see what Crime Scene comes up with, and where our cyber people are at on the phone's service carrier so we can find out who Maddison last communicated with before she left this room."

They turned their attention to the bed, still unmade and untouched from when Maddison last slept in it. Zubik and Asher took either side and felt under the mattress for anything concealed there, possibly a diary.

Asher then looked under the bed while Zubik sifted gingerly through Maddison's dresser drawers before he went to her closet and looked through her clothes, checking her pockets. Then he got on his knees and searched inside her shoes.

"What's in there, Stan?"

"Everybody has secrets, Fran. She could've been approached by her abductor before. He may have given her a gift, tricked her into keeping their relationship secret. Shoes and pockets can be hiding places."

Finding nothing, he took stock of all the walls, Maddison's posters of pop stars, then the shelves crowded with her stuffed animals. He picked up a white polar bear.

"Ice Baby," Asher said.

"Who?"

"Ice Baby, Stan. From Greer and Porter's briefing and the photo we've posted of her. Ice Baby is her favorite stuffed animal." Looking around, taking video and notes Asher said, "Stan, someone was in this room, someone who took her or lured her, and I'm getting a bad feeling. What do you say?"

"We gotta keep an open mind, Fran. It could've been someone lurking in the neighborhood stalking her. She also could've faked the whole thing to get attention, get back at her mother. Or it could've been staged to cover up another crime. We don't know." Zubik looked up at the fluorescent glow of the dark stars and moons on the ceiling.

They weren't glowing now.

Zubik didn't like being here in this little girl's room, touching her things, but it was his job. He'd looked upon corpses of children, and into the faces of killers. He'd touched death and confronted evil in all its forms. It was his sworn duty to learn the truth.

Wherever it leads me.

11

What's taking the detectives so long in the house?

Karen looked beyond her home to the dark woods of Lucifer's Green.

What did they find out there that Zubik thinks is potential evidence? Why won't they tell us anything?

Questions tormented Karen amid the upheaval surrounding her home, the helicopter, distant sirens and more people arriving to help. She felt like she was outside her body as she watched Cole directing volunteers and Jill, her hand on Tyler's back, comforting him as he and Dalton studied their phones.

Then Karen looked at her phone, pinging in her hand with supportive messages from friends but nothing that pointed to where Maddie was. It tore at Karen's heart staring at Maddie's smiling face on the screen.

My baby, my little girl, what happened? Did I say something that set you off? Did you run away with a friend to show me you're angry, to hurt me? Well, you showed me and you hurt me. But is this

*what you think being mature is? My God, you're
a twelve-year-old little girl!*

Karen's fingertips traced Maddie's face without touching it.

*Okay, I'm not perfect. I'm not a good mother,
I've made mistakes, I'm horrible, I'm "ruining your
life," but I'm doing the best I can and I love you
so, so much. Oh God, did some monster take you
in the night? What happened? Why won't anyone
tell us anything?*

Karen lifted her head from her phone, brushed
away her tears and saw Detectives Zubik and Asher
coming toward them.

Zubik pulled off his gloves.

"We'd like you to come with us now to our offices so we can talk further."

"Why?" Ryan asked. "We've told Porter and
Greer all we know."

"You gave them informal statements. We need
your help with other matters."

"What other matters?"

"We'll need formal statements from you, Mrs.
Lane and Tyler. And we'd like your consent to
allow our scene people to search and process your
home, to perform additional facets of our investigation."

"Like what?" Ryan said.

"Like tracking your daughter's phone, searching
for evidence on all the computers in your home,
all your phones, your vehicles, credit cards, bank

records, things of that nature. We'll need you to sign the consenting documents at our office. We'll also collect your DNA and fingerprints to compare with anything our techs find."

"DNA? Fingerprints?" Karen said. "Why do this with us?"

"To point us in the right direction to find Maddison."

"But shouldn't you be searching everywhere, knocking on doors?"

"We're doing that, Mrs. Lane, and we're bringing in more people. But we have to ensure the investigation is thorough, and for that to happen we need your cooperation."

"But you're treating us like we're the criminals!" Karen covered her face with her hands.

"I know this is upsetting, Mrs. Lane, but we need to proceed this way as quickly as possible so we can concentrate on the elements that will help us locate Maddison and bring her home to you."

"All right," Ryan told Zubik. "We'll do whatever you want, whatever it takes to find her."

Asher signaled officers to escort Tyler to them and summoned a patrol car for the family, an action that prompted Cole and Jill to join them.

"What's going on?" Cole asked.

"They want to take us downtown to get another statement and get us to sign off on searching our house," Ryan said.

"I'll go with you," Cole said.

"That's not happening," Zubik intervened. "You

know how this works, Cole. And so do the people you brought with you."

"Maddie's my niece, Stan," Cole said. "I'm going to do all I can to help find her. We're putting up a web page and offering a ten-thousand-dollar reward for information."

"We appreciate the help, but I suggest you work with our Missing Persons team on your efforts, keep them aware of anything you learn. You can help at the center, logging names, checking IDs, coordinating the neighborhood search and collecting reports."

Cole's jawline tensed as he nodded and said, "You've got to look at that residential reentry center on DeBerry and the registry."

"We'll look at everything, Cole." Zubik turned to the Lanes. "All set?"

"Wait, can I get dressed first?" Ryan looked down at his sweats and T-shirt.

"Can I change out of my work smock?" Karen asked.

"No, I'm sorry," Zubik said. "Your house is sealed. No one enters until it's processed and released."

"How long with that be?" Karen asked.

"No more than two days or so. You'll need to arrange a place to stay until then," Asher said.

"You'll stay with us," Jill said.

"Thank you."

After quick hugs, Tyler, Ryan and Karen went with the officers and got into a marked patrol car as the news crews captured images of the family being taken from the scene by police.

The back of the car smelled of air freshener and cologne, Karen thought. She looked at the plastic shield severing the front and rear seats, and imagined the types of people who'd sat in the back.

Criminals and anguished families like us.

She looked over to Ryan. He was lost in his thoughts. Tyler sat between them, and she held tight to his hand and offered him a weakened trembling smile. In her other hand, she squeezed a tissue so hard her knuckles whitened.

The police radio chattered with staccato, coded transmissions, all alien to Karen as she watched their neighborhood float by, like pieces of her life. There was the intersection where Ryan turned down the road that led to his shop. Their financial worries about the drywall business had been eclipsed. Now there was the avenue she took to her job at ShopToSave City, and the street that led to Tyler and Maddie's school. And only a few blocks back was Blue Sparrow Park, where she had taken Tyler and Maddie when they were little. They loved the wading pool, the swings, teeter-totter and sandbox.

They were so happy there, so safe.

Now, the streets rolling past outside the police car window began to blur as Karen was assailed by her greatest fear.

Will I ever see my daughter again?

12

The Syracuse Police Department's headquarters was in the Public Safety Building downtown on South State Street. The Criminal Investigations Division was on the third floor and consisted of a collection of cubicles, workstations and offices.

The Lane family followed Zubik and Asher through it like explorers who'd landed in a new world, navigating around municipal-style metal desks with veneer tops, some cluttered, some organized, all unoccupied. Steel file cabinets and bookcases holding manuals stood against the walls, which were pegged with maps, shift schedules, government notices, plaques and a large glass-framed poster of the department's crest.

The still air suggested carpet cleaner and stale coffee; the calm belied the family's desperation. The detectives sat the Lanes at a table. They waited with Zubik, and Karen put her arm around Tyler. Most days he'd shrug her off, but now he welcomed it. A minute later, Asher returned with a file folder.

"This is pretty routine." Asher placed legal papers and pens before Ryan and Karen. "Signing these gives us consent to examine your home and vehicles, all your contents, for evidence that could help us find your daughter."

"We'd also like your consent to clone your phones for the same purpose," Zubik said. "If you give your phones to us now, our Computer Forensic Unit can do it quickly and we'll get them right back to you."

"Doing this cloning gives you access to all the information on our phones?" Ryan asked, exchanging looks with Karen and Tyler.

"Yes. It will help the investigation if someone linked to Maddison's disappearance tried, or tries, contacting you."

Ryan weighed the request for a few seconds, then reached for his phone. "All right, we've got nothing to hide."

"Yes." Karen put hers alongside her husband's. "Anything to find her."

Tyler placed his phone on the table too.

"We're also in the process of getting a subpoena," Zubik said.

"A subpoena?" Ryan said.

"For your phone carrier so we can access the server for all of the messages on Maddison's phone. Our CFU people will determine who she was in contact with before she went missing. That should all happen quickly, but sometimes there are hold ups."

Ryan and Karen signed every needed document

as required. Zubik collected the paperwork with the phones.

"Later, we'll also get your fingerprints," Zubik said, "which we'll use as an elimination set when we search for evidence to determine who else was in her room and your house."

"Are we done?"

"Not yet," Zubik said. "Now we'll get formal statements from each of you and ask some questions. We'll talk to you individually. Karen and Tyler, we'll start by taking you to separate interview rooms."

"I can't be with Tyler?" Karen asked.

"No," Zubik said. "As I mentioned, we'll do this individually with each of you. Ryan, you'll have to wait right here, please."

Alone at the table, his pulse drumming in his ears, Ryan glimpsed some of the empty desks and the family photos detectives had next to their computer monitors. As the floor's ventilation fans hummed, he was pulled back to the moment in his life when he, Cole and their grieving mom were in Kraig and McWilloughbie's Funeral Home, selecting a casket for his father, who had never specified his choice. Ryan wanted mahogany, the same as his dad's desk. Cole wanted bronze. It lasted longer. Their mother settled it: oak, because it was the old man's favorite tree.

Why am I thinking of that now?

Ryan forced the thought from his mind as he

strained to understand what was happening to his family. His gaze shifted when he heard…

"…yes, Detective Martinez, Greg Martinez, Syracuse Police…"

Ryan turned; the voice was coming from behind a high-walled cubicle. Obviously someone was there working, talking on the phone.

"Yes, we're trying to locate Zach…that's right Zachary Keppler… I've called his phone and sent messages…just have him call me, Detective Martinez…"

Zach Keppler was the name of their babysitter's boyfriend, who Ryan suspected had been in the house, who'd come to pick up Crystal a few hours before Maddie disappeared.

13

Tyler was uneasy when the detectives opened the door to a windowless room. It was the kind of room where they took you if you were in serious trouble, he thought.

The walls were white, like the ceiling. In the middle was a solitary table with a chair on one side, which they asked him to take. The detectives sat in the two chairs across from him with their notebooks and files.

"I'm Syracuse Police Detective Stan Zubik, with Syracuse Police Detective Fran Asher," one detective began, stating the date and location. "We're here interviewing Tyler Lane. Tyler, are you nervous?"

He nodded.

"Son, see the camera up in the corner? This is being recorded so you have to say your answers out loud for us okay?"

"Okay."

"Are you nervous?"

"Yes."

"That's perfectly normal, that's okay. Let's start with you spelling your full name for us and giving us your date of birth. Could you do that for us?"

Tyler did.

"Good," Zubik said. "Now, I'll go over a few things. If you don't understand any of my questions or you're not sure what I mean, just ask me to explain, all right?"

"Yes."

"All we're looking for is for you to tell the truth about what you know and to be sure you understand that no matter what we ask you, it's a crime to lie to us, okay?"

"Yes."

"We need your help with our questions so we can find out what happened to your sister. You want to help us find Maddie, don't you?"

"Yes."

"Good. Okay, let's go back through what you first told Officers Greer and Porter earlier."

Tyler related in detail events of the night, starting with his parents leaving them with Crystal and on to when they ordered a pizza, watched a movie and went to bed.

"Where did you get the pizza from?"

"Zia Lorella's. We always get it there with Mom and Dad too. The delivery guy is Bennie and he's funny, always joking."

"Was Bennie alone when he came?"

"Yes."

"Did he come inside the house or anything like that?"

"Well, just inside at the front where Crystal paid him at the door. Maddie and I said, 'Hi, Bennie.' He smiled and winked at Maddie and said, 'Hey, beautiful,' that's what he always says to her, then we took the pizza and drinks to the kitchen table."

"Then after you ate, you watched the movie?"

"Yeah, *Jurassic Park*."

"Which one?"

"The very first one. We hadn't seen it, and my friends said it was good."

"What time did you start watching it?"

"I don't know. After we ate the pizza."

"Did you watch all of it?"

"Yes, and I ate some Doritos because I was still a bit hungry."

"After the movie, what did you do?"

"Maddie and I went to bed and I think, because I remember looking at my clock then, and it was maybe ten thirty."

"Did anyone visit your house during the evening, while you were eating, watching the movie, or after you'd gone to bed?"

"No."

"Do you know who Zachary Keppler is?"

"I think he's Crystal's boyfriend."

"Did he visit?"

"No."

"Did anyone visit?"

"No."

"Was Crystal talking to her boyfriend on her phone during the evening?"

"I don't know, but she was on her phone a lot, texting and stuff. I mean, she's always on her phone."

"You told the officers that you got up in the night and heard voices. Tell us about that."

"I was thirsty from the pizza and Doritos, and got up to get a drink of water from the bathroom."

"Did you know what time it was?"

"No, but it felt real late because the house was so quiet until I passed Maddie's bedroom door and I heard these voices talking softly."

"What were they saying?"

"I don't know."

"Did you recognize the voices?"

"I think one was Maddie's."

"What was the tone like, threatening, friendly, laughing or serious?"

"I don't know."

"Did you hear any screams, cries? Any sounds to suggest a struggle?"

"No, nothing like that."

"Did you see anything out of place or different?"

"No."

"What do you think was going on in your sister's room?"

"I don't know. I figured she might've been talking with Mom or someone on her phone, or playing a video."

"How would you say your mom and dad have been getting along lately?"

Tyler thought for a moment.

"Well, lately, like in the last few months, I overheard them arguing more and more about money and stuff."

"Like what?"

"About Dad's work having money problems. They never knew I could hear them talking about it. Whenever I came in the room, they talked about something else, but I could tell it was serious."

Tyler saw both detectives make a little note before Zubik resumed.

"Does your dad ever get mad?"

"Sure, sometimes."

"Has he ever hit you or your sister?"

"No."

"Have you ever seen him strike your mom?"

"No."

"What does your dad do when he gets mad?"

"He might swear, or get real quiet."

"And has he been getting mad lately?"

"No, I'd say he's about the same."

"How does your dad get along with Maddie?"

"Good, I guess. He calls her his little angel."

"What about your mom and Maddie? How do they get along?"

"Well, some days they get along fine but other days they fight."

"What do they fight about?"

"Maddie wants to date boys, but Mom says she's too young."

"Does Maddie have a boyfriend, maybe a secret one at school or online that Mom and Dad don't know about?"

"I don't think so."

"Do you know what sexting is?"

"Yes."

"Have you ever done it?"

"No."

"Do you think Maddie has done it?"

"I don't think so, no."

"Do you think Maddie could keep that a secret from you and your parents?"

"I don't know, I guess so, maybe."

"Would her girlfriends at school know her secrets?"

"Maybe. They're her friends."

"Can you tell us the names of her best friends?"

"I would say they're Brooke Carson, Lily Wong and Gabriela Rios. They all go to our school."

"Do you know if Maddie was ever bullied at school?"

"No, I don't think so."

"Did she ever bully someone at school or online?"

"No, she's not like that."

"She ever take drugs, or drink alcohol?"

"No."

"Have you?"

Tyler swallowed, casting his mind back to the warning about telling the truth.

"I tried pot and drank beer at a couple of parties I was at, but that's all."

"What else do you do that your parents might not know about?"

Tyler thought for a long time without speaking.

"Ever look at porn on your computer, Tyler?"

"No, my parents put controls on it and stuff."

"What about on a friend's computer?"

Tyler swallowed.

"Yes, I looked at it on some of my friends' computers a few times."

"Can you tell us the names of your friends?"

Tyler hesitated.

"I don't want to get anybody in trouble."

"Tyler, we need your help."

"Tate Sommer, Hunter Kent and Tristan Bryant."

"Okay, now, has Maddie ever run away from home?"

"Well, she sorta did."

"What do you mean?"

"A little while ago, a couple weeks I think. She and Mom got in a big fight, and Maddie was real mad. There was a lot of shouting and door slamming and stuff, and Maddie ran out of the house. I remember it was raining real hard, and Mom got Dad to drive down the street in his truck. He found her and brought her home. Maddie was crying and slammed the door to her room. It was pretty bad."

"Do you know what that fight was about?"

"Boys, I think. Maddie was telling Mom she was old enough to have a boyfriend because some of the girls her age at school have boyfriends."

"Were Maddie and your mom fighting yesterday?"

"A little, I think, but nothing big."

"Do you think Maddie ran away last night?"

"No."

"If she did run away, where do you think she would go?"

"I don't know, her friends', or maybe Uncle Cole's place, I don't know."

"What do you think happened last night?"

"I think someone took her."

"What makes you say that, given that she sort of ran away before?"

"This is different. I think someone got Dad's ladder, got into Maddie's room and took her."

"Do you think any of your friends may have taken her?"

"No."

"Anyone from school?"

"No."

"Anyone from the neighborhood?"

"No."

"Do you and Maddie ever fight?"

"Yes, once we had a fight and I hit her."

"You hit her?"

"With my pillow. I made some money cutting the grass for Mr. Sheridan, this old neighbor down the street. Maddie borrowed twenty-five dollars from me and didn't pay me back, and I got mad at her and hit her with my pillow."

"What did she want the money for?"

"I think to get some makeup and stuff, I'm not sure."

"Did she ever pay you back?"

"No. She cried and got sad, saying how she wished we were rich like Uncle Cole, Aunt Jill and Dalton. They give us nice presents. They gave Maddie a nice watch, once."

"And Dalton gave you those hunting knives in your room?"

"Yes, I like collecting knives."

"Those are real nice ones you have."

"Thanks."

"Ever use them to kill anything, Tyler?"

"No, but I wish I—" Tyler looked away.

"What do you wish?"

"That I could've used one of my knives to get whoever was in my sister's room. I would've fought them."

"You would've stabbed them?"

"Yes, to save Maddie."

Zubik looked at Tyler for a long time before he leaned forward.

"Suppose I told you that I didn't believe you?"

"What? What do you mean?"

"Tyler, did you kill your sister?"

"No!"

"Maybe you got mad at her for something, got

the ladder to make it look like someone else, then took her into the woods and killed her?"

"No!"

"Because we found something in the woods, you know."

"What?" Tyler's eyes widened, then went from Zubik to Asher and back in a futile search for an answer and his chin crumpled. "What did you find? Is Maddie dead?"

"I didn't say that. But you have to tell us the truth. Did you hurt Maddie?"

"I didn't hurt her! I didn't do anything to my sister!"

"What about your friends? Maybe they hurt Maddie?"

"No! I don't know who took her!" He began wiping his tears.

Zubik and Asher looked at him for a long silent time.

"It's all right, Tyler. We're finished for now," Zubik said.

14

Zubik and Asher would not reveal to Karen what they had found in the woods.

Something's wrong, she thought.

Just like it was that day Karen was thirteen and returned home from school to an empty house. It was odd, she thought as she called for her mother, who was always home. Then, glancing outside, Karen was happy to see her in the backyard working in her garden—until she looked again.

Why's Mom sleeping on the lawn?

Karen went into the yard. Something wasn't right. She tried to wake her but couldn't. Her mother was not breathing. Something was wrong. Alarmed, Karen called 911 then tried giving her the CPR she'd learned in school, all while begging her to wake up.

But Karen knew.

Her mom was dead.

Yet kneeling over her on the grass under a clear blue sky, Karen couldn't believe it was true. She sobbed against her mother's cheek, drank in her fresh soapy scent and cradled her in that faded print cotton top she wore and those torn, paint-stained jeans, smelling the soil, the flowers, kissing her forehead and screaming.

Come back! Mom, please come back!

Karen had felt so helpless that day. Nothing made sense. Nothing was real. She never heard the siren, never felt the paramedics gently pry her mother out of her arms. And now, as Karen sat in a stark interview room with Zubik and Asher staring at her, refusing to tell her what they'd discovered in Lucifer's Green, half-hearing their questions, she could feel disbelief and helplessness building and swirling inside her as they did that day. Only now her heart screamed for her daughter.

Come back! Maddie, please come back!

"Karen?" Zubik asked her again. "Is that correct?"

The detective had been relentless ever since he'd pointed to the camera and explained the process. Karen had answered question after question and had given them a time line covering the twenty-fours in her family's life before Maddie vanished. But Zubik kept going over everything again and again.

"In the hours prior to your daughter's disappearance you had an argument with her. Is that correct?"

"Yes."

"What were the issues of contention?"

"As I said, I told her she was too young to start dating boys."

"Was the argument about a specific boy?"

"No."

"Does she have a boyfriend?"

"No."

"Is it possible she has a secret boyfriend you're not aware of?"

"I doubt it because she'd tell me."

"You're certain of that?"

"Yes, I believe that."

"You don't think girls your daughter's age keep secrets?"

"I know my daughter."

"Did you ever lose your temper with Maddison?"

"Yes." Karen's voice weakened.

"What happens when you lose your temper with her?"

"We yell at each other."

"Did you ever strike her?"

"No."

"Did she ever strike you?"

"No."

"Are you being truthful to us, Karen?"

"Yes." She wiped her tears.

Zubik paged back through his notes.

"We understand that as recently as a couple of weeks ago, Maddison ran out of your home after an argument with you about boys and that you sent your husband to find her and bring her back. Is that correct?"

Somewhere deep inside, Karen felt a new emotional detonation and the room began spinning, casting her back in time to Maddie's face contorted in adolescent anger...

Why are you ruining my life? Other girls my age date boys! Other girls my age wear makeup and get piercings! I'm a young woman now! Why are you ruining my life? Why? Why? Why? I hate you! I hate you so much!

Maddie's words had pierced Karen because they were the same words she'd spewed at her mother the morning of the day she died, for the same reasons: wanting to dress the way she wanted, wanting to wear makeup and go out with boys. Karen soon realized that the things she'd said were hurtful, and all day in school she'd regretted it, was ashamed. They'd already endured so much pain. She had rushed home intent on apologizing and begging her mom to forgive her.

But it was too late.

Her mother died, and the last words Karen had said to her were hateful.

At the funeral, numbed by grief and guilt, Karen had watched her mother's casket descend into her grave, taking her away forever without her knowing the truth. Karen wanted to crawl into it with her, put her arms around her and say she was sorry, sorry for everything. Her father looked broken, and mourned with a bottle in his hand for the next three years until he died.

Karen went to live with her aunt and uncle, people she barely knew, or liked. Alone at night she cursed God for all that had happened to her family. First, the death of Cassie, Karen's younger sister, and the troubling questions that lingered over how she died. Then her mother's death. Karen had lost faith in life, drank, took drugs, had sex with most any guy who wanted it, didn't care what happened to her until a wise, patient school counselor saved her by making her take a good hard look at herself.

Karen stopped drinking, stopped taking drugs, stopped sleeping around and eventually took a few community college courses with a goal of being a nurse. But she dropped out when she got a full-time cashier's job at what was then Kleigermann's Supermart and shared an apartment with a girlfriend. Then she met Ryan and they fell in love. He was gentle, kind, hardworking and good-looking. His family became her family. Karen loved his parents and his brother, Cole, who was also easy on the eyes. Karen was thankful for her life. It was never perfect, it was never easy, but they were happy. They were ordinary working people doing the best they could.

"Karen?" Zubik said. "Did Maddison run out of your home?"

"Yes. We argued, she ran out in the rain. I sent Ryan after her. He found her walking in the neighborhood and brought her home."

"What makes you think Maddison didn't run away this time?"

"She didn't. Someone was in her room. There's the mud, the ladder!"

"Okay, but let's just say she did run away. Where do you think she would go? Where might she have been heading when she ran off a few weeks ago?"

Karen cupped her face in her hands and shook her head.

"A friend's house? I don't know if she was headed anywhere then, but I know that last night she didn't run away. She was taken!"

"All right. Now, you said Maddison wears a bra, started menstruating a few months ago, experienced mood swings and considered herself mature for her age."

"Yes."

"Would you say she's flirtatious, promiscuous?"

"No, she's twelve years old!"

"Does she use drugs or drink alcohol?"

"No."

"What kind of a personality does she have, outgoing or shy?"

"Outgoing, independent."

"Is she a good student?"

"I'd say above average."

"Did she spend a lot of time online, or on her phone?"

"No more than any other girl her age."

"You say your daughter was holding her phone in her hand and had fallen asleep while gripping it."

"Yes."

"Do you know exactly who she may have been talking to?"

"No. I'm sure it was a friend."

"Could she have met a stranger online and ran off to meet them or another friend?"

"It's possible, but we set up parental controls on Maddie and Tyler's phones and computers, so she only talked with people she knew."

"Do you have any idea who she communicated with before she went missing?"

"I'm guessing one of her friends, but I've contacted all of their parents and I also gave you a list of names of her friends and their families. Aren't your experts working on tracking down her phone?"

"Yes, they are. What about Crystal Hedrick. Do you have any concerns that she may have played a role in Maddison's disappearance?"

"No."

"Your husband suspects that, contrary to your wishes, Crystal invited her boyfriend, Zachary Keppler, to your home after the children went to bed. Do you share those concerns?"

"I have no concerns because Maddie and Tyler were asleep in their beds when I checked, and that was after Zach picked up Crystal."

"What about the possibility of Zachary returning in the night?"

"Why? It makes no sense. Have you talked to him and Crystal about his whereabouts?"

"We're looking at everything. We're not ruling

anything out yet. Now, did Maddison ever indicate any problems with her friends?"

"No."

"Any problems at school?"

"No."

"Other than the dating issue, arguments and mood swings, is there anything she complained about?"

"Nothing, really. I know she said that she was envious of her uncle Cole and his family because they have a bigger house and more money than we do. Maddie got frustrated when we couldn't do all the things they did, like go to Europe or Disney World."

"How was Maddison's relationship with her uncle's family?"

"Good. She worships her uncle as a hero and loves Jill, who treats her like a daughter. Dalton's a bit older than Maddie and Tyler. They look up to him as their cooler, worldly cousin because he's traveled places with his dad, has seen more and done more."

"All right, let's come back to your relationship with Ryan. Do you think he's ever lied to you?"

"No."

"Ever cheated on you?"

"No."

"Have you ever cheated on him or lied to him?"

"No, my God, what kind of questions are these?"

"Has Ryan ever struck you?"

"No."

"Has he ever struck the children?"

"Never."

"Does he ever lose his temper?"

"Yes, who doesn't? He runs his own business and is under a lot of stress."

"So there's tension in the home related to his business?"

"A little. He's going through a rough patch now, but it wouldn't have anything to do with Maddie."

"Do you think your husband's involved in your daughter's disappearance?"

"Absolutely not!"

"You think Tyler's involved?"

"No, that's ridiculous!"

"What about Maddison's uncle and his family, Jill or Dalton?"

"Are you crazy? No!"

"What do you think happened, Karen?"

"I don't know. There's that halfway house with convicts on the other side of the woods, there could be sex offenders living in the neighborhood, someone could've been stalking Maddie."

"Yes, all those are possibilities we're investigating."

"Why won't you tell me what you found in the forest?"

"What do you think we found?"

"Oh my God, you want to play guessing games with me? How can you ask such horrible questions? Why're you being so cruel?"

"I'm sorry, Karen, but the fact is we've got to be

careful with our investigation. Until we determine what happened, we have to ask every question you can imagine. What we found may be completely unrelated, but for now we're just not disclosing any information on that. Our goal is to find Maddison safe and bring her home to you."

"Is she hurt? Tell me if she's hurt, please!"

"We have no evidence to indicate that she's hurt. At this stage she's missing. She may have been taken or lured from her room, or she may have run off with a friend or stranger. We're doing all we can to get answers and to locate her."

Karen's eyes went around the sterile room before she stared into her empty hands. She was being punished again. A great karmic wheel had turned full circle, crushing her with agony for what she had put her mother through.

All Karen wanted was to protect Maddie, to keep her from making the same mistakes she had.

Oh God.

15

Unshaven, his hair wild, Ryan could feel his pulse drumming in his ears.

Zubik kept asking him the same things, going round and round, pulling him into a raging whirlpool until Ryan couldn't take it anymore and slammed his palms on the interview room table.

"I've answered these questions! Stop repeating them and tell me what you found in Lucifer's Green!"

Zubik didn't speak.

"The dog picked up Maddie's scent," Ryan said. "We heard the radios, saw the reaction. Whatever you found has to be serious. What is it? I have a right to know!"

Zubik and Asher stared at him for several seconds, their faces blank.

"Is she dead? Did you find Maddie out there? Tell me!"

"Ryan," Zubik said, "we didn't find your daughter in the woods. We're still searching there and everywhere. But we're not prepared to disclose at this time what we found. It may be related to the investigation. It may not. But for now we need to keep that aspect confidential. I hope you understand."

"Understand? Christ, we're talking about my missing daughter! I have every right to know what the hell you're doing to find her!"

"I appreciate that this is hard on you and your family, but we have a job to do and we have to do it properly at every step to ensure we find Maddison. You've got to work with us."

"Work with you? Someone climbed into Maddie's bedroom. Now she's gone, you won't tell me anything and you're telling me to work with you?"

"That's what you believe happened, that someone abducted her?"

"For God's sake yes. How many times do I have to tell you? She was taken. It's obvious. All the doors were bolted and chained from the inside. Mud streaks were on the carpet and near the window. You saw the ladder."

"But no one heard screams or a struggle?"

"Tyler heard voices in her room. Maybe the guy had a weapon and threatened her to keep quiet. Someone was in her room!"

"Yes, it *appears* that's what's happened."

"Look at Crystal's boyfriend! My gut tells me he was in the house at some point, and I don't trust that guy. Look at the halfway house, check the sex offender registries for creeps living around us."

"We're doing that," Zubik said. "Now, about

your brother helping you. Did you call him before you called police?"

Ryan hesitated. "No."

"What was the first call you made after discovering Maddie was gone?"

"We called her phone, then I called our service provider to locate her phone, then I called police."

"Then at some point you called your brother to help you?"

"Yes."

"He's a former Syracuse police officer, a decorated soldier, bestselling author, a somewhat famous figure, who now operates a successful private investigations company. He arrives with a team of investigators, all ex–law enforcement knowledgeable with police procedure. He puts up a ten-thousand-dollar reward for information that leads to the return of his niece. Cole sure looks like he wants to lead things. He's a take-charge kind of guy, wouldn't you say?"

A take-charge kind of guy?

Ryan considered the question, reflecting with ambivalence on his relationship with Cole, and in a flash remembered when they were both teens. Ryan had been happily heading off to work one morning to join his dad on a job site. In the kitchen, Cole said to him, *I don't know how you can do that, Ry, all the plaster, the dust, that backbreaking stuff. I could never do it, especially all day with* him.

His brother's words had pierced him. Even later when Cole told him that he just wanted to do something else with his life, Ryan understood, but in his heart he took Cole's feeling as a betrayal of their dad, of all he'd struggled for.

Ryan couldn't forgive Cole for that.

Even after Cole became a cop, then a soldier, even after he was blown up and lost his legs, and his will to live; even as he and Karen rescued him, brought him back from the edge; even after Cole triumphed, rebuilt his life with Jill, Dalton, wrote his book, started his business and achieved wealth to become a superhero.

All while Ryan struggled to keep his dad's dry-wall business afloat.

Ryan's resentment was still there. Only maybe it had hardened.

And now, Cole comes in with his people, his money, that there's-nothing-I-can't-handle drive of his, making Ryan feel helpless, and so damned obliged. Yes, Ryan loved Cole and needed his help now more than ever, but deep down he knew he could never shake his hard feelings, his bitterness.

And his envy.

"Yes," Ryan said, "my brother's doing all he can to help us."

"That's fine. We appreciate everyone's help, but we just don't want any complications where your brother's concerned."

"Complications? What're you talking about?"

"If he or his people discover anything that could be pertinent to the investigation, he must bring it to our attention immediately. Failing to do so could be construed as obstruction."

"Of course he would. Do you think we've got something to hide?"

Zubik let a moment pass before moving on.

"Ryan, are you given to losing your temper when you're under stress?"

He looked at Zubik without answering.

"Have you ever lost your temper with Maddie?"

"No."

"No? Come on, all parents lose their temper at some point."

"I may have raised my voice a few times when she didn't do what her mother and I asked her to do."

"Ever get physical with your daughter? Ever strike her?"

"No."

"What about in other instances? Have you ever lost your temper, ever resorted to violence?"

Ryan looked at Zubik and didn't answer.

"We understand your drywall business is in financial trouble."

Ryan said nothing.

"Things got out of control at the bank yesterday, didn't they?" Zubik opened a folder to a report. "How come you didn't disclose to Officers Greer and Porter, even your wife for that matter, how things ended after Henry Driscoll turned you down for a loan you desperately needed to help your business?"

Zubik referred to the report, summarizing what he was reading.

"When Driscoll rejected your loan request, you stood up in a threatening manner, picked up your chair, smashed it against the side of his desk and were verbally abusive. Driscoll summoned the security officer to his office. It happened that two SPD officers from Patrol Division, Simkin and Hughes, were in the bank at the time and assisted. You were asked to leave. Driscoll never swore out a complaint but conveyed your situation to the officers."

Ryan's face reddened.

"I was angry. I needed the loan."

"You're at risk of losing your business, aren't you, Ryan?"

"Yes."

"A business your father started and has been in your family for decades?"

"Yes."

"During your meeting with Driscoll, you'd mentioned your family's life insurance policies. We understand the benefit on each of the children is seventy-five thousand dollars. You were seeking a loan for sixty thousand dollars."

Zubik set the report down flat on the table and looked at him.

Ryan said nothing.

"It's interesting," Zubik said. "It's also interesting that in the time before you called police you were on your computer attempting to do something with Maddison's phone. Were you attempting to wipe it?"

"No!" Ryan sat straighter. "I was on the computer trying to locate Maddie's phone. And yes, I did lose my temper at the bank because I'm trying to save the business my father built! Why're you twisting things?"

Zubik said nothing, keeping a poker face while eyeing Ryan.

"I know this is unpleasant," Zubik said, "but in our effort to find Maddison, you don't want us to leave any stone unturned, do you?"

"No."

"That's why at this stage we can't rule out anything."

Ryan said nothing.

"Ryan, we may need you and your family to consent to polygraph exams."

"Polygraphs?"

"To help us rule you out as having had anything to do with your daughter's disappearance. Would you be willing to cooperate?"

Ryan looked long and hard at Zubik.

"We've got nothing to hide."

16

Syracuse police officers, county deputies and state troopers walked shoulder to shoulder, searching the woods behind Maddison Lane's home while her family watched.

Ryan stood with his arm around Karen. She held Tyler in front of her as they looked toward Lucifer's Green from their street. Juxtaposed against their house and the distant forest, the Lanes were a portrait of anguish that the news cameras had captured from afar in the moments after a patrol car had brought them back from police headquarters.

During the time they were downtown being questioned, the search for Maddie had grown. More volunteers, more police and more media had arrived. While coordinating his investigative team and the volunteer search, Cole Lane had become the family's contact, keeping the press far back, affording the family privacy so he could talk to them.

"How did it go?" Cole asked Ryan.

Without looking at him, Ryan dragged his hands over his face.

"They practically accused us of being involved, distorting and misinterpreting our lives. Then they took our fingerprints and swabbed our cheeks for DNA."

"That's to be expected."

Ryan turned to his brother. "They asked Tyler if he killed his sister. Then they suggested I wanted to kill Maddie for insurance money."

"They'd be sloppy if they didn't go hard on you. They've got to look at everybody because often in cases like this a family member is responsible for the crime."

Ryan shook his head and resumed staring at the woods.

"They won't let us go in there," Ryan said. "They say they've got to keep the public out to protect potential evidence. They won't tell us what they found in there, and that scares the hell out of me. So does that halfway house."

"If they found her, we'd know. You've got to stay positive. My guys will talk to their sources about the halfway house. We've also been combing through the registry. It doesn't look like any level twos or threes, the predator types at risk to reoffend, have moved into your immediate area."

"Can we be sure about that?"

"No system's perfect," Cole said. "We've also got something from Dalton. He's been talking to neighborhood kids. Seems two weeks ago, two fifteen-year-old girls three blocks from you were followed home by a creepy guy who wanted to know where they lived."

Ryan looked at his brother.

"We've passed it on to police," Cole said. "There's a lot happening. Your neighbors with home security are volunteering footage to police. We've got a new web page with tip line numbers, and Maddie's friends have blasted out appeals for help. Donations for the reward are coming in, a big one from Karen's employer. The total is now just over twenty thousand dollars. I promise you Ry, we're going to bring Maddie home."

Ryan looked at his brother then said, "Thank you."

Cole glanced toward the news crews and satellite trucks lining the street, some up on lawns or blocking driveways.

"I've been getting calls from the *New York Times*, the *Washington Post*, wire services and the twenty-four-hour news networks, using their local affiliates. They want a news conference with you and Karen, and we think you need to do it."

"We?"

"The police believe it can help and I agree."

"When?"

"As soon as possible." Cole searched the groups of people nearby then waved. "Syracuse PD has sent down their spokesman, Sergeant Roy Retler. Here he comes."

Ryan looked at Karen then said, "I don't know, Cole."

"You should do this press conference for Maddie," Cole said as Retler arrived and introductions were made.

"It can be very helpful getting solid information out there," Retler said. "I'll take most of the questions about the investigation. Ryan and Karen, just say a few words from your heart."

"That's right," Cole said. "I'll give you a few points to stress."

"We'll go in about ten minutes, and we'll keep it short," Retler said. "This will likely go live across the country, so it's important to bear in mind that whoever is responsible will likely see you. This is the best way to speak directly to them, and with everyone watching, it could lead to a break. You don't want to antagonize them. You just want your daughter back—stress that. Okay?"

Karen and Ryan exchanged nervous glances.

"We'll do it," Karen said.

A small portable podium stood on the sidewalk in front of the Lanes' house, making for an impromptu press area.

Near it, several TV news cameras topped tripods. Operators stood ready as did more than two dozen other reporters with camera phones, notebooks, recorders, and microphones with station flags. Last-minute calls regarding coordinates and feeds were made to networks as on-camera people primped and preened hair and teeth, checked earpieces and handheld mikes.

When he emerged with Ryan and Karen, Syracuse police sergeant Roy Retler began the conference by identifying himself and the Lanes, then outlining the case.

As he spoke, Karen slipped into a surreal state.

Maddie's gone, disappeared in the night from our home. Why is this happening? Oh God, please help me...

When Retler had finished summarizing events, he continued, "I want to stress that we have increasing resources committed to this investigation, and will be forming a multiagency task force with Onondaga County, New York State Police, the FBI and others. I'll take a few questions, then the Lanes will make a statement. Let's get started."

"Do you have a suspect at this time?"

"No."

"Is this a kidnapping for ransom, Sergeant?"

"At this point we don't know if it's for ransom, or not."

"Is it possible that Maddison is a runaway?"

"It's possible, but indications are that someone other than Maddison entered and exited the Lane home through her bedroom window in the rear, so we're treating this as an abduction."

"Is it possible she communicated with someone online, someone posing as a friend?"

"That's one line of the investigation. We're looking at all computers and devices used by her and her family."

"Does that include computers used by people employed at Mr. Lane's drywall business?"

"Yes. The family has been quick to volunteer all devices for analysis and cooperate with the investigation."

"Have you questioned and cleared any members of the family? Have you ruled anybody out?"

"We're not ruling out anybody until we concentrate on a suspect. We're looking at every aspect of this case. We're not eliminating anybody, but we have some strong leads that are outside the family that we're following."

"Can you say what those leads are?"

"No."

"Have there been any red flags from Maddison's school to indicate a fellow student, or teacher as a suspect? What about her coaches and instructors? We understand she takes gymnastics."

"We'll be interviewing everyone."

"Have you administered any polygraph tests at this stage?"

"I'm not going to discuss polygraphs."

"Have you interviewed inmates at the halfway house on the other side of Lucifer's Green?"

"That's part of the investigation."

"Do you know the name of the person Maddison Lane last had contact with?"

"That's under investigation."

"Have you obtained search warrants for anything related to this case?"

"I'm not going to discuss warrants."

"Do you have any items that have been sent to the lab?"

"I'm not going to discuss potential evidence."

"We understand something of interest was discovered in the forest after a K-9 unit picked up Maddison's scent. Can you indicate what that is?"

"Again, we're not prepared to discuss that."

"Do the Lanes have home security cameras?"

"Unfortunately no. They were planning to install a system prior to this happening, but hadn't yet."

"Is that a red flag?"

"I'm not going to speculate or discuss that."

"Has anything emerged from home security cameras in the neighborhood?"

"We're analyzing that."

"If this is an abduction, do you have any idea of what the motive might be?"

"Not at this time. Okay, before we end this we'll call on Karen and Ryan Lane to each make a brief statement. They will take no questions."

Exhausted and heartbroken, the Lanes stepped to the podium and into the brilliant TV lights. Ryan glanced down at the words on the folded sheet of notebook paper that Cole had given him, then looked into the cameras and cleared his throat.

"Maddie, if you can see or hear us, please know that we're doing all we can to help you. We want you to come home safely to us. We love you."

He turned to Karen and put his arm around her, pulling her tight to him. Trembling, she brushed a tear from her cheek, nearly overwhelmed by the cameras, the intense light glaring at her as if in judgment.

This is real. This is happening. My daughter, my baby's missing.

Karen's throat went dry. She glanced at Ryan then saw Cole. Both men nodded encouragement. She had to do this for Maddie.

At that moment, the cameras tightened on her, the lines on her face, her reddened eyes. Here was Karen Lane, the anguished mother, a working woman in her cashier's smock, whose daughter was missing.

Taking a deep breath, she unfolded her small piece of notepaper and as she spoke her voice quavered.

"Sweetheart, if you see me, or hear my voice, I love you. We're doing everything to bring you home safely. Please know that I love you so much. Whoever did this, please—" Karen's voice broke. Sobbing, she gasped for air. "Please let our daughter come home. I'm begging you."

17

Crystal Hedrick twisted her ring whenever she was nervous.

Now as her father faced the two detectives—the woman's name was Asher and the man's was Zubik—standing in their living room, Crystal twisted it more than she'd ever done before.

"We're going to do all we can to help you find Maddison Lane, but I want to know—does our daughter need a lawyer?" Her dad, a welder who feared nothing, stood between her and the police, his tattooed arms folded across his chest. "On the phone you said you wanted to interview her, but I know how these things can go."

"Mr. Hedrick," Asher said, "I assure you she does not require an attorney. We only want to talk to her about her time babysitting at the Lanes' home last evening."

"Daddy, I want to help," Crystal said, looking at her mother then the TV.

The sound was off, but it showed news footage of the activity at the Lanes' home, the news conference, the helicopter over the woods, worried neighbors searching for Maddie. Crystal wanted to rush to the Lanes' to help find Maddie, but the two officers who first came to their door to talk to her had requested that she remain home. Then a detective called to tell her dad they were on their way to talk to her some more, and he abandoned his plans to go to the auto show.

"Look," her dad said to the detectives. "I know how an 'interview' can turn into an interrogation. Crystal did nothing wrong. She's just the sitter, and those Lane kids were safe in their beds when she left."

"Mr. Hedrick." Zubik looked hard at him. "I'm sure it's not your intention to make it difficult for us to do our job, but we can interview your daughter privately here, or in our offices downtown. Which will it be?"

A moment of silence passed before it was broken by Crystal's mother.

"Would you like some coffee?" her mom offered the detectives.

"Yes, thank you," Zubik said.

A few minutes later, Crystal was alone with the detectives on the sofa in the paneled basement, the walls covered with framed photos of classic cars. The door was shut, and she was rotating her ring as they started by switching on a small digital recorder.

They saw the tears brimming in Crystal's eyes.

"Crystal," Zubik started, "it's okay to be nervous. I'm going to tell you right off that after we're done, we'd like you to volunteer your phone to us so we can clone it. That's important. Can you shut it off for now?"

"Okay."

"And we'll need your fingerprints later today. It's all standard and it will help us very much. You want to help us, don't you?"

"Yes."

"Good. All you have to do is tell us the truth," Zubik began.

For the next several minutes, Crystal detailed her time spent babysitting Maddie and Tyler. She answered every question Zubik asked about her knowledge of the children and the Lane family before he came back to ask again about last night.

"Crystal, did you invite your boyfriend, Zachary Keppler, into the Lanes' home last night even though it was against the family's rules?"

Crystal swallowed and twisted her ring.

"Yes." Her chin crumpled.

"Had you ever done this before?"

"Yes, a couple of times."

"And when you did it last night, was this after you put Maddie and Tyler to bed or before?"

"After. When the movie was over."

"When did Zachary leave?"

"Just before midnight."

"When Zachary picked you up, where did you both go?"

"He drove me home in his dad's car."

"What time did you arrive home here?"

"It was a little after midnight."

"Can anyone verify that?"

"My mom was up watching a movie on TV."

"Do you know where Zachary may have gone after taking you home?"

Crystal shrugged. "Home, I guess."

"You're not sure?"

"Well, I figure home because he told me he had to leave town in the morning."

"Leave town? Did he say why?"

"No."

"Did you ask him?"

"Yes, and he got a little mad. He said it was private and didn't want to talk about it."

"Do you know where he was going?"

"No, but I think he had to take a bus because his father would not let him drive his car outside of the city."

"Have you tried reaching Zachary on his phone this morning?"

"Yes. I texted and called but he hasn't answered."

The detectives each made notes.

"Did Zachary ever see Maddie last night?"

"No."

"Do you know if Zachary has ever met Maddie?"

"I think when we saw them once or twice at the mall."

"Was he attracted to her?"

"What? No, she's twelve."

"Did he ever speak of her?"

"Once he said she was real cute, that's all."

"Did he ever enter Maddison's room last night?"

"No. I was with him the whole time on the sofa or in the kitchen. He had some pizza and a soda."

"What did you do on the sofa?"

"Watched videos on our phones, we kissed and stuff."

"Did you have sex?"

All the color drained from Crystal's face.

"Crystal, you have to tell us the truth."

"Yes," she whispered.

"Was Zachary ever out of your sight the whole time he was in the house?"

She didn't respond; she was so worried so afraid.

"Crystal?"

"Yes, one time he went outside because I told him to go outside."

"Why did you tell him to go outside?"

"After we—after, you know, he wanted to smoke a joint, and I didn't want him to do it in the house."

"So you didn't go outside with him?"

"No. I don't like pot."

"Where exactly did he go to smoke?"

"I told him to go in the backyard."

"The backyard?"

"Yes."

"That's where the window to Maddison's room is, isn't it?"

"Yes."

"And after Zachary drove you home, he said he'd be leaving town in the morning but wouldn't tell you the reason?"

Crystal wiped away a tear on her cheek and twisted her ring.

"He didn't do anything wrong. I know he didn't."

18

Minutes after Zubik and Asher had returned to work at their desks in the Public Safety Building, their captain, Moe Tilden, approached them while reading an advisory on his phone.

"We grabbed Zachary Keppler before he boarded a bus for Rochester. They'll process him then bring him to you, Stan."

"That's a break," Zubik said.

"It is." Tilden was still looking at his phone. "Got a few updates for you. First is on the warrant for phone records. The Lanes' cell phone provider is sending us a log of the girl's messages. No content, just numbers, times. Last one she made was at 1:47 this morning."

"But we have the number she communicated with?"

"Yes." Tilden cursed as he read the update. "It's linked to a burner. That may dead-end us on who owns it. We'll get the FBI to help us on that."

"What about our crime scene people?" Zubik

said. "Any latents from what we found in the for-est? Anything from the ladder or her room yet?"

"Nothing yet. It's all ongoing. We're gridding the woods. We're also working with Onondaga to help us get people to the halfway house to start checking on the whereabouts of inmates, and we've got tips coming in, a lot on the go." Before Tilden left, he said, "We'll have a case-status meeting later today."

Asher called Zubik to her desk where she'd been digging into Zachary Keppler's background. "Take a look at this." She pointed her pen to the file on her monitor. "He's got no record, nothing, but this is interesting."

Zubik read the file then stuck out his bottom lip, looked up to see an officer standing before them. He was with the unit that had picked up Keppler at the bus station.

"We've just put your guy in number two," the officer said.

"Thank you," Zubik said. "Good work."

So this was Zachary Keppler, the kid who gave Maddison Lane's father a "bad vibe," Zubik thought as he and Asher sat across from him.

Keppler had an abundance of piercings, a nose stud, lip loops, an eyebrow ring and earrings. His arms and neck were laced with tattoos. Sitting there alone at the table, he looked like a scared seventeen-year-old.

"What's going on? Nobody will tell me anything. Can I call my dad?"

"I'm Detective Zubik. This is Detective Asher. We'd just like to talk to you, Zachary." Zubik nodded to the camera in the upper corner. "And you should know that this is being recorded."

Keppler cast an eye to the camera. "I like to be called Zach."

"All right, Zach. First we have to advise you that you have the right to remain silent..."

Keppler's jaw dropped as Zubik continued.

"...anything you say can and will be used against you in a court of law. You have the right to an attorney. If you cannot afford an attorney, one will be provided for you. Do you understand these rights?"

"What the f— Why're you telling me this?"

"Do you understand what I just said?"

"Yes, but what's going on? I didn't do anything. I don't need no lawyer to make me look guilty of something when I didn't do anything. Shit."

"If you'd like to help us and continue, then sign the form Detective Asher is providing you."

Asher slid the paper and pen to Keppler. He signed it, dropped the pen.

"Why's this happening? Why're you doing this?"

"Are you going to sit there and pretend you don't know what's happened to Maddison Lane, Zach?"

"Lane?" He thought. "Is that the family my girlfriend babysits for?"

"You know what happened. It's all over the news."

"No, I don't know. My phone's been dead."

"Maddison Lane is missing. She disappeared from her bedroom last night."

Keppler looked at Asher then back to Zubik.

"Seriously? She's missing?"

"You were at the Lane home last night, weren't you?"

Keppler hesitated.

"Weren't you?"

"Yes. I was there with Crystal."

"Why did you have to leave town this morning?"

"It was personal, private."

"You better tell us and tell us the truth."

"I was headed to Albion to see my mom."

"She's at the women's prison there," Asher said, glancing at her notes. "Doing three years for identity theft and fraud. Seems she was pretty good at hacking and stealing things online."

Keppler lowered his head. "I don't tell anybody that. Things aren't so good at home with my dad and stepmom. They're addicted to drugs, opioids."

"Why did you need to see your mom, Zach?" Asher asked.

"I go about once a month to see her. She did a bad thing, but she's a good person and she's my mom. We just talk."

"Were you going to ask her for help, advice?" Zubik said.

"Advice about what?"

"About the situation you're in?"

"What situation?"

"Let me paint you a picture," Zubik said. "You were inside the Lane home last night, correct?"

"Yes."

"Even though it was against the family's wishes, you were there."

"Crystal invited me."

"Maybe you suggested you come over so you could have sex?"

"No, she invited me."

"You like Maddison Lane, even though she's twelve, don't you?"

"What?"

"Don't lie. You think she's cute."

"I don't understand."

"You were standing outside her bedroom window last night, weren't you?"

"Is that what this is about? Because I smoked a joint outside?"

"Don't play dumb, Zach. You like Maddison Lane a lot, you think she's cute. You stood under her bedroom window thinking about her, and after you took Crystal home, you were still thinking about Maddison and that's why you came back, isn't it?"

"No, I never went back. I went home to bed."

"You like little girls, don't you, Zach?"

"This is bullshit."

"Is it? You like Maddison. You were in her

house, you were under her bedroom window—now she's missing and you tried to leave town."

Keppler shook his head.

"Make it easy on yourself, Zach," Asher said. "Just tell us what you did with Maddison. Maybe it was an accident, things got out of hand. Tell us what happened."

"Nothing happened because this is all your twisted fantasy."

Zubik let out a long breath. "We're in the process of getting warrants to search your phone, your backpack, your house, your dad's car. We'll see if you have other phones, if you tried to clean up any evidence. We're going to scour every inch of your life. Our crime scene experts are processing Maddison's room and the ladder, and if we find you've been lying to us, the district attorney will bring the hammer of justice down hard on you. But if you cooperate now, tell us everything now, well, maybe things will go better for you. What do you think, Zach? Are you ready to tell us the truth about what happened?"

Keppler blinked several times, glanced at the camera, at the detectives, then looked down at his hands as tears rolled down his cheeks.

"I want a lawyer now."

19

I've got to do something.

Ryan felt the steady continuous hum of alarm in the back of his brain.

It wouldn't stop.

They found something in that forest, but they won't tell us. I'm not going to stand here wringing my hands. I've got to do something.

After the news conference, Ryan, Karen, Tyler and Cole's family had walked the few blocks to the community hall that was being transformed into the search center. Tables had been set up, maps taped to walls. Cole and his people were helping police and the neighborhood groups register the volunteers streaming in to help look for Maddie. People talked on phones, were given flyers and assigned to areas to search.

A sense of controlled urgency filled the air.

Ryan was numb to the compassionate back pats by friends, deaf to the assurances of well-wishers. Then, across the room, he saw his brother holding Karen's shoulders. He saw her look up to him, nodding in her anguish. He knew they were close, knew that closeness went back to Cole's darkest days. In that moment Ryan felt a pang of resentment toward them. It subsided when he turned to accept a handshake. When he turned back, he saw that Karen and Tyler were now being comforted by Maddie's friends, neighborhood moms and Karen's coworkers.

Observing it all, Ryan felt an awful anger and panic swirling in his gut.

I've got to do something.

He stared at Maddie's picture in the flyer he held in his hands, folded it carefully and without telling anyone, left the building unseen through a back door.

I know what I have to do.

Seconds later Ryan was walking fast on Lime Tree Street toward his home, then before reaching it he turned toward the lane that led to the edge of Lucifer's Green. A helicopter was still circling the forest, and police continued their probe of the woods, which remained sealed.

Careful to keep his distance from any police vehicles, Ryan used parked cars as a shield to reduce chances of him being spotted as he stayed clear of the activity. Propelled by his anguish, he walked the perimeter of Lucifer's Green.

It's my fault Maddie's gone. I should've put up a better fence. I should've installed security.

As he covered the distance, he studied the forest, the only thing between his house and DeBerry

Street. Maddie's room and the halfway house were linked by those dense, hilly woods.

They found something in there, but they won't tell us anything. What if it's linked to that halfway house? We have a right to know and, I swear to God, one way or another I'm going to find out.

Some twenty minutes later, Ryan was on De-Berry.

Police and media vehicles dotted the side of the street bordering Lucifer's Green. Ryan steered clear. He hadn't had reason to be on DeBerry for a month or so, but he knew his destination, the three-story stucco building facing the forest.

When he came to it, he saw the sign: Residential Reentry Management Center. His pulse was throbbing from the walk and the anger pounding through him. A news box for a free community paper was out front, and he feigned interest in it, waiting until someone exited the building.

Ryan turned, caught the door and entered.

The clicking of a keyboard sounded as a man worked on the computer behind the front desk when Ryan walked by, exploring the facility.

Ryan was partway down the first hall when the clicking stopped.

"Excuse me, sir?" the front-desk man called. "You can't go down there."

Ryan took a breath, dragged his hands over his face and kept going.

"Sir!"

"I'm looking for my daughter. Someone here knows something."

Ryan stuck his head in the first room, an empty dorm-style unit with two beds neatly made. He moved on to next and heard a chair scrape behind him at the front desk.

"Stop right there, sir!"

"Maddie!" he called.

Someone grabbed Ryan's arm, and he turned to see the front-desk man.

"Sir, you can't be here. Come back. I'll get a case manager."

Ryan jerked his arm free.

"Don't touch me! You people know something!"

Drawn by the sound of a TV, Ryan moved to the end of the hall and came to a dining area where he saw several men, inmates, eating supper and staring at the screen suspended on the wall.

They were watching a weekend sports show.

A new man approached him. "Sir, my name is Burnham. I'm a case manager. We don't know who you are, but you can't be here and we need you to leave."

All the others turned.

"I'm Maddison Lane's father. Someone in this halfway house knows who took my daughter."

"You have to leave, sir," Burnham said.

"I'm not leaving until I get answers. Where's my daughter?"

Men moved to take Ryan's arms.

"Don't touch me!" He struggled against the men. "Let go of me!"

"Call the police," Burnham said to the man at the front desk.

"Maddie!"

More men moved to restrain Ryan, forcing him to the floor on his stomach, locking him in a cage of muscled, tattooed arms, smelling of cologne, deodorant and soap. Struggling was futile as Ryan battled his emotions.

"Tell me where my daughter is! Just tell me!"

The room fell quiet, except for the sports anchor's voice from the TV and a ripple of—"Who's that guy?"—whispered around the room.

Among the inmates staring down at Ryan was Kalmen T. Gatt, an IT expert finishing his sentence for white-collar crimes.

He knew exactly who Ryan was.

Gatt also knew something no one else in this world would ever know.

Gatt had a connection to Maddison Lane.

20

At the search center a circle of compassion had formed around Karen.

Her friends, her coworkers and mothers from the neighborhood had touched her, patted her, hugged her, and with eyes glistening offered heartfelt encouragement.

"Everybody's looking everywhere."

"We're going to find her, Karen."

"It's going to be okay."

"We just have to keep praying."

"You need to stay strong."

But Karen was drowning in their assurances. She didn't want sympathy right now. She didn't want prayers. She needed answers, and she searched the youngest faces to find them: Maddie's friends. When she spotted Amanda Morber, who'd known Maddie since they were six or seven years old, Karen broke from the circle.

"Amanda, sweetheart, I need your help."

"Yes, Mrs. Lane." Amanda was with her mom, Valerie, in a small group.

"You must've texted Maddie last night or used Instagram or something?"

"Yes." Amanda looked at her phone in her hand, then at her mom.

"Police are going to talk to all the kids, Karen. We've been notified," Valerie said.

"I know, I know, but Amanda, sweetie, please tell me what you and Maddie talked about yesterday before it got late?"

Amanda looked to her mom, who nodded.

"Just about clothes and shoes we saw online and wondering if they were at the mall."

"Is that it? Was there anything else Maddie said, or told you? Anything at all?"

Amanda blinked and she looked at her mother again, who nodded once more.

"Well, she said she argued with you about boys and stuff."

Karen swallowed. "Would you show me your phone, honey, let me see?"

Amanda's grip tightened slightly on her phone.

"Please, sweetie," Karen said.

Valerie encouraged her daughter. "Go ahead honey, its important."

Amanda took a breath and her fingers tapped on her screen. She passed her unlocked phone to Karen. Scrolling through it, Karen read her daughter's exchanges. They were made around 9:00 p.m. and concerned shoes, clothes, then boys, and arguing with her mother about dating.

She's so stupid, Maddie had said.

Why so harsh to your mom?

She doesn't get it.

Get what?

That I'm so old enough for boys.

Not all boys are old enough for you.

Ha ha. I hate her for ruining my life. She's such a bitch. Don't get me started on my dad.

Uh-oh, gotta go Mad. Later.

The exchanges ended.

Karen gave Amanda her phone and nodded her thanks.

"Mrs. Lane," Amanda said, "it's just stuff kids say."

Karen turned away, putting her hand to her mouth to gulp back a sob.

I hate her for ruining my life. She's such a bitch.

It was like a knife in her heart.

Jill found Karen, read the fresh pain in her eyes. "What is it?"

Unable to articulate the wound, Karen shook her head. She needed Ryan and searched the hall for him, wondering where he'd gone.

At that moment, there appeared to be a disruption outside the entrance, and Karen joined the people who'd moved toward it.

Outside in the parking lot, Ryan was being helped out of the back of a police car where Cole was waiting for him. Karen rushed to them. Ryan's hair was messed, his face was white and he looked exhausted.

"What's going on?" she asked.

"Ryan went into the halfway house looking for Maddie," Cole said. "He won't be charged. Everyone knows what he's going through."

"Let's get everybody inside," Jill said. "Have some coffee and something to eat. They've brought in some food."

They stayed at the search center well into the night.

When Karen was unable to bear another minute in the hall, she told Ryan, Cole and Jill she wanted to walk back to their house.

"I need to be there in case she comes home."

21

That night Chief Supervisor Vernon Pike stood at the front of the room, looking over the group seated before him in the Residential Reentry Management Center on DeBerry Street.

Everyone knew what was happening, but no one had spoken yet.

A few men coughed, others shifted in their folding chairs causing them to squeak, underscoring the tension in the center's meeting hall.

All forty residents were in the room—no exceptions, a full count.

All passes had been suspended, work, rec, school and job search, all of them. Everyone, including those out in the community, had been ordered to report back to the facility immediately.

"Listen up!" Pike looked over the men. "It is my duty to remind you that you are all still serving your sentences, you are all still confined, you are all still inmates and will abide by BOP rules or be subject to an infraction that could return you to prison."

Pike indicated the contingent of new faces standing alongside him.

"These people are with SPD and the Onondaga County Sheriff's Office," Pike said. "They've reviewed your case files as part of their investigation concerning the missing girl. Now they'll interview you individually and conduct any other actions needed to support their work. I expect that you *will* cooperate."

Chairs squeaked, a few residents coughed and Pike let a moment pass before he continued.

"I have to inform you that it's your right not to cooperate, but I would advise you to weigh the implications if you don't," Pike said.

Before ending, he added: "Your personal items will also be searched."

Kalmen T. Gatt was among the first selected for an interview. He was guided to the office of his case manager, George Pinson, where Detectives Carver and Balovitch waited with Pinson. Things were cramped.

"Have a seat, Kalmen," Carver said as he and Balovitch looked over the computer monitor and their phones. Carver also had a clipboard on his lap.

"You're coming to the end of your sentence for internet fraud." Carver kept his focus on the monitor, reading. "White collar fraud and investment stuff. You're a smart guy, doing well here at the center. Your reintegration back into society is going smoothly. Impressive, actually."

Gatt said nothing as Carver's attention shifted to him.

"Your passes are generous. Your curfew is 11:00 p.m."

Waiting for a question, Gatt said nothing.

"The surveillance camera and log shows you returned at 10:50 p.m. Where did you go last night, Kalmen?"

"The diner on the corner. I had some apple pie, sir."

"Do you have a receipt?"

"Yes, sir."

"I see your expertise is in IT and you're employed at a firm developing software, but you're blocked from access to the internet. How does that work?"

Gatt knew that police often knew the answers to questions they asked.

"I have access to only one computer, and it is not connected to the internet, sir."

"I see you own a cell phone, too. Does it have internet access?"

"No, sir. That would be a violation."

"What about the ability to take photos with it?"

"No, sir. It's an approved cell phone." Gatt glanced to Pinson to back him up, but Pinson's face was noncommittal. "I use my approved phone to receive and return calls and messages from my approved list in my file."

"Are you in possession of or have access to any other cell phones, laptops, tablets?"

Possession of any other devices would be a serious violation.

"Do you have any other phones, maybe a burner, Kalmen?"

"No, sir."

"You know we'll be conducting searches, and if you're lying to us and we find something, that's going to bring a world of trouble down on you."

"I have no other cell phones in my possession, sir."

"Where do you go on your rec passes?"

"I walk to the library to read or walk to Rose Garden Park, sir."

"What about the woods across the street, Lucifer's Green?" Carver pointed with his chin. "Do you walk there?"

"Yes, sir."

"What do you do there?"

"I go there to think about rebuilding my life. When you've been locked up, a place like that is like Heaven, sir."

"Do you exit the woods on the other side where houses back onto it?"

"No, I don't walk that far, sir. I follow one of the old trails. It runs about a quarter mile and it's circular."

"Were you in the woods in the last twenty-four hours?"

"No, sir."

"Do you know anyone who might have been in the woods?"

"No, sir. I keep to myself."

"Would you tell us if you knew?"

"Like I said, sir, I keep to myself."

"That doesn't answer my question, Kalmen. If you withhold information, that's obstruction and you go back to prison for a long time, so I'll ask you again: Do you know anyone who might have been in the woods within the past twenty-four hours?"

"No, sir, I do not."

"What about your roommate, Brandon Kane?"

"I don't know what he does when he leaves the center, sir."

Carver paused to flip through pages affixed to a small clipboard, tapping his pen on it as he read and consulted the monitor.

"All right." Carver exhaled. "I think we're done. You can go."

"Thank you, sir." Gatt stood to leave.

"Wait," Carver said. "One last thing. We're going to need your shoes."

"My shoes?"

"We'll take you down the hall to our forensic guys. They're taking photos and impressions of everyone's footwear, the ones in your quarters and on your feet."

22

It was close to 1:00 a.m.

The Lanes had left the search center to keep a vigil on their house from the street. They were not allowed to enter as it was still being processed.

They watched the silhouettes of investigators against the drawn curtains as they took flash pictures—making it clear to the family that it was no longer their home.

It was a crime scene.

"They're going to be at it all night," Cole said to Ryan, Karen and Tyler after the checking the time. "You need to get some rest. We should go now."

Ryan didn't react.

Karen shook her head slowly. "Leave? How can I leave? She has to come back. I can't leave." Somewhere deep in a corner of Karen's heart a sound began rising, a guttural aching that exploded into a moaning sob so powerful it buckled her knees. As Jill and Dalton caught her, Karen threw her arms around Jill's neck, locking on to her as if she were drowning.

"I'll call the paramedics," Cole said.

"No." Jill shook her head. "She needs a little time," she said, stroking Karen's hair, patting her back, offering her soft words of comfort. "I know, I know, it's all right. I know it hurts but we're going to find her. You'll see."

Ryan watched in silence as if he'd been turned to stone while Tyler grew terrified. His parents were crumbling before his eyes, leaving him alone to stare in shock at the detached pieces of his family.

After several agonizing moments, Cole and Jill helped Karen put one foot in front of the other. They got her and the others into their SUV, and started the drive to their home across the city. Cole's Land Rover was new, rich with the smell of leather seats, and it glided like a dream through the night. Lost in his nightmare, Ryan was numb with anger; anger at Maddie's disappearance; anger at himself for being helpless. He remained silent in the front passenger seat beside his brother.

As he drove, Cole spoke with his investigators using his hands-free mobile phone and earpiece. He kept his voice low.

"Vince, I want you to call our offices in Manhattan, Chicago, Seattle, Dallas, Los Angeles and Miami…we'll pull in more help for tomorrow…"

Jill and Karen were in the seats behind Ryan and Cole. Jill was rubbing Karen's shoulder; Karen rested her head against the window, weeping and lamenting. "Twenty-four hours ago I saw Maddie in her bed, I stroked her hair. I know we fought, we argued, but she's my little girl… Oh God, where is she? Where's my baby?"

Through her tears Karen searched the lights of Syracuse streaming by her window.

The boys were in the rear with Dalton on his phone reading texts from kids concerned about Maddie. Some offered prayers, some offered rumors—"there was this sketchy guy around our school"; "maybe it was devil worship freaks"— others offered suggestions or help—"her friends must know something"; "we asked people all day at the mall about her"; "we searched through Rose Garden Park."

Dalton held out his phone to Tyler, showing him some of the texts.

"See, Ty, a lot of people care. Don't worry, we'll find her."

Tyler nodded. He was trembling because of exhaustion.

And fear.

What had happened to Maddie was his fault for not checking out the voices in her room, for not alerting his mom and dad. He had to do something, anything to fix it. Staring into the night, he forced himself to remember the voice. Not Maddie's voice but the second voice he'd heard.

What was that person saying?

Once they had arrived at Cole and Jill's house, Jill helped Karen to one of their guest rooms, one that she and Ryan would use for the night.

"Thank goodness we're the same size." Jill collected some fresh clothes for her—pajamas, jeans, a top, and urged her to take a hot shower. "It might help you feel a bit better. I'll make some food and some tea. Please, you have to eat and rest before we go back."

Jill then got Tyler settled into the room next to Dalton's. She got him fresh clothes, and new underwear she'd bought for Dalton that was still packaged. She showed him where there were toiletries they kept for guests, then gave him a long crushing hug.

"We'll get through this, Ty," she said.

Cole and Ryan went to the spacious family room where Cole switched on the huge flat-screen TV that was suspended on one wall, tuned it to a twenty-four-hour news channel and checked his phone.

"Want a drink, Ryan—water, a beer, something stronger?"

Ryan covered his face with his hands. His eyes were bloodshot as he watched a report about hostilities in the Middle East without seeing it.

"I can't stay here." He stood. "I have to go back and search for her."

"We'll go back. You need to rest first."

"When we were at the search center, someone showed me a report about Justice Department statistics on stranger child abductions. Most kids are taken by pedophiles and are killed within four hours. If it's a ransom kidnapping, we'll hear within twenty-four hours. It's been that long already, and we've heard nothing."

"Ryan."

"And with each hour that passes, the chances of recovery shrink. We've got to get back out there and search for her!"

"We've got close to sixty volunteers who'll be searching all night. Twice that will show up in the morning. And with new donations coming in, the reward is now close to thirty-five thousand dollars. I've got my people coordinating things. Listen to me: Whatever it takes, we're going to find Maddie and bring her home. Now you need to have some food, get a couple hours of sleep and we'll go right back. I promise."

Ryan said nothing and sat down.

"Here." Cole held a glass with ice in it. "Drink this whiskey."

Ryan looked at it then swallowed it in one gulp, wiping his mouth with the back of his hand.

"What happened to her, Cole? Someone was in her room. Did she run off with somebody? With all this attention you'd think we'd hear from her, or a friend, right? Or maybe it's some animal from that halfway house, or some creep is holding her in a cage?"

"It could be any number of scenarios. We don't have all the facts. We don't know what the evidence shows."

"They found something in the woods, but they

won't tell us and I can't stop thinking that she's dead and—"

"Stop. If they found a body, the medical examiner's team would be out there, and they haven't been called. I checked. Now, what they found could be key fact evidence they're holding back to protect the case."

"It's my fault. It is. The business is nose-diving. I lost it at the bank, trying to get a loan."

"If you need money—"

Ryan shot a finger at Cole and shook his head.

"Don't! I'm just telling you that I've been consumed by my problems to the point of ignoring my family, leaving Karen to deal with Maddie, with everything." He ran his hand through his hair. "I should've put in a security system, should've replaced that old chain-link fence that was there when we bought the place. I thought it was good enough to keep the skunks and raccoons out. I figured we lived in a safe part of town. I was going to take care of it when I first heard the rumors they were going to open a halfway house at DeBerry. You told me when we moved in to replace the fence and install a security system, but I didn't listen and you know the reason."

"This isn't the time—"

"Because all my life I refused to take advice from you. Now look what it's cost me." His voice broke.

"Stop blaming yourself. It's not your fault."

Ryan blinked back his tears and exhaled.

"I know you'd never expect to hear this from me, Cole, but thank you, thank you for helping us."

"I can't bear to see you and Karen suffering."

Ryan shot Cole a glance as he continued.

"You know that I'm forever indebted to you both," Cole said. "I wouldn't be here if it wasn't for you guys. After I was blown up and lost my legs, I couldn't go on. I fell into a dark pit. You and Karen pulled me out. I swear to you we'll find Maddie and bring her home, because I owe you everything."

Ryan stared hard at his brother, struggling through his exhaustion and anguish, then looking around admiring Cole's home.

"You've done all right, haven't you?" Ryan said. "You've achieved so much. You've overcome so much. You got Jill, you got Dalton, you got your security business with offices across the country and you got money, fame. People look up to you. To them you're a hero. And you know what? You are a hero."

"Ryan, don't."

"You're a Purple Heart hero. And I am so proud of you, so honored to be your brother. But all these years I envied you and resented you at the same time. My brother the hero, and here I am with the little drywall business our old man gave his life to, barely able to keep it afloat. And another thing, about Karen—"

"Stop, Ryan."

"I see how Karen looks at you, how she sees

you, the hero, the protector who saves lives who knows what to do. I can't even protect our daughter. I've failed at so much. Don't you see? I'm so small next to you."

"Don't do this."

"The truth is that I love you, respect you for what you went through, so proud and amazed at how you fought your way out of hell to triumph, there's a part—" Ryan stopped to find the words. "No matter how hard I try, part of me will never forgive you for turning your back on dad. I just can't do it."

"Ryan, it had little to do with the business. Our old man was cruel and abusive. He hit mom and he hit me. You grew up in the same house. How could you not know that?"

"He never, ever laid a hand on me."

"You were his favorite, Ry. We both knew that, and we both knew what he was like. You can't tell me you didn't know about his dark moods, his wild temper. I think you just didn't want to believe it, refused to accept it, and I think I know why."

Ryan stared at Cole as he continued.

"My guys talked to their friends in the SPD. I know about your outburst at the bank. I think you have some of the old man's lack of control, and it scares you."

Ryan stared coldly at Cole but said nothing.

"Did Zubik ask you about your temper when he had you downtown?" Cole asked.

Ryan stared off at nothing.

"Did they ask you about your temper?" he asked again.

"Yes, they asked me."

"What did you tell them?"

"I've never laid a hand on Karen or the kids, Cole."

"Is that what you told them?"

"Yes."

"Is that the truth, Ryan?"

Ryan took a long deep breath then said, "About a week or so ago, Maddie stormed out of the house, screaming and crying. I didn't know, but it was after she and Karen had had a fight about boys. Karen sent me out into the pissing rain to find her."

"Did you find her?"

"Yes."

"Did you lose your temper?"

"Yes."

"Did you tell Zubik?"

"No."

"What did you do?"

Ryan was silent.

"What did you do to Maddie, Ryan?"

"I can't tell you what I did. But I'll have to live with it for the rest of my life."

23

Clouds of steam rose around Karen in the shower.

Lost in the mist, she was assailed with images of Maddie struggling, crying out. Then, as hot rivulets of water flowed over Karen, the images dissolved into a slow-motion vision of Maddie struggling underwater, her eyes bulging.

Drowning.

Karen's back slammed against the tiled wall, and she slid to a sitting, fetal position, sobbing in vain for ten minutes.

After the shower she remained exhausted and in pain.

Nothing felt real.

She'd become a zombie going through the motions of the living, pulling on a robe, drying and brushing her hair, unable to recognize the madwoman who was staring back at her from the mirror. Agony had clawed lines into her face, straining her reddened eyes with fear.

What if we never find Maddie? How can our lives ever be the same again after this?

She placed her hands on the counter to steady herself and wept until a soft knock sounded at the bedroom door and Jill entered carrying a small tray with tea, diced fruit and a sandwich.

"I can't eat, Jill, I just can't."

Karen sat at the foot of the bed.

"It's okay. It's here if you want. And I've brought two sleeping pills." Jill set the tray on the dresser and sat beside Karen. "Ryan and Cole are talking, so are Tyler and Dalton. We can talk a little but you should really sleep."

"How can I sleep with Maddie gone?" Karen lifted her tearstained face to the ceiling. "I keep thinking of her alone somewhere cold and dark, calling for me. Then I have these horrible images of her dead in a shallow grave, in the water. We have to go back out and search for her. I should be doing something!"

Jill pressed down softly on Karen's shoulders and rubbed her back.

"Shh-shh. We're going to find her. You need to rest."

"Last night I was asleep when someone was in my home stealing my daughter just down the hall. I can never ever forgive myself."

"You can't blame yourself."

"You know what some of the last words Maddie said to me were? 'Why are you ruining my life? I hate you so much!'"

"All young girls say things like that to their

mothers at some point. You have to stop beating yourself up."

"Oh but I deserve it," Karen groaned. "It's the price I'm paying for the sum of all the things I've done."

"No, it isn't. You're a good person, a perfect mother."

"Oh no, I'm not." Karen shook her head. "I'm not perfect, not like you. You don't know how much I wish I was like you."

"Me?"

"You're kind, beautiful, poised, smart and tactful, you've got Cole, Dalton and all this." She cast her hand to the house. "What you have is perfect."

"It's not. Believe me. It's anything but perfect."

"It is from where I sit, Jill." Karen shook her head. "You say I'm a good person, well, you don't know me. You don't know all that I've done, all that I'm guilty of."

"All that you're guilty of?" Jill repeated.

They searched each other's eyes as if probing for hidden fears, painful things unspoken. Jill knew that Karen and Cole had a special bond; that they were close, and while it sometimes made her uneasy, she accepted it as part of Karen and Ryan's helping Cole overcome his wounds. Yet, what she saw in Karen's face was unfathomable, like a revelation rising to the surface.

"Do you know about my family?" Karen said.

Jill hesitated, then nodded.

"I know your life's been hard, that you lost your mother and sister when you were young."

"I found my mother dead in our backyard."

"Cole told me. Karen, you don't have to talk about this."

"Before my mother died, we'd argued and some of the last words I spat at her were that I hated her. I was thinking about boys and arguing with my mom about it at a time when I should have been mourning the death of my sister, Cassie."

"Cole told me Cassie died accidentally."

"She drowned."

"I'm so sorry, Karen."

"I was there when it happened. I was playing a game."

24

Where's my sister?

Tyler picked up an old game controller and ran his fingers over it while fighting the throbbing knot in his stomach.

Where's Maddie? Where's Maddie?

Dalton's room was about three times the size of his and smelled nice like cologne. Tyler didn't get to see it often, but he liked coming here because his older cousin had the coolest stuff, the newest games, computers, clothes, cool knives and paintball stuff.

But none of that mattered now.

We've got to find Maddie.

Tyler was sitting at Dalton's desk, his brain tethered to one task as he and Dalton tried to figure out what had happened to Maddie and who might know. The food Aunt Jill had brought them was pretty much untouched. Dalton ate the chips but Tyler wasn't hungry, his stomach was jittery and he was shaky.

Ever since they'd arrived at the house, Dalton

had been sitting on his bed, texting people on his phone, checking for news alerts and grilling Tyler for details that might help.

"You gotta keep trying, Ty. You say you heard voices. How many?"

"I'm pretty sure one was Maddie's and one was a stranger's."

"Did that strange voice sound like anybody you know?"

"I really couldn't tell because they were talking low, kinda whispery."

"Could it have been more people, more than just Maddie and one other person?"

"I don't know. I was sleepy and I thought she was talking to someone on her phone or watching a video."

"So there's no way you know who was in her room?"

"No."

Tyler put his head down on Dalton's desk and tried not to cry. Dalton continued working on his phone until Tyler regained a measure of his composure.

"It's my fault, you know." Tyler lifted his head, brushed away his tears. "Because I should've done something, and now we don't know what's happened to her."

"She could've run away or something. Wasn't she always fighting with your mom?"

"Yeah."

Tyler searched Dalton's room, his attention

drawn to a shelf where there were photos of Dalton meeting a player from the Yankees, then a rock star, then some with his parents in Egypt and London and Disney World. There was a small photo of Dalton, Tyler and Maddie taken at Thanksgiving. Tyler half smiled and allowed the beginning of a laugh.

"You know, I think Maddie likes your hair, said it made you look like a rock star. I think she has a little crush on you. Weird, huh?"

Dalton looked at Tyler, looking at his pictures.

"What, you mean because I'm adopted and not really a biological relative?"

"I don't know. I don't even know if the crush thing is true. It's just weird."

"Yeah, pretty weird all right." Dalton went back to his phone. "Hey, there's a guy tweeting that he thinks Maddie's disappearance could be related to that halfway house on the other side of the forest."

"That was on the news. What do you think?" Tyler asked.

"Could be. Could be anything. Remember those girls who live near you said some creep followed them and wanted to know where they lived."

"Yeah."

"Tell me again. When police were interrogating you, did they tell you much? What did they ask you?"

"They asked me if I killed Maddie."

"Seriously? They seriously asked you that?"

"Yes."

"What else?"

"They asked me if I had ever hurt her, or if any of my friends had ever hurt her."

"What else did they ask?"

"Different stuff. Like, if I ever hit her, if Mom and Dad fought all the time, if they ever hit me and Maddie, if I ever looked at porn, if I knew our babysitter's boyfriend…"

"The babysitter's boyfriend? Why?"

Tyler shrugged.

"What's his name?" Dalton asked.

"Zachary Keppler."

"Do they think he's the guy?"

"I don't know."

"What else did police say?"

"They said it was a crime if I lied to them, so I had to tell the truth. They asked me to tell them exactly what Maddie, Crystal—that's the sitter—and I did last night, then if I heard any screams or noises in Maddie's room. They asked if I thought Maddie had a secret boyfriend, and if she would tell her best friends about it."

"Really? What did you say?"

"I said I didn't know, that maybe it was possible."

"Do you think this Zach guy was her secret boyfriend?"

"I don't know."

"Did the police tell you what they think happened?"

"No." Tyler turned to the door where his dad and his uncle were standing.

"All right, guys," Uncle Cole said. "Time to get some rest. We're going back to the search center in a couple of hours."

Alone in his temporary room, Tyler kept a nightlight on.

Guilt and fear kept him awake for the longest time as he cried for his missing sister. In the quiet he could hear Dalton talking softly across the hall, and it gave him a degree of comfort.

Dalton must be talking to people, working through the night, trying to help. Tyler was glad they were cousins because not only was Dalton cool, he was so worldly and smart.

He'll help us find Maddie.

25

The clock above the dry erase board in the meeting room in Syracuse Police Department headquarters read 12:06 a.m.—approximately twenty-four hours since Maddison was last seen.

The odds of finding her alive diminished with each passing minute.

Key facts, updates, questions and names of investigators assigned to tasks were written in block letters filling the board. To one side, easels displayed an array of enlarged color photos of evidence found in the forest behind her home. One easel held a photo of Maddison. Her eyes met those of every detective seated around the table. Most were parents themselves.

Law enforcement from various branches of the Syracuse police, Onondaga County, state police, the FBI and several other agencies were present. Ceramic coffee mugs and takeout cups, phones, tablets, notebooks and fast-food wrappers dotted the table as the first case-status meeting of the task force began.

Stan Zubik led the meeting. "Thank you all for getting us your reports. As you know, not everyone can attend because we've got people working through the night. We've got a lot of ground to cover here, so let's get started."

He went straight to the known facts. Checking his notes, he detailed the time frame of events, including Tyler Lane's account of hearing voices, up to the point he discovered his sister was missing.

Zubik said that analysis of the mud found in Maddison's bedroom shows it is consistent with traces found on the ladder and the soil under her window. Partial footwear impressions found under the window were still being processed. No useable latents were recovered from the wooden ladder, but analysis of latents found in the bedroom was ongoing.

"We're confident someone from the outside entered her room."

Zubik pointed to photos of a muddied and broken shoelace with pink polka dots, partial shoe impressions and aerial photos pinpointing locations.

"This is what we've found in a puddle in the woods known as Lucifer's Green. The lace and partial impressions are consistent with the size, style and model of Maddison's sneakers that her mother described. This places Maddison in the woods with the impression pointing northwest, away from her home."

"Were other impressions found with hers?" Len Reese, a county investigator, asked.

"There were some, but we can't make any determinations. They're being analyzed," Zubik said. "I want to stress this is all holdback. We'll move on to her last messages, and this is critical."

Zubik said that Maddison's phone had not yet been recovered, and it would be an advantage to have it. In working with the Lanes' cellular service provider, Unidique Global Tele-Systems in Texas, the SPD, New York State and FBI had determined that the last text sent from Maddison Lane's phone was at 1:47 a.m. Eastern Standard Time yesterday.

"Without the phone we don't know what that text, or any of them, say," Zubik said. "As most of you know, most service providers don't keep the content of phone conversations or messages."

In the case of the Texas provider, apart from privacy concerns, there were the issues of storage capacity and costs. Consequently, like most major providers, Unidique destroyed its copies of messages after they had been delivered. While Unidique did not keep the content of messages, it did store on its servers records of the parties to a text message, as well as dates and the times they were sent.

What investigators had discovered in Maddison Lane's case was that the text was the last in an uninterrupted series of exchanges with the same number that began earlier at 10:51 p.m. The number was 555-0116 and prefixed with an area code assigned to New York State. Records from the provider's server show that Maddison had communicated with the number intermittently over the last three months.

"The mystery number leads to a burner phone and the messages created with an app that had them self-destruct within sixty seconds of receipt. We're unable to determine the content of the messages or the person behind its number as yet."

"Have we talked to Maddison's girlfriends?" Vicky Bishop, with the Family Services Division's Missing Persons Unit, asked. "I mean, they'd know the boys she likes, or the boys who like her. Have we gone after Maddison's friends' phones to see if that mystery number pops up? They might be familiar with it."

"All valid points, Vicky. That aspect's being investigated," Zubik said.

"What about her communication with other people over the months leading to this?" Amy Benton, a state police investigator, asked.

"We have the complete list of numbers and already have determined most as assigned to her friends, family, automated texts from school, gymnastics class, notifications from pop stars she follows, things of that nature," Zubik said. "We're still working on the texts and tracking; triangulating cell towers for a geolocator of the burner phone. It's not emitting a signal, but we're working on it, focusing on the texts up to the time of her disappearance."

"Going beyond the phone, who're we interested

in at this stage?" Jan Ford, a Syracuse detective, asked.

"At this stage, we're interested in everyone."

"What about the babysitter's seventeen-year-old boyfriend who was outside her window in the hours before she vanished?" Ford said.

"Zachary Keppler. We've questioned him, and we haven't ruled him out. We're getting warrants for his phone, home and father's car. We've also searched trash bins near the bus station where we picked him up, and found nothing."

"What about that halfway house on DeBerry?" Mac Graham, a state police investigator, asked.

"No sex offenders or pedophiles reside at the center. So far, the pass logs and surveillance cameras show all the inmates are alibied. However, Onondaga County's got a good team helping us there, and we're still processing the center. So our work there is far from over."

"And the registry?" an FBI agent asked.

"We've got people working on nailing down the whereabouts of every registered sex offender residing in the city and the state," Zubik said. "It'll be a lot of work, but we'll request local law enforcement help us with each offender, checking alibis one by one."

"What about the Amber Alert and social media?"

"We're assessing the calls and messages that've come in. Nothing concrete or promising so far."

Going back to his notes, Zubik continued, relating that video from security cameras belonging to the Lanes' neighbors did not capture the backyard fully or clearly, and consequently showed nothing helpful.

"We're still processing the Lanes' house, garage, cars, phones and computers. We've also got the trash collection schedule for the neighborhood. Our people will go through everything before it's picked up."

Zubik said that friends, relatives, neighbors, teachers, coaches and people who worked with Ryan and Karen Lane, people who know them and their kids, would be interviewed.

"We're working our way through our list."

"And where are we with Maddison Lane's immediate family, their alibis, their background, the atmosphere in that home, Stan?" Paul Murray, a state investigator and old friend of Zubik's, looked over his bifocals.

Zubik consulted his notes.

"The father, Ryan Lane, age thirty-eight, is owner operator of Lane & Sons Drywall Contractors. Both parents deceased. The mother, Karen Lane, age thirty-seven, employed as cashier at ShopToSave City, both parents deceased. Also, her younger sister died at age ten. Cause was drowning. They are carrying a mortgage, credit-card debt balance and vehicle loans."

"Appear to be regular working folks," Murray said.

"Ryan Lane's got a rich, famous brother. Have

we looked into this being a kidnap for ransom of Cole Lane's niece?" Rob Van Buren, a state investigator, asked.

"We haven't ruled that out, but no ransom call has come so far," Zubik said. "Another concern is that there's tension in the Lane home on several fronts. Ryan Lane's facing financial strain with his drywall business, and had an outburst at the bank when he was denied a loan earlier the same day. He raised the issue of life insurance policies on his family, including a seventy-five-thousand-dollar death benefit on Maddison."

"That's got to raise a flag," Jan Ford said.

"It does," Zubik said. "Another troubling aspect is that Maddison has been arguing over the past few months with her mother on the issue of her wanting to date boys, which Karen refused to let her do."

"Are we going to spitball now, Stan?" Murray said.

Zubik turned to his partner, Fran Asher, and their captain, Moe Tilden, both of whom nodded.

"Go ahead, we'll open it up," Zubik said.

"Looking at what we have so far," said Murray, a case-hardened cop who'd cleared countless homicides, "Maddison was texting with someone she knew, and that 'someone' came to her house and left with her. And she left with her phone. That mystery phone number is the key. She knew who came, otherwise she would've screamed. Why didn't she scream?"

"I'll tell you why," Asher said. "The intruder could've entered quietly, while she was sleeping, and forced her into silence by threatening to kill her family if she did not come quietly. Tyler could've overheard that whispered conversation. We know of cases where that's happened. The intruder takes her phone, wipes it, gets rid of the memory card—essentially erases any record of their relationship."

"So it's a stranger rather than someone she knows?" Murray asked.

"She could've had an online relationship with a predator posing as an age-appropriate friend in love with her," Asher said, "say a sex offender, or predatory pedophile in the area, someone who could've easily flattered her into thinking she was mature enough for a relationship. Sexting could've been involved, and he could've guided her in how to keep it all secret, grooming her to agree to a meeting. He could've also extorted her, threatening to post her pictures if she didn't do what he demanded."

"Then he comes to her bedroom in the middle of the night?" Murray was skeptical. "I still think she'd scream."

"Not if she was asleep, or he had control over her," Asher countered.

Captain Tilden leaned forward with his thoughts.

"What do our FBI profilers think?"

"Well, it's early but based on the facts obtained at this stage," an FBI agent said, "it's a strong bet that she was not taken at random, that she was a target with some kind of connection to her abductor. But on the other hand, she could've run off, she could've orchestrated her own adventure."

"Agreed," Vicky Bishop said. "After arguing with her mother, Maddison could've summoned a boyfriend to help her escape into the night in an act of defiance, a Romeo and Juliet kind of thing, and now that the situation has exploded, as it were, she's afraid to come home and face the music."

Captain Tilden tapped his fingers on the table.

"Let's consider the statistics. Overwhelmingly, crimes of this nature are committed by a family member. What if Maddison and her mother, or her father or brother, argued? All had reason to argue, the boy thing with mom. Dad's stressed, short-fused and loses it. The young brother's owed money, or there's an offence she's committed against him. Maddison is accidentally killed, and the parents move to cover it up by staging her abduction. We've known of such cases."

Zubik took quick inventory of detectives around the table weighing speculation against the few facts they had.

"All of these theories are strong, and I'm sure there're others we haven't yet considered, but it's early in the case," Zubik said. "We have to give serious consideration to every lead, every piece of evidence and every possibility. Nobody and nothing can be ruled out until we have reason to rule them out. We've got mountains of work ahead of us, so we'll close this meeting and get at it again in a few hours."

26

After the case-status meeting, Fran Asher stopped the unmarked car in front of Zubik's two-story frame house.

"What do you think?" she asked her partner.

Zubik took in a long, tired breath and let it out slowly.

"We've got to go where the evidence points us, but keep our eyes open to all possibilities."

Asher reached into the back seat, got her bag, withdrew a slim folder and held it out for Zubik. "You should read this."

"What is it?"

"Cases similar to ours. It'll help you keep an open mind."

Zubik considered the folder, then took it. "All right."

"See you in three hours, Stan. We've got a long list of interviews. Get some sleep and recharge that old brain of yours."

When Zubik unlocked his front door, the creaking hinges echoed in the darkness. His home was as silent as a mausoleum. He felt a pang of longing for the familiar sound of Lucy's paws on the floor, her so-happy-to-see-you panting and her unconditional love, because no matter what kind of day he'd had, she'd soothe his heart.

In the kitchen he made a peanut butter and strawberry jam sandwich, got a cold glass of milk and sat at his table. He cut a lonely figure as he glanced at Lucy's bowls in the corner where he'd kept them like some sort of memorial.

Maybe I am living in a country song. Zubik shrugged as he turned to read the cases while he ate. Some reached back several years. He recalled most of them because of the attention they'd received.

The first happened three years back in St. Louis, Missouri. A twelve-year-old girl, who shared a room with her younger sister, was kidnapped by a man who'd done some contract painting with a crew on the family's home. He'd entered the home at night through a screen window, threatened the girl with a gun, threatened to murder her entire family as they slept if she didn't obey him. He'd ordered her to put on her shoes and jacket before abducting her.

The man was delusional. He was convinced the Apocalypse was imminent and wanted the girl to be his bride in what he called, "the new, pure life." The girl was rescued a year later living with the homeless man on the streets of New York City, physically abused and psychologically damaged.

Then there was the Florida case. The day before a family of four—mother, father, their fourteen-year-old daughter and ten-year-old son—were going to move to Alaska, a good friend and neighbor arrived to help. In the night their Florida home burned and the parents and boy were killed. The girl vanished, but left messages saying she killed her family because she didn't want to leave the thirty-eight-year-old neighbor with whom she'd fallen in love. Ultimately, the FBI determined the disturbed neighbor had killed the girl's family, forced her to write the untrue messages and abducted her to a remote cabin in Tennessee, where he was killed in an armed standoff. The girl was rescued.

The next case had happened in Montreal, Canada, where a thirty-year-old drifter spotted a pretty fifteen-year-old girl walking home from school near a park and became obsessed with her. For several days he stalked her until late one night he discovered a back door to her large home was unlocked. He entered, and while everyone was asleep he found the girl's bedroom, threatened and gagged her before abducting her. He lived in a van in a vacant lot, took her there and sexually abused her. He had planned to kill her and roll her body into a discarded carpet and toss it into the St. Lawrence River, but the girl pleaded and begged for her life with such fury she distracted him and escaped to a gas station nearby.

Zubik came to the last case in the batch, and it hit him like a gut punch.

Six years ago, a respected, wealthy couple, loved by everyone for their devotion and involvement with charities, had called 911 and reported their eleven-year-old son had been kidnapped in the night from his bedroom of their large, upscale home. They showed investigators a lengthy handwritten note demanding a one-hundred-thousand-dollar ransom within twenty-four hours. Detectives questioned the puzzling wording of the note, raising concerns about its authenticity. Fearful that time was ticking down on the boy's life, the family rushed to secure the cash, putting them at odds with detectives who insisted on first searching the property for more evidence.

Still, within hours of their 911 call, the mother made a horrible discovery, finding her son's body hidden in a basement storage room. He was gagged, his hands were bound and he'd been stabbed multiple times in his chest and abdomen. The family insisted an intruder was responsible. Autopsy results showed that the boy's death was due to his stab wounds, but that he was actually just barely alive for a time after being stabbed. The autopsy also showed that he'd first been rendered unconscious, appearing dead, by a traumatic blow to the head prior to his being stabbed. Nothing added up. Investigators wanted to question and polygraph the mother, father and their sixteen-year-old daughter, who was a high-achiever and destined for one of the country's top universities.

The family refused to cooperate.

Angered police didn't pursue the intruder theory, the parents got lawyers, refused to be polygraphed and hired their own private investigators, who wrote a report supporting the family's theory. But two years later the mother and daughter were found dead, due to an overdose of a powerful sleeping aid. In the note she left, the mother detailed how her daughter, in a fit of rage "over something inconsequential," had struck and killed her younger brother. The parents, fearing their daughter would go to prison—because at the time she would've been tried as an adult—panicked and covered up the crime, staging the whole thing, even stabbing their son. The mother said her dead son visited her in her dreams, and she could no longer live in torment and had laced her daughter's favorite food with the drug before taking it herself. The father admitted his role, pleaded guilty and received a fifteen-year sentence.

The tragedy, which had happened in Syracuse, haunted Zubik because he was one of the investigators. Like his colleagues, he couldn't forgive himself for allowing the family to deceive them in the early stages, to deflect suspicion, to have them focus on the case solely as if it were a kidnap for ransom.

I believe that little boy was still alive when we first got to that house. Even if the medical exam-

iner said it was unlikely, I can't shake the gut feeling that had we moved faster to take control we might have saved his life.

As far as Zubik was concerned, the lesson hammered home in all of these cases was that they could pull you in any direction.

You have to remember the basics. People think they know people. They don't. You never know what's in a person's heart. What they're hiding, what they're capable of when they're trapped in a bad situation and see no way out. Their first instinct is to lie and most of them do.

Zubik pulled out his phone and looked at the photos of Maddison Lane. Then he looked at the news photos of Ryan, Karen and Tyler. Then he studied pictures of them being comforted by Cole, Jill and Dalton.

Zubik took stock of all the facts he knew so far.

Was it an intruder? Is Maddison a runaway? Or is something going on with this family?

27

Jill Lane's sleep was fitful.

Worry for her niece plagued her, moreover she was troubled by what Karen had revealed about her past. Through the night Jill had grappled to comprehend how, as a young girl, Karen had found her mother dead, how she'd been with her younger sister when she drowned, and now this—her daughter's abduction.

My Lord, how much pain is Karen supposed to bear?

That thought triggered another, and Jill replayed the memory of seeing Cole consoling Karen at the search center. The subtleties of how he'd held her, how Karen looked at him, betrayed a closeness that secretly troubled her. Jill had to keep reminding herself that their bond was forged years ago during the time Karen and Ryan had helped Cole through his darkest days after his injury.

You've got to push that kind of thinking about Cole and Karen out of your mind right now because we've got another tragedy to overcome.

The lights on the clock at Jill's bedside read 4:45 a.m.

Cole's side of the bed was empty. Jill saw the glow at the table across the room by the window where Cole was working on his tablet and went to him.

"Any word?" she asked.

"Nothing. I'm just going through some of the tips."

"Did you sleep?"

"Some. You?"

"Not much, I was thinking about what Karen told me last night. I knew she'd lost her mother and sister, but I didn't know she was with her sister when she drowned. That's so horrible. Did she try to save her? Do you know what happened?"

"They'd gone swimming in the Monarda River with a group of friends. It was an accident, that's all I know. She doesn't really talk about it."

"That's understandable. She's endured enough tragedy for three lifetimes."

Suddenly their attention was drawn to the window and the car that had arrived. Neither of them recognized it.

"Is it one of your guys?" Jill asked.

"I'm not expecting anyone at this hour." Cole watched a man and woman get out of the car and approach the door. "It's Zubik and his partner."

"Maybe they've found her?"

Jill and Cole headed to meet them just as their doorbell chimed throughout the house. In seconds,

Karen, Ryan, Tyler and Dalton, desperate for news about Maddie, had joined Jill and Cole, who were standing in the foyer with the detectives.

"What is it?" Karen pressed them. "Did you find Maddie?"

"No, not yet," Zubik said. "We've got a lot of people working hard to help get Maddie home to you."

"We know that but are there any promising leads?" Cole asked.

"Nothing we can discuss here," Zubik said. "What about your team, Cole? They find anything you can share?"

"Nothing yet, but if we do you'll be the first to know."

"Good," Zubik said. "Listen, we're sorry to call on you so early, but we have a lot of work ahead of us." He nodded to Ryan, Karen and Tyler. "We'd like you to help us out by agreeing to take polygraph exams today."

Karen shot a look to Ryan then Cole, telegraphing her unease. Ryan put his hand on Tyler's shoulder as Zubik and Asher observed their reactions.

"I don't have a problem with that," Ryan said. "I told you before we've got nothing to hide. Right, Karen?"

"We'll do anything to help find Maddie," she said.

"Good. It'll be very helpful," Zubik said. "We'll need you back at our offices downtown at 1:00 p.m., okay? We can send a car."

"No need. We'll have them there," Cole said.

"All right. There's one other request," Zubik said. "We'd like to interview you, Cole, and your wife and son real soon, maybe later today if possible. We'd also request you volunteer your phones to us and consent to us searching your house, your vehicles. Would your family be willing to do that?"

"Yes. We'll cooperate."

"Thank you. That should be it for now." Zubik turned to leave just as Dalton casually brushed back his hair, briefly revealing the side of his face. Zubik stopped; his eyes landed on Dalton. "What happened to you, son?"

"What?"

"Those marks, those little scratches on cheek there." Zubik touched his own cheek near the back of his jaw and shot Asher a subtle glance.

"Oh." Dalton blinked, his face reddened. "I fell in a hedge at a party the other night."

Cole and Jill stared at Dalton's face. The little scratches had been hidden by his hair, and they were seeing them for the first time.

"You must've been having a good time," Zubik said.

"What do you mean?"

"Pull up your sleeves and hold out your wrists." Dalton tugged up the long sleeves of his hoodie.

"You get those at the party, too?"

"Oh, yeah. I fell pretty good."

Everyone saw little scratches around Dalton's wrists, then Asher took pictures with her phone.

"Hey!" Cole said. "What're you doing? What're you implying?"

"We're not implying anything, Cole," Zubik said. "We're just keeping a record of things. Is that a concern for you?"

Cole looked at Zubik for a long tense moment.

"No, not at all."

28

Kalmen T. Gatt stood with his back to the wall of his quarters and his arms at his sides as instructed.

The investigation concerning Maddison Lane had continued through the night into the morning, throwing off all procedure and schedules at the Residential Reentry Management Center on DeBerry Street.

Two Onondaga County deputies, two case managers and the center's chief supervisor, Vernon Pike, were searching the two-person room Gatt shared with Brandon Kane, a fraud artist from Cleveland.

As instructed, Gatt and Kane had laid out their personal belongings in an ordered fashion on the surface of their regulation-made beds.

The search commenced with Gatt.

Everything he owned was counted and reconciled on a clipboard against the center's official inventory of his listed property. Each article of clothing was squeezed, sifted and prodded, toiletries were checked and shoes were inspected. Every item was shaken, poked and felt by deputies wearing latex gloves before it was tossed to the floor.

The sheets of Gatt's bed were yanked, his pillow crushed and tossed, his mattress hefted, rotated and seams inspected.

After completing their search of Gatt's property, they moved on to Kane's. When they'd finished rifling through his belongings, they searched the bathroom, the toilet tank and lifted drain covers. Then they scoured the rest of their quarters.

They were nearly finished when a case manager entered the room.

"Vern, there's something your team needs to see downstairs."

On the center's main floor, in a rear section of the building, there were a number of utility and anterooms. Among them was a small, unlocked auxiliary room that housed supplies that were seldom used.

"Come inside," said Ross Nichols, the deputy who'd made the discovery.

The narrow room had one window that had been hidden by stacked storage tubs. The window was unsecured and large enough for someone to exit and enter.

"Okay," said Pike, turning to the other investigators who'd joined the group. "We have an unsecured window. We'll rectify that."

"There's more." Nichols led them from the room and nodded to the nearest corner and the suspended surveillance camera. "That's camera number nine. My partner, Bill, is going to stay here. Come with me."

Pike and the others followed Nichols across the center to the room that held the control panel for the surveillance cameras. The on-duty security officer overseeing them looked young enough to still be in high school. He'd put down his personal phone when Nichols entered and pointed to the rows of small TV monitors.

"See, number nine's aim doesn't capture the auxiliary room with the unsecured window." Nichols reached for his phone and called his partner. "Bill's going to show you that by crouching, twisting and ducking, it's possible for anyone to make their way through the center to that room without being recorded on the cameras."

The deputy spoke into the phone, and everyone at the control panel saw Bill in one monitor wave from a starting point, then he disappeared. Several moments passed and the deputy, phone to his ear, turned to the group.

"Bill's now in the auxiliary room at the window. But we never saw him on any of the cameras."

Pike's scowl deepened as he glared at his young acne-faced officer and the monitors of the control panel, cursing under his breath at the clear lapse of security.

"This is serious shit," Nichols said, pressing a number on his phone. "We're going to seal this room and the exterior. We'll have our evidence people process it to determine if your inmates have been leaving after curfew."

29

Grant Leeder, the former Syracuse detective working for Cole Lane, found Ray Velvet waiting in a back booth of the crowded coffee shop.

Velvet had long blond hair, a full beard and a craggy face.

"You look like crap, Ray." Leeder sat in the booth.

"I sleep in the day." He was nursing a tea and muffin.

"Right, the pimp shift."

"Where's my cash and what do you want?"

Leeder slid five twenties across the table to Velvet.

"We're looking for a twelve-year-old girl who was abducted from her family home, or may have run away. I want you to ask your people to get the word out on the street and help find her. She's on the news."

Velvet nodded as he chewed on his muffin and studied Maddison Lane's picture on Leeder's phone.

"Cute, has potential," Velvet said.

"Don't, or I swear I'll split you in two right here."

"Okay, calm down, old man. Send me her photo. I'll get the word out."

"You'd better, Ray." Leeder tapped on his phone. "I'm the reason you're not in prison right now. You owe me and I'm collecting."

"Right, I'm beholden to you. Try the vegan muffins—they're outstanding."

At that moment, Sally Beck, another of Cole's investigators, was waiting at a table in an empty corner of the True Light Shelter, reading the passage from Psalms 61 taped to the wall.

"From the end of the earth will I cry unto thee, when my heart is overwhelmed: lead me to the rock that is higher than I. For thou hast been a shelter for me…"

This was the fourth in the list of the city's missions and hostels Beck intended to canvass today. As a detective on the job, she'd worked in vice and with the Missing Persons Unit, and had built up a rapport with the people who operated the facilities.

Beck knew that young runaways often emerged at shelters, and wanted to get the word out about Maddison Lane, especially to kids living on the edge of society. April Kent, manager of True Light, had agreed to help, bringing two of the most recent clients, two teenage girls, to the table.

The girls, strangers to each other, had arrived at the shelter after running away from abusive homes—one in Utica, the other in Rochester. Beck thought that they didn't look much older than Maddison, and knew that April was working with social services to help them.

"We're just asking anyone for help finding this girl." Beck showed them Maddison's photo and information. After studying the picture, the girls agreed to ask around about Maddison. "Good, there's a reward." Beck smiled.

"I hope nothing bad happens to her," one of the girls said.

In the Syracuse office of Cole Lane's private investigation agency, Vince Grosso was traveling in a depraved realm of the dark web.

He'd already spent much of the morning alerting investigators in the company's offices across the country for help on Maddison's case.

Now, he'd set out to mine information from the most vile people on earth—pedophiles, human traffickers, pornographers and every freak imaginable. When he was a detective, Grosso had worked on cases involving cyber stalking of children. Posing as a pedophile online, Grosso had gained access to the most guarded sites where members exchanged and sometimes auctioned and sold images and information about children.

In the successful investigations, Grosso was able to lure and track down real pedophiles, which in some cases led to the rescue of their victims.

Now, as Smoothoperator4950, Grosso was at

work on Maddison's case, going to one of the most active discussion sites and posting.

Looks like we've got fresh meat out there from Syracuse.

Less than a minute later DirtyUncleLoveFace666 posted.

You mean this one? Posted with a link to Maddison's photo and missing person poster.

Oh my, RammerJammer911 posted. Would so love to meet her.

She'd be such a fun date, 1MillionSweetDreams4U posted.

So yummy. Wouldn't you love to have her locked up in your basement, to have and to hold as your slave forever? DungeonLord0000 said.

You're killing me!!! I just bet someone out there has her, Grosso posted. You can't keep that fresh piece of heaven to yourself. Anyone know if there's a chance to share!!!

Several moments of silence passed, then DungeonLord0000 posted.

Can't say yes, can't say no.

Oh, you're teasing now, Grosso posted. You know who's got her?

Another moment passed, then DungeonLord0000 posted. Is this the real life, or is this just fantasy? Ha ha.

That was it.

A few more players posted before the discussion ended with Grosso wondering if any of them really knew anything about Maddison.

Or if it was just fantasy.

30

Ryan scanned the sweeping view of metropolitan Syracuse, his gut clenched with desperation, as if he could pinpoint Maddie's location from the lawyer's office in the downtown skyscraper.

Cole had arranged for an emergency appointment with his attorney, Stewart Venter, to prepare Ryan, Karen and Tyler for their polygraph examinations.

"It's your right to refuse to be polygraphed," Venter, a seasoned criminal defense lawyer had said. "But it's better for you to cooperate and remove any doubt that you're involved in your daughter's disappearance."

With the Lane family seated across from his desk, Venter outlined the process. The Lanes would be given their Miranda rights. The results of the exam would be kept confidential and never be allowed in court.

"But your responses could be used to guide the investigation," Venter said. "There are three possible results. You're either untruthful, truthful or the results are inconclusive."

Then Venter looked at each of them.

"You must be aware that the detectives in this case will develop the questions, and I guarantee that some will be extremely brutal and uncompromising."

Venter let a long moment pass, allowing the Lanes to absorb the full weight of what he was telling them.

Hearing Venter's warning pulled Ryan back to that day in the rain…

…how I treated Maddie…the things I said to her…the awful thing I did to her… I begged her not to tell…and she didn't tell anyone…no one knows… no one must ever know… Oh God, Maddie, I'm so sorry…

Ryan rubbed his chin, his fingers trembling, maybe from stress, the lack of sleep, maybe from his crushing guilt over his failings.

Will I be able to endure this? Will I be able to hold it all together?

With Ryan lost in his thoughts, Karen turned to Tyler who had become withdrawn.

She reached for her son's hand, attempting to squeeze it, but he pulled it back.

"I'm okay, leave me alone."

His rejection stung, catapulting her back to her

arguments with Maddie and what Maddie had said to her.

Why are you ruining my life? I hate you! I hate you so much!

And again Karen felt the stab of Maddie's texts, those last words she'd written before she'd vanished.

I hate her for ruining my life. She's such a bitch.

The anguish pulled Karen's broken heart down, blurring through the years of her life to when she was young and took her little sister, Cassie, swimming at the Monarda River. She was supposed to watch over Cassie, but Karen was crazy about a boy and intent on playing a game with him, and it had ultimately led to Cassie's death.

Karen shut her eyes and took a breath.

Please, God, don't let this happen again.

Venter cleared his throat.

"Do you have any questions?"

They had no questions.

"Okay, I think that does it then," Venter said.

As he walked the Lanes to the elevator, he offered his encouragement and support. Venter never considered the possibility of their guilt, or their innocence, in their daughter's case. He was not representing them in any criminal proceedings. But as he watched the elevator doors close, he doubted that they were braced for what was coming.

31

A sense of gravity emanated from the Ruby Green Community Hall.

The building was named after a beloved champion of civil rights, and over time had been used for fund-raisers, local meetings and elections. Now, a billboard-sized photo of Maddison Lane stood above the entrance.

The photo was courtesy of a local print shop, and had served to transform the tired brick gathering place into the official search headquarters.

The growing effort to find Maddison had been ongoing through the night without pause. Syracuse police, Cole's private investigators and neighborhood officials were coordinating tips, updating map grids and reports arising from the ever-widening search that involved monitoring social media, physically circulating flyers, door-knocking, combing through fields, empty lots, parks, schoolyards, alleys and commercial and industrial sites.

When Zubik and Asher entered the hall to interview Maddison's friends, it was active. Volunteers at fold-out tables were registering and directing other volunteers. The detectives went to the table with coffee and food just as a tower of pizza boxes approached them.

The man behind it, Bennie, was donating another delivery of pizzas to the search effort. After setting the boxes down, he recognized the detectives.

"Hey, I saw you on the news," he said. "You're the cops on the case."

"That's right," Asher said.

"I saw Maddie when I delivered to her house," Bennie said. "She's such a good kid. This is so rough. You guys have to find her, okay?"

"We're doing all we can, and we're going to talk to you, too."

"For sure. My name's Bennie, Bennie Price, and I want to help."

"All right, thanks, Bennie." Asher turned as she and Zubik met Detective Doug Brentskov, who was fixing a coffee.

"Hi, guys. We've got it all set up. Grab a coffee and follow me this way."

Brentskov led them to the hall's administrative section. They came to four offices, a waiting area with bench seats and several small desks and folding tables.

"The ident people are moving in their fingerprint equipment," Brentskov said. "Stevens and I will log all personal data. While you talk to the kids, we'll keep the parents back here in these rooms well out of earshot."

Procedurally Zubik and Asher would've requested the parents of Maddison's friends bring their daughters and sons downtown for interviews. But they saw advantages to using the hall. It was closer to the scene, closer to where the friends lived and less intimidating, making it conducive to better results.

Amanda Morber, aged twelve, was first.

She entered the office alone, took her seat in the chair across from Zubik and Asher and rotated her phone in her hands as Asher spoke.

"Thanks for coming here to help us find Maddie. No one's in trouble, but we want you to understand it's important that you answer our questions as best as you can. Don't lie or hold anything back because even the smallest thing could help. And whatever you tell us will be kept confidential. You might already know that your parents have agreed for you to give us your phone when we're done talking so we can clone it, and that they can pick it up later today downtown. Are you ready, Amanda?"

She nodded, tears welling in her eyes. "Will you find Maddie?"

"We're doing everything we can to find her," Zubik said. "Now, would you say you're one of Maddison's closest friends?"

"Yes, we've known each other since second grade."

"Did you text Maddison last night?"

"Yes. A little."

"What about?"

"Clothes mostly, shoes I had seen at the mall."

"Did you ever text about boys with her?"

"Yes."

"Who specifically?"

"We both thought Caleb Langford and Noah Trell were cute."

"Does Maddison have a boyfriend?"

"No."

"Has Maddison ever gone on a date or secretly met a boy?"

"No, I would say no."

"Did Maddison ever talk about being unhappy at home?"

"Well, I know she argued a lot with her mother about not being allowed to date boys and got mad about it sometimes."

For the next twenty-five minutes, they asked Amanda questions. When they were done, she gave them her phone.

Nicole Webb, aged thirteen, was next. She'd already given her phone to Brentskov and gripped the sides of her chair as Asher outlined the interview.

"This is so scary." Nicole's voice wavered. "I've been texting her and texting her."

"Did Maddison ever talk about being abused at home, sexually, physically or mentally?"

"God, no. I think she's happy at home."

"What about with teachers, coaches or anyone older?"

"No."

"Does she have a boyfriend?"

"No, but she's a bit flirty, and she's so pretty and everything."

"Did you see her flirt with anyone in particular?"

"Logan. Logan Bostick. I know she thought he was kinda hot."

"Did she ever go out with Logan or meet him somewhere?"

Nicole shook her head. "No, she would've told me."

"Do you know if Maddison ever sneaked out of the house late at night?"

"No, she would've told me."

Following their session with Nicole, they continued with Brooke Carson, aged thirteen. After sitting down and hearing Asher's explanation, Brooke covered her face with her hands. Her fingernails had glitter polish.

"I can't believe what's happening to Maddie."

"Brooke, do you know if she has a boyfriend?"

"No, but she told me she wanted one."

"Did she tell you who she liked?"

"I know she thought some guys were hot. Caleb and Logan."

"Did she tell you secrets?"

Brooke hesitated. "I know how bad she wanted to start dating, and she told me how she had these big fights with her mom about it. It was hard for Maddie."

"Hard for her? What do you mean?"

"Well—" Brooke looked at Zubik, then Asher, unease in her eyes. "It's sort of embarrassing."

"It's okay," Asher said. "This is not the time to hold back."

"Well, because some girls our age *do* date and Maddie already had her period and wore a bra and thought she was a woman, you know?"

"Yes, we understand," Asher said.

"Brooke," Zubik said, "do you know if Maddie went online to pornographic sites, or places she shouldn't without her parents knowing?"

Brooke thought for a moment. "No, I don't think she did anything like that."

Their interview with Brooke lasted just over half an hour before the detectives went to the next girl, Lily Wong, aged twelve, who knew Maddison from her gymnastics class.

"This is a nightmare. Some kids are saying Maddie's dead," Lily said.

"We have nothing to prove Maddison's been hurt," Asher said.

"Some parents are afraid that what's happened to her could happen to another kid."

"Lily, do you know if Maddison ever used drugs or alcohol?"

"I saw her sip a beer at a party once. That's all I know."

They continued with Lily for some twenty minutes before Gabriela Rios, aged twelve, sat in the chair and sobbed through much of her interview.

"You've got to find Maddie! Please! I'm praying you find her."

"Do you know if she has problems at school?"

Gabriela shook her head. "She's smart."

"Does she have problems with other kids, teachers, anyone at school?"

"No, Maddie gets along with everyone. Everyone likes her."

After they concluded with Lily, Zubik and Asher moved on to the boys on their list, starting with Caleb Langford, aged thirteen, who struck them as quiet and reserved.

"Caleb, have you ever used a burner phone?" Zubik asked.

"No. Why would I want to, aren't those for drug dealers and gangsters?"

"Do you like Maddison?"

"Yes, I guess."

"In what way do you like her?"

"As a friend."

"Just as a friend? Don't you think she's pretty?"

"Yes."

"You talk to her at school?"

"Yes."

"Text her?"

"Yes."

"What do you text about?"

"Not much, just school stuff."

"Don't lie now."

"I'm not lying."

They continued questioning Caleb until they concluded, took his phone and started interviewing Logan Bostick, aged twelve, who struck them as extremely nervous. He kept rubbing the palms of his hands on his knees.

"Logan, have you ever texted Maddison with self-destructing messages to keep them secret?"

"No."

"You know if you mislead us we'll find out when we check your phone."

"No. I don't use that kind of messaging. I mean I tried it but, no, I don't use it with my friends."

"Have you ever gone to Maddison's house?"

"No. I didn't know where she lives until now. It's on the news."

They continued pressing Logan until it was time for their last interview, Noah Trell, aged thirteen, who kept running his fingers through his hair.

"Do you have a crush on Maddison?"

Noah didn't answer.

"Well, Noah?"

"I like her a lot, I guess."

"Do you know, or think, she has a crush on you?"

He shrugged and ran his fingers through his hair.

"That's not an answer."

He licked his lips.

"Some kids told me she might've had a crush on me."

"You ever meet up with her alone at a mall or someplace secret without anyone knowing?"

"No. I met her with a group of friends at the mall. She was with some friends, I was with some friends, and we all just met."

"Ever ask her to be your girlfriend?"

"No. I heard she wasn't allowed to date until she was older, which seemed dumb."

"Why's that dumb?"

"Because she's old enough and she wanted to."

"Ever suggest she meet you someplace without telling anyone?"

"No, I never did, but—" he looked off at nothing "—I wanted to ask her if she would go out with me but I never did."

They questioned Noah for another twenty minutes before concluding the interviews. Alone in the office, Zubik and Asher compared notes on what Maddison's friends had told them. They were underscoring several points, deciding on who would be reinterviewed and who they still needed to talk to, when Brooke Carson returned to the room and stood before them.

She was crying.

"What is it, Brooke?" Asher asked.

"There's something I need to tell you."

Asher got up, closed the door and helped her to the chair.

"Go ahead." Zubik got up, came around, crossed his arms and leaned on the desk.

"You said this was all confidential, right? No one will know what I tell you."

"That's right," Asher said.

Brooke squeezed her hands into fists, and she stared at her feet.

"She made me swear I'd never tell anyone."

"Who made you swear?"

"Maddie."

"She made you swear you'd never tell about what?" Asher said. "This is important, Brooke."

"She told me something was happening in her life."

"What was happening?" Asher asked.

Brooke shrugged.

"Well, did she elaborate?" Asher asked.

"No, no." Brooke shook her head. "It was like she let it slip, like she wanted me to know but then she didn't."

"Did she tell you anything more?"

"No." Brooke broke into sobs. "I'm so sorry."

She covered her face with her hands. Asher moved to comfort her, passing her a tissue, helping Brooke gain a measure of composure.

"It's just that when she told me—" Brooke blinked back her tears "—when she told me, she looked a little scared."

32

At the halfway house, an Onondaga County evidence technician carefully poured about two teaspoons of silver fingerprint powder onto a clean piece of paper.

She then selected a camel-hair brush from her kit and drew it across the powder. Using arching strokes, she gently applied the brush to the targeted surfaces to locate prints in the auxiliary supply room.

This was one step in a meticulous process.

She'd already photographed and measured the window, and inspected it for traces of hair and fiber evidence. Now, as part of the procedure to collect fingerprint evidence, she began brushing powder on the supply boxes that had been stacked in front of the window, working her way to the wall surrounding the window, the frame, the sill, the levers, the hinges and the glass.

Prints were evident everywhere.

They appeared first as smudges.

The technician continued. Once she had the

prints developed, she took more photographs before lifting them.

After completing her work inside, the technician went outside to repeat the process on the window's exterior. A colleague had started working outside earlier, and had already taken casts of shoe impressions from the soft earth surfaces directly under and around the window.

Word of the forensic work spread through the center and was soon known by every inmate in the halfway house, putting them on edge. One of them, a bank robber, stood in the hall complaining.

"All this is bull! Why they gotta convict us all over again? Man, this is going mess up my job, mess up my progress."

"Get back in your room," a case manager ordered him.

Soon after an update had circulated that the forensic people had finished, everyone heard a bark. Word burned through the center that a K-9 unit had been brought in.

It had detected a scent at the window.

Minutes ticked by, and the sounds of the dog and its handler working their way through the main floor grew more distinct as they reached the second floor. Then the unit hastened up the stairs to the third floor. The jingle of the dog's collar was unmistakable as the handler uttered soft encouraging commands. Panting and the tap of paws grew louder and nearer until Kalmen T. Gatt and Brandon Kane heard a yip and scratching at their door.

Static-filled radio transmissions crackled, then they heard a rumble akin to distant thunder as if an army had been summoned. The door to their quarters swung open. Armed officers swept in, guns drawn.

"On the floor! Hands behind your head, fingers entwined!"

Tail wagging, snout to the floor, the dog crisscrossed the room before stopping and barking.

With several case managers observing, Onondaga deputies got down on hands and knees, tapping the floor beneath and walls above the baseboard.

33

That afternoon, in the Criminal Investigations Division at police headquarters, Ryan Lane felt like a condemned man being strapped into an electric chair.

The polygraph chair was beige with a high back, wide armrests and a wired footpad, all fixed with hidden "seat activity" sensors. They were connected by a web of cables to the polygraph's system on the laptop controlled by Carl Kirby, chief polygraphist for the Syracuse police.

Kirby, a bald man with small round glasses, inspected the sensors he'd connected to Ryan's fingertips and chest. They would measure his blood pressure, heart rate, skin reflex and breathing on the polygraph chart displayed on Kirby's laptop.

"Are you comfortable, Ryan?"

Comfortable? How could anyone in my shoes be comfortable?

When Ryan, Karen and Tyler arrived at the Public Safety Building, Kirby had separated them for the pretest segment. Starting with Ryan, he'd outlined the process, how the polygraph worked, how he would analyze the results to conclude how Ryan fared.

Ryan was then read his rights and signed a consent form.

Kirby half smiled at him. "Ready to begin?"

"Yes."

"I'm cognizant of the fact you're uneasy. Take easy breaths and try to relax."

"Okay."

"Is your name Ryan Lane?"

"Yes."

"Were you born in July?"

"Yes."

"Do you lie to your wife?"

"What do you mean? Like with little things, or big things?"

"Just answer the question yes or no like we discussed, please. Do you lie to your wife?"

"No."

"Have you ever hurt anyone?"

"Physically? Verbally?"

"Yes or no, please. Have you ever hurt anyone?"

"No."

"Did you hurt Maddison?"

"No."

"Are you a violent person?"

"No."

"Do you lose your temper easily?"

"No."

"Before Maddison's disappearance were you under stress?"

Ryan hesitated and licked his lips. "Yes."

"Were you upset at the bank when you were rejected for a loan?"

"Yes."

Kirby eyed the chart flowing on his laptop.

"Did you lose your temper at the bank?"

"Yes."

"Were you violent?"

Ryan blinked then swallowed hard. "Yes."

"Do you know where Maddison is?"

"No."

"Did you kill Maddison?"

"No."

"Do you know who took Maddison?"

"No."

"Did someone in your family hurt Maddison by accident?"

"No."

"If someone in your family was involved in Maddison's disappearance, would you tell police?"

"Yes."

Kirby's questions continued for more than an hour. Some were posed differently, but they were still the same and relentless, like powerful claws ripping at his insides. With no sleep, little to eat and feeling emotionally empty, as they neared the end he felt numb.

How did this happen? One day I'm a working man, struggling to keep my business, now my daughter's missing and I'm treated like a suspect. God, tell me, will I ever see Maddie again?

Suddenly Ryan was pierced with a spear of truth—a flash of one horrible incident—that one terrible time with Maddie that he would never reveal to anyone.

It's my fault Maddie's gone.

Taking stock of the wires connecting him to the lie detector, Tyler felt the new weight of what was happening. He had listened to everything Kirby, the polygraph guy, had told him.

I've got to pass this test because it's my fault she's missing.

The guy checked to ensure Tyler's feet rested properly on the footpad. "Okay, that should do it," Kirby said. "Ready?"

Tyler nodded.

"Is your name Tyler Lane?"

"Yes."

"Are you thirteen years old?"

"Yes."

"Do you have a brother?"

"No."

"Do you have a sister?"

"Yes."

"Have you ever hit your sister?"

"Yes."

Kirby made a note while keeping his eyes on his laptop.

"Did you hurt your sister the night she disappeared?"

"No."

"Did you hurt her by accident?"

"No."

"Do you ever get mad at your sister?"

"Yes."

"Do you hate your sister?"

"No."

"Do you collect knives?"

"Yes."

"Do you ever think about stabbing a person with one of your knives?"

Tyler thought. He did think about stabbing the creep who was in Maddie's room, so: "Yes," he said.

"Did you kill your sister?"

"No!" Tyler shook his head.

"Did you convince her to sneak out her window the night she disappeared?"

"No."

"Did one of your friends or someone you know take your sister?"

"No."

"Do you know where your sister is?"

"No."

"Do you know who took your sister?"

"No."

"Did you hear voices in her room the night she disappeared?"

"Yes."

"Disregarding Maddie, do you know who the other voice belongs to?"

"No."

"Was Maddie being abused sexually or physically in your home?"

"No."

"Did one of your parents hurt Maddie then make it look liked she was abducted?"

"No."

"Did your mom, or your dad, or you, hurt your sister by accident?"

"No."

The polygraph guy kept asking Tyler questions like that for close to an hour before he said they were nearly done with only a few more to go.

"Are you protecting anyone who may have been involved in your sister's disappearance?"

"No."

"Are you happy your sister's gone?"

Tyler's chin crumpled. "No."

"Do you want her to return?"

"Yes." He started to cry. "More than anything."

"Please, take a breath and try to relax."

Karen was sobbing softly and trembling as Kirby connected the sensors to her fingers. She was not in an ideal state for a polygraph exam, but she told him that she wanted to go through with it.

"Would you like some water before we start, Karen?"

"No, thank you."

She blinked back her tears and readied herself as Kirby settled into his chair, studied his laptop and began the examination.

"Is your name Karen Lane?"

"Yes."

"Are you employed as a cashier?"

"Yes."

"Are you a mother of two children?"

"Yes."

"Have you ever lied to your husband?"

Karen didn't respond, and Kirby repeated the question.

"Have you ever lied to your husband?"

"Yes."

"Was there tension in your home before your daughter went missing?"

"Yes."

"Did you argue with your daughter before she went missing?"

"Yes."

"Were you angry when you argued with her?"

"Yes."

"Have you ever hurt anyone?"

"Yes."

"Did you ever hurt your daughter?"

"No."

Kirby paused as he watched the chart on his screen.

"Did you hurt your daughter by accident and cover it up by staging her disappearance?"

"No!"

"Do you know if your daughter is dead?"

"God, no!" Karen turned to Kirby. "No!"

"Do you know who took your daughter?"

"No."

"Do you know where your daughter is?"

"No." Her voice weakened.

Somehow Karen found the strength to keep herself together as Kirby grilled her for nearly ninety minutes. Some of his questions took her into the darkest corners of her life, leaving her raw and exposed. When it was over, Kirby disconnected the sensors and told Karen she could leave and join Ryan and Tyler.

But she didn't move.

It was as if she'd been ravaged as if all emotion, all feeling, had emptied out of her and she'd been cast into a bottomless black chasm. She was plunging, swallowed by darkness lit only by her sins and images of Cassie, then Cassie's casket being lowered into the grave; then her mother's casket being lowered into the ground and now Maddie was gone with Kirby's question hammering against her heart.

"Do you know if your daughter is dead?"

Karen never felt Kirby's hands, or those of the people he'd summoned to help her as she struggled against them in the polygraph chair and screamed for her child.

34

Still reeling from their polygraphs, the Lanes walked out of police headquarters.

Ryan searched for Chuck Field, who was going to drive them back to Cole's house. He didn't see Chuck. Instead, he'd spotted a young woman waiting outside the entrance. She saw Ryan and approached them.

"Excuse me, are you the Lanes, Maddison's family?"

She was in her early twenties, sunglasses perched atop her head. A nose ring pierced her right nostril. She wore a lot of makeup, and her eyes gleamed with a mix of anxiety and successful hunting.

Ryan nodded.

"I'm Daisy Miller, reporter for *Just Breaking Now*, online news." She held up an ID tag, then quickly held out her phone toward Ryan and Karen. "Will you be going to Buffalo to make the positive identification?"

Puzzled, Ryan and Karen looked at each other, then at Miller.

"We don't know what you're talking about."

"Our sources confirm that a girl's body was found in a wooded area in Buffalo and that they're confident it's your daughter. What're your thoughts at this time?"

Ryan went ashen; Karen's knees buckled. He and Tyler caught her before she collapsed as Chuck Field arrived and rushed to help them.

"What? Buffalo? What?" Ryan stammered while helping Karen. "We don't know anything about a body."

"I'm sorry to break it to you," Miller said. "It's happening now in Buffalo."

Karen moaned and began sobbing.

"We have nothing to say," Ryan said. "Leave us alone."

With Chuck's help Ryan and Tyler got Karen back inside the building.

Feeling everything inside him crack wide open, Ryan raced up to the Criminal Investigations Division on the third floor, stormed through it until he found Asher and Zubik at their desks. Asher was on the phone.

"Why didn't you tell us you found Maddie in Buffalo?" Ryan shouted.

Taken by surprise Zubik stood, holding up his open palms.

"Detective Asher is just confirming information," Zubik said. "How did you learn about Buffalo?"

"There's a reporter downstairs. She told us and Karen's destroyed. Goddammit, Zubik!"

"Hold on, have a seat. We just got the call, too. That reporter might have good sources but, Ryan, we need to confirm whether or not it's Maddison. Hold on."

His chest heaving, tears blurring his eyes, Ryan paced while Asher was on the phone. He rejected a bottle of water from Zubik as other investigators in the division came near, ready to subdue him if necessary.

Asher finished her call.

"All right." She exhaled. "The body found in Buffalo is not Maddison. It's a fourteen-year-old girl from Buffalo who apparently was hit by a train while walking on the tracks."

Zubik and the others watched Ryan absorb the news in silence. With each passing second the tension decreased. He ran his hands through his hair and shut his eyes.

"You should be with Karen. We'll go downstairs with you to tell her," Zubik said.

Ryan swallowed hard and nodded.

The silence in Chuck Field's Chevy Equinox was crushing. He found a classical music station and turned the sound low as they drove.

After Zubik and Asher had confirmed to the Lanes that the reporter's information was wrong, that the body found in Buffalo was not Maddison, they offered a small consolation. The Lanes would be able to return to their home the next day.

Now, as they rolled across the city to Cole's house, Karen gazed out the window, submerged in her pain.

Will I ever see Maddie again? Will I ever hold her again and tell her I'm sorry? Was she taken by a predator and killed? Is she lying in a ditch somewhere?

As they passed through a section of the city that was near the Monarda River, Karen found herself thinking of Cassie, of how she died. The agony of that time began swirling around her.

Not now. Please God, don't let me think of that now.

Karen then thought of the polygraph, how it had taken her into the corners of her heart where she'd hidden her deepest fears and darkest secrets.

She cried quietly.

As Chuck drove, the strains of a haunting piece by Mozart floated from the speakers.

Ryan's pulse continued hammering.

...like my wipers that day I got into my truck to search for Maddie in the rain...that awful day... I was enraged... I lost it that day...

As they passed the area that led to the Monarda River, Ryan glanced at Karen, lost in her anguish. Then he thought about what he'd learned about the statistics concerning abducted children. How most were killed within hours of being taken; how their encounter with that reporter had driven home the cold hard reality that Maddie was likely dead.

No, don't think like that. You're depleted because you've had no sleep and because of the polygraph.

The polygraph.

Will it bring us closer to the truth?

Closer to them finding out what I did to Maddie?

35

With each tap on the floor and walls, the deputies drove a new spike of fear into Kalmen Gatt's heart.

His face betrayed nothing.

But all the spit in his mouth had evaporated as he watched the deputies working with the dog along the baseboard near his roommate's side.

Kane flicked a look of trepidation to Gatt.

Gatt ignored him.

The dog, pumped with enthusiasm, crouched to sniff under Kane's bed, yelping and pawing near the wall's duplex electrical outlet. The deputies shoved Kane's bed aside. A screwdriver was produced, and the outlet's plastic plate removed.

A deputy drew his face within inches of the outlet, and used a penlight to probe the small space until an object was discovered. Gloved fingers were inserted into the gap, and after a few seconds of careful movement, the deputy delicately extracted clear plastic bags holding various items. Cash rolled into a tight cylinder, a cell phone, vials of pills, and small baggies of foiled items and powder were obvious.

The deputy set the discovery atop Kane's bedside table.

Another deputy was talking quietly on his phone. All eyes had shifted to Kane.

"We've just been told that your prints were found inside and outside the auxiliary supply room window, Kane," a deputy said. "I'll bet that phone's a burner, and you've been slipping out to deal. What else you been up to, Brandon? You're still incarcerated. You have no rights here."

Drops of sweat appeared on Kane's face. He said nothing.

"Turn around. Put your hands behind your back."

A metallic jangle, a clink and click as handcuffs were snapped onto Kane's wrists. As a deputy led Kane to the door, relief washed over Gatt.

But it died.

The dog yelped, turned and grew interested in something across the room, something on the floor.

He led the deputies to a grilled floor register for the center's heating and cooling system.

Again, a deputy got on his knees.

With gloved hands he pried up the metal register, which opened to the tin ductwork of the building's heating, ventilation and air-conditioning system. Getting flat on his stomach, the deputy searched the system with a flashlight. The center was an older building, and the ductwork was about a foot wide and six inches deep.

Seconds ticked by and it appeared he was about to abandon the effort when, there, nearly lost among the dust balls, the deputy discerned a piece of cord about two feet from the mouth of the vent. The cord was straight, and its end disappeared into the darkness.

He tugged gently on it.

Something of weight was tied to the far end.

He began pulling the object toward him.

Gatt's heart slammed against his chest.

36

At that time, across the city at police headquarters, heads turned from desks as Cole Lane walked through the Criminal Investigations Division.

Investigators stood to shake Cole's hand; he got the subtle head-to-toe look, smiles and back slaps. The new guys who knew only his story and the old-timers who'd known him from his days on the force greeted him with a mixture of reverence and condolence. A few commented about that god-awful false alarm out of Buffalo underscoring how intense the investigation was.

"Good to see you, Cole."

"Honor to meet you."

"We're going flat-out to find your niece."

"It's been a long time, pal."

After Cole introduced Jill and Dalton, he glimpsed Asher and Zubik waiting near the interview rooms. Their faces were taut; they held no time for heroes. They had work to do. Asher nodded to Cole and indicated an open door.

They'd start with him.

He entered the stark white-walled room and took a seat across from the detectives at the lone table.

"Is that chair going to be okay for you, Cole? I mean—will you be comfortable?" Asher acknowledged his prosthetic legs.

"I'm fine, Fran," Cole said.

Asher passed him forms to sign, consenting to volunteering his family's fingerprints, phones and volunteering their property to be searched as part of the investigation. He signed them all.

"Before we start, Cole, I want to make one thing clear," Zubik said. "We know you're running your own investigation, but this is our case. Is that understood?"

"She's my niece, Stan."

"I get that. I know all you've been through and what you're going through. But you better not interfere, or do anything to jeopardize or obstruct us. Do we understand each other here?"

Zubik's gaze drilled into him, and the muscles under Cole's jaw pulsed.

"Understood."

"Good. Now, we've got your informal statements," Zubik said, "and the questionnaire we'd sent you. Let's start with you taking us through a time line of the night Maddison disappeared, and how you heard."

Asher's pen was poised over her pad.

"Jill and I went out to dinner at the Inn on the Lake. We got home about ten thirty, ten-forty-five.

I was beat, so I turned in. She stayed up to wait for Dalton to get home."

"Where was Dalton that evening?"

"He'd gone to a friend's birthday party. He got picked up and was getting a ride home."

Asher took notes.

"What time did Dalton get home?"

"I don't know the exact time, but it was late, after his curfew. There was car trouble."

"Who was driving him home?"

"He got a ride with the older brother of his friend Donnie Slade. I think his name's Lennie Slade. I provided this information earlier."

"Where was the party?"

"On the far east side. It was supposed to be a big event. The friend was turning sixteen."

"Do you have the friend's name?"

"Jill knows it, but I think it's Jenna Guthrie. Her mom works in the mayor's office."

"And did you ask him how he got those tiny scratches on his face?"

"No, because I never noticed them, with the way his hair is."

"How did you learn about Maddison?"

"Ryan called me in the morning, and we rushed over to help."

"Do you know anyone who holds any ill will toward your brother or his family?"

"No."

"Do you think your brother or anyone in his family could've hurt Maddison?"

"No, I don't."

"Do you think anyone in your family could've hurt Maddison or be involved in her disappearance?"

"No."

"How would you describe your relationship with your brother?"

Cole thought before he said, "Complicated."

"How?"

"When we were younger, he wanted me to join him in our father's drywall business. I wanted to take a different road in life, and he resented me a little for it. We both acknowledged that and we still deal with it. We get along. When I got back home after being blown apart in Afghanistan, I went through some very rough times."

"I've read your book," Zubik said.

"Me too," Asher said. "You overcame so much."

Cole nodded slowly and looked away, for suddenly it all came back, and for a few seconds he was in the unforgiving mountains of Afghanistan with a fifteen-member team, following new intel to a remote Taliban camp...

Trekking to it, we near a small village. We're crossing a flat expanse when the air whips with the sound of bullets. The crack of gunfire. We're under attack. Exposed. Three of our guys go down. I find cover in a ditch behind a line of rocks with our medic and two other guys, and return fire.

Our radio's gone. We use the sat phone to call for help. It's an ambush. We count sixty Taliban firing on us. Our guys are down everywhere, wounded, bleeding, still returning fire, crawling toward us for cover. The Taliban bring out a machine gun and our rock cover begins chipping away, stone and shrapnel slicing into our guys, chewing up the ones who're exposed and can't make it to our cover.

We're reloading, returning fire, holding them off for as long as we can. Air support's coming fast. Three of our guys are dying yards away. I get our team to unleash cover fire and I crawl to them, dragging them to our cover, feeling bullets slice by. I get one, then two guys to safety and go for the third when I hear the choppers coming, see them fire from the sky as the Taliban bring out rocket-propelled grenades.

One RPG misses the chopper, but the Taliban aims the second at me. I see it come, everything slows, the flash-explosion, the heat. My body heaves into the air, I can't hear, breathe. One leg below my knee is hanging by charred skin; the other below my knee is gone. My world goes black.

I remember blue sky, being airlifted, medics working on me, the hospital, doctors telling me I had lost my legs below the knee but saved three lives. The hospital in Germany, the Purple Heart, surgery after surgery, my life changed...my life... gone.

Coming home to Walter Reed, getting new legs, therapy, struggling with mountains to climb...so hard. I can't do it, but Ryan and Karen are there, supporting me, pushing me. One person who is not there: my girlfriend, Brittany. She's devastated, they tell me.

She's devastated?

When I get back to Syracuse for more therapy, Brittany tells me she met someone new, but in my heart I know—it's a lie. She can't deal with me. The life she envisioned does not include a man who'd been blown apart. I'm not in that picture. She leaves me alone with a third amputation, an emotional one. I sink fast into the abyss. Ryan and Karen come to help me...you've got to hang in there, they tell me...but I can't...what's the point, look at me. I don't blame Britt for leaving me, I mean look at me...who could love me like this? I'm gone... I quit. Then Karen...taking my hand...don't ever say that...we love you, Cole...we need you... holding my hand...

"Yeah, well, Ryan and Karen got me through my darkest moments for which I'm indebted to them. They'd do anything for me. I'd do anything for them."

"Would you say Ryan is prone to violence?"

"No. I know he has a short fuse, but he's a gentle soul, a good man."

"How does your wife get along with your brother's family?"

"Good. She and Karen are good sisters-in-law."

"How would you describe Dalton's relationship with Maddison and Tyler?"

"All right. They're cousins. He's a little older.

They don't see each other that much but when they do, they get along fine."

"What do you think happened to Maddison?"

"I think someone abducted her."

"Who do you think did it?"

"Maybe a predatory offender, or someone she met online, or someone from the halfway house. Do you have any strong leads? I understand you're going hard on the halfway house and some other people?"

"We're looking everywhere," Zubik said. "What're your people doing?"

Asher was poised to take note.

"We're going through the publically posted sex offender registry," Cole said, "cross-referencing names and addresses, creating a map and list of offenders residing near Maddie's home."

"I think you should leave that to us. What else are you doing?"

"I've got my guys running down all their sources for any word on the street. And we're looking on-line with other sources to see if she surfaces on the dark web or porn sites. We're searching for any cyber predators, and we're helping coordinate the search and tips."

Asher took notes.

"You know you're required to give us anything you uncover," Zubik said.

"I'm aware of that, Stan."

Before they concluded, Cole asked Zubik a final question.

"Are you focusing on anyone in particular?"

Zubik considered Cole's question, his face betraying nothing.

"No one's been ruled out yet."

37

Jill twisted the tissue in her hands.

"It was around ten thirty when we got home from dinner at the Inn on the Lake." Her eyes glistened as she related the events to Asher and Zubik. "Cole went to bed. I stayed up and read while I waited for Dalton."

"Where was Dalton?" Zubik asked, not sharing what Cole had said.

"He went to a friend's birthday party."

"Who was the friend? Where was the party?"

"Jenna Guthrie, her sixteenth. Her mom is Celeste. She works for the mayor. They live on Republic Drive. I can get you the address."

"We can get it but sure, thanks."

"How did Dalton get there?"

"His friend Donnie Slade's older brother drove them there and back."

"What time was Dalton supposed to return?"

"Well, his curfew on Friday nights is midnight, but when it got late, I got a bit worried. He wasn't answering my texts, which frustrated me, so I got in my car and went out looking for him. He wasn't at the party, so I drove around looking for him to an all-night diner I knew he liked, but I couldn't find him and went home."

"Why not tell Cole, let him go looking or go together?"

"Because I had insisted that we try a different approach with Dalton, be more flexible, so I guess I felt a sense of responsibility." She sighed. "Anyway, he got home very late, after 3:00 a.m., maybe 3:30. I'd fallen asleep."

"Did you reprimand him for being late?"

"Lightly, because he said they'd had some car trouble and his phone wasn't working. I accepted that, but, well, Dalton's been having some problems."

Zubik and Asher exchanged a quick glance.

"What sort of problems?"

Jill considered the question.

"Over the past six months or so he's been caught a few times with alcohol on his breath, he got into a scuffle at school and he missed school assignments. After talking with his teachers and counselors, we decided that rather than being hard on him we'd try a period of respect and trust, to give him a chance to develop a degree of maturity and straighten out. Cole was reluctant to go along with that approach, but I supported it."

"Is it working?"

"It's challenging but we're hopeful. He's a teenager."

"And what about those little scratches he had on his face? Did you ask him about them?"

"No. The way he wears his hair, I never saw them until you pointed them out."

"Does he spend a lot of time online?"

"Yes. Like most kids he lives on his phone."

"Do you know if he sexts?"

Jill's face flushed.

"No, he doesn't because I force him to show me his phone under the threat of canceling it."

"Do you ever catch him visiting sites he shouldn't be visiting?"

"A couple of times I caught him viewing porn and came down hard on him, but he's a fourteen-year-old."

Zubik took a moment then resumed.

"How does Dalton get along with his cousins, Maddison and Tyler?"

Jill pondered her crumpled tissue.

"They look up to him, almost idolize him."

"What makes you say that? He's only a year or so older."

"Well, he's traveled all over the world with us. He's experienced more of life, I guess. He hangs out with older kids. Sometimes I wonder if Maddie has a little harmless crush on Dalton."

"Why do you think that?"

Jill smiled weakly. "Oh, just the way she looked up to him, as older, more like a young man of the world, I guess. I don't know." She shrugged.

"Did Dalton ever say anything about Maddison along those lines, or indicate feelings for her?"

"God, no. No, they're cousins."

"Does Dalton have a girlfriend?"

"He's been out on a few dates, and when we had to go to Paris for Cole's business, Dalton met the very pretty daughter of a French detective and I guess they had a little romance going. We know they were FaceTiming and texting a lot for months."

Zubik paused to let Asher catch up on her note-taking, then resumed.

"You say that you've talked with Dalton's teachers and counselors about his problems. Is there any thought as to what the source or cause of those problems is? Could you tell us a bit more about that, the atmosphere in your home with you, Cole and Dalton?"

"Me, Cole and Dalton?" Jill blinked several times and glanced up at the camera, aware she was being recorded. Then she looked into her hands.

Her thoughts rolled back to when she met Cole, working as an orthopedic physical therapist helping him with his postsurgical care. She liked him. He was a smart, good-looking guy, and she'd grown attracted to him.

She was heartbroken for him after she'd learned that his girlfriend had abandoned him. She was awed by how his brother and sister-in-law were relentless with their support and encouragement to see that he got through the breakup and that he continued his battle. Jill did all she could, too.

It took a long time and a lot of work, but Cole survived, like he'd found a new purpose. Like he was reborn, had become a new person. During this period, Jill got to know him all over again.

They fell in love. Got married and set out to start a family, but Jill suffered several miscarriages.

She was devastated.

But Cole was strong. He helped her; she leaned on him and they endured together.

"I guess that life in our home is much like anyone else's," Jill said. "Like everyone, we've had good times and bad times. I mean, I can't have children. We adopted Dalton when he was eleven months old. As he got older, he began studying family photos, then he started asking why he didn't really look like anyone in his family history. Cole and I gave it a lot of thought, then, eight months ago, we told Dalton he was adopted."

"How did he react?"

"Okay at first." Jill nodded slowly. "But it was after that, that he started having his problems, acting out, rebelling. So we felt a little guilty and wanted to give him some time and space to process everything."

"Who else is aware that he's adopted?"

"Ryan and Karen had known from the beginning, and my family. After we broke the news to Dalton, we let Ryan and Karen tell Maddie and Tyler. We left it up to Dalton if he wanted to tell people, that no matter how he chose to go, we'd support him."

Zubik looked at Jill, thinking for several moments before thanking her.

"I think that's it for now. An officer will escort you to where you can provide your fingerprints."

38

Dalton was familiar with police stations.

Given his dad was an ex-cop who ran his own private investigation agency, Dalton had been in a few with him. They pretty much looked the same.

But this visit was unlike any other.

And no matter how much the detectives sitting on the other side of the table smiled and tried to be nice to Dalton, he sensed their warmth was phony and he didn't like it. And he didn't like being in this bright, plain room. It gave him the same feeling as when he went to the dentist: the expectation that something unpleasant was about to happen.

"Are you nervous?" Zubik asked.

"Yeah." Dalton glanced at the camera up in the corner.

"That's okay," Asher said. "You want to help us find Maddison, right?"

"Yeah."

"Good," Zubik said. "All you have to do is answer our questions with the truth, all right?"

"All right."

"Good, and thanks for signing the papers and giving us your phone. Do you have any other phones, maybe old phones, a friend's phone, one you may have forgotten about?"

Dalton shook his head. "No, I only use one phone. The one I gave you."

"You probably know from your dad how these things go."

"I'm not sure what you mean."

"You know it's a crime if you lie to us," Zubik said. "And if you lie and we find out, it gets even more serious. You understand that, Dalton?"

He gave tense, short nods. "Yes."

"Were you communicating with Maddison in any way in the time before her parents reported her missing?"

"No."

"No texting?" Zubik asked.

"No."

"Do you ever text with her, or send messages or pictures?"

"No, not really." Dalton shrugged. "Maybe birthdays, and I'd send her and Tyler cool pictures whenever I went somewhere, like London or Australia. I mean Maddie's younger, and she's got her own friends. We don't see each other that much except when our families get together."

"How would you describe your relationship with her?"

"What do you mean?"

"Do you like her?" Asher asked.

"Yeah."

"In what way do you like her?"

"She's my cousin, part of my family, so I love her and I'm really worried about her, if that's what you mean."

"And what about how she feels about you?" Zubik asked. "Do you think she looks up to you?"

Dalton shrugged. "Maybe a little, I guess."

"Why do you guess that?"

"Maybe because I'm older and do stuff, I don't know."

"Do you have a crush on her?" Zubik asked.

"No, that would be weird."

"Do you think she has a crush on you?"

"I doubt it. That would also be weird."

"Are you involved in Maddison's disappearance?"

Zubik noticed that Dalton's hands had been flat on the table, but now his fingertips were pressing against the surface.

"No," Dalton said.

"Did you lure Maddie out that night?"

"No." Dalton's face creased a little as he glanced at Asher then Zubik.

"Did you hurt her, maybe by accident?"

"No. Why're you asking me this?"

"Do you know who's involved in Maddison's disappearance?"

"No."

"Who do you think might've taken her?"

"Some creep."

"Do you ever think about Maddison in a sexual way?" Zubik asked.

"No."

"Do you visit porn sites, Dalton?"

He swallowed and hesitated. "I've seen a few."

"Ever sext with anyone?"

Dalton didn't respond for a long moment. "That's private."

"We have your phone and our experts are good at finding deleted things, so tell us the truth. You're a good-looking young man who's seen the world. Ever use your phone to show a girl your junk, Dalton? Or ask a girl to show you hers?"

Taken aback by Zubik's questioning, Dalton's face flushed but he said nothing.

"Come on, Dalton, tell us the truth. Have you sexted with anyone, maybe that girl you like from Paris?"

Dalton swallowed and licked his lips.

"A lot of kids do it," Dalton said. "So, my answer is yes."

"Things will go better if you keep telling the truth." Zubik flipped through his notebook and repositioned himself in his chair before asking, "We understand you're adopted. Does that trouble you?"

The question seemed to wound Dalton. He was unable to mask the hurt that registered in his eyes as he stared at the table before him.

"I don't know," he said.

"Do you know much about your biological mother?"

Dalton hesitated then said, "Only that I was told that she died when I was born."

"We understand you've been having some trouble at school recently, getting into fights, not doing homework," Asher said, "that it started after your parents confirmed what you'd suspected, that you were adopted. Do you think your trouble is related to that?"

Dalton kept his eyes on the table and shrugged.

"Let's change gears," Zubik said. "Where were you and what were you doing the night Maddison disappeared?"

"I went to my friend Jenna Guthrie's birthday party."

"Tell us about the party."

"It was big, over a hundred kids. She lives in a big house in that new part of town way over on the east side."

"What time did you get there?"

"I think around eight thirty."

"How did you get there?"

"My friend Donnie Slade's older brother Lennie drove us."

"How old are these guys?"

"Donnie's fifteen and Lennie's seventeen, no, maybe eighteen."

"How do you know the Slade brothers?"

"I met them way back at a stock car race my dad took me to. Their dad is crew chief for K. T. Glory, the professional stock car racer. K. T. does commercials. I like hanging out with Donnie and Lennie and their friends. They're pretty cool."

"So the Slade brothers were invited too?"

"Yeah, we all went to the party. Jenna's sister goes to college, and she was there with lots of her friends. It was an epic party."

"Was there drinking and drugs?"

Dalton blinked several times then nodded. "Yes."

"Did you drink?"

"I had some beers, a couple."

"Did you have any drugs?"

Dalton was silent.

"Tell us the truth, Dalton."

"I had some pot."

Zubik took a moment to take stock of Dalton.

"And it was at this party that you got the scratches?"

"Yes."

"Tell us exactly how you got them again."

"We were standing on the garden wall, and I was playing this balance game with some guy. You press the side of your body against each other's shoulders and legs. Someone says go, and you push with all your strength to knock the other guy down, or off balance. I slipped and slid into the hedge and got scratched."

"Were other people watching?"

"Yeah."

"What time did you leave the party?"

"When it was close to midnight, I told Donnie

and Lennie I had to go, even though the party was supposed to go all night. We got in the car and left, but Lennie said he was hungry so we went to the all-night Whenever-Burger. Then when we were driving to my house, the car broke down."

"What kind of car is it?"

"A Dodge Challenger. I don't know the year."

"What was wrong?"

"I don't know. Lennie said it was making a noise. He pulled over, shut it off, tried to fix it, but it wouldn't start and I was real nervous because I was so late. Lennie had to call one of his friends to help him get it going and that took forever."

"Who was the friend?"

"George somebody, I don't know."

"Why didn't you call your dad to get you?"

"I was too scared to call him."

"Why?"

"First, because it was so late. Then, because I had been drinking and because there was beer and pot in the car. I was kind of freaking out."

Zubik looked at Dalton for a moment.

"So what time was it when you got home?"

"About three thirty, I think. I figured I was dead, that my dad was going to kill me, but only my mom was up and I told her what happened."

"Did you tell her about the drinking and the pot?"

"No, not exactly."

Zubik's icy, penetrating gaze bored into him.

"Is that the truth, Dalton?"

"Yes."

Zubik and Asher glanced at the door after someone knocked.

It opened to their captain, Moe Tilden, who called them out to the hall.

"Onondaga's got something from the halfway house that could break everything wide open," Tilden said.

39

Here was twelve-year-old Maddison Lane.

In her bedroom. In her bathroom. Dressing. Undressing.

Naked.

Zubik and Asher swiped through image after image on Rance Carver's laptop, the county detective who had been investigating the halfway house. Carver had downloaded the images from items found in the ventilation system of an inmate's quarters.

"We found a tablet with internet access, a digital camera and a telephoto zoom lens concealed in the ductwork." Carver held out his phone showing photos of the discovered items. "They're being processed now as evidence by the crime scene people."

Asher shook her head slowly while studying the photos. They were grainy enlargements, taken from a distance, and it was clear Maddison was not aware someone was taking them. In most of them she was in various stages of undress, or naked. "There must be hundreds."

"We estimate over one thousand," Carver said.

"And you've linked these items and images to the inmate—" Zubik consulted his notebook "—Kalmen Gatt?"

"Yes. We believe Gatt climbed a tree in Lucifer's Green and targeted the windows of the Lanes' home that faced it, and took pictures voyeur-style."

"Wait," Zubik said. "How did you connect this material to Gatt?"

"Fingerprint identification. Gatt's thumbprint opened the tablet."

Zubik nodded.

"We've got Gatt in a holding room, Stan. If you're ready, we can get to work bringing you and Fran up to speed as quickly as we can."

Over the next couple of hours, Carver, along with other detectives, senior SPD brass, case managers from the halfway house and those who managed Gatt in prison scrutinized every aspect of Gatt's life.

They studied Carver's notes from his initial interview with Gatt, his crime file, his prison records, pysch reports, exams, assessments, his above-average intelligence, his computer expertise, his new job, his good behavior and pass access, and the security breach at the halfway house window that allowed inmates to circumvent the surveillance cameras.

When they finished, Zubik downed the remnants of his coffee.

Gatt's our number one suspect, he thought. *But if he took Maddison, there's little chance she's alive. If she is, the clock's ticking down on her.*

Zubik and Asher headed to the holding room.

Dread fluttered up in Zubik's chest, and he whispered a prayer for Maddison.

Whatever condition she's in, this could be my best shot, my only shot, to find her.

Kalmen T. Gatt sat in a chair at a table in metal handcuffs wearing orange prison scrubs, the uniform of the County Justice Center.

His wrist cuffs were fastened to a steel ring bolted to the table, and his ankles were fettered.

Zubik and Asher sat across from him.

After introducing himself and Asher, Zubik said, "Because you're currently in custody, Miranda rights are not necessary. Do you understand, Mr. Gatt?"

The suspect looked at him with a blank expression.

"You're going back inside to do more time," Zubik said. "Accept it."

Gatt gazed at the cop for a moment and blinked.

"Kalmen, if you cooperate with us we'll put in a good word with the district attorney. No guarantees, but it could lessen your sentence."

Gatt's face remained devoid of expression.

"We have evidence linking you directly to Maddison Lane."

Still he continued to stare at Zubik.

"Where is she, Kalmen?"

Gatt's jawline pulsed.

"Did you hurt her?"

Wearing the face of a man standing on the edge of an eternal chasm, he didn't answer.

For more than an hour, Zubik continued questioning him, but Gatt remained silent. Then the detective took the step of showing Gatt the photos of Maddison they'd found on his tablet in an effort to trigger a response. As Zubik swiped through them slowly, he studied Gatt. The suspect's eyes were drawn to the images, his nostrils flared ever so slightly as his breathing deepened.

One by one Zubik fed the images to him.

"This is what happened, Kalmen—you were out on your pass when you first saw Maddison. Maybe she was walking down the street. Maybe she smiled at you. She's very pretty. You fell in love. You wanted her, but you were afraid because you have urges no one knows about."

Gatt's gaze was welded to the pictures.

"You locked on to where she lives, and you began your secret game of capturing her image from the forest so you could enjoy her privately, have her to yourself. But it only made your urges stronger, painful, as you dreamed about her. You were in agony and had to do something, anything, to satisfy your urges."

Gatt swallowed.

"That's when you saw the ladder in her yard, and your fantasies about her evolved into a plan to have her for real. You came in the night and took her, but like all plans, things didn't go well. She was afraid, maybe she was going to tell, maybe she hit you and you hit her back. You didn't mean it. It was an accident. You had to hide her. Maybe you didn't kill her. Maybe you locked her up somewhere so you could enjoy her a little while longer."

Zubik stopped, stood and drew his face to within inches of Gatt's.

"You never meant to hurt her, did you, Kalmen?"

Gatt blinked, and for an instant he went somewhere in his mind, then returned shaking his head.

"No."

"It was an accident, wasn't it?"

"No, no, no accident."

"No?"

"I never touched her."

"Don't lie. You're smarter than that."

"I never touched her. I only took pictures. I swear that's all I did."

"Why're you lying when we have the evidence?"

"I didn't take her. I only took pictures."

"Think of her family. Unburden yourself. What did you do with Maddison Lane?"

An odd change came over Gatt.

He looked up at the camera in the ceiling corner,

then at Asher, then at Zubik. Then he shut down, remaining motionless with an unblinking stare.

Time passed without anyone speaking before Gatt shifted in his chair and said, "I've got to take a leak."

Zubik frowned. "No, you don't."

"Want me to piss myself right here?"

Zubik muttered under his breath then nodded to Asher, whose chair scraped as she stepped into the hall and summoned two deputies. Keys jangled as a deputy released Gatt from the table's handcuff ring. His shackles jingled and they took him into the hall, leaving Zubik and Asher behind.

With one deputy on Gatt's left and a second on his right, they escorted him toward the restroom at the end of the hall. At this time, a meeting of the units from traffic, patrol and the airport had broken up, and officers streamed toward Gatt and his escorts.

One of the uniformed officers stopped at the water fountain, bending over to drink just as Gatt and his escorts were passing. Gatt's eyes went to the cop's holstered sidearm and he lunged for the gun, seizing it with his cuffed hands. Years earlier, before he was convicted, he had studied retention-type holsters in online police equipment manuals. He knew to release the thumb break, to slightly twist the weapon to clear the trigger guard lock, accomplishing it all in a terrifyingly swift motion, grabbing the gun in both hands.

In that same instant the deputies and the officer reacted, struggling with Gatt who in a rush of adrenaline was turning the gun toward one of the men, succeeding in raising the muzzle up, up, up until it was pressing into the cop's throat. The officers battled with Gatt for control, as his finger was moving ever closer to the trigger.

In those seconds another officer rushed at Gatt with his weapon drawn, and shot him five times.

The chaos drew Zubik and Asher into the hall, where they saw Gatt lying on the floor in a growing pool of brilliant red blood. People were shouting about a "gun grab," someone was calling for an ambulance. One officer was kneeling over Gatt giving him rapid chest compressions.

"We need that prisoner alive!" Zubik shouted.

In the mayhem, paramedics arrived.

"He still has vitals!" one of the medical crew said as they tended to Gatt, stabilizing him before loading him into the ambulance and rushing him to hospital.

After three hours of surgery, they put Gatt in the intensive care unit.

A tall doctor with a somber face joined Zubik and Asher in the corridor outside.

"The patient has a ten percent chance of surviving his wounds," the doctor said. "It's anyone's guess when, or if, he'll regain consciousness. I'll allow you to keep a bedside vigil as you requested."

The doctor nodded to the uniformed officer, and Gatt's door was opened for the detectives. The suspect was on his back. A series of small screens above his bed monitored his blood pressure, his heart and other vital signs. A breathing tube and plastic mask covered his mouth and nose. An IV pole with a drip stood next to his bed. A nurse was next to it, tapping information into a tablet.

Zubik and Asher settled into cushioned chairs.

Night had fallen, and as they watched the city's lights twinkling, Zubik reviewed Gatt's prison file.

Prison psychiatrists had measured his IQ at 138, noting that he possessed very superior intelligence. Gatt had been subjected to various psych assessments to determine his sexual preferences in order to uncover any cognitive distortions, or desires concerning having sex with children. The findings had raised no concerns. Results showed that he was a thirty-five-year-old heterosexual male whose sexual desires were for heterosexual women aged twenty-five to forty-five.

That turned out to be wrong, Zubik thought, because it was clear Gatt desired women younger, much younger.

He must've learned how to feign his responses to the assessments because if Gatt's true nature had been discovered, he never would have qualified to serve the last six months of his sentence in a halfway house. This guy fooled everyone, and now he's our only hope of finding Maddison.

Every now and then Gatt's monitors would bleep, giving Zubik momentary false hope that he would awaken.

Every few minutes the detectives checked their phones for any word from other investigators who were working through the night questioning inmates at the halfway house about Gatt and Maddison.

As the time flowed by, Zubik and Asher sipped coffee from ceramic mugs the nurse had brought them and studied their case notes. It was well after midnight when the detectives heard a muffled, dried croaking.

Gatt was waking.

A nurse swept into the room, and with smooth, professional care tended to him, removing his mask and helping him drink water through a straw. She spoke in soft tones while helping Gatt, who couldn't move.

Then she turned to Zubik.

"Detective, I think this is your opportunity."

Asher and Zubik each took a side of the bed with Asher using her phone to record. Gatt's eyes were closed but he was awake.

"Kalmen, this is Detective Zubik. Can you hear me?"

Gatt's eyes flitted and he made a slight nod.

"Kalmen, do you wish to make a declaration?"

Gatt gave a nod.

"Did you kill Maddison Lane?"

The monitor beeped and Gatt clenched his eyes.

"Only took pictures," he said.

"Did you work with someone else to take her?"

"Only took pictures. So pretty—so…"

"Kalmen, where is Maddison?"

"Only took…so pretty… I see her now…"

The monitors bleated with alerts, and the detectives cleared away for the nurse, then a doctor and other critical care staff to respond. They worked on Gatt for several minutes.

The tracking lines on the monitors flattened. Gatt was dead.

40

At the moment Gatt died, Karen sat alone in Cole's house, losing her grip on her sanity.

She had not slept since Maddie's disappearance. How could she, not knowing where her daughter was?

It was so late.

She had not taken the sleeping pills Jill had given her, thinking that it would be wrong for her to rest when Maddie was out there somewhere in the night.

That reporter had nearly destroyed them all. Karen felt locked in a cage of fear and pain. The polygraph had been an evisceration.

"They can be rough, like an emotional autopsy on the living," Cole had said before they'd urged Karen to get some sleep. But she couldn't sleep. Her entire body ached. The only way to battle her pain was to stay awake, think about Maddie and mentally reach out to her.

Keep hope alive.

No one saw Karen when she left the house

through one of the rear entrances. Inhaling the crisp night air, feeling the soothing lawn under her feet, she walked around the big house to the long driveway lined with apple trees that scented the air.

In this quiet part of the city, there was less light from other buildings; the sky was beautiful and lit by a half moon. Karen sent love to her daughter.

Are you seeing the same moon where you are, sweetie? Wherever you are, I'm keeping you in my heart, holding you safe there until we're together again.

The polygraph had taken a terrible toll, forcing Karen to exhume the long-buried, painful things she'd done. She remembered how she had battled with her mother, the same way Maddie had battled with her.

She remembered the price she'd paid.

Oh God.

Alone in the night, she felt herself going back to when she was thirteen years old and took Cassie swimming with friends at the weir in the Monarda River.

At the time, Karen had a crush on a boy, Gibb Wallerby. She wanted to be his girlfriend, but her mother would not allow her to date boys.

At the weir, the older kids played a game called "the wall crawl," where they'd go into the water and let the pressure flatten their bodies against the weir; it was made of railroad ties and they were slippery, kind of greasy. The kids would slide under, doing a Spider-Man crawl, open their eyes and touch the bottom, then crawl back to the surface while the water was pressing them against the weir. But older kids, girls or boys, would then flash their privates to each other while underwater.

Karen had done the wall crawl a few times. Cassie wanted to do it, too, but she was too small, not strong enough. Karen wouldn't let her do it.

"I'm going to tell Mom that you're trying to make Gibb Wallerby your boyfriend if you don't let me do it!" Cassie said.

Karen thrust her finger under Cassie's nose.

"You wouldn't dare because I'd kill you if you did!"

When Gibb invited Karen to do it with him, she agreed. It was her chance to steal him away from Marla, his girlfriend at the time.

Karen and Gibb went under together, and they showed each other their privates then surfaced to see Marla watching them as Karen adjusted the strap on her top. Marla confronted Karen about stealing her boyfriend with Cassie witnessing their exchange.

"I'm going to tell Mom on you," Cassie said afterward.

"Fine. Go do the wall crawl if you want, but you can't tell," Karen said.

That's when an ice-cream truck came to the weir and most of the kids went to it.

Except Cassie.

Karen couldn't find her sister.

Cassie! Where is she? What happened to her?

Karen called and called her name.

And now, standing in the dark under an indifferent moon, Karen called out again, only now it was for her daughter.

"Maddie! Maddie!"

Her calls grew louder, becoming screams as she called.

"Maddie! Maddie, come back! Please come back! I'm so sorry!"

Between great gulping sobs, Karen screamed into the night.

She screamed until Ryan, Jill and Cole found her and got her back into the house.

41

Zubik had managed to eat a sandwich, get two hours of sleep, a shower and coffee before Asher picked him up in the morning for the next case-status meeting at headquarters.

As Asher drove through the city's empty streets in the predawn, one question weighed on Zubik.

Are we closer to finding her?

In the elevator Asher saw the dark lines pulling at the corners of his mouth, the new wrinkles near his eyes signaling his frustration.

"Gatt's our guy," she said. "We know it's him, and we're going to find her, Stan."

Zubik said nothing.

An air akin to defeat permeated the task force meeting room.

Gatt's death had left investigators with questions and theories, but nothing pointing to where Maddison Lane was. No one in the task force was surprised that interviews of halfway house inmates conducted through the night by state, county and Syracuse investigators had yielded nothing.

"The inmates adhere to the code of silence," said deputy Rance Carver. "Each one of them claims to know nothing about Gatt's connection to the girl or her whereabouts."

"What about Brandon Kane, his roommate?" Captain Moe Tilden asked. "Didn't he want to leverage what he might know to help with his own beef?"

Carver shook his head. "Kane had nothing."

"So that leaves us with Gatt's last words that he never touched Maddison Lane, that he only took pictures of her," Asher said.

"Based on experience," Tilden said, "we can all agree that guilty people lie. Even those on death row convicted irrefutably by DNA will proclaim innocence with their dying breath." Tilden surveyed the detectives around the table. "I suggest we consider Gatt's denial a lie."

"I agree," Asher said. "Gatt chose Maddison. He had motive, and opportunity through his passes and the unsecured window at the halfway house. We've got his photographs and his admission of taking them. We're looking at his movements to see if he shared them with anyone."

"But what if Gatt was telling the truth?" asked Earl Reid, a state police investigator. "What if all he did was take pictures of her?"

"Why believe him?" Asher said. "Gatt's deceived everyone for years about his sexual desire for children."

"You've got nothing putting him in her room," Reid said. "And she didn't scream or struggle."

Asher glanced at Zubik, who'd steepled his hands in front of his face while listening to the arguments.

"Maybe Gatt established an online relationship with her," Detective Jan Ford said. "He was a cyber expert with above-average intelligence. Maybe he convinced her he was a boy from school using a burner. Or a secret admirer who suggested a Romeo and Juliet meeting and she bought into it?"

"But you can't put him in the room," Reid said again. "You've got no prints, no shoe impressions and no phone with the mystery number she'd been communicating with."

"He could've been working with someone else," Ford said.

Earl Reid shook his head. He wasn't buying it.

A moment passed while the investigators absorbed the debate, with Reid looking at Zubik. "Stan, you're the lead, what do you think?"

After consideration Zubik said, "We're still building the case against Gatt. We're getting warrants for the computers at Gatt's job and interviewing people there. His camera, his tablet are still being processed by IT. Forensic people are still working on Gatt's room, and on the ladder. Crime Scene's wrapping up at the house and processing every print lifted there. We're working as fast as we can to locate Maddison. We'll continue gathering facts and evidence and following every lead.

We can't forget we've got plenty of other vital work in this investigation to resolve. Let's move on."

Ties were loosened, shirtsleeves were rolled up and coffees were freshened as the task force provided updates on other facets of the case.

Polygraph results for Ryan, Karen and Tyler Lane were expected later in the day. The results of polygraphs done on the babysitter, Crystal Hedrick, and her boyfriend, Zachary Keppler, showed them to be truthful. Arrangements were being made for Cole, Jill and Dalton Lane to be polygraphed.

More investigators from Syracuse drug, vice and robbery units were being brought in and the FBI, Onondaga County and state police were adding more resources to the task force.

One key assignment was the need to reinterview Maddison's friend Brooke Carson, who had told Zubik and Asher that Maddison had appeared "scared" after confiding to her that, "something was happening in her life." This needed to be followed, Zubik noted.

Moreover, time lines and alibis were being checked for everyone connected to Maddison and her family.

Nothing significant had arisen after checking the whereabouts of Maddison's friends and schoolmates, including the boys she liked: Caleb Langford, Logan Bostick and Noah Trell. It was the same in checking the backgrounds and movements of her teachers and gymnastics coaches, as well as neighbors and the men and women who worked with Ryan and Karen Lane.

So far, examination of all the phones and computers volunteered to the task force had not yielded any communication with Maddison deemed to be suspect, nor had they pinpointed the source of the mystery number of the last person she'd communicated with before disappearing.

The Computer Forensic Unit, the FBI and state police IT specialists continued working on the burner phone number, and had applied for new warrants to track cell phone towers that may reveal the phone's location when it was used to communicate with Maddison.

Task force investigators confirmed that Cole and Jill Lane had dined at the Inn on the Lake in the hours before Maddison was last seen.

Jenna Guthrie and several friends confirmed Dalton Lane was at her birthday party and did fall into shrubs during horseplay with another boy, and that Dalton left the party near midnight with the Slade brothers. A receipt for Whenever-Burger was found in the Slades' Dodge Challenger, and the boys confirmed loose cable posts had caused the engine to stall, which delayed them getting Dalton home by his curfew. They admitted to having open beer and pot in the car.

They'd double-checked all the security camera footage provided by the Lanes' neighbors. Nothing useful had emerged.

Upwards of one hundred tips and reports from the public needed to be followed. Additionally, at least twenty tips from other police jurisdictions with similar cases across the country were being pursued and analyzed.

As the meeting wound down, Lieutenant Tim Milton checked his phone and said, "We're going to put out a bare bones news release this morning stating that Gatt died in custody after seizing a police officer's weapon—that Gatt, a resident of the halfway house on DeBerry Street, was being questioned as part of the ongoing investigation into Maddison Lane's disappearance. We won't say anything more while our work continues."

Notes were gathered, sleeves were rolled down and jackets slipped on as the meeting broke up. Asher's phone vibrated, and she took a call while Zubik used his phone to stare at Maddison Lane's photo, knowing in his heart that the odds were overwhelming that she was dead.

I will never give up until we find you.

A shadow fell over Zubik and he turned to Carl Kirby, the SPD's chief polygraphist, who had not attended the meeting but wanted to catch Zubik.

"Stan." He handed him a sheet of paper. "I wanted to give you the polygraph results for her family. I just completed them. I've got to get back to work on the others. Please remember exhaustion and anguish can have an impact on a subject."

The sheet of paper read:

Tyler Lane: Truthful.

Karen Lane: Inconclusive.

Ryan Lane: Inconclusive.

* * *

Zubik stared long and hard at the results. Then he folded the paper, put it in his pocket and turned to Asher, who had finished her call.

"You'll never guess who that was," Asher said.

"I've got no time for games."

"Roland Franz."

"Rollie? Didn't he retire about ten or twelve years back?"

"That's right, living in Tucson, now. No more Syracuse winters. He just saw the news on the Lane case. He says that back in the day he'd been assigned to work on the Cassie McHenry death with the Onondaga County medical examiner."

"Karen's younger sister."

"Right. Rollie says that even though the little girl's death had been ruled accidental and the cause was drowning, in light of the new case, we should revisit that old file. He says he'd be happy to take any calls on it. What do you think, Stan?"

"I agree."

42

"Oh my God. I don't know how much more I can take, Ryan."

Karen stood in their living room, her mind swirling.

A uniformed officer in a patrol car had driven the Lanes from Cole's place to their home, where the crime scene experts had finished processing their house. It looked like a muddied football team had charged through it.

Silver graphite fingerprint powder was everywhere: on the walls, the windows, the TV, light switches, lamps, doors, doorknobs, door frames. In the kitchen it was smudged on the sink, the stove, the fridge, cabinets, counters, the dishwasher, tables and chairs.

"Wow," Tyler said, staring with his parents in disbelief at the aftermath.

Every piece of furniture had been shifted, and was now out of place after investigators had rifled through their entire home, hunting for evidence tied to Maddie's vanishing.

Karen went to Maddie's room where the scene was more intense. The walls and the window were coated in the blackish powder; it was on Maddie's door, shelves, drawers, closet doors. They'd rummaged through her belongings.

It felt like a violation.

Karen lowered herself to sit on Maddie's bed, tracing her fingers over the pillow. It seemed like a lifetime since her daughter was asleep and safe in this bed. *Where are you?* Karen could not stop the ceaseless onslaught of fear, entwined with images of Maddie struggling, underwater, and Karen unable to save her.

Please make it stop!

Karen thrust her hands to her face and sobbed as if she were broken.

Ryan joined her on the bed, putting his arm around her.

"We've got to be strong, Karen," he said. "We'll get through this."

She didn't respond.

"I called Cole," Ryan said, "to find out what's happening. He's at the search center with Jill and Dalton. They're on their way."

Through her tears Karen looked at her daughter's room while shaking her head.

"They hook us up to the lie detector, they ask the most horrible, accusatory questions like we're the criminals, like we did something!" She gestured to the powder everywhere. "They do this to our home! I can't take it anymore!"

Tyler appeared at the doorway, reading his phone.

"Mom, Dad, my friends just found this. You better see it."

He showed them the Syracuse news release on Kalmen Gatt.

Ryan and Karen read the short release quickly, then read it a second time, grappling to comprehend its ramifications.

"Does this mean a convict from the halfway house over there took her?" Karen pointed toward Lucifer's Green.

"I don't know what it means." Ryan pressed numbers on his phone. "I'm calling Zubik."

"Mom." Tyler sat by his mother. "It doesn't say this guy took her."

Ryan's call went to Zubik's voice mail, and he left a message, on the verge of shouting, wanting answers about Gatt. Then he called Detective Asher. He got through and demanded to know more about Kalmen Gatt.

Asher tried to calm him. "I understand this is upsetting, but we can't tell you much more. It's still under investigation."

"But did you find Maddie? Is she, is she—"

"No. We still have no evidence to prove that she's not still alive."

Ryan shut his eyes, swallowed and ended the call just as their doorbell rang. Cole, Jill and Dalton had arrived.

"Cole, there's a police statement on a convict and Maddie," Ryan said.

"We saw it, too. I'm trying to find out more. My people have been pushing their sources on the task force."

Cole's phone rang, and he turned to take the call. Dalton and Tyler looked in dismay at the condition of the house while Jill went to Karen. Then Ryan's phone rang. Without checking the number, he answered. It was Sarah Silver at Channel 53, seeking reaction to the news release.

Ryan glanced to Cole, busy on his phone, before telling Silver, "We've got nothing to say at this time except that we continue praying for Maddie's safe return."

Ryan dragged his hand over his face, staring at the window and the forest, knowing the halfway house was on the other side of the woods. Again he was stabbed with guilt for not erecting a better fence and installing a security system.

Finished with his call, Cole turned to the others.

"Okay, according to our sources on the task force, Gatt had a camera with a long lens and would go into the woods on his passes and take pictures of Maddie changing in her bedroom and the bathroom. She was naked in many—"

"Oh my God!" Karen shouted.

"But before he died he denied abducting her."

"And they believe a convict?" Ryan said.

"They're still investigating his connection and Maddie's possible whereabouts."

"Was he a sex offender, a pedophile?" Ryan asked.

"He was in for fraud, white collar crime. That's all we know."

"A convict took pictures of Maddie from out there!" Karen shouted, her voice breaking. "And we don't know if he took her! If he killed her, if he left her to rot somewhere!"

Cole sat beside Karen, stared into her eyes before embracing her tenderly as Ryan and Jill watched.

"Karen, listen to me," Cole said. "So far there's no proof Gatt physically harmed Maddie. We can't give up hope. I swear, we'll find her alive and bring her home." He continued staring hard at her until she nodded. "I've got my people here and in every office across the country digging into Gatt's history. Someone somewhere will know more about him." Cole looked at Ryan, then Tyler, then Dalton, Jill and Karen again. "We're not going to stop until we find her and bring her home."

Ryan nodded and watched as Karen hugged Cole, hard for a long moment before he followed Dalton's gaze to the window and the forest.

Cole then said, "The Gatt development has drawn more attention to Maddie's story, and national news networks have been calling to have you do interviews." He looked at Ryan. "I think you should do one together."

"We'll do whatever you think is best," Karen said.

Ryan's phone rang again. The number was blocked, but he answered.

"Mr. Lane, Jack Gannon with the World Press Alliance in New York."

"Yes, if it's about Gatt we're not—"

"No, sir, it's not just that. Sir, sources have confirmed to our wire service that you and your family submitted to polygraphs and that you and your wife did not pass them, which suggests you've not been ruled out as suspects in your daughter's disappearance."

Ryan's face whitened.

"Sir?" Gannon said. "What is your response?"

Ryan hung up.

43

The file on Cassie McHenry's death was slim.

A staff member in Records had pulled it from the archives and placed it on Zubik's desk, so the file was waiting for him when he and Asher returned.

After studying it carefully, it was clear the little girl's death had been ruled accidental and the cause was drowning.

But Zubik's attention was drawn to a few handwritten notations.

Witnesses reported Karen arguing with Cassie. Did K kill C as act of retribution?

Zubik had the file scanned and sent to retired detective Roland Franz.

Asher and Zubik worked on the list of witnesses Franz had interviewed, the name of the pathologist who handled the autopsy, tracking them down, getting contact information.

While that was in progress, Zubik made coffee then returned to his desk and pulled up the full report on Karen Lane's polygraph. He zeroed in on specific questions Karen had been asked and the polygraphist's notes on her responses.

Have you ever hurt anyone?

Yes. (truthful)

Zubik pondered that excerpt, thinking: *Could it include her little sister?*

He moved on to other questions.

Did you ever hurt your daughter?

No. (inconclusive)

Did you hurt your daughter by accident and cover it up by staging her disappearance?

No! (inconclusive)

Zubik stared at the polygraphist's notes, wondering what the death of Karen's younger sister may have to do with Maddie's disappearance, if anything. Again, he read Franz's analysis and the autopsy report, not sure what to think until Asher waved him over, her other hand covering the mouthpiece of her landline.

"Got Roland Franz here, Stan."

Zubik took the phone and exchanged quick small talk with Franz about old cops: Who's still on the job, who got sick, who retired and who died. Then they got to the McHenry case.

"What's up with that note, 'Did K kill C'?" Zubik asked.

"That's why I called," Franz said. "It had been gnawing at me since I saw the news about Karen's daughter. Well, in Cassie's case, some of the kids who were at the weir when it happened told me that Karen and Cassie had argued nearly the whole time they were there. They also said Karen had argued with another girl, too. No one was certain of the timing up until the time Cassie vanished from the riverbank."

"What did you make of that, Rollie?"

"I couldn't verify any of it. To my mind it was a very sad accident. Kids never should've been swimming at that weir and playing that stupid crawl game. The city shoulda fenced the thing. Those were different times. But you should follow through on this, Stan. One girl you should try from my list is Annie Jacobi. She tried to help save the McHenry girl. Say hi to Moe for me, and good luck on this, pal."

After the call Zubik looked for Asher who was nowhere in sight.

He saw her on the phone in an empty glass-walled office with the door closed, signaling for him to join her.

"Okay, Annie," Asher said into the phone, nodding to Zubik as he entered. "I'll put you on Speaker, and you can tell both of us." Asher whispered to Zubik. "Annie Jacobi is married. She's Annie Schallert now, lives in Brooklyn."

"Like I was saying." Annie's voice crackled through the speaker. "It's something you can't ever forget. Yes, Karen had had this spat with another girl about her boyfriend. And yes, Karen argued with Cassie, too. I don't remember much of that, something stupid. But right after that Karen looked around for Cassie. Someone said Cassie had gone into the water alone to do the crawl. I was one of the better swimmers, and Karen asked me to go in the water with her to help look for Cassie. We went under and down the wall. It was about ten feet to the bottom, and that's where we found Cassie, struggling."

"Was she alone?" Zubik asked.

"Yes. She was pinned. Her little foot was wedged somehow between two of the beams, and no matter what Karen and I did, we couldn't get it out. Cassie was hysterical, screaming and swallowing water. Karen and I tried to give her air from our mouths. It wasn't working. Karen and I yelled for help at the surface. Some of the older boys tried to help. Someone ran to a phone to call for help. It took firefighters or police divers with tools a long time to get Cassie's body out."

"You never saw Karen go in the water with Cassie?"

"No. Can't say for sure, but I'm pretty certain nobody did. It was all a terrible tragedy, one I'll remember for the rest of my life. And now you tell me Karen's daughter's missing?"

"Yes, Maddison. She's twelve."

"Oh no, no," Annie sobbed. "I'm going to pray with all my heart that you find her."

"Thank you."

Asher tapped a pen on the desk as she and Zubik weighed what they'd learned from scrutinizing the file, the polygraph results and their calls.

"What do you think?" Asher asked.

Zubik rubbed the bridge of his nose then shook his head.

"It just doesn't fit that Karen killed her sister," he said. "We've also got Gatt and his pictures, we got the fact Maddison had argued with her mother, and the mystery number. I just don't know, Fran."

Zubik's focus shifted to the door. Asher followed it to a uniformed female officer. The nameplate over her right pocket said B. T. Bridges.

"Excuse me, Detectives. My lieutenant suggested I talk to you."

"What about, Officer Bridges?" Asher said.

"My aunt lives near the Lane family, and a few weeks before Maddison went missing she saw the father, Ryan, with her out front of her house, on the street."

"And?" Zubik said.

"My aunt says they were arguing, and he abducted her from the street."

"Abducted her? How does a father abduct his child?"

"It appears he grabbed her from the street and struck her."

Zubik and Asher exchanged a look before Bridges added, "I brought my aunt here if you'd like to talk to her. She's downstairs."

"Give us a minute then bring her up to number one," Zubik said.

Bridges nodded but stopped midturn.

"Oh, we also have video of it from her home security system."

44

Maddison Lane is walking fast in the pouring rain along a sidewalk, and stops when a pickup truck suddenly rolls up beside her. The lettering on the truck's door reads Lane & Sons Drywall Contractors. The driver's window is down, and Ryan Lane is waving for Maddison to get in. She refuses and remains standing in the rain. Ryan rushes from the truck, grabs Maddison who fights him, arms swinging, legs kicking, as he drags-slash-carries her into the truck. The angle captures enough of the inside of the cab to show Maddie kicking at the dash and Ryan striking her before the pickup does a 180-degree turn out of frame.

"One more time," Zubik said.

Asher replayed the short scene again.

Officer Bonnie Bridges had downloaded the footage from her aunt's security system to her tablet. Bridges's aunt, Meredith Craig, sat patiently as Asher and Zubik studied it. She'd returned home from a Caribbean cruise yesterday.

"When Bonnie told me about the Lanes' tragedy, my heart nearly burst." Craig twisted her wedding rings. "Then after I told Bonnie what I'd seen in front of my house before my trip, she insisted we check my security cameras. We did, then we alerted you."

"Yes, that was the right thing to do, Meredith," Asher said.

"I know the Lane family. They live a block away. They're a nice family. But when I looked out my window that rainy day I was shocked. It was disturbing. I mean it was none of my business but dear Lord, that's so troubling, especially now in the wake of what's happened."

"We'd like to take a formal statement from you, and we need you to sign some forms for us, for the video," Asher said.

"Yes, of course. I want to help for Maddison's sake."

The video was a damning piece of evidence against Ryan Lane.

Zubik and Asher reexamined Ryan's statement, those of Karen and Tyler, and the analysis of his polygraph.

"It's all here in Karen and Tyler's statements," Asher said. "They acknowledged that Karen and Maddison argued, that she ran out and that Ryan went after her and brought her home."

Zubik massaged his temples.

"Take a closer look at Ryan's statement when we questioned him about ever being physical with his daughter, ever being violent. He either said no, or didn't answer. Then go to his polygraph analysis when Kirby asked him if he'd ever hurt Maddison, if he was a violent person, if he lost his temper easily. Each time Ryan's response was no, but Kirby flagged those responses as inconclusive, meaning Ryan could be telling the truth or he could be lying."

"Right," Asher said.

"Then weigh that against Ryan's actions in that video."

"Not good."

"Damn right, not good. We need him down here," Zubik said.

45

Why call me down here again?

Sitting alone in the same white-walled room at police headquarters, Ryan looked around. He hated being in this place—it gave him a bad feeling.

Maybe they found Maddie? Maybe she's dead and they need me to identify—

The door opened and Zubik and Asher entered.

"Thank you for coming down," Asher said as Ryan strained to read the detectives' faces. "I want to remind you that you're still under the Miranda warning that was given to you for the polygraph."

"Miranda? Why, what— Why am I here?"

"We need your help." Zubik's chair scraped as they sat across from him. "New information has come to light."

"What new information?"

Asher was busy tapping and swiping on her tablet.

"We're going to show you video footage recorded by the security cameras of one of your neighbors a couple of weeks ago," Zubik said.

Asher angled her tablet for all of them to see, then played the video.

Ryan froze.

There was Maddie walking in the rain and there he was in his truck, angry, hauling her kicking and screaming into his cab where she kicked at the dash and he struck her. Staring at that entire raw, horrible scene, Ryan's emotions hammered at his heart, breaking it into a thousand pieces.

The detectives observed him, their faces void of sympathy. Zubik opened a file folder.

"In your polygraph statement, you were asked if you'd ever been violent or lost you temper with Maddison. You said no." Zubik continued. "You were asked if you'd ever struck her. You said no."

Zubik's gaze drilled into Ryan.

"Now, having seen recorded evidence to the contrary, we can conclude all of your answers were lies, weren't they?"

Ryan said nothing and lowered his head.

"We want the truth," Zubik said. "Look at me, Ryan."

He looked at Zubik.

"The truth. Do you know where your daughter is?"

"No."

"Did you help someone in your family cover up an accident?"

"No."

"Did you kill your daughter?"

"God, no!"

"Why should be believe you now when we know what you did in the time before Maddison disappeared? The footage clearly shows what you're capable of. The incident at the bank shows what you're capable of. Why should we believe you?"

"Because it's the truth!"

"Bull!" Zubik said.

"Yes, I was violent with Maddie. I was so pissed off that day, stressed over money and the business, then the crap with Karen and Maddie. I was nearly out of my mind with anger at having to go into the freaking rain to find her—that she refused to get in the truck. When I got her in the truck she was out of control, kicking the dash, mouthing off about Karen, calling her mother a bitch, and I just lost it and smacked her with the back of my hand, told her to shut the fuck up."

Tears rolled down Ryan's face.

"I told nobody what happened and Maddison said nothing about it, but I knew I'd crossed the line with her. I'd never, ever struck her before. My God, she's my little angel. I apologized to her later. I was ashamed that I'd lost control. I never told you because I was so deeply ashamed."

Zubik and Asher were silent as he continued.

"I swear I had nothing to do with her abduction, but I'm guilty of failing her as a father, as a protector."

Ryan wiped at his tears, his chin crumpled.

"I slept in my bed while someone came into my house and took my daughter." He shook his head as his voice broke. "And the last thing I may ever have to remember is that rainy day and how I treated her."

The detectives looked upon Ryan sobbing before them without compassion for they hadn't decided if he was a distraught father.

Or a monster.

46

Two days later, under glaring TV lights set up in the search center near the Lanes' home, a makeup artist touched up Karen's and Ryan's faces.

"To take the shine off when you're on," the artist said.

The couple was seated close together, holding hands. Their clip-on microphones had been sound checked, and the voice of Morgan Stone, the national network's famous anchor, came through their earpieces.

"Karen and Ryan, I want to thank you for doing this at such a difficult time," Stone said from network headquarters in New York. "Just look into the camera and think of this as a conversation with friends."

"Okay." Karen offered a nervous smile and Ryan nodded.

Three minutes later Stone began the live interview. She introduced the Lanes, provided some general background while images of Maddie and her case flowed on half the screen and activity in the center continued behind them.

"Thank you for joining us," Stone said to the couple. "We can't imagine the anguish and pain you as parents are enduring at this time."

"Thank you," Karen said, glancing quickly to Cole, Jill, then Dalton and Tyler, who were watching off camera a few feet away.

"For viewers who might be learning of this case for the first time, take us through those horrible hours when you discovered Maddie was gone."

After Karen and Ryan related events, Stone asked, "What do you think happened?"

"We think someone came into our home and took Maddie," Ryan said.

"Do you think it was the halfway house convict, Kalmen Gatt?"

"Based on what we know," Ryan said, "and we only know what we're hearing and what's in the press, everything points to Gatt."

"Yes, but police have stated that while they continue investigating Gatt, which is challenging now that he's dead, they've ruled nothing out and everybody remains a suspect."

"Yes, we understand that." Karen squeezed Ryan's hand.

"We understand your family and extended family have submitted to polygraphs."

"Yes," Ryan said. Remembering Cole's attorney's advice, he was careful to withhold anything incriminating. "We're cooperating fully with police."

"What do you think of the theory that Maddie ran away?"

"We don't believe it for a second," Karen said. "Yes, she's a headstrong, energetic young girl, but she wouldn't do this."

"You're her mom and you'd know her best."

"Yes." Karen wiped a tear away.

"Donations to the reward for information leading to Maddie's return have been incredible," Stone said. "It's now at one hundred thousand dollars. What do you make of the response?"

"It means the world to us," Ryan said. "Words fail to express our gratitude to everyone here at the center, Maddie's school friends, teachers, neighbors, our coworkers, volunteers and strangers. The messages of support and prayers from across the country mean so much."

"If by chance Maddie's watching, what would you say to her, or the person who knows what's happened to her?"

Karen's voice quavered. "Maddie, sweetie, we love you, honey, and we're doing all we can to find you."

Ryan put his arm around Karen and said, "To the person or persons who know what happened, we only want our daughter back."

"In our hearts," Karen said through her tears, "we believe and feel that Maddie's alive, and we're begging that whoever knows where she is, get word to authorities. Please don't hurt her. Please do the right thing."

Stone let a beat pass before resuming.

"Ryan, Karen, I know this is difficult, but how do you deal with the fact that statistically family members are implicated in most cases like this? And that police sources tell our network that among their working theories is that Maddie's disappearance was staged, perhaps to cover up a family accident because no one heard a struggle or heard her cry out."

"We're aware of the speculation," Ryan said. "But these are the facts—our son heard voices in Maddie's room, her window was unlocked, there was a ladder on the ground under it and mud streaks on Maddie's carpet and the walls near the window. I can't go into detail, but we know that Gatt, a convicted criminal, had an interest in our daughter."

"We are not involved and we're cooperating with police," Karen said.

"Karen, our researchers have discovered that your sister, Cassie, drowned tragically when she was ten in a swimming accident."

Karen blinked several times as Stone continued.

"And not long after that, your mother died. Some say of a broken heart over Cassie's death. You were with them both at that time." Stone sighed, her eyes glistening sympathetically. "And now your daughter's missing. So much tragedy for you. Where do you find the strength?"

Karen was at a loss and Ryan held her close.

"I don't know. I don't know. It's hard. All of this is so hard."

Karen touched a tissue to her eyes, and Stone gave her a second.

"You're so brave," Stone said before moving on. "Now, Ryan, Karen, we'd like your response to some video footage our network has obtained through our sources. Take a look."

The network crew directed Ryan and Karen to watch a monitor that began rolling the security camera footage of Ryan violently dragging Maddie into his truck and striking her. Karen's eyes widened—she was seeing it for the first time. Before it ended, Ryan saw Zubik and Asher in a corner of the search center watching the interview on a TV and his jaw clenched.

"That footage was recorded shortly before Maddie disappeared," Stone said. "That's you and Maddie, Ryan. What's your response to these dramatic images?"

A few seconds passed and Ryan, stunned that someone had leaked the footage to Stone, cleared his throat.

"Maddie," he began. "She'd had an argument with Karen and walked out of the house. It was the only time she'd done this. I was upset and stressed, and when I found her she refused to get out of the rain and into my truck and come home. I forced her into the truck. She was upset. I lost my temper."

Stone said nothing.

"We're not perfect people," Ryan said.

"What do you mean?" Stone said.

"Just that we're a normal family with normal family issues and like any family. We're not perfect."

Stone let a moment pass before concluding.

"Karen and Ryan Lane, I'm sure our viewers join you in your prayers to find your daughter and bring her home. Thank you for being with us."

47

"You're going to burn in hell for what you did."

The anonymous email that included the televised video clip of Ryan dragging Maddie into his truck was among the scores of hate-filled messages the Lanes had received immediately after their interview with Morgan Stone.

Each one pierced Karen's heart, but they were eclipsed by the revelation that Ryan had struck Maddie, and she confronted him with it when they got home.

"How could you hit her? How could you do that?"

"You know how it was that day. You two were arguing, she ran out and I had to find her. I had to drag her into my truck. She called you a bitch and—" Ryan's voice broke, tears brimmed in his eyes. "I've got a temper. I'm cursed with my old man's mean streak, and I just lost it with her. I swear it was just that one time. And I'm going to have to live with it."

"You should've been able to control your temper! You're the adult! You crossed a line, Ryan, and oh God—"

All the things that she had said to Maddie, that she had done, and that she had sent Ryan into the rain to bring Maddie home… She had set things in motion. Karen broke down.

Ryan embraced her.

"I'm so sorry," Ryan said.

He deleted the email.

But they kept coming, part of the fallout from appearing on national TV. It had sparked an online debate on the case. Some of it pointed to Kalmen Gatt as the suspect, but most people alleged that there was a cloud of suspicion over the family. And it didn't help that nothing new had emerged from the investigation to confirm Gatt as Maddie's abductor.

Still, when Cole came to their home after the TV interview, he urged Karen and Ryan to remain positive.

"That video is not good, but the Morgan Stone appearance has given the case a national profile," he said. "We've got our investigators across the country and subcontractors digging into every other conceivable element. We're going to find her and bring her home."

But Cole's words fell like water against the stone-cold reality of life without Maddie. Her absence was a gaping hole in their existence.

For much of the day, Karen, upon learning that police had finished searching Lucifer's Green, wandered alone in the woods as if expecting Maddie to somehow materialize there. She followed the path Maddie might have taken only to find nothing but pain and a desperate notion that Tyler could help her. She hurried back to the house, nearly out of breath.

"Tyler, you've got to ask her friends for help. I need to know what she was thinking before she was gone."

"Mom, her friends are sad but they don't know anything."

"Maddie had her phone in her hand when she went to sleep. They must know what she was saying what she was thinking."

Tyler stared blankly at nothing.

"Tyler?"

"That video of dad is everywhere," he said, his voice breaking. "How could he hit Maddie like that?"

Karen grabbed his shoulders. "Listen. What your father did was wrong. Completely wrong and he's sorry."

"How could he be so mean to her? I just don't—"

"Honey, I know. It was a horrible day with Maddie, me and dad. It's my fault, too and I'm so, so sorry. If we could go back in time, things would be different. But it's because of that, because of everything, you've got to help me by asking Maddie's friends what she was thinking."

"Mom, I can't."

"Please, Tyler, they won't tell me but they'll tell you. You've got to try."

"Mom, don't make me."

"Why not?"

"Because this is what the kids at school are saying after you were on TV." Tyler showed Karen a message.

Hey Lame Brain Lane! Everyone now thinks your family faked your sister's disappearance to get that big fat reward. Is that true?

Karen turned away, defeated.

Ryan had retreated into his own anguish. That video was everywhere.

His shame was overwhelming; he'd been emotionally gutted. He ached to have Maddie back so he could hold her and tell her how sorry he was and how much he loved her.

He felt like a cursed man living with a terrible dark affliction, and it tore him up inside—because it was true.

He was a guilty man.

The things I've done are unforgivable.

The Lanes got a call from police services who

were offering to arrange for counselors, but Ryan reached for whiskey as the emails kept coming.

Ryan Lane: We saw you on Morgan Stone and that video on TV. It's obvious you two killed your daughter. Why don't you confess?

48

"Maddison Lane is dead..."

Zubik listened to the female caller's muffled voice, which had been recorded on the tip line.

"Maddison was kidnapped by a serial killer named Barabbas. He dismembered her and burned her remains. He is on the hunt for other victims. This information was channeled to me spiritually. Goodbye."

Zubik's gaze shifted to Asher who shook her head.

"The claim is unfounded," Asher said. "The caller is a troubled woman in Iowa who boasts of having cosmic, mystic, psychic abilities. She often calls on high-profile cases."

In the wake of the Lanes' interview with Morgan Stone, investigators had received an influx of tips that continued into the morning after the show was broadcast. The task force had said little publicly other than that it continued to study all aspects of the case. But behind the scenes Zubik feared that the investigation had stalled with Gatt's death.

As for Ryan Lane, as disturbing as the video was, at this stage they had nothing to harden their suspicions that Ryan was involved. Besides the footage, they had the inconclusive polygraph results, financial stress in the family, Karen's argument with Maddison, but it was still all circumstantial.

And it was the same with Kalmen Gatt. They had the photos he'd taken but no evidence to put him inside her bedroom or at her window, nothing strong enough to close the case. Their search of every alley, lot and abandoned building around the halfway house had come up empty. Interviews with inmates, coworkers and others who knew Gatt had so far yielded nothing more linking him to Maddison.

Did he do more than take pictures from the woods?

One theory held that Gatt had killed and buried Maddie. Investigators were planning to go back into Lucifer's Green and conduct a new search using cadaver dogs and ground-penetrating sonar.

That would take time.

Forensic examination of the window, the bedroom, the ladder provided no new leads. Of course, Ryan's, Karen's and Tyler's prints were found everywhere in the house. And, as expected, so were Cole's, Jill's and Dalton's in every room, because they often visited before Maddison vanished.

And everyone they had interviewed—Maddison's friends, teachers, coaches, neighbors, Ryan

and Karen's coworkers, the babysitter, her boyfriend, even Bennie Price, the pizza delivery
man—had been alibied.

Zubik continued reviewing the files and notes.

They'd followed up with Maddison's friend
Brooke Carson who'd told them how Maddison
had seemed troubled, cryptically confiding that
something was happening in her life shortly before she'd disappeared. They'd pressed Brooke to
provide additional information or context. But that
second interview ended with Brooke in tears because she couldn't remember more details.

Zubik moved on to other reports.

A retired schoolteacher told police that she'd
seen Maddison in a car in a mall parking lot in
Watertown, New York, and got the plate number.
Follow-up investigation showed the girl did resem-
ble Maddison but was not her. The Watertown girl
was fifteen and with her family at the mall.

In Cleveland, a male caller said he'd overheard a
paroled ex-friend at a bar claim Maddison's abduction was a robbery gone wrong, and he was holding her for ransom. Cleveland FBI followed up and
found the claim to be without substance. Drunken
bar talk, Zubik thought, moving to review another
call when Jay Tomkins, with the Computer Forensic Unit, approached him.

"Just sent you something, Stan. Open it up."

Tomkins had been working with the county,
state and FBI cyber experts along with service
providers on the mystery burner phone number,

the last number Maddison had communicated with before she vanished. They obtained warrants to track cell phone tower signals to reveal the phone's location when it was used to communicate with Maddison.

Now Tomkins had the results.

Zubik went to his mail, opened a map of greater Syracuse with a dizzying display of colors and cone-shaped patterns superimposed on it.

"Okay," Tomkins said, pointing at the monitor as Asher joined him. "We triangulated the signal from the burner phone in the time before her disappearance, and we've been able to chart the path of the burner phone's user and the times. That's the bright yellow dotted line zigzagging everywhere. In some cases we got as close as twenty-five feet of the location—in others the distance is much greater. And there are gaps, so in some spots we're guessing. But you'll see by the distance and time that the user had to be mobile, definitely in a vehicle, not on foot."

The map showed locations near the halfway house on DeBerry, and on the other side of the woods close to the Lanes' home and all over the city.

"But you don't have an ending point?" Zubik asked.

"Not a clear one. Somewhere downtown," Tomkins said. "The phone was likely switched off, the battery and memory card removed. We're going to canvass and check security footage of every possible address along the way."

"It's the proverbial search for a needle in a haystack," Asher said.

"And finding them is how we solve cases," Zubik said.

"Okay, with that in mind," Asher said, "let's consider the people who were the last to see her."

They had Ryan Lane, the disturbing video, his financial stress. They had Karen Lane, with her tragic history of being present at the deaths of her sister and mother, her arguments with Maddison, and the fact Maddison had fled the house in anger; and that the parents' polygraphs were inconclusive. Then they had Tyler, her brother, with his knives and admission that his sister owed him twenty-five dollars, and the fact he was awake in the night when she vanished.

"And the others," Zubik said.

Zachary Keppler, the babysitter's boyfriend, admitted to being under Maddison's window earlier that night. He thought she was "real cute." But he was solidly alibied and passed his polygraph.

They had Bennie Price, the pizza guy, who'd made a delivery to the Lane home earlier that night, greeted Maddison and her brother. But Price was alibied, making deliveries until 4:30 a.m. before going home.

Asher went over the long list of other people. Cole, Jill and Dalton Lane—all were alibied. Maddison's school friends, the boys she liked and the boys who liked her. All alibied.

Again the detectives contended with theories, ranging from the likelihood a sex offender took Maddison, to the possibility she was killed in the home and her disappearance staged.

"We still can't rule out anything, or anybody," Asher said.

"That's right. We can solve this case," Zubik said. "It's just that…"

Zubik's chair creaked as he sat back to take stock of the files, reports, the map on his monitor, those on the wall. Then his attention went to the large photos of Maddison Lane smiling back at him, and he blinked thoughtfully at her.

"But what, Stan?" Asher said.

"At this stage, I just don't know how." He nodded to his desk. "Maybe we missed something, overlooked something. Maybe the answer's right in front of us."

49

Karen stood alone at the edge of the school yard.

The bell would soon sound the end to classes.

This was sixth day of Maddie's disappearance. Karen was losing her mind and had come here to find answers. She'd been moving through time feeling like an open wound, and didn't know what else to do.

She glanced at her phone, the phone that never rang or vibrated with a message from Maddie. But Maddie's face was there, staring back at her, and Karen nearly touched it with her fingers. She found a measure of comfort viewing recordings of birthdays, Christmas, Maddie learning to ride a bike and her first day of school.

Karen tapped the screen on her favorite.

"Okay Mommy, I'm gonna sing a song for you!"

Maddie, age four, her hair held back with two pink butterfly barrettes, standing in the living room holding her toy microphone in both hands.

"Which song, sweetie?" Karen asking off camera.

"'You Are My Sunshine'!"

Maddie begins, twisting her little body, eyes sparkling like diamonds, putting her whole heart into it...

Tears rolled down Karen's face. She could almost feel Maddie, almost smell her. She ached to hold her and never let go for she was broken without her. This morning Karen didn't know the stranger in her mirror, a haggard, wretched woman who looked twenty years older.

Is this the price to be paid for all the things I've done, the mistakes I've made, the secrets I've kept and the lies I've told? Is this my torment?

The memories of them haunted her: Maddie's disappearance, her mother dead in the garden, her sister underwater. For even when sleep came in short bursts, Karen was tortured by her dreams, dreams of her sister at the weir...

Cassie's eyes ballooning with horror...her foot stuck in the weir... Karen fighting to pull it out but it won't move, oh God, it won't budge! Karen giving Cassie air but Cassie struggles, a bubbled scream explodes from her mouth, life drains from her eyes; eyes that stare at Karen. Cassie's hair flowing Medusa-like...the water gracefully swirling to reveal Maddie's face...her lifeless eyes... accusing Karen...

The bell rang, jolting her.

School was over, and students began flowing from the building to the pickup zones, one for parents waiting in cars, one for school buses. Karen moved closer to the activity, her pulse picking up as she scanned the young faces amid the chatter of hundreds of conversations.

Last night Tyler had learned from other kids about a rumor that one of Maddie's friends had told police something Maddie had told her before she'd disappeared. But Tyler was unable to find out more because police told the friend not to tell anyone.

That's why Karen was here, moving among the streams of children.

I need to know what Maddie told her, what was in her heart.

Moving, turning this way and that, Karen searched dozens and dozens of faces until at last she found the face of Maddie's friend.

The one she needed.

"Brooke!"

Brooke Carson's smile melted into surprise as she ceased talking with another girl.

"Mrs. Lane. Hi."

"Brooke, I need to talk to you about Maddie. It's very important."

The girl with Brooke gave a little finger wave and left.

"Sure." Brooke shifted under the shoulder strap of her backpack.

"You're one of Maddie's best friends. She talked to you, she told you things, right, honey?"

Brooke hesitated. "I guess so."

Karen looked around to a low brick wall and indicated they sit there.

"I really should be going." Brooke pulled on her strap.

"Please sit with me. I just need a minute."

Brooke sat, noticing how Karen's two-handed grip on her phone had whitened her knuckles. She tried not to stare at the lines carved into Karen's face, the red veins webbing her eyes.

"Brooke, I need you to tell me, was my daughter mad at me?"

"Mad at you?"

"Yes, I need to know what she told you."

"I—" Brooke shook her head. "I don't know."

"Was she angry at me for being too strict with her about boys?"

"Maybe a little, but I really don't know."

"Did she tell you that we argued about boys?"

"A little, I guess."

Karen gulped back a sob. "Did she forgive me?"

"Forgive you?"

"Did she say that she loved me?"

Unease and worry began rising in Brooke's face. "Mrs. Lane…"

"I thought I knew Maddie. I know we argued and she's rebellious, but she's a good girl, isn't she?"

Karen gripped her wrist.

"Why didn't I know my own daughter? What didn't I know?"

"Mrs. Lane, you're squeezing too hard." Brooke looked off as if she wanted help.

"I thought we were close. What do you know

that I don't know? You have to tell me—there has to be something!"

"Please, Mrs. Lane, you're scaring me."

"Tell me!"

"Karen." Monica Carson, Brooke's mother, gently loosened the woman's grip on her daughter's arm. "We understand how painful this is, but Brooke's just a twelve-year-old girl. You're frightening her."

"Brooke knows something about Maddie! Maddie told her something!"

"Karen, we're with you, we support you. But you must go through proper channels for information. Don't do this to Brooke."

Karen looked into Brooke's eyes. "I'm Maddie's mother! I deserve to know!"

Brooke fought her tears in the face of Karen's anguish. "But police told me not to tell!"

"Tell me!" Karen screamed.

"Stop this, please!" Monica said.

"All Maddie said to me was that something was happening in her life," Brooke said.

"What was happening? What?" Karen said.

"I don't know, I don't know." Brooke sobbed into her mother's arms.

"Karen, she doesn't know," Monica said. "We're so sorry, but she doesn't know."

Karen stared at them: A mother comforting her twelve-year-old daughter. A girl Karen had terrified. Her mother holding her, loving her the way a good mother should love her child.

The world began blurring, spinning, and Karen's mind raced.

Did Maddie love me? Was I too hard on her about dating, forcing her to rebel the same way I rebelled? Did my sister die because of me? And now my daughter...gone...

Again, the haunting images tortured her, finding her mother dead in the garden, Cassie dying underwater and Maddie's empty bedroom.

What have I done?

Monica and Brooke caught Karen as she collapsed.

BOOK TWO

FOUR YEARS LATER

50

Lana Compton was certain that she and Pearl, her seventy-six-year-old mother, were going to die.

Hurricane Zeus was bearing down on them.

The storm had Category 5 strength with winds reaching 180 mph, and had already churned through much of the Caribbean, killing twenty people. It would hit Florida's east coast within hours. Evacuation orders had been given, and millions had fled or sought refuge in shelters.

Not Pearl. At first she'd refused to leave her South Florida home. "I've lived here all my life, and if it's God's plan that I die here, so be it."

But after seeing TV news reports of the devastation in the Bahamas, Pearl agreed to go with Lana to the nearest storm shelter in Greater Miami—the gym of a new high school, built to withstand hurricanes.

But now, as they neared its doors, Lana slid her arm tight around her mother's waist, knowing they were too late. The rain was coming down in torrents, the lashing winds hurled palm fronds at them, and they stumbled. The last reports had put the wind speed near 50 mph and climbing fast. Miami-Dade County officials had made it clear: when the winds reached speeds of 40 mph, shelter doors would be closed.

With one arm around her mother, Lana pounded her fist on the doors.

"Please! Let us in! Please!"

The winds howled with increasing velocity, peeling pieces of roofs off the houses nearby. Pearl screamed when a metal sign from a gas station knifed through the air, missing them by inches, crashing into the wall. Sheets of plywood followed, along with metal trash cans and hubcaps.

In her panic, Lana saw a body hunched in a ball behind a stone planter, a teenage girl. She didn't have a poncho, just a polo shirt, shorts and shoes.

"Honey, are you okay?" Lana shouted.

Terrified, the trembling girl raised her head, her face webbed with blood and matted hair. She was sobbing. Lana kicked at the door and, still holding her mother, moved closer to the girl, taking her hand. Then the doors pushed open against the pummeling winds and two men pulled all three women inside.

"This girl's hurt—you've got to help her," Lana said.

"She's with you?" one of the men asked.

"No. Don't know who she is. She was just outside."

"Let's get to the registration table. We need to

sign everyone in," one of the men said but, growing concerned, he looked at the girl, patting her wound with a towel, telling her to keep pressure on it.

"What's your name?" he asked at the table where staff members were poised to list her.

She shook her head.

"Do you have a wallet or identification?" a staff member asked.

Again, she shook her head.

"She's alone, hurt her head and bleeding. She needs help now," Lana said. "Maybe she's got family in here?"

"Okay, we'll take care of her." One of the men spoke into a walkie-talkie. While a staff member recorded the girl as a white, unaccompanied child, aged fifteen to seventeen, as well as her injury and time of arrival, two emergency volunteers emerged. One helped keep pressure on her wound with the towel. They draped a blanket around her and guided her through the large gym where more than a thousand people were sitting on sleeping bags and mattresses. Some were talking or playing cards, some were checking their phones and some were sleeping.

The volunteers brought the girl to the shelter's medical unit with its treatment stations behind curtained walls. They got her out of her wet clothes and into a paper gown. A nurse in a flowered smock began cleaning her head wound.

It was a four-inch laceration. The edges of the

wound were not separated. It looked like she'd been cut with a sharp, straight edge.

"What happened?" The nurse was shining a light in the girl's eyes.

"I don't remember. Something hit me hard on the head."

The nurse looked at her.

"What's your name?"

The girl blinked, looking off as if traveling back in time.

"I think it's Maddie?"

"You think? What's your last name, Maddie?"

The girl began crying again. "I can't remember."

"Don't move. I'll be right back." The nurse returned with a man wearing jeans, a Dolphins T-shirt and a stethoscope around his neck. "This is Dr. Shirer. He'll take a look at you."

He examined her wound, which did not penetrate her skull. He placed the bell of his stethoscope on her back. Then he felt her skull, her jaw, shone his light in her eyes and checked her nose and ears.

"So you got a bump on the head from something?" He had a kind face.

"It hurt. I saw stars and I felt I was spinning. Maybe I fainted."

"Do you have a headache?"

"Yes."

"Can you tell me your name?"

"Maddie… I think it's Maddie?"

"Your last name?"

"I can't remember."

"How old are you, Maddie?"

"Sixteen, I think."

"Do you know where you were when it happened, or what happened?"

"No."

"Are you here with family?"

"I don't know."

"Where do you live?"

"I can't remember."

"Do you know what day it is, or who the president is?"

"No." She covered her face with her hands and cried. "Why can't I remember anything?"

"Well, Maddie, you've suffered a pretty good head injury, a concussion. Probably hit with debris in the storm. Memory loss is a common symptom. It could be short-term, or it could last longer."

"Don't worry, sweetheart," the nurse said. "We'll get you some dry clothes and get you reunited with your people here."

Dr. Shirer patted the girl's leg.

"We'll give you some ibuprofen for your headache and patch you up. You won't need stitches. But when it's safe, I want the paramedics to get you to Holy Palms Memorial as soon as we can for X-rays and a scan to check the severity of your concussion. It'll be done through emergency relief. I'll sign all the papers. We'll get a protective services person to watch over you. Don't worry, okay?"

The girl nodded while crying. "Thank you."

"Meantime, while you're here, we're going to

put your name and picture up on the gym video board, so that your family or friends can find you."

Less than fifteen minutes later, the mystery girl's face stared from the video board at all the people in the shelter. The message under it said: "This is Maddie. If you know her, please come to the medical station."

51

Anna Croll kept looking at the video board and the picture of the girl known only as Maddie.

Something about her is calling to me, and I don't know why.

"It's been up for hours," Croll said. "They must not have found her family."

"Maybe you should check it out, Anna," said Mitch, her husband, who was playing board games with their daughter and son. "We'll be fine, go."

Croll kissed her family then left their space on the gym floor. Navigating her way to the shelter's admin tables, she had second thoughts. Was she overreacting? Had she misread her instinct? Croll was a mother, a wife, and an attorney who helped the South Florida chapter of Searching for Lost Angels, a national missing children's group.

Mitch is right. I just need to know that she's okay.

Croll showed her laminated ID to several shelter staff, a nurse and Red Cross officials who were huddled at one of the tables. Rita Salena was among those who knew Croll and her organization.

"Has anyone come for her?" Croll indicated the video board. "Has she been reunited with her family?"

"No one, Anna," Rita said.

"What's the girl's story?"

"She was found alone outside with her head bleeding." Rita typed on a keyboard and was reading from a monitor. "She suffered a concussion and memory loss. We got her to Holy Palms. They'll keep her there for a while. We checked our databases with other shelters to see if anyone's looking for her. We've put out a notice with her photo. Nothing so far. She had no wallet, ID or phone in her clothes."

"Maybe she was assaulted and robbed? Who's with her at Holy Palms? Did protective services assign someone to her?"

"Denise Perry. Want her contact info?"

"Yeah, I'll call her. Here's mine." Croll handed her a card. "Keep me posted."

The next morning after the hurricane had passed, Anna Croll left the shelter with her family, counting her blessings: they were safe and their home had sustained little damage.

Other than toppled trees, smashed car widows and debris scattered everywhere, much of her neighborhood was unscathed. It was the same for most of Croll's relatives in South Florida. She was grateful because so many people had lost so much.

Throughout it all, Croll had never forgotten about Maddie, the mystery teen at her shelter. By midafternoon she called Denise Perry who was still at the hospital with the girl.

"No," Perry said, "aside from the bump on her head, the medical staff found no sign she's been assaulted, and we've had no luck so far identifying her."

"Do you mind if we take a shot at it, Denise? I could be there with another member this afternoon, if you'll allow it."

"All right. With the storm's aftermath everybody's stretched right now, and we could use any help we can get."

Next, Croll called Penny Metcalf, her sister-in-law, and asked her to meet her at Holy Palms to help try to identify the teen.

"Oh, Anna, we've got so many storm-related calls. I'm not sure I can book off the time," said Metcalf, a Miami-Dade police officer and a member of Croll's missing children organization's chapter.

"This is storm-related and it won't take long."

Metcalf considered her reasoning and sighed.

"You're like a dog with a bone, Anna. I'll meet you there."

Later that afternoon Croll and Metcalf waited in an office near a nurse's station before Perry brought the girl to them.

Maddie was dressed in jogging pants, a T-shirt, sweater, sneakers and was hugging a stuffed teddy bear. Some of her hair had been cut away where her head had been bandaged. She grew apprehensive as Perry introduced Croll and Metcalf.

"We're all here to help you find your family." Croll smiled.

"The doctor said her scan results were good. No signs of neurological damage. But that it's impossible to know how long her post-trauma memory loss will last." Perry brushed Maddie's hair behind her ear. "Maddie says little bits are coming back, isn't that right, sweetie?"

Maddie nodded.

"That's good," Metcalf said. "We'd just like to ask a few questions, okay?"

Maddie nodded.

Croll and Metcalf turned to the table where they each had laptops and another device that looked like a mobile credit card machine.

"We'll start with this fingerprint scanner." Metcalf placed Maddie's right thumb on a sensitive square on the screen, held it there as a light flashed. Then Metcalf entered some commands. "We'll see if you're in any of our regional or state databases, maybe for a school thing, a job, or if you got into trouble or have been reported missing, anything like that. It'll take a little while."

While the machine searched, Metcalf asked Maddie questions.

"You're certain your name is Maddie?"

"Yes, pretty sure."

"And you're sixteen?"

"Yes, I think so."

"What's your last name?"

Maddie shook her head while hugging the bear.

"Do you know what happened, how you got hurt?"

"No."

Metcalf's fingerprint machine beeped, showing a No Hits response on the screen.

"Hmm, looks like you're not in the Florida system," Metcalf said, then went to her laptop.

"Maddie, do you have any memory of where you live?" Croll asked. "A landmark, or the sound of the town or city's name? Maybe you're in Florida visiting, or on vacation, or staying in a hotel?"

Blinking, she touched her cheek to the bear's head and thought.

"I think it had the word *New* in it?"

"The hotel?"

"No, the city, I think."

Croll began searching the state database of missing children files or news reports for New Port Richey, New Smyrna Beach and any others she could think of. The search yielded no results.

"What about the files for New Mexico, New Jersey and New York?" Metcalf suggested.

Croll's keyboard clicked with rapid typing as she submitted the name "Maddie" then "Madison" with spelling variations for the smallest state first. Nothing for New Mexico. Then she moved on to New Jersey and her computer flashed: One file found. The case of Bradley Madison, aged five, from Atlantic City, had been closed. He was found a year earlier.

With Metcalf watching over Croll's shoulder, she queried the database for New York State. Her screen flashed: One file found.

Croll opened it.

The page filled her screen with a Missing Child—Possible Abduction headline over the name Maddison Lane and two color photos, a description and a case summary that read:

Maddison Lane was last seen in the bedroom of her home in Syracuse, New York, at age twelve. It is believed she may have been abducted. Maddison's photo is shown age-progressed to sixteen years old.

Croll and Metcalf studied Maddie, then the age-progressed photo, not believing what they were seeing.

Denise Perry walked around the table, saw the file, then looked at the girl in the chair. Her hand flew to her mouth.

"Honey—" Croll moved closer to Maddie and lowered herself "—can you pull up the cuff of your pants so we can see your right ankle?"

Maddie swallowed and slowly tugged up the

right leg of her jogging pants, revealing a half-moon-shaped birthmark.

"Oh my God," Perry said. "It's her. It's Maddison Lane!"

52

"You'd asked me to call if anything unusual happened with the Lane policy?"

The Lane case?

Zubik had just answered a call from Nathan Hurst of American Eagle Federated Insurance. He glanced at the cardboard boxes filled with Lane case files, which he'd hadn't archived, stacked on top of his filing cabinet. Zubik demanded they remain there as a monument to his refusal to surrender.

He reflected on all those Saturday-morning meetings with Asher in their usual booth at Big Ivan's Diner, and how they reviewed the case. Now, Asher was poised to leave town for a job with Homeland in Washington. Time had flowed like a river, and they still hadn't cleared the case.

"Yes, Mr. Hurst, the Lane case. What do you have?"

"Ryan Lane visited me the other day. He seemed quite, well, a mess. I could smell alcohol on him. He was a man on the edge…"

"His daughter's disappearance has taken a toll over the years." Zubik glanced at the small photo on his desk of Rosie, the black Lab he'd adopted a week earlier from a shelter. Then he swiveled in his chair. Asher was across from him, talking on her phone to a Florida cop named Metcalf.

"...but what was more troubling," Hurst continued, "is that Mr. Lane asked me how long he needed to keep paying premiums on his daughter's policy and how long before she was declared dead. Well, I..."

Zubik watched Asher's face turn serious, and she stood.

"What?" Asher said, her eyes widening as she absorbed the information on her call, waving at Zubik to end his call now.

"Excuse me, Mr. Hurst, I'll get back to you," Zubik said as Asher's call ended.

"Oh my God, Stan—you are not going to believe this!"

53

Ryan Lane was extending his measuring tape along the wall of a new house in the suburb of Willowind when he got Zubik's call.

"Police in Florida have a girl that they're convinced is Maddie."

Ryan froze, not understanding or believing.

"Say that again."

Zubik repeated the news, and as he relayed details Ryan's heart rose. He stuttered a quick, thankful goodbye to Zubik with a promise to call him back. Fingers trembling, Ryan then called Karen at the store. She was at her register when he told her their daughter had been found *alive*, and her scream startled customers in her line.

"Oh God, is it really true, Ryan?"

"Zubik said it's her. It's Maddie!"

"We have to go now! I need to see her. I have to hold her today!"

Events began unfolding fast.

Cole arranged for tickets for Ryan, Karen and himself on the next plane to Miami, where the airport had just reopened after the storm. Tyler stayed with Jill and Dalton. Cole had alerted his investigators in Miami to keep him updated.

The Miami bureau of the Associated Press broke the story, and got a call to Ryan and Karen just before they boarded, requesting reaction.

"It feels like a dream," Ryan told the reporter. "We need to see her."

Karen sat in the middle seat of their 737 looking at the photos of Maddie that police had sent. They included close-ups of her half-moon-shaped birthmark above her right ankle, unmistakably Maddie's. Karen smiled at it like she did when Maddie was a baby.

Yes, this was Maddie, but she was older; her face had changed from the twelve-year-old little girl Karen last saw. It was fuller, tanned, somewhat hardened but looking so much like the teenager in the age-progressed picture. Karen was unable to imagine what had happened to her in all those years. Was she cared for? Was she mistreated? Where had she been? Who had she been with?

Maddie was alive. Karen thanked God for that. Her daughter was alive.

Tears filled her eyes and she squeezed Ryan's hand, relieved he'd only been drinking sodas on the plane. He'd shaved, he looked better, hopeful, but had retreated into his thoughts, leaving her to wonder if they could ever overcome the damage inflicted by Maddie's lost years.

The agony had strained their marriage to the

breaking point. Ryan had been able to keep the drywall business afloat but he drank too much, and Karen went through the motions of her life like a ghost, like she wasn't there. Tyler was still undergoing therapy and was determined to leave home and join the military, to see combat as soon as he could.

Throughout it all, Cole had been unfailing in his search for Maddie. He'd helped arrange age-progressed photos of Maddie. They were used by police, by the national support groups and his investigators in their search for her across the country.

But the heartache of missing Maddie was overwhelming for Ryan, Karen and Tyler. It had left them broken people.

Will we ever be happy again?

Karen looked at Cole beside her, working on his laptop, assessing information his investigators had sent him, and was struck by the dark truth she shared with him.

Will we be able to keep our mistakes buried?

As if reading Karen's mind, Cole gave her a furtive look and touched her hand as the jet began its descent.

At Miami's airport they were met by nearly fifty news people. Cameras flashed, microphones were thrust at them and Ryan repeated what he'd said to the wire service while they hustled with Van

Brophy, one of Cole's Miami investigators, to a waiting SUV.

It whisked them across the metropolis to a Miami-Dade police office.

More news crews were waiting for them as they hurried through a side entrance to meet Detectives Chad Powers and Julia Castillo, who ushered them and Cole to a small office.

"We're going to take you to her," Castillo said, "but there are a few things you need to know."

Karen struggled to concentrate and keep from bursting as Castillo updated them.

"We've been talking to her with the lead Syracuse detectives on video conference, trying to determine her place of residence, how she came to Florida. But she's suffered a head injury and remembers very little about anything, so we've been unsuccessful. Syracuse police will follow up in New York on formalities, like fingerprinting or DNA. We all believe this girl is your daughter, but once you confirm it for us, we'll have you sign a few papers, release her to you and you can take your daughter home. Karen, Ryan, we're happy for you." Castillo smiled. "Most cases don't end this way."

Karen cupped her hands to her face as they were led down the hall to a meeting room, glancing at Ryan then Cole.

Four years, she thought. *Will she recognize us?*

Inside, sitting in a chair between Anna Croll and Officer Penny Metcalf, was Maddie.

Slowly, she stood in silence before them, wearing shorts, a pink T-shirt, sneakers. A bandage about the size of a playing card was affixed to one side of her head. Karen took quick inventory, relieved to see the birthmark above Maddie's ankle. She had grown so much. Her face was rounder, her shoulders, chest and hips had developed. Maddie, their little girl, was now a young woman. Karen saw Maddie's chin quivering and searched her eyes, which were glistening as Maddie said, "Hi."

"Maddie!" Karen shrieked, taking her into her arms, feeling Maddie's fingers clawing into her back as Ryan suddenly crushed them both into his arms, snuggling his head into theirs, gasping for air as he sobbed.

"It's you, it's you! Oh Maddie, it's really you!"

54

The next day they returned to Syracuse.

At home, Maddie stood in her bedroom, looking around like she had arrived in a strange new world. Nothing was familiar. She ran her fingers along the bed, glanced at the posters on the wall, the gifts stacked in one corner. Then her attention shifted to her reflection in her dresser mirror.

She touched her bandage, struggling to mentally grasp all that had happened. At the Syracuse airport they'd met privately in a room for a moment with the two detectives who'd tried to find her all these years. The man said, "This is Fran Asher, I'm Stan Zubik. We're happy you're home safe, Maddison. We'd like to talk to you in a few days, when you're ready."

Then her family tried to rush her by another cluster of reporters, lights blazing and flashing, with Maddie's father only saying, "We're so happy our nightmare is over."

They made it home where more of her family embraced her. It was overwhelming, and they'd decided to let everyone see her one at a time. So much was happening so fast, like a new kind of hurricane, filling her with anxiety. She saw it in herself in the mirror. Now, she saw Karen's face beside hers, joyous and glowing.

"I keep telling myself it's real, I'm not dreaming you're home. I feared I'd never see you again, but deep in my heart I knew you were alive. It's really you!"

Maddie gave her a nervous smile.

"You really don't remember, honey? You don't remember us, your life before?"

Maddie pursed her lips, shook her head, blinking.

"The doctors in Florida said it might take time for everything to come back. We'll get a doctor to help you here. We'll talk to your school. We'll go shopping for new clothes and—" Karen nodded to the gifts "—we'll catch up with birthdays and Christmases. We'll have a big celebration."

Maddie gently raised her palms.

"Oh, sorry," Karen said. "Too much, too fast. I'll back off, give you space. But I need to tell you something before the others talk to you."

Maddie was listening.

"We're never, ever going to argue again, okay?"

Maddie nodded, smiling, and they held each other.

Alone for a moment, Maddie went to her window, seeing it reinforced and secured with white bars with a decorative scrollwork design. She looked through it to the backyard, the high fence and the forest beyond.

"The fence and window guards are new. Uncle Cole and I put in a new high-tech security system, too," Ryan said from the doorway. "You're safe here."

"That's good," she said.

"But if you're uncomfortable in your room because of what happened, Tyler will swap rooms with you."

"It's okay. I think I'll be okay here."

"Look, honey, I know you're having trouble remembering what happened to you, but you have to know that whatever comes back to you, whenever it comes back, that I love you with all my heart."

Maddie turned, rushed to him and they hugged for a long time.

After Ryan left, Tyler came to her room and sat on her bed. Looking at her, he said, "Your voice sounds deeper. You got taller. I guess, I did, too."

She smiled at him.

"This is weird." He let out a little laugh. "But in such a good way."

"I know," she said.

"You really can't remember stuff, like what happened to you?"

"No. I wish I did."

"Do you even know where you've been all this time?"

"No."

"How you got to Florida?"

"No."

"What about here? Can you remember any of it?"

"Not really. People seem worried and it's all scary, kinda crazy, like there was this life I had but I don't remember it."

Tyler thought, nodding. "A lot happened," he said. "Like Gabriela Rios, one of your best friends. She got cancer and died about two years ago. And Logan Bostick, a guy you liked, he moved to France with his family."

Maddie shook her head. "It all sounds sad, but I don't remember them."

"Some things haven't changed. Bennie still delivers pizza, just like he did that night." Tyler smiled. "Oh, yeah, and as for me, I'm going into the army later this year."

"Oh." Maddie sounded even sadder.

"Yeah, well, things got pretty rough living here when you were gone. I never ever stopped thinking about you. I begged God to bring you back. I got this to give to you for the day you came back."

He pulled out a bundle of tissue paper from his pocket and unfolded it, revealing a pink woven fabric bracelet with a small gold metal charm bearing one word: *Hope*.

"I'm really sorry I didn't do anything that night, but I never gave up hoping you'd come home." He was crying.

Maddie smiled, put the bracelet on and hugged Tyler. "Thank you."

Her aunt and uncle were next to see her.

"You're our miracle." Jill embraced her, kissed her cheek. "We all prayed so hard. Your uncle Cole and his team, everyone over the years, worked so hard to find you and now you're here, like an answered prayer!"

Jill kept hugging her.

"And you've become this beautiful young woman."

Cole handed Maddie a new top-of-the-line cell phone.

"I had my people rush this over for you," he said. "Ty will show you how to use it, if you need help. My numbers are programmed in there. I want you to contact me at any hour for anything, anything at all. We're all here to help you."

Maddie thanked them and, after they left, Dalton visited her.

"Everyone's insanely happy you're home," he said, glancing at the door to be sure they were alone. Then he softened his voice. "Maddie, do you remember me at all?"

"No, not really, sorry."

He looked at her for a long time.

"My dad said you talked to police at the airport. What did they ask you or tell you?"

"They want to talk to me in a couple days. Why?"

"I was wondering, that's all." He bit his lip, glanced at the window, the fence and the forest.

"Do you remember what happened the night you disappeared?"

"It was a long time ago. I'm not sure what I remember."

He gave her a long, uneasy look, as if he were searching for something in Maddie's eyes and unable to find it.

55

Maddie's heart was pounding a little faster now, sitting in the chair of the interview room at Syracuse police headquarters.

The detectives, Zubik and Asher, sat across from her, as they had done four years ago with the suspect, Kalmen T. Gatt, her family, her friends, with every person who might have known what had happened the night she'd vanished.

It had been several days since her return.

During that time, her family had been inundated with requests to interview her by media from across the country and around the world. Being protective, they'd declined each one, telling journalists, "We need some time to absorb it all." But when her parents agreed to bring her downtown to talk to Asher and Zubik about her disappearance, they'd insisted on being at her side.

"We understand your concerns," Asher had told Karen and Ryan, "but our procedure is to interview her alone. You're welcome to wait in the unit reception area."

Now, after Asher and Zubik explained to Maddie about the camera and ensured she was comfortable, they began.

"Maddie, it's important for us to know what happened to you and who was involved," Zubik said. "You understand?"

"Yes."

"We know," Zubik continued, "that you've been seeing a doctor and a psychiatrist and that you're starting to remember a little."

"Only in teeny bits, I guess."

"What do you recall about that night?"

"I remember eating pizza and I remember going to bed."

"Anything else? Anything at all?"

"No, I'm sorry."

"How did you get to Florida?"

"I don't know."

"Is there anything over the last four years that stands out in your mind, any names, faces, locations, landmarks?"

Maddie thought hard, licked her lips, coughed.

"No, nothing really." She coughed again.

"Are you thirsty?" Asher asked. "Would you like a soda or something?"

"I like cola."

Asher left and returned with a can of cola and opened it for her. She and Zubik watched as Maddie pulled down the sleeves of her hoodie, covering her hands before she cupped the can with them and sipped.

She smiled. "I'm a little cold."

"Maddie," Zubik said, "do you think it's possible you ran away?"

"No, I don't know. Why would I do that?"

"Do you remember problems at home?"

"I don't know. I don't remember."

"What has your family told you since your return?"

"That they love me, and they're sorry if they made me feel bad before."

Asher shot a quick glance to Zubik.

"Did they say specifically what they did to make you feel bad?"

"No, not really. I think they're just happy I'm back."

Zubik and Asher let a moment pass before Asher turned her laptop to Maddie. On the screen were photos of Kalmen T. Gatt.

"Do you know who this is? Have you ever had contact with him?"

As she looked at it they studied her reaction.

"No, I don't think so."

Next they showed her pictures of Zachary Keppler, then pictures of boys from school Maddie had liked, or who liked her—Caleb Langford, Logan Bostick and Noah Trell. All were pictures from the time she went missing ranging to more recent ones.

"Do you recognize any of these people?"

"No, I'm sorry."

The interview continued for nearly an hour but yielded little, and Zubik closed his notebook.

"Thank you, Maddie," he said. "We'd like to keep trying. Call us anytime day or night if you remember anything, please?"

"Okay."

"Before you leave, we'll take you down to our ident people so we can get your prints and a cheek swab for DNA, for the case. There was a glitch in Florida. They didn't save or send us your prints for ID, so it's just a routine thing."

"Okay."

In the hall they met Karen, Ryan and Cole, who'd joined them.

"How did it go?" Karen asked.

"Fine," Asher said. "She doesn't remember much, but it's a start. We're just taking her down-stairs for fingerprints and a DNA swab for the file."

Karen, Cole and Ryan exchanged glances. Karen put her arm around Maddie, pulling her close as if shielding her from a threat.

"No," Karen said. "We don't want that. She was already fingerprinted in Florida, confirming her identification. We confirmed it and signed."

Zubik and Asher looked puzzled.

"But her Florida prints have gone astray. It's a formality," Asher said.

"No, you're not going to start treating her like a criminal," Karen said. "My God, do you realize what our family's been through, how you treated us, how this thing nearly destroyed us? We're not putting her through that!"

"But it could help us find out where she's been, how she disappeared, what happened in the time she was gone, who was behind it."

"We said no," Ryan said. "We have her back home, safe, alive. That's all that matters now."

"Is it?" Asher said.

"All right." Zubik ended it. "We don't need to do any of this now. That's fine. We just need to be patient and wait for her memory to come back."

During the exchange, Maddie had remained silent, watching the faces of Ryan, Karen and Cole, who had not spoken, something that was not lost on Zubik.

56

Maddie's psychiatrist had an aquarium in her office, and Maddie liked watching the fish glide in the water.

It was calming.

"How are you doing today?" Dr. Emily Hartley asked on this, Maddie's third visit since her return over a week ago.

"I keep trying to remember but it's hard. I lie awake at night trying to bring it all back, and when I fall asleep, I try to dream it all back but it just doesn't come." Maddie touched a fingertip to the aquarium glass, and a little blue fish bubbled up to it. "My parents keep showing me videos and pictures, telling me who's who, but hardly anything's coming back and I don't know what to do."

"Don't stress over it." Hartley removed the large glasses she wore attached to a beaded chain, letting them rest on her chest. "We know head injuries like yours cause memory loss, or what we call post-traumatic amnesia. In some cases, it only lasts a few hours while in others it lasts for months."

"Months?"

"Yes, and in some cases, longer," Hartley said. "The trauma can manifest itself in a multitude of ways. It can take a toll on your sleep, your appetite. It can even alter the color of your eyes and hair."

"It can?"

"Yes, and yours is an unusual case possibly linked to other, unknown trauma. It's quite possible that subconsciously your brain is suppressing troubling memories, terrible things you've experienced, as a type of protection. But as I've said, it's unlikely your memory loss will last forever. Everything will come back to you in time."

At home, the calls from newspapers, online media outlets and TV networks wanting to interview Maddie and her family had not subsided. Friends, neighbors, strangers who'd helped search for her also wanted to see her and her family.

A few of Maddie's friends and Ryan and Karen's coworkers were allowed to see her in what were short, teary hugging sessions. Still, her parents remained steadfast, protecting her privacy. Eventually, after discussing it with Cole and Jill, the family decided to have a celebration event where Maddie could make a statement, but nothing had been finalized yet.

For now, Maddie spent most of her days in her room using the new laptop her uncle Cole had bought her to look at family photos and videos.

Here she is at age four singing, "You Are My

Sunshine," for her mother; here she is at six with her family at Christmas, then blowing out the candles on the cake at her eighth birthday party. Here she is on a school trip at Lake Placid with friends; now here she is at Uncle Cole's family barbecue, at the pool with Dalton and Tyler. Here she is messing around with Tyler in his room, looking at all those knives in his collection. With each image Maddie fought to remember, tried to put herself in those moments. But nothing worked.

It was as if she was never there.

Then her concentration shifted, and she began researching news reports online about her disappearance.

She devoured headlines, TV news videos and story after story about the search, the reward, her parents pleading for her return, her distraught friends, police dogs, helicopters and people scouring the woods, going door-to-door.

She came to the stories about the convict, Kalmen Gatt, who died while grabbing a police officer's gun after being questioned about her when they found pictures he'd taken of her.

Oh my God! Who was this creep, lurking out there in the woods? Taking pictures. That's so gross! At least he's dead.

Maddie then digested the in-depth newspaper pieces and anniversary features that examined the speculation, theories and rumors concerning her disappearance.

Then she came to Ryan and Karen's TV interview with Morgan Stone, Maddie's pulse pounding as she absorbed it all, parts of it bursting upon her like emotional fireworks.

How everything pointed to Gatt, the pervert in the woods; how Karen begged for her life; how some people suspected her family was involved in her disappearance; and how Karen and Ryan had denied any part in it. Then came the security camera footage of Ryan violently dragging her into his truck and striking her. She was stunned as she watched. Then came Ryan's explanation and response, which ended with "We're not perfect people."

Maddie stared at the screen for a long moment before continuing and coming to a headline and article about Karen: Missing Girl's Mother Has Tragic Family History. She read the article about how Karen was present at the deaths of her sister and mother.

Maddie caught her breath.

Transfixed by all she had seen and read. Tears rolled down her face.

57

Pop music throbbed from the Ruby Green Community Hall.

Just a few blocks from the Lane family home, the brick building that once served as the Maddison Lane search center was now a place of celebration.

The parking lot was jammed. Cars lined both sides of the street, and a new billboard-sized photo of Maddie stood above the entrance.

Inside the packed hall, the air was jubilant. Bunting and colored lights looped from the rafters and stretched the length of the main room. Music flowed from speakers suspended on walls covered with rainbow-colored crepe-paper streamers.

At one end, a line of buffet tables offered a variety of food donated from local restaurants, including a never-ending supply of pizzas. At the opposite end was the stage and a podium adorned with flowers. High above it was a massive banner that read: Welcome Home Maddie!!!

Maddie, her family and several people joined

her uncle Cole onstage as the music died and he got things started.

"Are you guys ready?" Cole nodded to the news cameras. He'd made an arrangement with the media—local, national and international were there—that they were welcome but would leave after Maddie's statement.

There would be no interviews at this time.

"Thank you everyone for coming to help us celebrate. I'll try to keep it short," Cole started. "You all know that when my niece vanished four years ago, a light in our world went dark. Ryan, Karen and Tyler suffered the agony of her absence every day. So did everyone who cared about her. Not knowing where she was, if she was alive, was almost more than any of us could bear. Believe me, I know. I also know, from my own life, that with faith, courage and the help of others, nothing's impossible." Cole pushed back his tears and tightened his grip on the podium. "We know it's true because a couple of weeks ago, thanks to Anna Croll, a miracle happened in Florida and we got our angel back. We flew Anna up to join us here now, so we can present her with a check in the full amount of the reward. Anna."

Croll hugged Cole to the sound of applause, accepted the envelope then said, "Words cannot describe our gratitude and happiness for Maddie and her family. I'm happy to announce that this full amount will be donated in her name to our nonprofit national missing children's organization, Searching for Lost Angels."

"Okay, now," Cole said, "what you've all been waiting for—Maddie will say a few words. But first, as most of you know, she's endured some trauma and has not yet recovered her full memory, so it will be short."

Maddie smiled and with Karen and Ryan at each shoulder, holding her arms, she went to the podium. A long moment passed as she stood in the glare of the news cameras taking in the audience, their joyful faces, and the news people, all staring at her. At the back she saw detectives Zubik and Asher. Watching.

She took a breath, unfolded a single sheet of paper and read.

"'I'm so, so grateful to be home. I know how lucky I am, how loved I am and I want to thank my family, and, and—'" Maddie's tears gushed and her mother crushed her tighter "'—and everyone who searched for me, worked so hard to find me and prayed for me. I love you all with all my heart. It's good to be home. Thank you.'"

The hall shook with thunderous applause and cheers. Cole, Jill, Tyler and Dalton joined them and helped Maddie from the podium as Cole waved, the music thudded and the party began.

After Asher got some wings then joined Zubik, who'd heaped potato salad onto a paper plate, Cole, Ryan, Tyler and Dalton arrived at their table.

"This is a nice way to thank everyone," Asher said above the music.

"We didn't expect to see you here," Cole said. "Any new leads?"

Chewing slowly, Zubik said, "We're working on it. We need to keep talking to Maddison, see what she can recall."

"In the meantime, have you thought of an apology?" Cole said.

Zubik's eyes narrowed. "A what?"

"An apology. For the hell you put my brother and his family—all of us—through."

"No."

"Why not?"

"Why not? Because we were, and are, investigating a disturbing case. If things got unpleasant, it's because they were unpleasant for everyone. We were doing our job, Cole. You better than anyone would know that. Above all, we're happy that Maddison is safe and home with her family." Zubik looked at Cole, then Ryan, Tyler and Dalton. "We still need to know what happened, and until we do this is an open case."

A few seconds passed.

"Fair enough, Stan," Cole said. "Been a tough four years for all of us."

"It has, Cole."

"I had to release a little steam. No hard feelings." Cole offered his hand, which prompted a round of handshakes for everyone. "I hear you're leaving for DC, Fran," Cole said.

"Not for another eight weeks. I may extend it to see this case through."

Cole nodded, then said to Zubik, "You gotta be thinking about retiring, Stan."

"I'm thinking about a lot of things, Cole."

"Oh my God!" Amanda Morber threw her arms around Maddie.

Maddie was in a corner of the hall encircled by some of her friends who knew her best before she disappeared. They were juniors and seniors in high school now.

"You look so different than you did when you were twelve." Caleb Langford showed Maddie an old picture on his phone.

Nicole Webb started taking selfies. "That's because she's older, we're all older. It's been four years, you idiot."

"I never stopped thinking of you, Maddie," Amanda said.

"So you really don't remember what happened?" Lily Wong asked.

"Not really," Maddie said.

"There were all kinds of reports and rumors, like everyone thought that convict killed you." Noah Trell had a picture on his phone. "His name was Kalmen T. Gatt. See?"

"Yeah, he was creepy," Amanda said.

"We thought you were dead," Caleb said.

"So much has happened," Amanda said. "You

know Gabriela Rios died and Logan Bostick moved away?"

"Tyler told me."

"So what do you remember?" Brooke Carson asked.

"Not much at all. It's kinda scary," Maddie said.

"We heard you were coming to school. Is that true?" Amanda said.

"Yes, my folks talked to the school. They're going give me some tests to assess me or something, then put me in some classes, I guess."

"How the hell did you end up in Florida?" Noah asked.

"I don't know."

"Somebody take you from your room?" Noah asked.

"I'm not sure. I can't remember."

"You remember us, though, right?" Brooke said.

"A little. I mean, at home when I saw pictures it started to come back a little. It comes in bits. The doctors said it could be a month or so before it all comes back."

After several more minutes of questions from the group, Brooke Carson grabbed Maddie's arm, taking her aside.

"I need to talk to my girl," Brooke told the others. Then, when they were alone, she said, "Maddie, do you remember anything about what you told me just before you went missing?"

Maddie shook her head, and Brooke stared

at her without saying anything. "No, what is it, Brooke? What did I tell you?"

Brooke looked around, bit her lip, then spoke into Maddie's ear.

"You told me something big was happening in your life that I couldn't tell anyone. You seemed scared. Do you remember telling me that?"

Maddie looked at her then shook her head. "I don't. What could it be?"

"I don't know," Brooke said.

"Hey!"

A man with a ballcap and ponytail had joined them.

"Hey, Bennie," Brooke said. "Maddie, you remember Bennie, the pizza man?"

"Oh, I'm sorry to interrupt you ladies," he said. "I was just making another delivery to the party, and I had to see for myself."

"See what?" Maddie said.

"That it's really you." Bennie searched her eyes, then assessed her from head to toe, becoming lost in the wonder of what he was seeing. "How could this be? It just can't be."

"What do you mean, Bennie?" Brooke said.

"I just can't believe this," he said. "It's the most amazing thing I ever saw." Tears came to his eyes. "I just can't believe it's you standing here. It just can't be." He shook his head. "Okay, gotta go. Thanks." He touched his fingers to the brim of his hat in a causal salute, turned and left the hall.

"What was that all about?" Maddie asked.

Brooke rolled her eyes. "That's Bennie. He's weird. That's what happens when all you do in life is deliver pizzas." Brooke looked around. "Think about what I said. I'm going to get a drink. Want anything?"

"No, thanks."

In the moment Maddie was alone, her cousin Dalton found her.

"This is great, don't you think?" he said.

"It's kinda overwhelming."

"I'm Dalton, your cousin." He had a handsome smile.

"I know. We already talked. I mean, I know who you are."

"Just teasing," he said. "So, still having trouble remembering what exactly happened?"

She rolled her eyes and groaned pleasantly.

"That's all anyone asks me. Yes, I'm still having trouble remembering."

"Is the shrink helping much?"

"Yes, she's very nice."

He thought for a moment, glanced around then back at her.

"Maddie, I'm going to ask you something that I really need to know."

"All right."

"Do you remember anything at all about that night, anything specifically?"

She swallowed, thinking for the longest time, staring at him, unable to answer as the music hammered into the night.

58

Alone here in my darkness...remembering what I want to forget...traveling back...years and years... always pulling me back to that night...

Crystal came to watch us...we had pizza... Bennie delivered it... "Hi, Bennie"... Bennie winking, waving, saying, "Hey, beautiful"...

We watch the movie... Jurassic Park...*dinosaurs chasing people, gulping them down... Tyler loving it...then bed...the darkness...my secrets lit by the light of my phone...my secret desires.*

Mom knows nothing... I'm old enough to know what I'm doing...my pulse is racing...pretending to sleep when Mom checks on me...the secret messages keep coming...my heart is beating so fast...

59

"We just got these new images of Maddison."

Miami-Dade Detective Julia Castillo tapped on her keyboard, and the video played on the large flat screen in the boardroom.

"It's from the security cameras at a strip mall about three blocks from the shelter in the hours before Zeus hit full force."

Hopeful to unravel the mystery of Maddison Lane's return, Asher and Zubik sipped coffee and studied the video clip of the mall's parking lot.

Street signs are dancing to and fro, vibrating. Palms are bending, a traffic light swings, debris skips off parked vehicles, flying like shrapnel as Maddison, wearing a polo shirt and tan shorts, runs alone through the lot, leaning into the wind-driven rain, holding her head.

She's visible for about four seconds.

Castillo's keyboard clicked.

"Then, a few minutes later, we pick her up here in the shelter's security camera."

Maddison arrives staggering in the wind hold-

ing her head, crouching behind a planter where she's discovered by two women before they are all taken into the shelter.

"How did she get to that strip mall?" Detective Chad Powers asked. "We've got nothing leading up to that point."

"And exactly how was she injured?" Asher asked.

Zubik had made notes then said, "Julia, can you run the strip mall again but super slow this time?"

The images appeared in a stop-start manner. Zubik leaned forward, looking at the vehicles and Maddison's movements just as she entered the frame. After Castillo ran the clip a few times, even zooming in and out, Zubik shook his head in frustration.

"All right," Asher said. "She arrives at the shelter injured but with no phone, no wallet, no ID. Was she robbed? Was she fleeing from someone? Where did she come from?"

It had been two days since Zubik and Asher had landed in Florida to search for answers to Maddison Lane's disappearance and how she emerged. In that time they had followed Maddison's known path, interviewing everyone who had contact with her before she'd returned to Syracuse.

Lana Compton and Pearl, her mother, the women who'd found Maddison at the shelter, remembered little. "She was bleeding and drenched," Lana said. Shelter officials, the medical team on duty there and at the hospital tried but couldn't offer anything new. They went over the statements given by Anna Croll and Officer Penny Metcalf without uncovering anything they didn't already know.

Zubik and Asher faced additional challenges arising from the fact that the fingerprints collected from Maddison at the time were lost because of an IT issue. And while her prints were run with no hits through county and state databases, they had not been submitted to the national databases, which may have provided leads had they surfaced for any reason in another jurisdiction.

"Everyone was preoccupied with Zeus," Powers said. "We were also dealing with reports of burglaries and looting."

"What about DNA? Did you do a cheek swab?" Asher asked.

"No, we didn't. Our hands were full, and we were comfortable with her identity being confirmed by her parents and by her birthmark with the understanding that any follow-up would be done in New York."

Asher exhaled her frustration.

The Syracuse detectives had also reached out to Van Brophy, a private investigator with the Miami office of Cole Lane's agency.

"You can believe we did everything we could to help find her, and to find out what happened. From the get-go we'd circulated Maddison's information to law enforcement, the press, missing children's groups, child services, everyone down here," Brophy had told them when they met him at a local

Starbucks. "We also pushed every street source we could. Cole wants us to find out how she got here, too. We're doing all we can to get answers."

Today, after viewing the new video, Zubik and Asher interviewed people at the strip mall with little luck. Then they ran down plates of the vehicles that were in the parking lot at the time Maddison passed through it. They'd interviewed the owners, a long shot that yielded nothing.

Late that night, after dinner with Asher, Zubik relaxed on the bed of his motel room with his laptop on his stomach replaying the footage of Maddison in the strip mall lot.

Again and again.

From the beginning, he ran it stop-action, frame by frame, certain he caught the faint hint of a blurred image of a person near Maddison.

Is she running from someone? Running for her life?

60

Everyone stared those first days as Maddie walked through the halls.

Going to school was unnerving.

Most of the time she'd kept her head ducked down, holding her books close to her chest like a shield against her uncertainty, confusion and the reaction of the other students.

Like when two girls gawked as she passed by them.

"It's really her," one of them said to her sidekick. "The famous girl who disappeared."

Others were less like circus-goers and a bit more mature.

"Hi, Maddie, I'm Hannah Merton. You likely don't remember me. We were in sixth grade together." Hannah jotted her number on a scrap of notepaper. "Let me know if you ever need any help with anything."

No matter how hard Maddie tried, she could not shake feeling like an alien in a foreign land. While many kids were welcoming and warm to her, others regarded her as a celebrity, an oddity, or something to be mocked.

"Remember me, Maddie? Gwen?" A nervous freckle-faced girl giggled. "We had history together back in the day."

Another girl had swiped to a photo on her phone and showed it to Maddie: two girls wearing leotards, laughing in a gym. "It's me, Sophie Verdes. That's us when we were in gymnastics together, remember?"

As the days passed, Maddie lost track of how many times people wanted to show her old photos or take selfies with her. Her teachers were understanding, but treated her like she was made of glass. They gave her special attention, in those first days when she sat in on classes, always asking, "Are you comfortable with this?" or, "Is there anything you need, Maddie?"

Tyler was the ever protective big brother, the future soldier, always texting, needing to know where she was, how she was doing.

"Where are you?" he'd ask. "Everything good?"

"Geography. Yes, I'm okay."

And sometimes that was true, particularly when she was with the kids she knew, the ones she felt most comfortable with, like Amanda and Lily. They were nearly bursting when they'd showed her the draft of the page they were going to run in the yearbook for her.

"It started out being a page of hope for you when you were still missing." Amanda showed it to Maddie on her tablet, pictures of her when she was twelve and a nice one taken only days ago. "Now we're turning it into a welcome home Maddie page, see, with fireworks, confetti and balloons!"

But not everyone was enamored with Maddie's return. It may have been juvenile envy, but some couldn't hide their resentment at the attention she'd gotten. One girl touched her arm and said, "Gosh, Maddison, how are you going to get into college after missing all those years?"

Another girl snickered. "You'll probably end up working beside your mom. Better practice saying 'Price check on canned peas!'"

Then there were others, like the boy who said, "Did you get a movie and book deal yet? Some people think this is all fake news, that you faked the whole thing so you could cash in."

All Maddie could do was shake her head and walk away.

But more kids grew curious about her and her ordeal. As time passed, their reluctance to press her on it melted, until one day in the cafeteria a group who'd seemed friendly beckoned her to join them. As they ate lunch things started off all normal, then one popular jock, Vin Dubner, shot a glance to the others before he stared at Maddie.

"So what the hell happened to you?" Vin asked. "Where were you for four years and how'd you end up in Florida?"

"I guess I was taken from my room, but I still don't remember much."

"Still can't remember?" Vin shook his head. "Man, I don't know."

"You know, we think you look older," Vin's pal, Reed Lanski, said.

"I am older. We're all older—it's been four years," Maddie said.

"Naw." Vin crossed his arms. "We think you look older than sixteen."

Maddie didn't respond.

"And different, look." Katie O'Conner swiped through her tablet then turned it. "Here's your picture when you were twelve before you disappeared." Katie held the tablet next to Maddie's face. "Look at your nose and eyes now. We think you look different."

Maddie swallowed and studied the older photo.

"I know," Maddie said. "The doctors told me that the stress of what I went through could do things to me."

"Really?" Vin was deciding to believe her.

"Yes, it's some kind of medical thing. You can look it up. I should go."

"Wait," Vin said. "You really don't remember anything?"

"Only little bits." Maddie was barely audible.

"It's all so weird," Vin said.

"I'm sorry. I have to go." Maddie gathered her things and stood, fighting tears as she left.

61

Karen selected a serrated knife from the drawer.

She was at the kitchen counter making Maddie's favorite, an egg salad sandwich, while Maddie waited at the table. It was Saturday. Ryan had taken Tyler to help him clean up on a job, so for now it was just the girls.

"Want to go to the mall, Maddie?" Karen drew the knife across the sandwich, cutting it in half. "There's a sale on some cute outfits at—" She pivoted with the plate and froze.

Her daughter's chair was empty.

"Maddie?"

Karen set the sandwich down and checked the living room. Nothing. The hall. Nothing. The bathroom. Nothing.

Karen's pulse picked up when she entered Maddie's bedroom. Relief and concern rolled over her when she saw her through the window, standing outside at the fence facing Lucifer's Green.

Karen went to her.

Tears brimmed in Maddie's eyes.

"What is it, sweetheart?" Karen stroked her hair. "Want to talk?"

She was silent. Birdsong floated from the woods. Butterflies flitted over the tall grass.

"It's been almost a month now, and I know it's been hard," Karen said. "I'm worried about you, honey. You've been so quiet and you're not eating. I know we need to be patient, but I can't help worrying."

Maddie brushed at her eyes and blinked back her tears.

"Why can't I remember anything?"

"Maybe you're suppressing things you don't want to remember, like Dr. Hartley said."

Maddie ran her fingers through her hair and shook her head.

"It's more than that."

"What else? Tell me, sweetie."

"It's the things people say, the way they look at me and it's all the news stories I've read, the new ones, the old ones, about me, about Dad." Maddie speared her with a look. "About you."

"About me?"

"How when your mom died and your little sister died, you were there with them each time. Some articles kinda implied you were responsible for their deaths, and that just bothers me so much."

"It bothers me, too." Karen stared at the sky for a moment. "Cassie drowned. It was an accident. My mother's health was failing, and the stress of losing Cassie was a factor in her death. I nearly went crazy. Sometimes I felt like I was cursed to keep losing the people I love. It's why I argued with you so much, because I was afraid I was losing you. And when we did lose you, when you vanished, my world shattered. I thought I was being punished for the things I'd done."

"What things did you do?"

Karen looked at her.

"I'm not perfect. I'm not a perfect mother, or a perfect person."

"I don't know what that means," Maddie said.

Fighting her own tears, Karen took Maddie in her arms.

"It means God has given us a chance to start over, a chance to make everything right, the way it should be, and I'm never going to lose you again. We just need to be patient, okay?"

Maddie looked at Karen for a long moment.

That afternoon after returning home, Ryan went to Maddie's room where she was watching videos on her tablet.

"Mom told me you were having a rough day."

Maddie tugged out her earbuds, stared at him, took in a breath and let it out slowly. "Since I've been back I've been trying to figure things out."

Ryan nodded.

"I've looked at the family pictures and videos a million times, but it's so hard for me to remember."

"I understand."

"I also read all the news stories I could find

about me, my family. Some of the stuff I found is alarming, you know?"

"Yes, I do. It was devastating when we lost you. We were hollowed out. Your mom and I went through our lives like the living dead. I drank way too much because we were in so much pain."

Maddie shook her head. "No, it's not that. I get that."

"What then?"

"This." She tapped on her tablet, turned it to him so he could see the security footage of him dragging her into his truck in the rain four years ago. "This scares me."

"Oh," he said, barely audible as it played. "I see."

When it ended, Maddie waited for him to respond.

"Maddie, if I could turn back time and do things differently, I would." He dragged his hands over his face. "Yes, I pulled you into my truck after you ran off. You mouthed off pretty bad about mom and I lost it. I struck you one time that day because I was angry. I was under so much pressure with my business. It's no excuse for my behavior that day. It's one of the regrettable things I've done that I'm not proud of."

"One? There are others?"

Ryan scraped the back of his hand across his lips like a man who suddenly craved a drink. He had cut back since her return, but something was twisting his insides.

"Look, honey, I think it's best if we leave the bad things of the past in the past," he said. "We've got a second chance here to be better people. Not everybody gets that."

In the days that followed, Maddie came out of her room less and less except to go to school.

She barely spoke to her family and picked at her meals.

Then one night at about 2:00 a.m., Tyler, Ryan and Karen were awakened to screams coming from her bedroom.

Ryan had a baseball bat and Tyler a hunting knife when they rushed in to find Maddie flailing and shrieking.

"NO! STOP! GET AWAY! PLEASE!"

Karen, still gripping her phone to call police if necessary, scooped Maddie into her arms and soothed her.

"Honey, wake up. Wake up. It's just a bad dream."

In her stupor, Maddie blinked then squinted at the faces of her mother, her father and her brother, as if seeing them for the first time.

It was just a bad dream.

Still, the incident gave Karen pause as she comforted Maddie, soothing her until she fell back asleep.

62

Two days later, Karen Lane's cell phone rang.

"Hi, Karen, this is Fran Asher. Stan and I would like to visit with you, Ryan and Maddison as soon as possible. Could we drop by today?"

Fran and Stan? All casual, like old friends. Karen was wary.

"Why? What's this about?"

"We just returned from Florida, still trying to fill in the blanks, and we have something we need Maddison's help on."

"What?"

"I'd rather not say over the phone—it's something we need to show her."

"Just a minute." Karen muted her phone for several seconds to consult Ryan before she came back to Asher. "All right, six thirty this evening."

Tyler got the door when the detectives arrived, and any traces of smiles dissolved on their faces when they saw Cole Lane with Ryan, Karen and Maddison in the kitchen.

Ryan gestured that they'd talk at the kitchen table, an indication that he didn't want them to be too comfortable.

"Coffee?" Karen offered.

"Sure, thank you," Zubik said.

"Yes, please," Asher said, nodding to Maddison. "How're you doing?"

Maddison shrugged.

Zubik found a smile. "We understand you've been getting counselling?"

"She has. That's no secret," Karen said. "To help her recover from what she's been through."

"That's why we're here." Zubik kept his eyes on Maddison. "We'd like to know what you've been through. Have you been able to remember anything new?"

Maddison began shaking her head slowly.

"No, she hasn't," Ryan said. "What's this about? On the phone you told Karen that you had something to show her."

"We do." Asher worked on her tablet. "We've just returned from Florida where we were talking to people, and we want to show Maddison these security camera images." Asher cued them up. "Come closer have a look."

"Where did this come from?" Cole asked.

"Security cameras at and near the shelter," Asher said.

Maddison watched as Asher played the short sequence from the shelter then the strip mall parking lot. Her family drew nearer to view them.

"This is you," Asher said. She'd set up the clips so they replayed over and over and slowed them down to stop-action speed. "What do you think? Does this help you remember what you were running from, where you were in the time before these images?"

Cole studied Maddison as she concentrated on the images, then shook her head.

"Look—Fran, can you stop it here?" Zubik pointed with his pen to the blurry dark image near Maddison at the beginning of the strip mall footage. "We've enhanced this. It looks like it could be a person just exiting the frame. Does that help you remember? Do you know who that is?"

She shook her head. "I'm sorry, I don't."

"That could be anything," Cole said.

"Exactly," Zubik said. "That's why we're here for help." Then to Maddison he said, "Has your therapist tried hypnosis to help you remember?"

"No, she hasn't."

"Hey, what's this about?" Ryan asked.

"We'd like Maddison to undergo hypnosis to help her remember."

"Just hold on," Cole said. "Hypnosis has drawbacks. You know about confabulation, false memories, Stan."

"No, to be clear," Asher said, "we're talking more about a cognitive interview, Cole."

"Yeah, that's right," Zubik said.

"We know a cognitive interview reduces distortions and inaccuracies," Asher said. "It can be very effective."

"No, no," Karen said. "She's been having an extremely hard time. Her doctor says she may be suppressing traumatic events she doesn't want to remember. I'm afraid this kind of thing could cause more damage to her."

"We understand that," Asher said. "But Karen, Maddison, everybody, we all want and need to know what happened when she disappeared from this house four years ago, what crimes were committed."

"But we've got her back," Ryan said.

"Yes, and thank God for that," Asher said.

Zubik steepled his fingers and touched them to his mouth. "Think about this. What if whoever took Maddison has also taken other children, is holding them somewhere, is harming those children now as we sit here in your kitchen? Maddison's memory could be the key to helping us save them."

A silence fell over all of them until it was broken by Maddison.

"I'll do it. I'll let you hypnotize me."

63

"Are you comfortable, Maddison?"

"Yes."

Maddie was lying on top of her bed in her room where Dr. Vera Granov conducted the final segment of the session.

It was night. The lighting had been dimmed.

Granov, a psychiatrist from the university, had worked with the FBI, state and Syracuse police, helping witnesses remember details using a method known as a cognitive interview.

Earlier that day, Maddison had met the white-haired grandmotherly woman in her office, where Granov's cat, Pasha, took to Maddison. She liked the doctor, who, after reviewing police and news reports on Maddison's case, had initiated the first stages of the interview process.

Granov took notes while Maddison relayed the little she could recall about her ordeal while Pasha padded through the office. The doctor was going to help Maddison reach into her mind to recover more details of her disappearance. Granov said that while studies showed that "on the scene" sessions increased the accuracy of memories and the chances of unlocking suppressed details, they would not be able to travel to Florida. They would instead start in Maddison's bedroom, re-creating the time and conditions, then use the Florida security footage.

Granov would help Maddison reach an intense state of concentration by guiding her to be cognizant of details in the moments leading up to her departure from her bedroom—the weather, the sounds, smells, her emotions and her thoughts. Maddison agreed to do her best but had requested her psychiatrist, Dr. Hartley, be present for the final interview segment in her bedroom.

"Shall we proceed?" Granov said.

Now, along with Granov and Hartley, Zubik and Asher were also present, filling Maddison's room. The detectives were recording the session. Asher adjusted the tripod and camera. Maddison closed her eyes in the soft, tranquil light of her room. The camera's recording light was blinking. The tablet on Granov's lap was filled with notes. She made a formal evidentiary introduction on the video then began.

"As we discussed, Maddison, I want you to think, reach back to that night in this house, in this room, and tell me what you remember. Start with the first thoughts you have."

"I smell pizza…we had pizza…and we watched

a movie about dinosaurs—*Jurassic Park*...pretty scary..."

Maddison talked about the movie for a moment.

"Good. I'm guiding you to your bedroom, this room now...what are you doing..."

"I'm changing...getting ready for bed...pretty tired...my window's open and there's a nice breeze... I hear the quiet..."

"And your phone. Where's your phone?"

Eyes closed, Maddison raised her hands a little.

"Phone?" Maddison repeats.

"Yes, where is your phone? Are you communicating with someone on your phone? Are you using self-destructing messages to keep them secret?"

Maddison's fingers began to move in slow motion, mimicking texting.

"I can't... I don't..."

"That's okay. What happens now?"

"The ladder... I remember a ladder...at my window..."

"Who put the ladder there? Who's at your window?"

"I don't... I can't...outside... I'm outside now... leaving my yard...running...running...through the forest...dark...it's so dark..."

"Who are you with? Think of voices, sounds, smells, colors. Who?"

Maddison was silent. Eyes closed, she shook her head.

"What's happening Maddison? What're you doing? Who's with you?"

Tears rolled down Maddison's face.

"I can't. I can't…so dark…so dark…please no…no more…"

"All right, it's okay," Granov soothed her. "Take a breath. Take your time. We'll shift to Florida, like we discussed." Granov worked on her tablet, opening the Florida footage of Maddison from the strip mall and the shelter, which had been merged into a single, short video. "All right, Maddison, are you ready to look at the pictures of you in Florida during the storm?"

Maddison's face glowed in the light of Granov's tablet as she watched.

"Go back. Think of the sounds, the smells, your thoughts. What can you tell us? What do you recall?" Granov asked.

"Rain…" Maddie said. "Rain and wind…howling, loud wind…stuff is flying everywhere…and smells…it smells like tropical air…not like Syracuse…and warmer…"

"Go back. Take your mind back to where you came from just before the shelter, Maddison. Where were you before running to the shelter?"

"Running… I've got to run…the hurricane's coming…run…"

"How did you get to the parking lot? Who was with you?"

"…just run…run…my head…"

"Was anyone with you?"

"…run…keep running…"

"Who is with you? Do they remind you of anyone you know?"

"...run...something hit my head..."

"How? How are you hurt? Did someone hurt
you? Who hurt you?"

Maddison shakes her head from side to side.

"No... I'm so afraid... NO!"

Maddison screamed. Then cried.

Granov moved to console her.

"It's okay, we're finished. We're done, Maddison."

Zubik looked at Maddie, his expression betraying nothing.

64

"What happened? Is she going to be all right?"

Karen's face was etched with worry when the psychiatrists and detectives closed the door to Maddie's room after leaving her there.

"We gave her a mild sedative. She'll be asleep soon." Dr. Granov touched Karen's shoulder, glanced at Ryan, Cole and Tyler. "Let's go to the living room."

After everyone was seated, Granov continued.

"It was difficult for Maddison, but unfortunately little emerged from the session."

"Did it do any damage to her, hurt her in any way?" Karen looked at Granov then Hartley.

"No, I don't believe so," Hartley said.

"Did she remember anything?" Cole looked at the psychiatrists, then the detectives for answers. "Anything from that night? Anything from Florida."

"Like Dr. Granov said, very little emerged," Zubik said.

* * *

Zubik and Asher drove Dr. Hartley home first. Then after dropping her off, they stopped at a coffee shop with Dr. Granov.

Their server brought the detectives coffee, and tea for Granov.

"So what's your take on this?" Asher asked.

"The research on memory retrieval shows us that everyone stores their recall of events differently." Granov dipped her teabag in her cup of hot water. "In Maddison's case, after tonight's session, I would conclude that she was blocked."

"Blocked?" Asher looked at Zubik.

"Yes," Granov said. "It would appear she's experienced something traumatic. That trauma is refusing to allow access to the information you need, refusing to allow us to unlock her memory to recover it."

"So what does that mean?" Asher said. "You try more sessions?"

"Perhaps, but I sense reluctance on the part of the parents to continue," Granov said. "It's understandable. Maddison appears to be in a fragile state, and it's important to note that memory deteriorates over time."

"What're you saying here?" Zubik said. "In plain English."

"What I'm saying, Stan, is that instead of trying to remember, the girl may be trying to forget."

Zubik's jaw tensed.

He turned away, looked to the window and into the night.

"So we don't know what happened to her," he said. "Where does that leave us?"

65

The house was a custom-built, two-story colonial with a deep, private backyard, a tall fence, trees and big shrubs.

It sat back from the curb in an upper-class Syracuse neighborhood.

This is a thief's dream, he thought as he worked at disabling the security system. Easy if you knew what you were doing, and he did. He'd been at this for years, and he'd never made a mistake.

As always, he'd done his surveillance.

No barking dogs nearby. He knew who lived in the house, knew the family's cars, knew their basic schedule, their routine. He'd followed the family online.

They were on vacation.

He had to smile. One thing he'd learned about places with security systems—it was a flag that there was something of exceptional value inside. In this case, the father often mentioned his collection of rare coins online.

Pop!

He'd broken the lock on the back window that

was nearly obscured in shadows. Contorting himself into the house, he moved quickly, taking stock, looking everywhere.

I want those coins.

First he'd see what other treasure he could get. Cash, jewels, credit cards. He'd amassed a lot of money in his career. Much of it was tucked away in offshore accounts. He was ready to slow down, maybe even retire with his perfect record—except for that one incident he'd witnessed. At times it still gnawed at him. That's the trouble when you're a compassionate thief.

Forget what you saw. It's in the past. Get to work.

As usual, he searched everywhere because he knew people hid things in unlikely places. He searched the washer, the dryer, the freezer, the fridge, the stove, toilet tanks, bookcases, spice racks, in cereal boxes, sugar and flower canisters, before moving on to the standards. He searched the study, the living room, sofa cushions, wall paintings then the bedrooms.

He'd worked his way through the master bedroom and was in the walk-in closet, checking the pockets of the clothes, when there was a sudden diffusion of light.

He turned.

A mountain of a man stood in the doorway.

He was holding a gun, pointed at him.

"Don't move, asshole!"

He slowly raised his gloved hands.

"Della!" the gun man shouted. "Call 911 now! We got an intruder!"

"Oh my God, Dan!" a woman shrieked.

"I want you to get out here," the gun man—Dan—told him, "on the floor. Get on your stomach or I'll put a bullet in your head."

He didn't move. His world had stopped. This was how it would end. The homeowners had inexplicably returned, and he'd never heard a sound.

"Move, asshole! Now!" Dan waved the gun and stepped back.

He moved with caution from the closet into the bedroom, got down on the carpet, the citrus scent of the cleaner hitting him with the realization that the life he knew, the life he loved, was over.

No, it can't end like this!

He felt a hand pawing him, patting him for a weapon. He felt the soft vibration on the floor of someone running up the stairs, someone approaching. Without thinking he twisted, kicked in a lightning attack that knocked Dan to his knees and sent the gun bouncing, sliding across the carpet, stopping several feet away.

He dove for it, but the now gunless man moved fast, blanketing him, crushing him with his body, sliding his arm under his neck, locking him in a choke hold just as a woman appeared. She picked up the gun and pointed at his head as he coughed for air.

"Freeze, you son of a bitch!" she screamed.

"Please," he gasped. "Can't breathe."

The man loosened his death grip. The panting of all three soon gave way to the sound of sirens approaching.

66

In the morning Karen knocked on Maddie's door.

"You're going to be late for school, honey."

No response.

Karen opened the door. Maddie was under her blankets with her back to her.

"I'm not going."

Karen sat on the bed. "Are you not feeling well?"

"My mouth is kind of sore."

Karen touched the back of her hand to Maddie's forehead. "Want me to give you something?"

"I just want to be left alone."

"Are you upset after the session last night?"

"I don't know. I'm confused about everything."

"Want to talk?"

"I just want to be alone."

Karen thought then said, "That's okay. I'll stay home with you."

"It's not necessary."

"No arguments, young lady," Karen joked, smiled and kissed her cheek. "I'll be in the kitchen."

Alone in her room, Maddie was admiring the Hope bracelet Tyler had given her, then staring at the sunlight filling her bedroom window when her phone vibrated with a call.

It was her uncle Cole.

"How's it going today, Maddie?"

"It's hard, really hard."

"Are you bothered by last night?"

"It wasn't easy. It's very stressful."

"I know, but you've got to keep doing your best."

"I'm not sure I can, Uncle Cole."

"Yes, you can, sweetheart. You can. Everybody loves you. We're all pulling for you. You can do this."

"But it's not easy, especially with the kids at school."

"What about them?"

"Most are nice but some are asking questions, like how come I can't remember anything, and some are saying mean things."

"Well, you're famous, and that kind of reaction from people comes with the territory. I know how it is. But kids will be kids and you just got to shake it off. Keep going. Take each day one at a time because that's how they come, and remember to do one thing."

"What?"

"To realize how blessed you are."

After her uncle's call she thought about what he'd said, not knowing how much time had passed before Karen returned with a tray she set on the table beside the bed.

"I want you to eat something. Come on, sit up and talk to me."

Maddie inventoried the scrambled eggs, bacon, yogurt, fruit, toast and juice. She picked up a strawberry.

"I know it's hard but talk to me, honey, please. What's troubling you?"

"I'm scared about a lot of things. I had this whole life here, and I don't remember it."

"It's going to take time."

"But it feels like I'll never connect with it. People tell me things, like I had a friend who died of cancer. Don't remember her. There was a boy I liked who moved to France. Don't remember him, even when I look at pictures of them."

"It'll come back. It takes time to process, like Dr. Hartley said."

"And the bad stuff I've learned about you and Dad, your tragedies, arguing with me, Dad pulling me into the truck in that video. That all scares me."

"I know. We have to work through that together. Try to concentrate on all the happy times our family's had, look at those pictures of us at Christmas, birthdays, Uncle Cole's barbecues—"

"But that's just it. I can't because I'm so afraid."

"What're you're afraid of?"

Maddie looked at her window.

"I'm afraid that whoever took me will find me and take me again."

67

Darrell Robert Nybee.

Aged twenty-nine.

They processed him downtown—fingerprints, mug shots, an array of charges. They submitted his prints to the state's computerized criminal record index then checked him for any prior criminal records.

Nothing came up.

Good-looking, clean-cut, no tattoos, possessing an air of intelligence, Nybee cooperated without speaking unless it was necessary.

His life as he knew it had irrevocably changed.

Furious with himself for what had happened, he took no comfort in the snippets of conversation the homeowners had given to the responding police unit. "Canceled flight…changed our plans…come home to find…" And the gun man he'd fought with was limping, grunting between curses before an ambulance took him away.

Nybee hadn't appeared before a judge yet. But bail was likely, the lawyer he'd called had told him.

Now, sitting in his cell wearing an orange jump-suit and waiting for her to arrive, he assessed his situation. He was jammed all right, but he had an ace up his sleeve.

A big one.

And this is the time to play it.

A series of electronic buzzes sounded, followed by clanking and jangling. Then the cell door opened and a guard appeared.

"Lawyer's here, Nybee, let's go."

68

In my darkness... I hear the soft bump of the ladder at my window...a dark shadow...a face in the night outside my window... I lay still... Oh God I'm frozen with excitement...thoughts galloping like wild horses... It's really happening...

69

The guard escorted Nybee to the secured visiting area and placed him in one of the small booths. Each side had a phone. A glass partition separated him from Wendy Bloom, his criminal defense attorney.

She looked to be in her late thirties, had a stylish bob with a side bang, wore a suit and looked all business when she pulled a legal pad with notes and paper-clipped reports from her briefcase.

She picked up her phone. He picked up his.

"Hello, Darrell, I'm Wendy Bloom." She gave him a business smile.

He nodded, thinking she had nice eyes as she glanced down at her notes. "I've got a summary of your background. I've read your information. No priors. You haven't seen a judge yet, haven't been arraigned. We have a good case for bail, but your charges are likely to be enhanced."

"Why?"

"You fractured the homeowner's knee when you assaulted him."

"I didn't mean to hurt him. I just didn't want him to exercise his legal right to kill me."

"Darrell, on the phone you indicated there's something I should know."

"I want you to negotiate reducing the charges and work a deal."

"And why should I do that? The case against you is pretty solid."

"I have information to offer on another case."

"Which case?"

"The case of Maddison Lane."

"The missing Syracuse girl?"

"Yes."

"But they found her in Florida."

Nybee explained what had happened a few years earlier when he was working on a house in the new Willowind subdivision. What he'd witnessed and what he'd recorded. He didn't tell anyone at the time because it would've put him at the scene of a crime. As he recounted details, Bloom's skepticism evaporated and she made notes. When he'd finished, she tapped her pen on her pad.

"What do you think?" Nybee asked.

"There could be something here to work with, but I'd have to see this evidence you claim to have before I consider approaching the DA."

"You will, as soon as you secure bail and get me out."

70

I am not alone in the dark anymore...he's really there...thoughts twirling in my head...swirling... making me dizzy...he really came...he's at my window...standing on a ladder like Prince Charming... my window's opening wider...slowly...wider... slowly...he's in my room... Oh my God you came... Dalton!... Dalton! I can't believe you're here in my room... I can't believe it's happening...so exciting... he came just like he said he would... "Want to go to cool party with me, Maddie? No one will ever know. We'll keep it secret just like the pictures we show each other... Come with me...it'll be so fun..." It's like a dream...like I'm Dalton's girlfriend...so cool...so exciting... I grab my shoes, my hoodie, my phone... I'm climbing out my window into the night with Dalton, the coolest cousin in the world...my heart's thumping so fast. I can't stand it...

71

Asher got two empty boxes with lids from the photocopy room and placed them under her desk.

"You know it breaks my heart when you do that in front of me, Fran," Zubik said after watching her.

"Don't look so forlorn. I'm not leaving for weeks. I'm doing this now because Nick Colson's been scooping up all the good boxes since he sold his house."

"Yeah, whatever." Zubik loosened his tie and spread his hands over his files and keyboard. "It's not you, it's this case."

"Lane?"

"Yes, Lane. We've hit a wall. The cognitive interview was a bust. The girl can't remember anything useful. How long has she been back, and we've got nothing. Nothing on who took her, what happened in the four years she was gone. Nothing on how she ended up in Florida."

Asher settled in at her desk and began working on her computer.

"Something will break. It always does, Stan."

"No, not always." Zubik sifted through the case file folders. "Did you make those follow-up calls to Castillo and Powers in Florida to see if they found any new video, anyone who had contact with Maddison before she got to the shelter?"

"I did this morning and nothing. But they're working on it."

Zubik began reading tips called in and shaking his head.

"So many unfounded reports that lead nowhere," he said.

"Also, once again," Asher said, "I submitted Maddison Lane's fingerprints, the ones we collected from her room when she vanished to AFIS, NCIC, Interpol, every database we can in case she'd been processed in another jurisdiction. Zero results."

"Look at this." He held up a page. "Another unfounded confession from a disturbed individual who says he abducted Maddison Lane into his spacecraft and is holding her hostage on Mars."

"Stan, we could try another recanvass of the mystery number, you know, the last number she'd communicated with before she disappeared, track the path on the map for the cell phone tower signals?"

Zubik didn't respond. He was reading another tip report.

"What is it?"

"A woman whose daughter attends the same

school as Maddison says there's a rumor flying around that the girl who returned to Syracuse from Florida might not be Maddison Lane."

Asher stuck out her bottom lip. "That's a new one. What do you think?"

Zubik dismissed it and tossed it back in the file.

"I think that one's nuts, too. That girl is Maddison Lane. We saw the birthmark, the age-progressed photos. It's her. This is just the seed of a wild conspiracy theory, from the tin-foil-hatted community."

"Stan." Asher smiled. "What happened to checking out every tip, every lead, no matter what, because that's what good detectives do?"

"All right, we'll check out this one right after we go to Mars."

Zubik's landline rang and he answered.

"Stan, Lorenzo Bartucci at the DA's office. I've been talking with a lawyer for a guy on burglary assault."

"Yeah?"

"Her client claims he's got solid evidence in the Maddison Lane case."

Zubik rolled his eyes. "And how many times have we heard such things over the years?"

"Well, his evidence is a video."

"A video?"

"The lawyer just showed it to me. It looks legit, and it's very troubling. You need to see it, Stan."

72

Karen finished washing dishes at the sink.

She looked out the window to the forest, happy and grateful to have Maddie back. But it pained her to see Maddie unable to adjust and connect with her family and the life they had.

In a corner of her heart, Karen tried to suppress the tiny concern that her daughter seemed different somehow than what she'd expected since her return. Karen hadn't seen any of her or Ryan's mannerisms or family traits in Maddie—not as she did when she was younger. It must be a result of the trauma she experienced. The doctors had warned that it could take a toll in a number of ways.

It tormented Karen that they didn't know what had happened to her in the four lost years. She couldn't bring herself to imagine what Maddie might have endured. And when Karen replayed what Zubik had said, how whatever happened to Maddie could still be happening to others, she grew terrified.

God, please help us find the answers we need.

Karen dried her hands on a dish towel, turned and was startled.

Maddie was standing in the kitchen, hand cupping her jaw and cheek.

"I've got a toothache and it hurts so bad."

Collecting herself, Karen took Maddie's shoulders. "Open up, let me see."

Maddie groaned and opened. It wasn't good. Everything was swollen and inflamed along her lower right gum. She wailed when Karen gently pressed her cheek.

"It really hurts!"

"Okay, get dressed. I'll call the dentist. We'll go right away."

"I saw a listing for a new dentist who specializes in emergencies," Maddie said. "Dr. Foley. Ow."

"Okay, I'll check."

Maddie got ready and Karen went online, made a quick call for an emergency appointment, then changed. In the car, Maddie leaned her head against the window, moaning as they drove to the practice of Dr. Samantha Foley. It was located in a new, small office complex.

When they entered the office—thick with its antiseptic smell—the receptionist hurried around her desk and greeted Maddie with a big hug.

"Oh my gosh, there she is! Our little hero!" The receptionist smiled. "I followed all the news about you. This whole city worried and prayed."

Stifling her pain, Maddie threw a questioning glance at Karen. The awkward moment was not lost on the receptionist, who had large-framed glasses and dangle earrings.

"Oh my gosh, I'm sorry! It's me, Kitty Marie. I used to work for Dr. Bannister, remember? Why didn't you go there? I mean we're happy to see you but he's your regular dentist."

"He's never been able to take us for emergency appointments in the past," Karen said, "and Dr. Foley's site said she welcomed walk-ins."

"She does. Sam just opened up here last month. She's from Albany—her husband's a doctor there and she's still back and forth until he opens his practice downtown. I left Dr. Bannister to work here because I live two blocks away. Oh, I'm such a gossip. Enough gabbing. Let's take care of Maddie. Karen, if you're still at the same address, I can set up a new account here if you'd just give me something official with your address."

Karen handed her family's health plan card to Kitty. "So we'll start with an entirely new file here for Maddie?"

"That's right. Have a seat. It'll just be a minute before the assistant will take Maddie into a room. Karen, you can go in with Maddie, if you like."

"Do you need me to be with you?" she asked her daughter.

Maddie shook her head.

"Sam's just finishing with another patient and will take you next." Kitty Marie returned to her desk and resumed working.

* * *

Veronica, the dental assistant, wore a face mask, hairnet, protective plastic glasses and gloves. After she guided Maddie into a treatment room where soft music was playing, Veronica made her comfortable in the patient chair.

Dr. Foley came in, also dressed the same way, but with glasses that had small headlights like those of a surgeon. She had very nice eyes and was smiling behind her mask.

"I hear you got a heavy-duty toothache," Foley said. "Let's have a look."

They reclined the chair until Maddie was lying flat. They swung the blinding dental light into position. Maddie opened wide and Foley examined her mouth.

"Does the tooth hurt at night?"

Maddie nodded.

"When was the last time you visited a dentist, or had X-rays?"

Maddie shrugged.

Foley made several technical comments to Veronica who made notes in the new chart they'd created for Maddie.

"You've got a few cavities there, and a few other issues, but your pain is from an abscess in the lower right. We're going to take some X-rays, then I'll freeze it and we'll take care of it, okay?"

Maddie nodded.

*   *   *

While waiting for the freezing to take effect, Dr. Foley reviewed Maddie's radiograph and the notes in her chart.

There were signs of gingivitis, a little plaque accumulation and tartar buildup. Judging from the cavities, Maddie showed a pretty high sugar intake. The radiograph showed some bone loss. Maddie might need a root canal and a crown or two down the road.

It appeared as if she hadn't seen a dentist in a long time.

Maddison Lane. Why is her name familiar?

It rings a bell, but I've been so busy these last weeks, bouncing between here and Albany. I'd like to see her records from the last time she visited a dentist. For now we'll treat her, take care of her pain, make appointments for future work and get her home.

Maddison Lane. Maddison Lane. I know I know that name...

73

After watching Maddie and Karen leave the dental office and get into their car, Kitty Marie smiled.

"Boy, that was something," she said as Dr. Foley and Veronica finished some paperwork at the reception counter.

Veronica pulled off her mask. "Yes, it breaks my heart to think of what that child's been through."

"Hold on." Dr. Foley pulled off her mask and removed her glasses. "Is that the girl who was missing all those years and was found recently?"

"Yes, Maddison Lane," Kitty said.

Foley nodded. "That's why her name's familiar."

"I know the Lanes from when Maddie was a patient at Dr. Bannister's." Kitty typed a few commands on her keyboard. "I got my friend Sally over there to transfer Maddie's old records to us. You've got them now, Sam."

"Thanks, I'll take a look. You got consent from the Lanes, Kitty?"

"Um, not yet, but Sally knows me. I'll send the

consent form to Karen, and we'll get it signed. It'll be okay."

Foley thought for a second. "Kitty, you know the rules about confidentiality and patient consent. We have to follow them. I'll let this go this time because it was an emergency and you worked at Dr. Bannister's office, but don't ever do this again. I want you to secure consent and stick to the rules every time. All right?"

Kitty's cheeks reddened. "Yes, Doctor. I got caught up in the excitement of seeing Maddie. Sorry."

"Okay, who've we got next?" Foley said.

"Ida Mahoney for a checkup and cleaning in twenty minutes."

"Thanks, Kitty. I'll be in my office."

Foley shut the door to her office, still a little rattled from Kitty cutting corners on the transfer of patient records.

This kind of thing could result in some pretty severe penalties, including the loss of her license.

What's done is done. We'll have to get things rectified. Foley took in a long breath and let it out slowly. She began working at her computer. As long as she had Maddison Lane's previous records, she might as well look at them and make notes for the next visit.

The radiographs had been downloaded with her digital chart.

Foley began reading them, comparing the results

with her new radiographs, when she stopped. She blinked several times, enlarged the images and leaned closer to her monitor.

Something's not right here.

In the radiographs from Bannister when Maddie was twelve, two of Maddie's first molars have resin restorations in them. Foley went to the radiographs she just made today. Those same teeth show no restorations at age sixteen.

What's going on?

And look, at age twelve she's got a missing adult premolar and a retained primary molar in its place, but at age sixteen the missing adult tooth is suddenly there?

"No, this is wrong. These are the wrong records. And this only makes matters worse," Foley said to the monitor, then got up and went to the front desk.

"Kitty, your friend at Bannister's office sent the wrong records."

"What? No, I'm sure she didn't. Sally's good at her job."

"Call her right now, please, and double-check."

Kitty reached for her phone, punched the number. Dr. Foley drummed her fingers on the counter, waiting as Kitty consulted with Bannister's office, looking at her computer monitor, checking, nodding several times before ending the call.

She put the phone back in its cradle. "Sally absolutely confirms that the records she sent belonged to Maddison Lane."

Foley stared at Kitty, thinking for a long time.

"All right," Foley said, and returned to her office.

Foley sat alone at her desk, studying her monitor.

She was staring at the dental records. Both sets were clearly labeled Maddison Lane, but the records were those of two different girls. Her stomach tightened. What does this mean for the family, for the girls involved, the case? The questions began spinning in Foley's mind.

She went online to read stories about the case, coming to a recent in-depth feature in the *Washington Post*. Her attention went to the part about the detectives having yet to determine who, or how, Maddison Lane disappeared from her bedroom, what had happened to her in the four years she was gone and how she surfaced in Florida.

The girl that was in my chair was not Maddison Lane.

Is that why the mother didn't take Maddison to Bannister?

Veronica knocked on Foley's door.

"Sam, I've got the next patient ready for you."

At home alone that night, Foley poured herself a glass of wine. Sipping from it, she read more news stories about the Lane case.

She'd also accessed her practice's drive from her home computer and studied the dental records again.

The tightness in her stomach had evolved into a knot. She didn't want to risk losing her license over this, and was struggling to determine the right course of action when her phone rang.

"It's me, got your message," her husband said from Albany. "Sorry, it's been one of those days."

Foley recounted everything in detail to her husband.

"Wow, Sam, that's just—my God. I agree you can't sit on this."

"I'm going to call your sister."

"Candy?"

"Yes. She'll know what to do, how to proceed."

Her husband thought about it. "Okay, I agree. Call her, then call me after you talk to her."

"All right."

Foley had her sister-in-law's business card next to her tablet and looked at it again before dialing *Special Agent Candice Young, Federal Bureau of Investigation. Los Angeles Division.*

74

They'd set up in a small boardroom at police head-quarters.

Lorenzo Bartucci from the district attorney's office had brought his laptop, and Asher helped link it to the large, wall-mounted monitor at the end of the room.

Along with Zubik, the new captain, Eric Flynn, a seasoned veteran promoted through the ranks, and Lieutenant Tim Milton had joined them at Bartucci's request to view the video.

"We're good to go, just play it," Asher said, shutting the door and dimming the lights.

The images were slightly grainy on the larger screen, but visually the video was strong and clear. The footage was taken from a second-floor window and showed a pickup truck parked in front of a rural house. The name on the side of the truck was clear: *Lane & Sons Drywall Contractors*. A man was standing at the front door of the house. In the bed of the truck were tools, including a shovel, and a tarp. It appeared that no one answered the front door. The nervous-looking man went to the back of the truck. The camera pulled in on the tarp, with its bulge and what appeared to be blood seeping from under the tarp. The man seized the shovel. As he turned his face, he was recognizable as Ryan Lane. He walked to a small forest and started digging, as if rushed. Then he came back and collected the tarp and whatever was under it, carrying it in both arms, walking back to the hole he'd dug in the forest.

"Well, that sure as hell is interesting," Milton said.

"This is why I thought you should see it," Bartucci said. "This was recorded by a man who was burglarizing the house near Willowind at the time."

"Why did he sit on this?" Milton asked.

"Self-preservation. In his mind, it would've put him at the scene of a crime and ended his successful career as a thief. He figured he could play his ace when he needed it," Bartucci said.

"And now he needs an ace," Milton said.

"Now, he's facing burglary and assault charges, and is angling for some kind of plea deal in exchange for this evidence and testifying, should it lead to charges."

"What do you think, Stan?" Flynn asked.

Zubik was flipping through a file with reports and notes. "Lorenzo, your summary says the video's date-stamped the day before Maddison disappeared."

"That's correct."

"But we've got witnesses," Asher said, paging through her notes. "The babysitter, Crystal Hedrick, her boyfriend, Zach Keppler, the pizza guy, Bennie Price, who all saw Maddison in her home the night before, so that should rule out any possibility that it's her under that tarp."

"Maybe, maybe not," Flynn said.

"Well, and this is puzzling," Zubik said. "Our crime scene reports indicate no traces of blood in Ryan's pickup or the family vehicle."

"I get that. I've been through the file too, and you and Fran have done great work, but we have something critical with this video." Bartucci loosened his tie. "As for the witnesses, they could've been mistaken, or the girl's disappearance could've been staged to cover for another crime. As for getting rid of the blood, Ryan Lane could've used a detergent containing active oxygen, could've washed the truck. The thing is, and I think all of us here agree that one day before his daughter disappeared, dad here, who in the past had struck her, who admitted money and temper problems, who did not pass a polygraph, is acting exceedingly suspicious in the video, and this footage is revelatory to everyone involved in the investigation. Wouldn't you agree, Stan?"

Zubik was nodding slowly.

"Oh, I agree all right, Lorenzo. This video changes everything."

"Yeah." Flynn clicked his pen. "This is a stunner. We need to determine exactly what Ryan Lane was doing. Let's get out to that property and see who he buried. All right, Stan?"

"Definitely."

At that moment, Milton's phone vibrated with a call.

He took it at the far side of the room, keeping his voice low as he listened. It didn't take long before his expression grew serious, and he turned to the others as if the call involved them.

"Okay, thanks for calling."

Milton ended his call, returned to the group. "You won't believe what's happened."

"After seeing this video, try us," Flynn said.

"That was a friend of mine with the FBI. We've got a dentist in town who needs to talk to us confidentially as soon as possible."

"A dentist?" Flynn said.

"She just treated Maddison Lane. Or, not. She says that the teen recently found in Florida who returned to Syracuse is not Maddison Lane, and she can prove it. She wants to meet us here with her lawyer."

"What the—" Asher looked at Milton and Flynn. "This case is busting wide open." Then she looked at Zubik.

He was staring at the image frozen on the large monitor, of Ryan Lane digging what appeared to be a shallow grave, and nodding.

"Wide open," Zubik said.

75

Gray Easton, the bow-tied attorney for Dr. Samantha Foley, withdrew a large laptop from his briefcase, set it on the table, entered commands until it displayed records in the case of Maddison Lane.

Easton then angled it, giving detectives Zubik and Asher a clear view.

"As we discussed, my client Dr. Foley will provide her analysis," Easton said.

Foley cleared her throat, then, pointing with a pen, began.

"On the left we have Maddison's radiograph taken at age twelve. On the right is Maddison's radiograph taken at age sixteen, yesterday, when her mother brought her in for emergency treatment of an abscess."

For the next several minutes, Foley pinpointed the differences in the records, concluding that they had been verified and cannot possibly be from the same girl.

"Is Karen, Maddison or the Lane family aware of your finding?" Asher asked while making notes.

"No, only my office and that of Dr. Bannister, who treated twelve-year-old Maddison, know. We've consulted with Dr. Bannister, who signed off on some administrative expediency regarding the transfer of records. We are all bound by confidentiality."

"To reiterate," Easton said, "my client is volunteering this, shall we say, preliminary information, but will retain the records until compelled by warrant to release them. She will then fully cooperate to give a formal statement and testify to her role in discovering what appears to be an impostor."

Zubik stared long and hard at the two sets of records, then thanked Foley and her lawyer.

Just like that the case pivots, Zubik thought. It was an astounding break, but they had to be careful against becoming overconfident.

76

Moving fast through the night...over the fence into the cool dark forest... I trip...my lace is undone... I break it... Dalton grabs my phone... "I can fix it so no one will know where we go."... We keep moving fast, his phone flashlight showing the way...branches smacking me...so thrilling, this is wild...we come out of the forest, a car is waiting... bigger boys, older boys, laughing, drinking beer... one moves the front seat, tells me to get in the back where another boy sits... I'm in the middle, Dalton's beside me...the music's throbbing...the car goes like a rocket through the city...they pass me a can of beer...the boys have drugs too...

"Drink up, baby," one of them says over the music...we drive and drive... "You didn't lie, Dalton, she's a hot little piece of ass!" Someone grabs my leg in the dark... I smack his hand away... I don't know where we're going...where's the party? Where're we going, Dalton? I can't hear, the music's so loud...we're going so fast, flying through the night...

We're far away from my home...in the country...the headlights find only woods...what's going on? We turn off the pavement, bumping down a road...we stop...nothing here, no one here...the music stops.

All is quiet. The doors open. They keep the car lights on. Everyone gets out, laughing, drunk, some are burping, some are peeing. Where's the party? Through the woods I hear the roar of waterfalls in the distance. "This is the party, baby, just you and us because you're such a cute piece of tail." "What? No!" One of the boys unzips his pants, grabs me so fast, forcing me to my knees, shoving my head into his...down there...

"Come on, you know what to do!" Pulling my hair. I fight. I struggle. They laugh. No, no, Dalton, why? No, I'm screaming. Dalton yells at them to stop. The other boys are bigger, stronger than Dalton, but he's fighting them. I'm fighting them, screaming. "Shut the fuck up!" I'm hit in the head... I see stars... I keep fighting. Dalton tries to help me... I'm fighting, kicking, biting, scratching, gouging, breaking free...running into the night, to the river, to the falls. Running for my life...

77

In the minutes after meeting the dentist and her lawyer, Zubik and Asher went to their captain's office where he and their lieutenant were waiting to be briefed on the case.

"The dentist just proved that Maddison Lane from Florida is not our missing girl from Syracuse," Asher said. "She's an impostor."

The captain and lieutenant traded glances.

"Unbelievable," Lieutenant Milton said. "So we could pursue criminal impersonation charges against the girl."

"Yes, but there has to be more to this," Zubik said. "Some things are starting to connect, fit and make sense. Let's go through the facts."

The detectives went through key points of the case. Since Maddison's return, the Lanes had resisted requests to fingerprint her. Perhaps they were fortunate that the Florida prints went astray, or they possibly had help. Consider how fast Cole Lane moved to pay the reward to Anna Croll, the Florida woman who helped identify Maddison,

Zubik suggested. The detectives also noted how during their interview of Maddison after her return, she held the soda without leaving prints on the can. They noted how the cognitive interview had failed; that, since returning, Maddison had been unable to recall, or provide, details of her experience; that they'd been unable to track Maddison's trail in Florida; the school rumor that the returned girl is not Maddison. And that they could never place the suspect, Kalmen Gatt, in her room. Then there was that disturbing video of Ryan Lane hauling Maddison into his truck and striking her in the time before she'd disappeared; there was Karen's arguing with her; and that the Lanes' polygraph results were inconclusive.

"All right." Milton took a challenging position. "What about the mystery phone number Maddison communicated with before she left? Where does that fit?"

Zubik shook his head. "Don't know, yet."

"Okay, then why?" Milton asked. "Why welcome this impostor into your home and pretend that she's your daughter? Why would the Lanes do it?"

"To cover up an accident, or some crime," Zubik said.

"But why?" Milton asked. "It's been four years and they've gotten away with any possible crime in the home all this time. So why accept an impostor to pose as their daughter?"

"Maybe something happened that risked expos-

ing them? Something that forced them to go the
impostor route. Something that we haven't discovered yet."

"Like what?" Milton asked.

"Could be anything. We just don't know. Let's
go back to the theory that the disappearance was
staged to cover something up," Zubik said.

"But the grave-digging video dates are off,"
Milton said. "That's a flaw."

"Maybe," Asher said, "Ryan was preparing a
practice grave?"

"A practice grave?" Flynn repeated.

"Maybe?" Asher said. "We don't know what he
put into the ground."

The room fell silent except for the creaking of
Flynn's chair as he rocked gently in it, thinking on
the next steps in the investigation.

"This is where we're at," Flynn said. "We can't
arrest or charge anyone, not just yet. We need more
strong evidence. We need everything documented
and locked."

"But we're close," Zubik said.

"We're very close but we need this to be solid.
Big pieces have come together, but we need to nail
everything down tight. We'll request warrants for
the dental records, and we should have the warrant to search the property by Willowind at any
moment now. I've already set things in motion to
marshal our resources out there."

"What about the Lanes?" Asher asked.

"We'll put an unmarked car down the street to

surveil the Lane house for activity," Flynn said as his phone sounded with a message. He read it. "And there it is. We've got our warrant for the property. Let's go."

78

For more than two centuries for as far as you could see, before the new Willowind subdivision emerged, the region produced corn, potatoes, onions, apples and other crops.

Dairy farms dotted the gentle rolling hills, and a few operations still remained alongside the rows of big new cookie-cutter houses.

After Zubik and Asher had arrived and served the surprised property owner with the search warrant, Zubik surveyed the area.

"Back in the day, I'd come out to this way with my old man to buy milk and cheese directly from a farmer who lived around here," Zubik said.

"And now it's a crime scene," Asher said.

Everything moved fast after the warrant. Syracuse police had cordoned off the section to be searched. Guided by the tipster's video, Blane Pierce, who led the forensic unit, had his team concentrate on the small grove near the property's edge.

The air hammered as the Onondaga County helicopter thudded overhead, taking aerial photographs. A cadaver dog had been brought in, and they unloaded ground-penetrating radar equipment from its trailer and moved it into place.

"With all this activity," Asher said as they tugged on coveralls, "how long do you think before word of our search gets out?"

"Not long."

Zubik watched the officer with the radar cart. The device looked like a lawn mower, and could detect where the earth had been disturbed beneath the surface by emitting electromagnetic energy into the ground. If it detected an object, it sent signals back to the surface where they could be read. Zubik was familiar with the model. It could penetrate some thirty feet.

The operator slowly crisscrossed a patch near the grove that approximated the area seen in the four-year-old video. Back and forth, back and forth, for nearly twenty minutes before he stopped, raised one arm and pointed to the ground with the other.

"He's got something," Pierce called to Asher and Zubik.

The operator inserted a series of small yellow flags into the ground outlining the target area. Two officers in coveralls headed toward it carrying shovels. Careful to use the same path into the scene, Zubik and Asher followed, stopping to observe from the edge of the flagged area.

As the first shovel bit into the earth, Asher turned to Zubik.

"After all these years, Stan, is this where it ends?"

79

"Oh, come on, pal, you know you can tell me."

Justin Rice smiled as he tried to massage information from one of his sources downtown. Phone pressed to his ear, Rice sat in his ten-year-old Toyota Corolla, knowing he had to get the smashed left taillight fixed. He looked at the blank screen on his tablet. He also knew that last week's fire at the east side bar was arson, but just needed confirmation for his story.

"Maybe tomorrow, Justin. Check with me tomorrow."

The source ended the call. Rice cursed and looked through his windshield at the boarded-up ruins of the bar. He knew the owner had torched the place to pay off a gambling debt that was tied to something bigger. Rice would not give up on the story, just like he wouldn't give up on being a reporter, despite being downsized in New Jersey.

He'd come back home to live in his mom's basement while struggling to sell stories as a freelancer and stringer for big national news organizations.

Problem was that while the rent and meals were pretty much free in Syracuse, the stories, the kind he needed to get his name on the front pages in New York, were scarce.

In the seven months since he'd been back, Rice was zealous, reconnecting with every source he'd ever known while connecting with a lot of new ones. "Justin will never burn you," that was the credo he lived by. He'd out-hustled a lot of the locals and had sold a few pieces to the *Washington Post*, the *New York Times*, *USA TODAY* and a few others. But it wasn't enough, and he was getting worried. He went online and checked his bank account again. His buyout package was almost gone.

Rice tapped his pen to his chin, thought again about moving to Los Angeles and staying with a friend, when his phone rang.

The number was blocked.

"Rice," he said.

"Hey there, muckraker."

Rice recognized the voice of one of his best sources, a guy plugged into the courts, law enforcement, all things crime-wise.

"Hey, how you doing?" Rice said.

"Great. Listen, Riceman, you should get your butt out to Willowind at the edge of town. Got one helluva story for you out there, and so far ain't nobody else knows a thing about it—all hush-hush."

"What's going on?"

Within minutes of being tipped, Rice was pushing his Corolla past the speed limit on his way to the scene. He was relieved when he saw an array of police and emergency vehicles, confirming that something was happening. At the same time, a court source gave him a summary over the phone of a search warrant for the property and warrants concerning dental records—"all related to the case of Maddison Lane."

After getting the standard "cannot confirm or deny" line from investigators at the scene, Rice, from a distance, took photos of police probing a site in the ground, then returned to his car, consulted his notes, sent off an email and began writing.

A moment later his phone rang.

"Justin, this is Lee Durrant, National Desk, *New York Times*. What is it you have there?"

Working to keep calm, Rice could not hide the nervous excitement in his voice as he relayed all he knew. It concerned the case of Maddison Lane, the Syracuse girl who drew national attention when she vanished at age twelve four years ago, but recently returned. Rice said new information had surfaced and detectives were working on a fresh lead that the teen found in Florida was not Maddison Lane; that the real Maddison Lane may have been killed, buried in a rural grave, and her abduction staged to cover it up, her parents inviting an impostor into their home.

"Wow," Durrant said. "Okay, we need to confirm everything. And it's all yours so far?"

"Yes, so far."

"I'm going to put some of our people on it to help you. Keep at it. I want you to keep me posted. Good work, Justin, and thanks for calling the *Times*."

80

Karen scanned the frozen ham, not noticing that the laser light hadn't read the bar code.

"Excuse me," the customer, a man with white hair and glasses, said. "I'd love a free ham, but it would be dishonest of me not to point out that you didn't charge me for it."

Karen was poised to bag the ham. She stopped, checked the display scroll on her register's monitor. The ham wasn't there. She entered the price manually. "Sorry, thank you." She gave him a distracted smile.

She'd been dwelling on Maddie for most of her shift. Karen had felt that Maddie had recovered from the dentist yesterday and insisted she go to school today. Still, Karen was anxious. When she'd texted Maddie asking how she was doing, all she got back were one-word answers.

"Fine." Or, "Good."

As Karen passed the man his receipt and coupons, her phone vibrated in her pocket with a call.

No customers were in her line so she took it, even though the store frowned upon personal calls.

"Is this Karen Lane, the mother of Maddison Lane?"

The number was blocked. Not recognizing the voice, Karen thought it might be the school.

"Yes, this is Karen Lane, Maddie's mother."

"Hi, Karen, this is Sue Landers with the *New York Times*. I'm calling for your reaction to the latest development in your daughter's case."

"Development? What development?"

Landers summarized what the *Times* knew, and Karen's knees weakened. She gripped the counter to steady herself.

"Mrs. Lane? What are your thoughts on this development?"

Clenching her eyes shut, Karen swallowed hard and barely voiced the words. "This can't be— It just— I have no comment."

She hung up, then called Maddie but got her voice mail. Fingers shaking, she texted her. Come home now! Don't talk to anyone! She then texted Tyler. Find your sister and bring her home now, do not talk to anyone!

Karen closed her till, rushed to the admin office.

"Bill, I have to go. Something's come up with Maddie."

"Karen, what is it? Can we do anything to help?"

Covering her face with her hands, she shook her head. Hurrying to her car, she tried to reach Ryan, but her call went to his voice mail.

She texted him. Come home now!

Climbing behind the wheel, Karen's entire body shook.

She fought her tears, her knuckles whitening as she drove home.

Ryan was on a job on the twentieth floor of a new office building, smoothing the outer edges of a joint to make the seams of the drywall sheets invisible, when he glanced at his phone, realizing he had accidentally switched it off during his coffee break. When he turned it on, it rang in his hand. Weird coincidence, he thought, and answered.

"Hello."

"Ryan Lane?"

"Yes."

"John Reeger, *New York Times*. We're seeking your response to…"

Reeger outlined the information he had. Stunned, thinking hard and fast, Ryan tightened his hold on his phone.

"None of this is true. I've got nothing else to say."

Confused, Ryan hung up, cursed, looked at his phone in disbelief. Without checking his texts or voice messages, he called Karen. She didn't answer. He texted. Don't speak to the press if they call. Meet me at home now.

Ryan hollered to Chuck that a family emergency had arisen and he had to leave.

On his way down the building's elevator, his mind raced.

An impostor? Willowind? A grave? What is this? It can't be true.

He couldn't think clearly. His thoughts shifted when he checked his voice mail and text from Karen, then he got a new text from her.

The New York Times just called me. I told them nothing. Meet you at home now!

On the ground, phone to his ear, Ryan trotted to his truck as the line clicked through to his brother's number. Heart racing, he told him about the calls from the *Times*.

"What the hell's going on, Cole? Do you know anything about this?"

"No. Let me see what I can find out. I'm on my way to your house. I'll call Jill and Dalton."

"Maddie! Maddie!"

Karen was the first to arrive home and rushed through the house looking for her. Maddie wasn't in her room.

Okay, Karen thought, maybe she was early and Maddie was on her way home with Tyler. *Why didn't I go to the school and get her?* Karen wasn't thinking straight; she had to take a breath and clear her mind. But it was futile. What that reporter had told her was a monstrous lie.

It had to be.

Karen heard the door as Ryan arrived.

"What's going on?" he asked. "Is she home yet?"

"No." Karen was on her phone. "I'm calling and texting the kids again."

"I called Cole." Ryan ran his hands through his hair and searched the house. "What did the guy from the *Times* tell you?"

"There's no answer from her."

"Karen? What did the reporter tell you?"

"It was a woman. She said they've learned that police think Maddie is an impostor, and they're digging for something near Willowind."

"Yeah, yeah, that's what the guy told me, too. I told him it wasn't true. I don't know what the hell's going on."

At that moment, they saw Cole pull into their driveway. He was talking on his phone as he approached then entered their house, finishing a call.

"Cole, what is it? What the hell's happening?" Ryan asked.

"All right, this what I've got so far." Cole rubbed his chin hard. "They've received some sort of new information. They executed several warrants, one to search a property out near Willowind and another for Maddie's dental records, suggesting the girl we found is not Maddie."

"Oh my God! That's— I took her to the dentist yesterday—but—" Karen lowered herself to the sofa, her hand covering her mouth. "This has to be some sort of horrible mistake!"

Tyler arrived home alone, concern blossoming

on his face as read the alarm in his parents and uncle's expressions.

"What's going on?" he asked.

"Tyler, where's Maddie? I told you to bring her home!" Karen asked.

"I asked around. No one saw her at school. I figured she was taking another day off."

"She didn't come home?" Karen rushed back to Maddie's room, examining it now with deeper apprehension. Her big backpack was gone. Many of her clothes, shirts, underwear, brushes, makeup and toiletries were gone, haunting Karen, knotting her stomach. For it pulled her back to that awful morning four years ago when Maddie vanished.

"Oh God, no." Karen nearly collapsed on the bed as the others joined her in the room. "She's gone!"

"I found this pinned to my pillow." Tyler held up the Hope bracelet he'd given his sister with a small note that said only: I'm so sorry, Tyler.

"I don't understand." Ryan looked at everyone, helpless.

No one spoke. The silence was broken when the doorbell sounded at the same time a phone vibrated with a message.

"That's mine," Tyler said, and raised his phone to check. His jaw dropped. "It's from Maddie. She sent me something."

81

Digging at the site near Willowind was slow and meticulous.

The investigators were mindful of removing layers of earth inch by inch. The excavated soil was placed carefully on the surface to be sifted and screened later for evidence.

They'd gone down four inches.

Nothing.

Then eight inches.

Nothing.

They'd gone down a foot when a tiny curl of tan-colored material broke the surface.

"Hold it," said Blane Pierce, the forensic team leader.

At this stage more photographs and measurements were taken as the excavation proceeded, akin to an archaeological dig. Smaller tools and brushes were used until the entire object was revealed: A canvas tarp, rolled into a small bundle of around two feet in thickness and close to five feet in length.

Adolescent size. Maddison Lane's size.

Asher turned to Zubik as the forensic team continued measuring and photographing. The detectives were beginning to get anxious, glancing back to the crime scene tape in the distance where other detectives had stopped someone. Somehow, some reporter, tipped to their break in the case, had arrived on the scene asking questions. If the press knew, it wouldn't be long before the Lanes found out, too.

After several long minutes, Blane Pierce gave the okay to remove the tarp and its contents from the hole.

82

"It's a video." Tyler stared at his phone.

"A video?" Karen went to him. "What does it say? Where is she?"

"It's slow to load. Hang on."

Cole answered the door. Jill and Dalton had arrived and joined them. As Cole updated them, Jill put her arm around Karen.

"It's loading, it's loading," Tyler said.

"Ty, come out to the living room," Ryan said. "Play it on the big TV."

Ryan switched on the set, and Tyler refreshed the video after the app on his phone connected to the television. Within seconds Maddie's head and shoulders filled the fifty-inch wall-mounted screen. Karen stepped closer to it, half reaching to touch Maddie who wiped at her tears before her voice filled the room.

"Okay, this is so hard." She blinked rapidly, staring at the ceiling. "Um, I don't know how to start. The truth. I'll start with the truth."

Maddie looked into the camera.

"Ryan, Karen, I am not your daughter."

Karen gasped.

"Tyler, I am not your sister. This is the truth. I swear to God, I don't know what happened to the real Maddie, or where she is, but I am not her. Okay, that's the truth. Who I really am doesn't matter. You, everyone, have been so good to me— that's why this is so hard. I'm sorry for all the pain I've caused, but I cannot go through with this anymore. I have to leave. Please forgive me. Don't try to find me."

Karen stepped back, sunk to the sofa, her eyes locked on the TV. Jill went to her.

Ryan stood frozen in disbelief.

Tyler shook his head, struggling to make sense.

As Cole dragged his hands over his face, he felt Dalton's eyes drilling into him.

83

At the site, two forensic investigators, suited head to toe, carefully hefted the rolled canvas from the ground.

They placed it down gently on a plastic sheet. Gloved hands delicately unfolded the soiled tarp, revealing the decomposing carcass of a large dog.

"A dog," Asher said.

It appeared to be a German shepherd. The sight of it angered Zubik.

"Why would Ryan Lane do this? How does it fit?" he said. "Why keep this from us? What was he up to, Fran?"

She shook her head while gazing at the remains. "That poor animal."

Photographs and measurements were taken.

In keeping with procedure, investigators resumed excavating the grave, digging down another foot. Then they used a metal detector and the mobile component of the ground-penetrating radar equipment to ensure nothing else had been buried under the remains. Nothing else was found.

"It's all clear," Pierce said.

"Thanks, Blane." Zubik made notes, reached for his phone to inform his lieutenant and captain, but turned to Asher before calling. "This whole case now smacks of something staged with a cover-up. We need to bring in Ryan, Karen and the girl posing as Maddison Lane."

At that moment, Asher received a text from the detective in the unmarked car watching the Lane residence.

"We better hurry, Stan. The unit sitting on the Lanes' house says there's a lot of sudden activity, people arriving, and I'm thinking with the press on us, it's going to blow up any moment now."

84

The girl's face was frozen on the Lanes' TV.

Karen shook her head, rocked back and forth, hugging herself on the sofa. "No, no, I don't believe this." She looked up at the face looking down at her. "Maddie's confused. She's having a breakdown. Look at all she's been through. She doesn't know what's real anymore."

Ryan stared at the screen as if waiting for the girl in the video to step from it and say that this was all a bad joke. When that didn't happen, he turned to his brother.

"Cole, what the hell's going on?"

"I don't know."

"Is this true what this—this fake—is saying?" Ryan said.

"Stop! Don't call her that," Tyler said. "That's Maddie—that's my sister! Mom's right. She's confused, she's flipped out. We've got to find her. Help me locate her phone, Dalton."

Tyler was texting, trying to reach Maddie on her phone. Dalton worked on his for several seconds then said, "Looks like she's disabled it. Shut everything down."

Ryan went back to Cole. "What the hell's going on here? Did that girl, whoever she is, set something up with the people in Florida to grab the reward money?"

Cole was shaking his head.

"I don't know."

Ryan turned to his sister-in-law. "Jill, what do you think is going on here?"

She shook her head, her eyes brimming with tears as she rubbed Karen's shoulders.

"Dalton? Do you have any ideas?"

He glanced at his father, then the others, then the TV.

"I don't know what's going on, Uncle Ryan."

Cole had gone to the window, took a breath and let it out slowly.

"Get ready," he said. "Two marked and two unmarked cars just arrived, and there's a TV news van coming up the street."

85

"You have the right to remain silent…"

Sitting across from Zubik and Asher, Ryan's world was coming apart, just as it had four years ago in this very room at police headquarters.

"Anything you say can and will be used against you in a court of law…"

The wounds he'd suffered when they'd first lost Maddie had been ripped open, and the same fears slithered around his heart.

She's gone, she's really gone. How much more can we take?

"You have the right to an attorney. If you cannot afford an attorney, one will be provided for you. Do you understand these rights?"

"Did you find Maddie?"

"Ryan, do you understand your rights and do you wish to have an attorney present?" Asher asked.

"I understand and I don't want a lawyer." Ryan signed the form, slid the pen to Asher, then said, "This is all a horrible mistake."

"You think it's a mistake?" Zubik flipped open his folder. "We've got dental records confirming the girl found in Florida is not your daughter. We've seen the video the impostor sent to your son. Now, we have another video to show you."

Asher turned her tablet to Ryan so he could see the footage of him approaching the rural house at Willowind, then taking the canvas from the bed of his truck and burying it.

"What were you doing at Willowind the day before you reported Maddison missing?" Zubik said. "And why did you fail to tell us about your activity there?"

Ryan's Adam's apple rose and fell as he looked at Zubik then Asher.

"I drove out to Willowind that morning to see about a contract in the new subdivision. I was behind this large truck, going around a curve when I saw the truck hit the dog. I honked, flashed my lights, but the truck kept going. So I stopped, got out and ran to the dog. It was so badly hurt. I got my canvas from my truck and wrapped the dog, I tried to comfort it. I put my ear to its chest, and there was nothing. The dog died in my arms.

"So I began knocking on doors to find the owner, but I couldn't. No one was around. I was upset. I couldn't just leave it. So I buried it and went on to my meeting with the builder, even though I was late. We didn't get that particular job, which put my company in a financial bind. I went right to the bank, was turned down for a loan, and then Maddie disappeared. With everything that happened, I completely forgot about the dog."

"That's your story, Ryan?" Zubik said.

"That's the truth."

"That's a good story. We believe you, but there's a problem," Zubik said.

Asher then played the video of Ryan pulling Maddie into his pickup truck and striking her. Then they played a clip of one of Ryan's earlier interviews with the detectives admitting to being violent with his daughter. His voice sounded tinny in the clip.

"When I got her in the truck she was out of control, kicking the dash, mouthing off about Karen, calling her mother a bitch, and I just lost it and smacked her with the back of my hand, told her to shut the fuck up... I told nobody what happened and Maddie said nothing about it, but I knew I'd crossed the line with her."

Zubik stared at Ryan without expression as he rolled up his sleeves.

"Here's what we think happened." Zubik stood, put his hands on the table and leaned into Ryan. "There was a lot of tension in your home with Maddison, with your business. When you and Karen came home from the movie that night, and after the babysitter had left, there was an incident with Maddison in the night. Something got out of hand, something went wrong and Maddie was hurt."

"No—"

"She was hurt so bad she died."

"That's a lie—"

"Maybe you lost control, Ryan. Maybe it was Karen, or Tyler. But you panicked. You remembered burying the dog the day before, so in the middle of the night you buried Maddison somewhere out there, too, where no one would see you. And if anyone did see you, you could say that you only buried a dog. That's why you never told us about Willowind, because you didn't want us looking out there. That's why your polygraph was inconclusive. Then you came back and set things in motion to make it look like Maddison was abducted. You put the mud streaks in the room, the ladder was in place, you took her phone into the woods, turned it on and off, then destroyed it. Maybe you carried some of her clothes into the woods for a scent, left one of her broken shoelaces."

"No, no, that's all bullshit!"

"And then this impostor surfaces in Florida, looking just like Maddison. Everyone believes she's Maddison. You don't question her identity, and you won't let us confirm it. You take her in because she's the perfect cover for your crime."

"No, no, you're twisting everything. You've got to find that girl, talk to the people in Florida who got the reward money."

"We're doing all that, Ryan. Got the FBI helping us."

Zubik stopped, drew his face even closer to Ryan's.

"It must've been so hard for you living this lie for all these years. Now's the time to unburden yourself, be a man and tell the truth. Where is your daughter?"

Ryan shook his head slowly.

"Ryan?" Asher's voice was soft. "Don't you think you owe Maddie that much?"

Shaking his head, biting back on his anger, Ryan looked around the room, feeling as if the walls were closing in on him.

86

"Just tell us the truth, Karen."

Karen refused to believe this was real—that it was happening again.

After reading Karen her rights, Zubik and Asher spent the next fifteen minutes hammering point after accusatory point into her heart. The fragile crust of whatever was holding her together was disintegrating, and she was losing her hold on reality.

"Karen?" Asher said.

"No, I don't believe any of this. It's all wrong."

Zubik and Asher observed her.

"We've seen the dental records, spoken to the dentists," Asher said.

"There's a mix-up, a mistake. Someone gave you the wrong records," Karen said.

"There's no mistake. The girl you took into your home, the girl you took to the dentist, is not Maddison," Asher said.

"No, no, it's Maddie. She's just overwhelmed. She was struggling to adjust, so she ran away. We have to find her."

"Karen," Asher said.

"That girl is my daughter!"

"Karen, she is not your daughter," Asher said. The detectives let a moment pass.

"It's time to stop the deception," Zubik said.

"Deception?"

"You're not telling the truth about what happened that night in your home." Zubik leaned forward. "Something bad happened to Maddison. Something went horribly wrong, didn't it?"

Karen said nothing.

"Things always seem to go tragically wrong in your life."

"What?" Karen's voice broke.

"Look at your history," Zubik said. "Those closest to you have died when you were near."

"What're you saying?"

"Your sister, Cassie."

"That was an accident."

"Your mother."

"Stop."

"And now Maddison."

"No, stop."

"You were arguing with Maddison, weren't you? You lost your temper, you snapped and something happened. You just lost it and you struck her. You didn't mean for it to happen. It was an accident."

"Stop."

"We found a grave."

"Oh God!"

Asher played the video of Ryan burying something wrapped in canvas in Willowind without revealing to Karen that it was a dog.

"Ryan took care of it, then planned the abduction story to cover it all up," Zubik said.

"Oh my God, no, no, it's not true."

"Then sometime over the years, somewhere along the line, something went wrong, something that threatened to expose everything, leaving you with no choice. You had to do something. Didn't you?"

"No!"

"That's why you needed an impostor. Maybe you hired her, maybe you had help finding her, but you needed her to ensure that no one would ever suspect the truth—that you hurt your daughter."

"No, no, stop!"

"And it almost worked didn't it?"

"Please stop—"

"And when this impostor emerged in Florida, you welcomed her into your home. Yes, we all believed it was Maddison," Zubik said. "She looked like Maddison in every way, right down to her birthmark. But 'looking like' someone is not proof. Yet you and Ryan were steadfast in your refusal to allow us something as basic as a fingerprint check to confirm she was Maddison because you didn't want us to know the truth."

Karen said nothing.

"It is a fact, Karen, that the Florida girl is not your daughter. She's not Maddison," Zubik continued, "because Maddison was killed in your home, wasn't she?"

Still Karen was silent.

Zubik slammed his palm on the table. "Tell us the truth!"

Karen's face went blank, her eyes emptied, she stared at nothing.

"The truth?" she whispered. "I don't know what the truth is anymore."

87

Hope.

Tyler looked into his hands. He was holding Maddison's pink fabric bracelet with the metal charm that bore the word. Then he returned the gaze of the detectives.

"Did you kill Maddison?" Asher repeated.

"That's a ridiculous question because she's not dead."

"Come on, Tyler. We've been over everything, the dental records—"

"They're wrong. Some clerk messed up. I told you, and the whole world knows. We found Maddie in Florida, brought her home, she had a hard time getting back into her life after four years. She had a breakdown and just ran away."

Zubik took in a long breath then let it out slowly.

"Why don't you tell us what really happened that night in your home when you heard voices in Maddison's room?"

"I already told you everything."

"You told us your mother and sister argued. Did

your mother hit your sister? Did your dad lose his temper? Who hurt Maddison that night?"

Tyler shook his head and rotated the bracelet in his fingers.

Zubik nodded to Asher, and they played the grave site video for him for the first time. As Tyler watched, his face whitened then went blank.

"Now," Zubik said after it ended, "you can see with your own eyes your dad buried something out there. So why don't you tell us the truth, now?"

"I don't know what that video is—" Tyler nodded to Asher's tablet "—or if it's even real, but I told you everything I know."

"Did you help your mom and dad cover up an accident?"

Tyler said nothing.

"You know the truth about what happened that night, don't you?" Zubik said. "And you know it's against the law to lie to us."

Still, Tyler was silent.

"Tell us the truth, Tyler. Who killed Maddison and where is she?"

Tyler kept rotating the bracelet with his fingers and staring at it until tears rolled down his face.

88

As the Lanes were being questioned, the search for Maddie's grave, and for the fugitive who'd assumed her identity, had intensified.

More investigators had converged at the Willowind site, where the operation had been expanded. Uniformed officers walked shoulder to shoulder, scrutinizing the ground for signs of a burial. More K-9 units had been brought out; maps were being reviewed.

Police called for more ground-penetrating radar equipment. In some spots soil samples were being tested for disturbance. The Onondaga County helicopter continued its work while aircraft chartered by news teams recorded the operation.

Across the city, alerts had been issued for the girl who'd claimed to be Maddison Lane. Her picture and description were circulated online and at the airport, the bus terminal, the train station and to the city's transit and cabdrivers.

In the Lanes' neighborhood, officers went door-to-door looking for her, and combed through the woods of Lucifer's Green, just as they had done four years earlier when the real Maddison Lane had disappeared, said one TV news journalist, reporting live from the scene before throwing to her anchor on the desk as they cut away to a news conference.

Downtown at the Public Safety Building, in the room used for major news events, Captain Eric Flynn took his place at the podium while other law enforcement officials stood behind him.

On one side of Flynn, an enlarged head-and-shoulders shot of Maddison Lane's impostor stared from a tripod. On the opposite side were enlarged photos of Maddison Lane at age twelve, and her age-progressed photos. The resemblance with all the photos was remarkable.

Flynn took stock, estimating upward of seventy news people had packed into the room.

"We'll get started," he said as blazing white light washed over him. Cameras clicked and flashed, and he began by giving a summary of the new developments in the Lane case, which repeated the points in the statement every journalist had received upon arrival.

"Not long ago the SPD received new information confirming that the individual who'd recently been located in Florida and thought to be Maddison Lane is in fact not Maddison Lane. We are in the process of attempting to identify and locate that individual for questioning. We can confirm that

Maddison Lane remains a missing person, and the investigation into her disappearance remains open and active. We're appealing to the public, to anyone with any information on this matter, to contact us. With that, we'll take a few questions now," Flynn said, opening the floodgates.

"Sir, the *New York Times* has published a leaked video showing Maddison Lane's father digging and burying something near Willowind. Did you find her remains and do you suspect he killed his daughter?"

"We're talking to all members of the Lane family. That is all we can say at this time."

"Do your investigators feel duped by the impostor?"

"No, because at the time the individual had emerged we had no real grounds to question her identity."

"But we understand she provided you no information about her whereabouts for the past four years."

"Yes, the individual appeared to have suffered trauma and memory loss and was undergoing counseling."

"Why wasn't her identity confirmed in Florida?"

"Florida officials did collect her fingerprints, but they were lost in a computer malfunction during the post-hurricane period. We must note that her birthmark was absolutely consistent with Maddison Lane's, and her parents had confirmed her identity, as well. At that stage we all wanted to believe, and did believe, that Maddison Lane had been recovered safely."

"How did you determine that the Florida girl was not Maddison?"

"We had official confirmation that we can't discuss."

"Was it fingerprints, DNA?"

"We're not going to discuss that at this time."

"What're you doing to identify the impostor?"

"We're analyzing fingerprints we have recently collected and DNA."

"We've heard the impostor left the family some sort of confession video. Do you have it and did the impostor have a role in Maddison's disappearance?"

"We've obtained the video, and determining the impostor's role in the case is part of the investigation. We're working with Florida law enforcement and the FBI."

"Do these developments cancel the reward? Will you request its return?"

"We'll work with the group behind the reward to determine where this falls into the investigation in terms of charges, or return."

"Are you looking at other suspects? Does this resurrect your interest in Kalmen Gatt, the inmate who was under suspicion early in the case?"

"In light of what's happened, we'll revisit every aspect of the case, follow up on all leads. All right, we'll wrap this up after one more question."

"Captain, do you believe we'll ever know what happened to Maddison Lane?"

Flynn took a moment to absorb the question, glanced at the large photo of Maddison taken before she'd vanished, then answered from his heart.

"I believe that we will find out exactly what happened to this twelve-year-old girl, and I believe it will be soon. Thank you."

89

I'm running...running...heart slamming against my ribs... I need help. The waterfall is getting louder. Running...falling...so dark...hard to see...sliding down the hilly ridge to the river...water misting on my skin...the banks, rocks are wet...slippery...

"MADDIE!" *Someone's calling...gaining on me...don't stop...the water roars like the whole world. The rocks are rough. Got to move faster to the slope ahead...the cold spray of the falls on my skin...my shoe wedges, foot slides out...*

"MADDIE!"

Oh God...can't find my shoe...

"MADDIE!" *They're gaining...the water's so loud...keep running... One foot cold, wet, the rocks biting into my sole...running to the slope...going uphill...grabbing, clawing at the tall grass, pulling up, faster, move, move to the top...the road... the paved highway...*

Running...running down the road...running and sobbing in the night...

Panicked, afraid, running, bleeding, aching, scrambling for my phone...call home for help...

No phone! Dalton took it.

Lights. Headlights, an approaching car. Standing in the middle of the road, waving my arms. Oh God, please stop, help me. The car slows, stops. Driver gets out. "Help me, please!" I know the driver! Oh God, I'm saved! Thank God! I'm safe now...

90

Everything was unraveling.

In his study, watching the news conference on his tablet, Cole grappled with the images and fear blazing through his mind.

The impostor's video, the hunt for her, the search at Willowind for a grave, that damning footage of Ryan burying something—and knowing that right now, Zubik and Asher were questioning Ryan and Karen about it all.

Cole's phone kept ringing with media calls—CNN, the Associated Press, *USA TODAY*—but he never answered.

Battling to stay calm, he glanced at his treasured photos of Jill and Dalton, his medals and awards—all he had achieved in his life. The phone rang again. He was under attack just as he was that day in Afghanistan, and just as he did that day, he took action to protect lives.

That's what he did.

I had to do it. There was so much at stake and there was no way out.

Jill appeared in his study, terror in her eyes. "Cole, what's happening?"

He looked at her without speaking.

"Dalton's going out of his mind. He's crying. I've never seen him like this, and I can't get anything out of him," she said. "He's scaring me to death. He said that you knew from the start that the girl from Florida was not Maddie. How could that be?"

Cole didn't respond. He searched his wife's eyes, but failed to find the words to begin.

"Cole, please. I'm so afraid! What do you know about Maddie?"

Unable to face her, he lowered his head then glimpsed his gun safe in the corner, noticing a slight shadow at the door's seam, noticing with rising concern that it was not locked, and he always kept it locked.

Always.

"Jill, did you go into my gun safe for any reason and not close it?"

"What?" Jill followed his attention as he stood, quickly checking the inventory.

"My Glock's gone."

"I never touched your gun safe. Who would take your gun?"

They looked at each other for answers as alarm coiled up Cole's spine.

"Where's Dalton?" Cole said. "You said he's upset. Where is he?"

"In his room." She read the fear in Cole as he shot past her, and she followed him to their son's room.

They found Dalton.

He was sitting on the edge of his bed, contemplating his lap where he was holding his father's handgun.

His computer was on, with the news coverage of Maddie's case flashing on the monitor and a reporter's voice sounding small from the headphones.

"Son." Cole moved toward him slowly. "I want you to give me the gun."

Dalton didn't move.

Jill came in behind Cole. Both hands flew to her mouth.

"Give me the gun," Cole said.

"No, you stay right there," Dalton said. "Don't come any closer!"

"Son, please. Look at me." Cole inched forward.

Dalton raised his head, a strange look on his tearstained face. "This whole thing is my fault. I've been living with it all these years, ever since that night."

"Listen to me, son. It's *my* fault, but we're all going to get through this."

"I've carried this secret for all these years. It's been tearing me apart."

"Please, Dalton, give me the gun and we'll talk."

"Ever since I discovered the truth about me."

"What are you talking about?"

"You lied to me," Dalton said.

"Lied? About what?"

"My real mother tried to flush me down a toilet when I was born. She was a crackhead whore. She didn't even know who my father was."

Cole and Jill exchanged looks.

"Who told you this?" Cole said.

"I found out myself four years ago—that you lied, telling me my mother died giving birth when you told me I was I was adopted. I looked in your office. I found some papers about me, my adoption and my mother. Then I searched for her."

Cole and Jill were silent.

"That time when I supposedly went to Newark with friends for a concert, I found her in Brooklyn. She's an *exotic dancer*. She cried then offered me money, then drugs. It made me sick, so angry that I came from that disgusting world, that I was worthless."

"Oh, Dalton, no, you're not worthless!" Jill said. "You're everything to us. We were trying to protect you."

"I never understood who I was, where I fit in. I was angry. I didn't give a shit about anything, about anybody. I was drinking getting into trouble. That night with Maddie, I wanted to have fun, impress my older, cooler, so-called friends. It was stupid. You know what happened to her. I told you the truth, everything."

"Son, please."

"And I don't know what you did or how you did it, but now everything's worse. It's replaying all over again…it's like we killed her twice." Dalton seemed distant, lost.

"Oh my God!" Jill groaned. "What're you talking about—"

"And it's my fault!" Dalton screamed. "My fucking fault! I was never meant to be here!"

Dalton thrust the gun to his temple, his finger on the trigger. Cole leaped at him as Jill screamed. Cole shoved Dalton's hand, pushing as the muzzle flashed, the room exploded—POP! The round missed Dalton by a fraction, smashed into the ceiling and Cole crushed down on his son, twisted the gun from his hand, stood and unloaded it.

Jill took Dalton into her arms and held him as he sobbed.

"It's over." Cole gasped for breath, inspecting the gun. "I'm going to put an end to it all."

91

Cole Lane stepped from his SUV as a news helicopter thundered over his brother's house, hovering above Lucifer's Green where officers were searching the woods.

Police units, media cars and trucks lined the street, forcing Cole to park over a block away, just as he had done that awful day four years ago.

Taking quick stock of Dalton and Jill, he steeled himself and they walked to Ryan's house.

Before they'd left their home, Cole had told Jill everything—everything that Dalton had done, everything that he had done. Overcome, she'd rushed to the toilet and vomited. She locked the bathroom door and sobbed on the floor for a long time before she managed to find a veneer of composure. Numbed by the revelation, her skin had whitened. Now, depleted and destroyed, Jill was robotic as she stepped toward the coming storm.

Cameras turned when reporters spotted them and fired a rapid line of questions.

"Do you think Maddie's disappearance was staged to cover a crime?"

They didn't answer.

"Cole, do you think your brother's family killed your niece?"

"Did they try to cover up Maddie's murder?"

"Where's the real Maddie?"

Cole waved them off without responding as they got to the door and entered amid a final volley of questions and camera flashes.

Inside, Ryan greeted them with traces of alcohol on his breath. Karen, tearful and trembling, hugged them all. Tyler exchanged embraces with his aunt and uncle as they went to the living room.

"This is a horrible, horrible, nightmare," Karen said.

"Zubik's saying that one of us killed Maddie because I buried a dead dog in Willowind, and now they're talking about charges— I just— I just—" Ryan's voice was breaking.

"Hold on, just hold on." Cole took his brother's shoulders and directed him to the sofa. "You all need to sit because it's time you knew the truth."

"The truth?" Karen asked. "What're you talking about?"

"Listen, first I want you to know that Jill, and for most part Dalton, had no knowledge of what I'm going to tell you, and that I've already contacted my attorney and we'll be telling Zubik everything. We'll be confessing."

"Confessing?" Ryan said. "I don't understand."

"*I* arranged to have Maddie found in Florida."

"You *what*?"

"Half a year ago or so, I got my people who were searching for Maddie across the country to use the age-progressed pictures we'd created to find someone who would look just like her now."

"I can't believe this," Karen said.

"It took time. They eventually found a girl named Maya Starr Gagnon living in a homeless shelter in Los Angeles. She was Canadian. She'd just turned eighteen. She wanted to be an actress. She was smart, independent and had run away from abuse in a broken home."

"But her birthmark—"

"We had that tattooed on her," Cole said. "I convinced Maya to assume Maddie's identity, promising her a good life with a good family. When the time came, we thought it best that she surface as Maddie during the chaos of a natural disaster like the hurricane in Florida, with no memory of what happened. And through friends of friends with access to the right databases, I had them remove her fingerprint records and make it look like an IT issue."

Ryan was breathing hard, glaring at his brother. "You— How could you—" He rubbed his temples. "Why would you do this when we still had hope of finding Maddie? Why the hell would you do this?"

"I had to."

"Why?"

Cole turned to Dalton, put his hand on his shoulder, and everyone's gaze shifted to him.

Dalton began shaking his head, tears filled his eyes.

"I can't, I just can't," he said.

Jill took his arm. "You have to, Dalton. It's the only way."

Ryan, Karen and Tyler struggled to comprehend what was happening as Dalton brushed at his tears.

"Maddie had a crush on me and I liked it," Dalton said. "We texted, then we started sexting a few times using self-destructing messages. I showed her how to keep things secret, and I had a disposable phone I used. She told me she wanted to start dating, that she argued with Aunt Karen."

Karen covered her mouth with her hands. "Oh my God! You sexted with her?"

"I liked her. Maddie wanted to have fun, so that night when I was going to go to Jenna Guthrie's birthday party with some of my older friends, I started texting Maddie about it. She wanted to sneak out and go with us. I told my friends, and they said that it would be fun to get Maddie drunk for the first time."

"Jesus," Ryan growled, barely containing himself from launching at Dalton.

"We parked on the other side of the woods so no one would see. I came to the back of the house. I knew the ladder was there. I was the one who got her to come with me—she wanted to come with me. I disabled her phone so no one would know where she was."

Ryan kept shaking his head, seething.

"We got into the car. The other guys were drinking, doing drugs." He paused then continued. "We gave Maddie a beer. I don't think she drank more than a sip. I don't think she liked it. We drove out to Ranger Falls to get her drunk there, then go back to the party for a while then take her home, but it didn't happen that way. My friends were pretty drunk, and when we got to this isolated place in the bushes near the falls, one of the guys, he—he—"

"He what?" Ryan shot at Dalton.

"He tried to force Maddie to go down on him, and she screamed and fought back. I tried to fight him, too, tried to stop it, but the other guys were older, bigger and they all had the same idea. I swear I fought them and so did Maddie. That's how I really got scratched up that night."

"What happened to Maddie?" Ryan was quaking, on the verge of erupting.

Dalton blinked at the memory as if he had been pulled back into the events. He began breathing harder. "She got away and ran fast into the woods toward the falls. It was so dark out there but I chased her. I wanted to get her, help her and find some way to get her home. I followed her down to the river, just below the falls. You know how it rushes so fast, the rapids, and the noise. I saw her running in the distance, then she was gone. I found her shoe, but I couldn't find Maddie. We looked until we knew that she must've—"

"Must've what? Where is she?" Ryan shouted,

taking a step closer toward his nephew. "She must've what, Dalton?"

"She must've fallen into the water and got carried downstream to the hydroelectric complex and got sucked into the big turbines. I'm so sorry, I'm so sorry." Dalton dropped to his knees, sobbing. "I'm so sorry."

Karen was crying, gasping, screaming. "Oh God, oh God!"

"You're sorry?" Ryan exploded. "You and your perverted asshole friends, and my fucking *brother*, knew our child was dead, keep it secret all these years—"

"Let me explain," Cole said. "I didn't know until Dalton told me half a year ago. I was stunned, devastated. I didn't know what to do. Yes, my first instinct was to turn him in, but that would've destroyed both of our families."

"So you were thinking of yourself, again!" Ryan's eyes narrowed.

"No, Ryan, listen! I realized you had already suffered so much for four years and that Maddie wasn't coming back, and we'd likely lose Dalton, too. That's why I did what I did."

"All these years," Ryan said, "all the pain we've been through all these years, being accused of killing our own child. Then you bring her back, give us hope, only to take it all away and leave us with nothing but lies!"

"You and Karen were dying day by day from the pain of Maddie's disappearance. Yes, I knew she was gone, so I did what I did to protect lives, to pull you all out of the darkness just like you pulled me from mine. I had to do something! So I thought I could give Maddie back to you and hang on to Dalton. I know it was stupid, it was wrong, but I was blinded, too."

"You bastard!" Ryan stood toe to toe with his brother. "What? Do you think we should thank you? Maybe give you a medal for playing God with our lives to protect your perverted kid who's responsible for killing ours?"

"I was wrong."

"You, you—"

Ryan drove his fist into Cole's face, sending him sprawling to the floor, then straddled his chest, seized his head in his hands, leaned to his ear and hissed so only he could hear.

"And I know you fucked my wife, asshole!"

Adrenaline pumping full bore, Ryan's hands blurred as he landed punch after punch on Cole's head. His brother didn't fight back. He was barely able to cover his face with his arms as the blows rained down with such savage force, it took every bit of strength Karen, Jill, Tyler and Dalton had to pry Ryan away. He stood over Cole, chest heaving, tears and spittle flying as he screamed.

"Get out of my fucking house before I fucking kill you!"

92

Cole's and Dalton's confessions resulted in a massive search along the Ranger River for new evidence in the case.

Drones flew along the banks and over the rugged brush and fields surrounding the area where Dalton had found and hidden Maddie's shoe years ago. Searchers walked side by side along the river, combing the terrain for traces of Maddie. Cadaver dogs trained to find human remains were used, along with ATVs and horses, to scour the undergrowth.

Police divers tethered by ropes probed the dangerous rushing water in an extensive search encompassing the Ranger Dam and the hydroelectric complex. Authorities operating the facility had agreed to shut down its big turbines to allow technicians and police to examine all of the equipment for any evidence of human remains.

Every aspect of the plant's turbine system was meticulously scrutinized, inspected and swabbed, the propellers, the blades, the gears, teeth and shafts, despite the odds. Given the volume of water, and the velocity at which it would have traveled through the system over four years, it was unlikely anything would be found.

Nothing was.

The search continued downriver for miles.

Dalton and Cole Lane had been charged with obstruction of justice.

More charges were coming, pending further investigation.

After they were processed and had made their respective court appearances, they were granted bail.

The investigation led Zubik and Asher to reinterview Jill Lane for more details of that night. Jill knew nothing of Dalton's and Cole's acts, reiterating how when Dalton missed his curfew, she'd driven into the night looking for him in vain.

The investigators still hadn't located the impostor, Maya Starr Gagnon. No new aspects of the case had emerged from Florida.

But Zubik and Asher had tracked down and arrested the others who were involved in Maddie's disappearance: Donnie Slade, his older brother Lennie, but not their friend George Street, who had been killed in a motorcycle crash the previous year. The Slade brothers were also charged with obstruction for lying in their statements and interviews with investigators, and concealing evidence about Maddie's disappearance.

But as with the Lanes, additional and more serious charges were also coming for the Slades.

Lorenzo Bartucci at the DA's office was working on it, putting in long hours every day. He was wrestling with a complicated case, given the circumstances and the ages of the victim and the others at the time. Certainly for Dalton and the Slades, there were grounds for charges related to kidnapping, possible criminal sexual acts and for causing the death of a person under the age of fourteen in the course of committing other specified crimes. He was building a case for second-degree murder with a sentence of life, or at least twenty-five years, in prison.

But considering how this case had evolved, with its twists and turns, Bartucci needed it to be rock-solid. And it wasn't. Not to his way of thinking. Compounding the challenge, in his view, was the fact that so far no body had been recovered, which, at this stage could render much of the case circumstantial.

The story was back in the national spotlight. Again.

This time reporters eviscerated the Lane family's troubled history, generating a social media storm. People across the country and around the world pilloried the family as criminal frauds who had murdered a twelve-year-old child.

Others were sympathetic.

"This is a horrible tragedy, and our hearts are

broken all over again for Maddie and her family," Maddie's friend Amanda Morber said.

A national TV network had interviewed Amanda during a candlelight memorial for Maddie at the Ruby Green Community Hall. It was the same building that had become the official search center when Maddie first went missing; the same building that held the celebration when everyone believed Maddie had been found. Now, it was the place where those who loved her had come to remember her in death.

Again, large photos of Maddie at age twelve were displayed.

"I just can't believe this," Maddie's friend Nicole Webb sobbed before the camera. "My heart goes out to her family for what they've been through. They're absolutely shattered and I pray for them."

News cameras recorded Ryan, Karen and Tyler supporting each other as they walked the few blocks from their home to Lime Tree Street and the community hall to take part in the service.

The flickering flames of the candles they held lit their grief-stricken faces. Karen and Tyler were too distraught to address the gathering.

They went to the makeshift podium where Ryan struggled but managed a few pain-filled words.

"Thank you for your love and for your support," he said. "We pray that Maddie is at peace in Heaven and making God smile."

During the service, Tyler's free hand was pulled into a fist.

From time to time he opened it. He was holding the bracelet he'd given Maddie upon her return. In the candlelight the small gold metal charm glittered with one word:

Hope.

93

Lewis Perez didn't move as fast as he used to.

At seventy-three, Perez, a Vietnam War veteran—Private First Class Infantry—seemed to discover a new ache every morning he took Buster, his beagle, for their morning walk.

They strolled through their quiet section of Syracuse, slivered between the neighborhoods of the Southside and the Near West Side, a community where life was not easy. Most folks struggled to get by, like Perez who survived on a fixed income.

It saddened him too that so many people he'd known had died over the years. Like Sonja, whose house they were nearing. Sonja had died, oh so many years back. Was it three, no, four now? She was a lovely woman who always came out to her porch or the sidewalk to gossip, always had a treat in her pocket for Buster. He still wagged his tail every time they passed her place, expecting to see her and get a treat.

This morning was no different.

Only this time he kept barking and pulling harder than usual.

"What's gotten into you, Buster? You know Sonja's not there anymore."

She had lived in her house with her grown son, and it was a shame how he'd let the place go after his mother's death, Perez thought as he felt the tension on Buster's worn old leash tighten before it snapped and the dog ran onto the property. He'd never run into the yard before.

"Jeez! Buster, get back here!"

The dog bolted to front the porch, barked at the door, then ran around to the side of the house. That cheerful, short-haired hound was good company, but he was also very nosy.

Perez started after him, assessing the old two-story wooden house. It was an American Four-square, a style built in the 1920s, with a full front porch and a roof that had a central dormer.

But it was falling apart.

The yard was overgrown, shingles were missing from the roof, paint peeled and blistered along the walls, some of the exterior shutters had slipped from their mountings and the glass in a few of the windows had fractured. The mailbox was jammed with flyers.

Yes, a damn shame Sonja's son had let it go. Perez sighed as he walked along the driveway, looking at the dilapidated garage set back in Sonja's deep, narrow lot. A tired-looking, rusting sedan was parked in front of the garage. Buster was barking and scratching at the side door of the house, when suddenly his weight pushed it open and he vanished inside.

"Buster! Get back here! That's an order!"

Perez got to the door and called again. No sign of him, but the side door creaked open wider as if inviting Perez to enter.

He recoiled when a wave of air carrying the stench of human waste and garbage greeted him as he stepped into the side entrance. Not good, Perez thought, covering his nose and breathing through his mouth.

"Hello? Buster?"

He came to the kitchen first where flies strafed the unwashed dishes piled in the sink. The table was heaped with newspapers and fast-food containers. He moved to the dining room, glanced at the spiders, wriggling along their webs on the windows and the hutch. In the living room he saw piles of empty soda cans, stacks of stuffed plastic garbage bags, then one, two, three mice scurried across the stained, worn area rug.

Something above him creaked, and he heard a faint bark.

"Hello! Anyone home? Buster!"

Perez found the stairs and climbed to the second floor.

The stench grew even more penetrating as he came to the first bedroom still holding his nose and breathing through his mouth.

Towers of sagging cardboard boxes with the

word *Mother* scrawled on them teetered along one wall. Beyond that, the room was empty.

In the second bedroom he found clothes heaped on the bed, shoes lined around it. Otherwise the room was empty.

The bathroom: empty.

Then he heard the scratching of Buster's claws on hardwood, panting and barking, drawing him to the next bedroom.

Perez froze.

He saw an overturned wooden chair, then a corpse above it hanging from a rope affixed to a hook screwed into the top of the door frame.

Its wide eyes stared down at him.

Jolted, Perez stepped back in shock. The gagging stench forced him to press his hand harder over his nose and mouth, and he mentally recited a prayer. Man, this was so sad.

It was Sonja's son. Perez struggled to remember his name.

Bennie.

In his life, Perez had seen death in all its forms. He figured Bennie had been dead for a long time. He was no expert, but he guessed maybe a week or so.

This must've been what had Buster so curious. All right, keep calm. Perez knew what to do. *Don't touch anything. Call police.* He slid his free hand into his pocket for his phone when he heard a faint cry from lower in the house.

Buster barked and darted down the stairs.

Perez went after him, guided by the sound of Buster's barking. He'd returned to the kitchen and closed a pantry door, which, when open, had blocked the door to the basement.

"What the hell?"

The basement door was barricaded. Steel brackets bolted to the frame held a section of standard two-by-four-inch board. The length blocked the door from opening, sealing whatever was down there.

Buster was barking and scratching.

Perez considered options—number one: calling police and waiting for them. Perez bit his lip. He wasn't afraid; he wasn't stupid. But he was, like Buster, inquisitive. He needed a weapon to defend himself. Thinking, he glanced around, opened a utensil drawer and selected a meat cleaver. Then he lifted the two-by-four and opened the door to the yawning, stinking darkness.

Buster yipped and ran fearlessly down the stairs into the black.

"Hello down there?" Perez called while searching for a light switch.

The sound of a chain moving made the little hairs on the back of his neck stand up.

Buster was growling.

Perez fumbled for his phone and used its flashlight. The first step creaked as he stepped on it.

"Who's down there?"

A chain moved again.

Buster was panting and making nervous yips.

The light from Perez's phone found a workbench, a furnace, shelves with jars and jars of what might've been jam or preserves, discarded trunks, food wrappers, empty water bottles, then stacks and stacks of pizza boxes.

The windows were painted black and secured with metal bars.

Perez's light found a portable toilet then another bucket, a mattress and the chain he had heard. He followed chain to a human ankle. In the light he saw Buster's eyes reflected—then a second pair of eyes.

They belonged to a girl who was hugging Buster and whimpering, trembling.

"Dear Jesus," Perez said.

The girl was sobbing softly and trembling.

"Help me, please help me. My name is Maddie."

EPILOGUE

Three Syracuse patrol cars converged on the house.

An ambulance rushed Maddie to the hospital where she was admitted through emergency. Zubik and Asher waited in the hall to interview her as she underwent several tests, including a DNA swab, then a rape-kit exam conducted by a female nurse.

Doctors found that Maddie had been sexually assaulted.

They compared her DNA with that of the dead man found in the house to determine if he, as most believed, was her attacker. The medical team's examination had also determined that Maddie was emotionally distraught, emaciated, malnourished and dehydrated.

"But remarkably, her vital signs are good. We'll run an IV and feed her intravenously for a short time," Dr. Olivia West informed the detectives as she uncollared her stethoscope. "You can go in and talk to her. You'll have a little time before we give her a sedative."

Despite her weakened state, Maddie managed to tell the detectives everything; how she'd fought with Karen, how she'd had a secret sexting relationship with Dalton, how she'd wanted to go to the party and how things went horribly out of control with the other boys and how Dalton had tried to intervene.

She stopped often to sip water because her throat was dry.

Maddie recounted how she escaped back to the highway and how miraculously Bennie, the pizza guy, was in the car that stopped. She was so relieved because she knew him.

After telling him everything, Bennie said he would protect her from the bad boys, and the best way to do it was for Maddie to spend the night at his house. Bennie didn't want to take her home because it was so late and her parents would freak out. He said he could take her home in the morning and help her explain. Maddie didn't want that. She screamed, demanded Bennie take her home, but he hit her and she lost consciousness. When she woke up, she was chained to a mattress in his basement.

The next morning Bennie had told Maddie that her case had turned into such a big deal that he could never take her home because he'd go to prison. Maddie cried her heart out, begging and pleading. Bennie cried, too. He said that ever since his mother died he was so lonely in the house that he decided he would keep Maddie to be his forever-friend. During her time in captivity, he fed her, gave her books to read, even a big dictionary and encyclopedias. Maddie tried to educate herself by reading them all, and the whole time, even when Bennie did terrible things to her, she begged and pleaded for him to take her home every day, saying how she ached to be with her family again. Sometimes she felt that she had died and her basement prison was hell. Sometimes she would relive the details of that horrible night in her mind over and over.

Maddie said it felt like a week since Bennie had last visited with her. Before that he'd seemed so sad all the time. He complained that he had headaches and would sit in front of her mumbling how his dead mother was calling him to be with her. Just babbling and not making sense. He kept holding his head, finally telling her that he was going away for a while. He left her some extra water and food and was gone.

When the detectives told Maddie that Bennie was dead, she stared at them without an expression.

"He was my only link to the world. I don't know what I feel, or if I feel anything at all for him," she said.

"Let me see my daughter now!" Karen Lane's anguished voice echoed down the hospital corridor.

Upon leaving Maddie's room, Zubik and Asher saw half a dozen uniformed officers and medical staff contending with her overwrought family. Dr. West waved for the detectives to join her as she guided Karen, Ryan and Tyler into an empty office. Then as the doctor gave the family a sensitive but accurate assessment of Maddie, including the most horrific aspects, Karen sobbed and Ryan and Tyler held her.

"But she survived," West said. "And given all that time, all she's endured, she's in good condition. With care and counseling, Maddison will recover."

West said that when Maddie woke in a couple of hours her family could see her.

During that time, Zubik and Asher summarized some of what Maddie had told them. And this time around, they would compare her DNA with the DNA they'd collected from Maddie's hairbrush in her room four years ago, to confirm what everyone knew to be true—that this was the real Maddie.

It seemed like a lifetime had passed before a nurse informed the Lanes, "She just woke. We'll give it five minutes, then you can see her."

When they went into Maddie's room, they were thunderstruck.

The person sitting up in the bed was much bigger, older and different from the Maddie they'd known. It was if they were staring at a ghost, someone who had come back from the dead. They approached her in wondrous disbelief.

Maddie's smile was watery but bright when she saw them. "Mom, Dad, Tyler…"

"Is it really you, honey?" Karen touched Maddie's hands, her arms, shoulders, her cheeks, to confirm she was actually real.

"Yes, Mom, it's me."

Ryan stared in amazement, his eyes scanning her as if to assure himself she was not an illusion.

"I missed you so much," Tyler said.

Maddie slowly raised her open arms, and they moved toward her gently in a tearful group embrace.

"I never thought this day would come," Maddie sobbed. "I prayed for it, but I never thought it would come. I thought I was going to die in that basement."

Tyler wiped his tears.

"I never stopped hoping we'd see you again," he said, reaching into his pocket and tenderly pulling out the pink fabric bracelet he bought for this moment.

"This is for you."

Maddie accepted it and rubbed her fingers over the gold metal *Hope* charm.

She slid the bracelet on and continued hugging her brother, her mother and father as tight and for as long as she could.

Crimes had been committed. But the Lane case was fraught with complexities, and the judges involved had to look closely at all aspects.

Because of Dalton Lane's age at the time of the offence, the presiding family court judge considered the context and Dalton's acceptance of responsibility and remorse for his actions. Through his lawyer, Dalton had entered into an agreement with the district attorney and pleaded guilty to obstruction. The judge approved and consequently sentenced Dalton to ninety days in a nonsecure juvenile detention facility, a youth group home, along with one year of probation.

In his case, Cole Lane and his attorney also entered into a plea agreement approved by the judge.

Cole took responsibility for his actions and expressed profound remorse as he pleaded guilty to obstruction. The court considered all the elements at play at the time of the offence as well as Cole's character. He was an outstanding citizen with no criminal history, a former law enforcement officer and decorated soldier who made an extraordinary sacrifice saving lives in the protection of the country, and overcame Herculean challenges as a result.

"That said, the offense of obstruction, as well as facilitating the impersonation, cannot be overlooked," the judge said and sentenced Cole to ninety days in Albany County jail within a special jail block holding military veterans. Part of Cole's sentence was to help counsel the other incarcerated veterans who were dealing with an array of offences and personal issues.

Through their attorney, the Slade brothers also pleaded guilty to their offences. Again, the judge had to weigh their ages at the time as well as other factors. As a result, the brothers each received a three-month jail sentence in addition to one year of probation.

Darrell Robert Nybee, the burglar, was sentenced to one year in prison.

And as for the drowning of Karen's ten-year-old sister, Cassie. After their review of the case, Zubik and Asher affirmed that Karen had no direct or criminal role, agreeing that Cassie's death was a tragic accident.

Nearly two weeks after Maddie Lane's rescue, Maya Starr Gagnon stepped from a Greyhound at the Syracuse bus station, took a cab to the home of Karen and Ryan Lane and rang the doorbell.

"I have something to tell you," Gagnon said.

Astonished, Karen invited her inside, where she sat in the living room before the family, including Maddie. She was stunned to see the older girl who had impersonated her, adopted her life and lived in her room.

"I've been watching the news reports, and I couldn't go on living the way I was any longer," Gagnon said. "I apologize to all of you for what I did. For a long time now, I've been lost in this world and Cole offered me a real family. He said I'd be helping you ease your pain over losing Maddie, that she was gone forever. I know now that I only deepened your suffering, and I'm so sorry."

The Lanes traded glances.

Karen touched Gagnon's hand. "When you came

into our lives, our pain was unbearable," she said. "For that brief time, you took it away. That you came back to acknowledge what you did and apologize means a lot to us."

Gagnon said she was going to surrender to police and face charges.

Karen called Jill, who contacted Cole in jail and he agreed to provide Gagnon with a good attorney. She pleaded guilty. Her surrender was taken into account, and she was sentenced to sixty days for criminal impersonation and obstruction charges, and was given six months of probation.

A few days after Gagnon had returned, Asher advised Ryan and Karen that DNA testing confirmed Maddie was their daughter.

"There is no doubt whatsoever," Asher said. "We made further confirmation through her fingerprints."

For an hour after Asher's call, Karen grew pensive.

Ryan pressed her on the matter, and she took him alone into their bedroom where they could talk in private. Then after searching for the words, she pushed back on her emotions.

"I can't keep this inside any longer," she said. "I have to tell you about me and Cole."

"That you slept with my brother?"

Karen's jaw dropped.

"I always suspected it, Karen. But I never

wanted to know. You two had a closeness you couldn't hide. I wouldn't be surprised if Jill suspected it, too." He looked away and let a long moment pass. "I told Cole that I knew when I was beating him. Deep down my suspicion is likely the real reason I always resented him."

"I'm so sorry," Karen sobbed. "It was one time. He was at his worst. He had just come home after losing his legs. Brittany had left him. He was suicidal, believing no one could love him, that he was no longer a man."

"Stop. I get it." Ryan dragged his hands across his face. "I'm not okay with what you two did. Believe me. I'm not. Maybe we can get past it. It won't be easy, but if everything else we've been through couldn't break us, then this shouldn't either. I never stopped loving you, Karen."

"I never stopped loving you."

Ryan stood, went to the window to look at the backyard and Lucifer's Green beyond as if looking into a forest of regret and past mistakes.

"We've all done things we're not proud of," he said. "I honestly don't know if I will ever forgive Cole, or Dalton, for what they did. I don't know. But now, now that we have Maddie back, it feels like a second chance to start over, to be better people." He turned to her. "I think we should take it. One day at a time."

Karen flew to him, and they nearly crushed each other in their arms.

* * *

Maddie's case continued making headlines for weeks.

In Florida, where she had been following the news and at times was interviewed for stories, Anna Croll called a meeting of her nonprofit organization, the South Florida chapter of Searching for Lost Angels.

She arranged for the executive members from headquarters in Washington, DC, to be on the line, and after a short discussion, it was decided to give the reward money it had received in the Lane case to Lewis Perez, the veteran who found Maddison in Syracuse.

The move drew more media attention when Mr. Perez told the Associated Press that since Buster his beagle was the real hero who'd found the girl, he would only accept the amount needed to buy Buster a new leash, collar and bag of dog treats.

"I think the rest should stay with that Lost Angels group. They sound like a good bunch of folks," Perez said.

Stan Zubik and Fran Asher stood at a small mound of earth alongside a grove near the Willowind subdivision.

A few weeks had passed since they'd wrapped up the case, and Zubik, who'd cleared everything with the property owner, insisted they come here.

They stared down at the small granite wedge

and steel plaque that was only six-by-six inches. It read: In Memory of an Unknown Friend.

Zubik had it made and wanted to be sure that the dog that was buried here had received the respect it deserved.

"This is a good thing you did, Stan," Asher said.

"If I've learned one thing as a detective, Fran, it's that every step is a step toward resolution. This animal played a role in the case, and I wanted him remembered for it."

They drove back to headquarters in silence before Asher suggested they stop at Big Ivan's Diner.

She smiled. "One last time."

They found their usual booth and made their usual order.

"So." Zubik let out a long breath. "All packed up, all ready to go?"

"Leave this weekend."

"My loss is Homeland's gain."

"Thank you, Stan." Asher gazed into her coffee. "I want to ask you something."

"Shoot."

"Martha and I are getting married in DC in three months. Going to make it legal. It would mean a lot to me if you came. Would you consider coming?"

Zubik looked at her. "Just try and keep me away, Fran." He winked and patted her hand.

She stood up, went around the table and gave him a hug.

When Jill picked up Dalton the day he was released from the youth home, he made one request.

"Can you drive me straight to Maddie's house?"

"Do you think that's a good idea? I mean, she's been getting a lot of counseling. Isn't it a condition of your sentence that you not see her?"

"No, it's not a condition, Mom. You can call the DA. It's not."

Jill knew it wasn't a condition. She also knew that the families needed space and distance to move forward. Between visiting Dalton and Cole during their incarcerations, she'd become emotionally drained. She could only imagine what Ryan's family was enduring.

"Please take me there, Mom. I need this."

They drove to the house and, at Dalton's request, Jill went to the door and asked if Maddie would come to the driveway where Dalton was waiting, leaning against their car.

Ryan and Karen stared uneasily at Dalton for a long time. Their feeling of protectiveness for their daughter was as strong as ever. Ultimately, they'd said the decision was Maddie's to make.

About ten tense minutes passed before Maddie came to the door and, with her parents and aunt watching, walked slowly toward Dalton.

But halfway there she stopped.

She stood there looking at him, seeing him for the first time in four years since that night.

He was a man now.

"Hello," he said.

She could see he was struggling.

"I'm so sorry," he said at length. "I was so messed up back then. It was my fault. I didn't know those guys were going to do what they did. But it doesn't matter because I'm to blame. It was my fault. I tried to stop them, but it— I don't deserve forgiveness, and I'm not asking for it. I just need you to know that no matter what happens I will always hate myself for what happened to you, Maddie."

She looked at him for the longest time while gently twisting her bracelet. She had no words for him. She looked down at her wrist and sniffed because she was crying, her tears splashing on the gold charm.

Maddie turned to her family then back to Dalton.

Since that night so much had happened and so much had changed. A lifetime had passed for all of them.

The only thing they had left was hope.

* * * * *

Acknowledgments and a Personal Note

As a former crime reporter I have a basic understanding of police investigations. But please know that with *Missing Daughter*, I took creative license with procedure, jurisdiction, technology and geography.

I have visited Syracuse, New York, which is a great city especially if you're a literary tourist. F. Scott Fitzgerald, Stephen Crane, Shirley Jackson and L. Frank Baum are among the few masters with ties to Syracuse. I make no claim to being an expert on the city and most of the places mentioned in *Missing Daughter* exist only in my imagination.

In bringing the story to you I benefited from the hard work, generosity and support of a lot of people.

As always, my thanks to my wife, Barbara, and to Wendy Dudley, for their invaluable help improving the tale.

Very special thanks, Laura and Michael.

My thanks to the ever-brilliant Amy Moore-Benson and Meridian Artists, the super-talented Emily Ohanjanians, and the incredible, wonderful editorial, marketing, sales and PR teams at Harlequin, MIRA Books and Harper Collins.

I want to give particular thanks to Dr. Geoffrey Gay of Ottawa, Canada, for suffering my imposition with questions on dentistry. If the dental aspects of *Missing Daughter* ring true for readers who are expert in the profession, it's because of his kind help. If they fell short for you then blame me—the mistakes are mine.

Again, creative license.

This brings me to what I hold to be the most critical part of the entire enterprise: you, the reader. This aspect has become something of a credo for me, one that bears repeating with each book.

Thank you for your time, for without you, a book remains an untold tale. Thank you for setting your life on pause and taking the journey. I deeply appreciate my audience around the world and those who've been with me since the beginning who keep in touch. Thank you all for your kind words. I hope you enjoyed the ride and will check out my earlier books while watching for my next one.

Feel free to send me a note. I enjoy hearing from you.

Rick Mofina

Facebook.com/RickMofina
Twitter.com/RickMofina
RickMofina.com